1/05

LOOKING FOR IT

Books by Michael Thomas Ford

LAST SUMMER

LOOKING FOR IT

MASTERS OF MIDNIGHT
(with William J. Mann, Sean Wolfe and Jeff Mann)

Published by Kensington Publishing Corporation

MICHAEL THOMAS FORD

LOOKING FOR IT

KENSINGTON BOOKS
www.kensingtonbooks.com

KENSINGTON BOOKS are published by

Kensington Publishing Corp.
850 Third Avenue
New York, NY 10022

All Kensington titles, imprints and distributed lines are available at special quantity discounts for bulk purchases for sales promotion, premiums, fund- raising, educational or institutional use.

Special book excerpts or customized printings can also be created to fit specific needs. For details, write or phone the office of the Kensington Special Sales Manager: Kensington Publishing Corp., 850 Third Avenue, New York, NY 10022, Attn. Special Sales Department. Phone: 1-800-221-2647.

Kensington and the K logo Reg. U.S. Pat. & TM Off.

Library of Congress Card Catalogue Number: 2003116205
ISBN 0-7582-0407-8

First Printing: August 2004
10 9 8 7 6 5 4 3 2 1

Printed in the United States of America

For John Scognamiglio,
who waited

the world is big
the world is bad
but I will find the beauty
I see a vision in my head
I am looking for it now
oh, I am looking for it
oh, I am looking for myself

ACKNOWLEDGMENTS

Thanks and love, as always, to the man who takes care of business and so much more, the divine Mitchell Waters. And for listening, nagging, commiserating, and tolerating: Jill Terry and Christian Muncy, Robrt Pela, Katherine Gleason, Nisa Donnelly, Michael Rowe, Michael Elliott, Jennifer Williams, Lynn Brown, Maureen McEvoy, Stephanie Krmpotic, Mike Lever, Vince Smith, Laura O'Heir, and most especially, Patrick, Roger, and Andy.

CHAPTER 1

"Another fireman. That makes five."

John Ellison took a sip of his vodka tonic and regarded the man in the yellow slicker and red plastic helmet with an air of weary disdain. "You'd think they'd at least try not to look like overgrown kindergartners."

Mike Monaghan, preoccupied with trying to remember the order the nun waiting at the other end of the bar had just given him, nodded absentmindedly as he poured gin over the ice in a glass, neatly popped the caps from two Rolling Rocks, and searched beneath the counter for the bottle of vermouth. *Damn it, Paulie,* he thought, silently cursing the barback whose duty it was to set up before the evening rush. *Why can't you ever put things back where they belong?*

"I know this is the Engine Room, and I'm sure they think they're being very clever, but can't they show a little more imagination?" said John.

"Actually, engine rooms are on ships and submarines, not in fire stations," Mike remarked as he grabbed a pile of napkins to hand to the nun along with his drinks. "Technically, they should be dressed as sailors."

"That makes it even worse," said John, draining his glass. "Not only are they unoriginal, they're ignorant."

"Well, it was very original of *you* to come as Mr. Rogers," Mike told him, eyeing the blue cardigan John had buttoned almost all the way up. "I know I definitely want to be your neighbor."

"Fuck you," John shot back. "For your information, this is what all self-respecting high school science teachers wear."

"The stuff of teenage boys' wet dreams," joked Mike as he took John's empty glass and refilled it.

"What have I missed?"

A man took the seat next to John at the bar. Leaning over, he kissed John quickly on the mouth.

"Nothing," said John. "Just the annual Halloween Faggot Parade and Masquerade Ball."

"Russell, I don't know how you live with this bitter queen," Mike said. Anticipating the request he knew was coming, he poured a rum and Coke and slid it to the man who had just joined them.

Russell took the drink, lifted it to his lips in salute, and took a deep swig before replying. "I'm just with him for the sex," he said, earning a laugh from Mike and a roll of the eyes from John.

"How was the sale?" asked John, changing the subject.

Russell groaned. "Three hundred overweight women all insisting they were size fours," he said wearily. "I barely made it out alive."

"Oh, the perils of retail," said John.

"I didn't even have time to come up with a costume," said Russell.

"Thank God," John told him, sounding relieved. "There are enough cowboys, Batmen, and lumberjacks here to recreate an episode of *Let's Make a Deal.*"

"Actually, I think those lumberjacks are lesbians," Mike teased. "And since you're asking, I'll take what's behind door number two."

Russell laughed. "You don't have to be so uptight," he said to his lover. "Halloween is supposed to be fun."

John snorted. "Excuse me if I'm a little tired of this nonsense. All day long I had to teach chemistry to children dressed as gangbangers and hookers," he said. "Not that *every* day isn't like that."

"You should have gone as Grand Master J," suggested Mike. "Pimp Daddy of the science lab. You could show them how to make their own street drugs. That would get them interested in chemistry."

"I don't see you in a costume," John retorted. "If you think this is so much fun, how come you're not dressed in some inane getup?"

"I *am* in costume," Mike said. "Can't you tell? I'm a straight guy."

Russell laughed as John shook his head. Mike, noticing a ghost waving a ten-dollar bill at him, excused himself to attend to the customer.

"Can we go now?" John asked Russell.

"Go?" Russell said. "They're just about to start the drag show."

"That's exactly why I want to go," said John. "I've got a splitting headache, and being here isn't helping."

Russell looked down into his drink. "Yeah," he said quietly. "We can go. Let me say good night to Mike."

John stood up. "I'll be outside," he told his partner.

As John pushed his way through the crowd toward the door, Russell finished his drink and set the empty glass on the bar. He caught Mike's eye and waved.

"You're leaving?" asked Mike, coming over and automatically sweeping the empty glass into the plastic tub beneath the counter.

Russell sighed. "Her majesty has a headache."

"So send him home by himself," suggested Mike.

Russell shook his head. "It's okay," he said. "I'm pretty beat anyway. I'll see you later."

Mike nodded and watched as Russell left. Russell and John had been coming into the bar regularly for the six years Mike had worked there, and still he hadn't figured out what kept them together. One of these days, he thought, he'd unravel the mystery. But tonight wasn't the night. Tonight he had too much else to do.

He turned his attention to the customers lined up three deep at the bar. Within moments he was busy mixing drinks, his hands finding the bottles, ice, and wedges of lime as his mind ticked off the orders: three martinis for Wonder Woman, a shot of Jack Daniels and a Cosmo for the scarecrow, and a Budweiser for the devil with the wicked smile. Then he was on to a new set of faces and the next round.

"What's an old queen have to do to get a sidecar around here?"

"Simon!" Mike said, leaning across the bar to kiss the cheek of the man addressing him. He eyed the old-fashioned black dress and powdered wig Simon was wearing. "What are you supposed to be?" he asked as he began putting together the sidecar.

"What did I just say?" asked Simon primly. "I'm an old queen."

Seeing Mike's confusion, Simon shook his head. "You children have no sense of history," he said. "Victoria. I'm Queen Victoria."

Mike nodded. "Oh," he said. "I get it."

Simon took his sidecar and handed Mike a five. "Don't feel badly about not knowing," he said. "Someone else complimented me on my Zsa Zsa Gabor costume. There are, I'm afraid, disadvantages to being the oldest one in a room."

Behind Simon a drag queen sporting a pink-sequined dress, enormous breasts, and a beehive hairdo that added a good two feet to her height stepped onto the small stage that had been erected for the evening. Taking up a microphone, she flashed a red-lipped smile, batted her false eyelashes, and addressed the crowd.

"Happy Halloween!" she shouted. "Welcome to the Engine Room. So, what will it be tonight, tricks or treats?"

"Tricks!" shouted the crowd.

The crowd around the bar thinned as people turned to watch the show. Simon pulled out a stool and sat down. "She got that from Walter, you know," he said to Mike.

Mike knew. He'd heard Simon's stories about Walter many times. Everyone in the bar had, particularly in the year since Walter had died.

"He was so lovely," Simon said, speaking to no one in particular. "So beautiful."

Mike looked at Simon's face. Caked with makeup, it reminded him of a crumbling painting. How old was Simon, he wondered? Surely he must be almost seventy. And Walter had been even older. Mike, picturing Walter, tried to imagine the wrinkled little man with the white mustache who'd worn corduroy trousers and neatly pressed plaid shirts dressed in drag.

"I remember the first time I saw him," Simon said. "It was at a party given by my friend Harold Carver. We didn't have a bar to go to back then, but Harold was wealthy and had a big house in Saratoga. Every weekend we went there. Escaped, really. From our lives. One weekend someone brought Walter along as a guest. Friday night he made his entrance to dinner dressed in a beaded gown, and I fell in love with him."

Simon looked at Mike and smiled, the pancake makeup on his cheeks cracking and flaking off. "I know it all sounds terribly fey," he said. "But he wasn't playing at being a woman. It was just his way of having fun." Simon sighed deeply. "It all seems so much easier now, doesn't it? We have our bars, and parades, and we're on television for everyone to see. People talk about how terrible it was back then, how we had to hide who we were. But they forget that it was also magical. We had our own secret world. Maybe we were afraid sometimes, but we weren't unhappy."

Simon looked down into his glass. "We weren't unhappy," he repeated. "Not then."

"Would you like another one?" Mike asked him, nodding at the empty drink. "It's on the house."

Simon shook his head. "Thank you, but no. One makes me maudlin. Two will make me positively morose. I think I should probably take myself home before I become a spectacle."

"You're going to miss the costume contest," Mike told him.

"That is a misfortune I will have to live with," Simon said, standing up. "I pray that I am up to it."

He waved away the change Mike had placed on the bar. Mike pocketed it as Simon turned and melted into the crowd. With only a few customers waiting, Mike enjoyed the relative quiet. The drag show was in full force, but he was able to block it out. It was a trick he'd developed during years of bartending in places whose clientele favored the cover of blaring music over the ability to communicate with those around them. He simply tuned the noise out, losing himself in his work or his thoughts.

He observed the action from within this sphere of artificial silence, surrounded by the chaos that was Halloween at the Engine Room but at the same time removed from it. As he straightened the bottles and restocked the napkins, he watched the faces of the patrons. Many of them he recognized, but others were strangers to him. This was to be expected. The Engine Room was one of only three gay bars in a two-hour radius. The towns of upstate New York had many charms, but the availability of entertainment for the queer community was not one of them.

Oddly, this was one of the things that appealed to Mike about life in Cold Falls. He'd lived in larger cities, Albany and Syracuse for several years and a brief three-month stint in Buffalo one summer, but he preferred the quieter atmosphere of the smaller towns. Not that Cold Falls was merely a flyspeck on the map of New York State. An hour north of Utica, it shared with that city a history and economy based in brewing. Founded a hundred years earlier, Cold Falls Ale continued to be the bar's best seller, beating out Coors and Budweiser by almost three to one. An image of the falls that gave the town its name graced the label, and the brewery's motto—"Give me a cold one"—was regularly shouted out by customers, each of whom Mike rewarded with a friendly laugh suggesting that it was the first time he'd heard such cleverness.

He didn't mind. He liked his customers. Like the town itself, they had quickly become familiar to him, until he knew their faces and names in the same way that he knew the most recognizable of Cold Falls' landmarks: the brewery, the falls, the statue of the town's lone celebrity (Cuthbert Applewhite, a dairy farmer who had distinguished himself in 1892 by preventing an assassination attempt against presidential candidate and former fellow upstate New Yorker Grover Cleveland during a campaign stop, and who after Cleveland had secured his second, improbable, term in office had been awarded a medal of distinction that he wore for the rest of his life, even when mucking out the barn).

In addition to their names, Mike knew their stories as well. He fell easily into the time-honored role most bartenders held along with their ability to mix drinks, that of father confessor and unpaid therapist. The tips he received were just as often tokens of appreciation for the advice he dispensed as they were for the strength of his cocktails, even if all he'd done was nod sympathetically during a patron's rambling, boozy dissection of a recent breakup.

Stories. It was all about stories. Everyone had one, and almost everyone wanted to tell it. All he did was listen to them, and for that his customers were thankful. He was like a book they were writing, recording the events of their lives in his head. Maybe, he thought occasionally, one day he would write them all down. But who, he asked himself, would want to read it? To whom would the individual stories of heartbreak and joy be of any interest besides those who told them? It was, Mike thought as he washed and dried a wineglass, one of the less appealing characteristics of human beings, the ability to be completely uninterested in the lives of those around them while desperately longing for someone to pay them attention.

A burst of cheering made him look up. On the stage, the beehived drag queen was putting a crown on the head of a muscular man halfheartedly dressed as a pirate, the primary clues to his identity being the patch on one eye and the stuffed parrot somehow affixed to his shoulder. Apart from these props he was nearly nude, which Mike assumed was the reason for his popularity.

"How about showing us your Jolly Roger?" the drag queen teased, shamelessly pawing the pirate's chest as the crowd roared.

"Can I get a cold one?"

Mike looked away from the action to see a skeleton standing at the bar. He wore a black turtleneck and pants painted with crude representations of bones. His hair was slicked back and his face, too, was painted black and white to resemble a skull. His eyes were misshapen white spots above a ghostly mouth, and the overall effect was unsettling.

"Great costume," Mike remarked as he pulled a beer from the ice-filled chest and handed it to the man.

"Thanks," came the short reply. "How much?"

"Two bucks," answered Mike.

Three dollar bills were slapped on the bar. Then the skeleton man turned away, scanning the crowd.

Mike took the money, putting two of the bills into the register and adding the third to the rest of his tips. The man, he guessed, wasn't one of the regulars, otherwise he wouldn't have had to ask the price of a beer, which hadn't changed in well over a year. Probably he was one of the visitors who came in only on nights like this, when they could hide behind the anonymity of a costume. Maybe there was a wife at home, perhaps a kid or two. Mike saw a lot of guys like that. They came to the Engine Room from other small cities, driving an hour or more to ensure invisibility while they spent a night living other lives.

Usually he saw them only once, but sometimes they showed up at regular intervals. Apart from their nervousness and unfamiliarity, they were easy to spot. Often they forgot to remove their wedding rings. He glanced at the left hand of the skeleton man. It was bare. Still, that meant nothing. Not all of them were married, of course. Some were simply afraid of who they were.

The man moved away, out of Mike's sight. Looking for something, Mike thought. He was looking for something. They all were. That's why they came there.

CHAPTER 2

What was it with faggots that they liked to dress up like women? Pete Thayer stared at the drag queen standing on the stage. He was rambling on and on, grinning at everyone and throwing his hands all over the place. Pete couldn't stand to look at his face, painted up like a clown's. Someone needed to take the queen out back and show him how a real man acted.

That was the problem with fags; they wanted to be women. Not all of them, but most of them. That's why so many of them were wearing dresses or girly costumes. Even the ones dressed as men were trying too hard to look masculine, hiding their sissiness behind military uniforms and football player getups. But Pete knew that once the clothes came off, the masculinity would fall with them to the floor of the bedroom, discarded like so much make-believe.

He took a swig of his beer and leaned against the wall. His eyes scanned the bar, looking for anything to relieve his boredom. The possibilities were few and far between. There was a cowboy by the pool table who wasn't too bad, and at the back of the room a guy dressed as a baby wearing nothing but a diaper. The costume was a turnoff, but the guy at least had a hairy chest and didn't seem too swishy.

Pete decided to give the baby a shot and started walking toward him. Halfway there he found his way blocked by a guy in a devil outfit. The devil looked him up and down and smiled.

"Nice costume," he said.

Pete nodded. He wasn't in the mood to talk.

"That paint sort of glows," the devil continued. "Is it fluorescent?"

"Yeah," said Pete curtly. Fluorescent? Who the hell cared? It was paint. He'd grabbed the bottle from the back room at the shop. The costume was a last-minute thing, pulled together in about ten minutes.

"You should have won a prize," the devil said, grinning broadly. "It's really cool."

Behind the devil Pete saw the baby getting ready to leave with someone dressed as Dorothy from *The Wizard of Oz*. He quickly looked for the cowboy, but he, too, was gone.

"Can I buy you a drink?" the devil asked him.

Pete looked at the guy. He was shirtless, like the baby, although his chest was smooth. But at least it was well muscled. His skin was painted red. On his head was perched a set of horns, and he had a goatee. He was wearing red boxer briefs and black work boots. He would do.

"I have a better idea," Pete said. "Why don't you and I take a little trip to hell."

The devil looked at him, confused.

"Let's get out of here," Pete explained.

The devil nodded. "Oh," he said. "I get it. Funny. Well, I'm sort of here with some friends. I should—"

"Okay," Pete interrupted. "No problem."

He turned to go, but the devil grabbed his arm. "I guess I could leave a little early," he said.

"Then let's go," Pete told him.

He walked toward the door, knowing the devil would be right behind him. They always were, predictable as Monday morning. As the door of the Engine Room closed behind him, the devil was there beside him.

"I'm Mark," the devil said.

"Dan," Pete told him. "Where's your car?"

"Over here."

Pete followed Mark to his car, waiting for Mark to unlock it and then getting in. When they were inside, Mark leaned over and tried to kiss him. Pete put his hand on the back of Mark's head and pushed it down to his crotch instead.

Mark's fingers fumbled with Pete's zipper, pulling it down and reaching inside. Unrestrained by underwear, Pete's dick slid out easily. A moment later Mark's mouth was sliding up and down it hungrily and

Pete was growing hard. He leaned back, shut his eyes, and lost himself in the warmth of the mouth that serviced him.

When he felt himself begin to come, he said nothing. His load exploded into Mark's mouth and he felt Mark gag for a moment before swallowing hard. When he was done, Pete pulled his softening cock from Mark's mouth and zipped up. He opened the car door and got out, leaving Mark looking up at him with a puzzled expression.

Pete shut the door quickly, blotting out the sight of Mark's face with its smeared red makeup and the horns hanging askew. He walked briskly away from the car toward the one he'd driven to the bar. It wasn't his; it belonged to a customer from the shop. He would never drive his own car to a fag bar. It was too recognizable.

He got into the borrowed car and left the parking lot. He was home within fifteen minutes, where he parked the car in the garage and shut the door. Once safely inside the house, he went to the bathroom, where he turned the shower on, stripped off his painted clothes, and stuffed them into the small garbage can beneath the sink.

The water was too hot, but he left it that way. It would help wash away the dirt. Maybe, he thought vaguely as he soaped himself, it would also kill anything the queer's mouth had left on his dick. He scrubbed his skin hard with a washcloth, wiping away the oily drugstore makeup he'd bought to create his skeleton face. He watched it run down his body and into the drain, a milky stream that ran clear after several minutes. Still he scrubbed, making sure he was rid of any lingering taint. You could never be too careful.

Turning the water off, he stepped from the shower and dropped the washcloth into the trash on top of the clothes. Grabbing a towel from the hook behind the door, he dried himself and walked into his bedroom. He flopped onto the bed and reached for the remote on the bedside table.

The TV came on with a click. Another push of a button set the tape inside the VCR whirring, and a moment later the image of a big-breasted blonde getting fucked from behind filled the screen. Pete stared at the TV, idly playing with himself while the girl's partner, an unattractive but hugely endowed man, thrust in and out of her pussy. The girl's tits jiggled and her lipsticked mouth was open in an expression of ecstasy as squeaky little "ohs" and "yeahs" filled the air.

After a few minutes the camera moved in, moving behind and

above the couple to focus on the pink folds between the girl's legs. The man pulled his cock out and rubbed the swollen head against the girl's asshole. Pressing it against the pinkish-brown pucker, he slid inside her, the length of him disappearing between her cheeks.

Pete lay back and spread his legs. His cock angled across his belly, untouched, as he wet a finger and slid it beneath his balls and began to rub his asshole. His eyes were fixed on the dick that was pounding the girl's butt. It moved in and out with increasing force, stretching her wide. The skin was slick and shiny with lube. He wondered what it felt like for the girl to have such a thing inside her.

He'd fucked a girl like that once. Like the girl in the film, she'd had blond hair and store-bought tits. He'd met her at a party. Fourth of July, maybe. He couldn't remember. What he did remember was how he'd been fucking her from behind and suddenly wondered what it would feel like to stick his piece in her ass. Without asking, he'd done it. She was so drunk she hadn't even really noticed, groaning a little at first and then going right back to mumbling some foul-mouthed crap she apparently thought was sexy.

He'd blocked out her voice, concentrating on how tight her ass felt around him. He'd come quickly, before he was ready, and it had made him angry. He'd left the girl on her hands and knees, pulling on his jeans and leaving before she could ask him where he was going.

What would it feel like to have something as big as a cock in your ass? He slid his finger inside himself, poking gently. Just a finger hurt a little. He couldn't imagine what a dick must feel like. Especially one as big as the one on his TV screen. Christ, it had to be a good ten inches long. His own was eight. He knew because he'd measured it once just for the hell of it. Eight inches. Man, those faggots loved his big cock. They always said so when they sucked him off.

He'd never fucked a guy. Some of them had wanted him to, but he wouldn't do it. Who knew what kind of shit you could get from that. Not that the idea didn't have some appeal. The girl—what was her name, Amy? Kelly?—had been virgin tight. Probably a guy wouldn't be, though, especially some queer who'd been plowed by everything he could get in there.

He slid more of his finger inside himself. His ass tightened around him and he felt his balls give a jump. He moved in and out a little, fucking his own ass. In the film the guy was pulling almost all the way out and slamming back in. The head of his dick would appear for a moment, the girl's asshole almost closing. Then he would push back into her, his balls slapping against her as he nailed her.

Pete added a second finger to the first, gritting his teeth as he stretched himself open. How did those fags stand it? He was about to pull his hand away when suddenly his ass relaxed, as if something had stopped resisting and opened up. The pain ebbed and his fingers were simply surrounded by heat. He could almost feel the blood pounding in his ass.

He started to fuck himself with his hand, matching the motions of the guy in the movie. With his free hand he gripped his cock tightly. He imagined fucking the girl. His fist was her ass, tight around his dick. She was moaning as he pumped her. He was giving it to her hard, the way he liked it.

Behind him was a guy. Maybe the man in the film, maybe someone else. A cock was pressing against his asshole, pushing its way inside. As he fucked the girl, he too was getting fucked. He closed his eyes and imagined it, the three of them rocking together on the bed, his dick and the other guy's moving in tandem, sliding in and out like the pistons of an engine. It was like they were both fucking the girl, the other man's dick connected to Pete's inside.

He heard loud moans and opened his eyes. On the screen the man had pulled his dick out of the girl's ass and was spraying a thick load over her back. Pete pumped himself harder and came too. His ass tightened around his fingers and he erupted with a shout. Cum splattered across his chest in thick drops, leaving behind a pearly trail caught in the dark hair of his stomach.

He pulled his hand away from his ass and reached for a T-shirt on the floor. He used it to wipe the stickiness from his skin, then tossed it back on the floor. The TV was shut off and he was left in the darkness of the room, looking up at the ceiling.

He reached for the pack of Marlboros on the bedside table. Pulling one free, he flicked his lighter to life and lit it. The smoke felt good as he drew it into his lungs, a cloudy darkness that surrounded his thoughts. The end of the cigarette glowed redly in the dark like a star.

He exhaled, blowing the smoke into the air. He lifted his fingers to his nose and inhaled the scent of himself. It clung to his skin, thick and ripe, like the smell of leaves in the fall. Is that what he smelled like inside? He had expected it to be different, dirtier. But it wasn't; it was rich and dark, like the smoke that fell over him like invisible rain.

He licked a fingertip, expecting to taste something sour. Again he was surprised. The taste that met his tongue was nothing like that. Instead it had a sweetness to it. He sucked on his finger, drawing it inside. Minutes ago it had been inside his ass, filling him. Now he was tasting himself. He was both repulsed and thrilled by the act. He thought about the times when girls had sucked him after he'd pulled his cock from their pussies. Watching them lick their own juices from his skin, he'd wanted to fuck them all over again.

He was no girl, though, he told himself. He didn't get fucked. His fantasy had been about something else. What, he wasn't sure and didn't want to think too much about. It was just something that had popped into his head, that was all. He'd just wondered what it might feel like. Nothing more. And now he knew.

He removed his finger and took a long drag on his cigarette, blotting out the taste in his mouth with the bitter kiss of tobacco. In a few minutes he would get up and wash his hands. He would use lots of hot water and soap, just like his mother had made him do when he was littler. "You can't be too careful," she'd always said as she watched him to make sure he didn't just run his hands under the tap to fool her.

"You can't be too careful." He repeated the phrase out loud. It was the guiding principle of his mother's life, and like a good boy, he followed it himself. Well, mostly. He suspected his mother wouldn't approve of certain aspects of his life. But still, he was careful.

He'd almost totally forgotten about his encounter with Mark earlier in the evening, but now the guy's face came to him. He recalled the red skin, the two little horns.

"You got a blowjob from the devil," he told himself. He laughed. The idea was so ridiculous he couldn't help but find it funny. After all, he was a nice Catholic boy. He'd done altar service, gone through CCD, all that crap. Sometimes he still went to Mass, at least on holidays or when his mother demanded he accompany her. What would Father Fitzpatrick think about his former altar boy getting a knob job from Satan? Maybe he was a cocksucker himself, although Pete doubted it. Despite the recent rash of abuse revelations, he could honestly say that Father Fitzpatrick had never once done anything like that to him or, as far as he knew, any of his friends.

Maybe he would stop by the church tomorrow, he thought. It was, after all, All Saints' Day. He could light a candle for his grandmother. It had been a while since he'd done that. His mother would like it if he did.

He stubbed out his cigarette in the ashtray and got up. Going into the bathroom, he turned on the water in the sink and began to scrub.

CHAPTER 3

"You are no longer strangers and sojourners, but fellow citizens with the saints and members of the household of God."

Father Thomas Dunn looked out at the congregation. There were a surprising number of them given that it was six o'clock on a rainy Wednesday morning. Then again, most of them were elderly. They had nothing else to do, nowhere else to be. The chance that they'd spent the previous evening trick-or-treating or attending Halloween parties was remote. Probably they'd locked themselves in their houses and turned off the porch lights to discourage any children who might come around.

It was an unkind thought, and he admonished himself for having it. The members of Saint Peter's Episcopal Church were, for the most part, kind people. In the ten months that he'd been there, most of them had invited him to dinner at least once. Several had even attempted to interest him in their unmarried daughters, offers he'd so far managed to sidestep. They came to the church, and to him, because they were searching for something that presumably they found there.

He refocused on the service, uttering the words of the Confession of Sin. "Beloved, we have come together in the presence of Almighty God our heavenly Father, to set forth his praise, to hear his holy Word, and to ask, for ourselves and on behalf of others, those things that are necessary for our life and our salvation. And so that we may prepare ourselves in heart and mind to worship him, let us kneel in silence, and with penitent and obedient hearts confess our sins, that we may obtain forgiveness by his infinite goodness and mercy."

Obediently, the people knelt with a muted rustling of papers and the rasping of the wooden prayer benches against the floor. He imagined he heard elderly joints creaking in the cold confines of the old stone church, echoing dimly off the ceiling high above them where spiders swung like tiny many-eyed angels and trapped in their webs the prayers that floated heavenward.

"Most merciful God, we confess that we have sinned against you in thought, word, and deed, by what we have done, and by what we have left undone." The words of the confession came easily, burned into his memory by daily repetition until they had become almost meaningless. "We have not loved you with our whole heart; we have not loved our neighbors as ourselves. We are truly sorry and we humbly repent. For the sake of your Son Jesus Christ, have mercy on us and forgive us; that we may delight in your will, and walk in your ways, to the glory of your Name. Amen."

Standing, he lifted his hand toward the people.

"Almighty God have mercy on you, forgive you all your sins through our Lord Jesus Christ, strengthen you in all goodness, and by the power of the Holy Ghost keep you in eternal life. Amen."

They stood once more, looking at him expectantly. He smiled and felt a collective sigh ripple through the sanctuary as the newly forgiven sank into their seats.

"The Lord is glorious in his saints. Come let us adore him."

He led them through the reading of the Psalm, only half listening as their mingled voices followed his in the call-and-response. When it came time for the reading of the first lesson, he relinquished his place at the pulpit to George Edderly, who removed a pair of bifocals from the pocket of his red flannel shirt before beginning to read in a shaky voice.

"A reading from Ecclesiasticus. 'Let us now sing the praises of famous men, our ancestors in their generations . . .' "

The old man's voice faded into the background as Father Dunn stared at the pattern of the carpet beneath his feet. It was a pattern of vines and flowers, red and purple on a blue background. He chose one particular vine and attempted to follow it with his eyes, but when it circled around itself and became entwined with the petals of a rose, he grew confused and lost interest.

"The word of the Lord."

The ending of the reading brought him back to the moment. Along with everyone else in the church, Father Dunn gave the familiar response. "Thanks be to God."

Another lesson, this one from Revelation, was read by Jenny Parish. A pretty young woman, her clear, pleasant voice bespoke of the terrible things that would come when the angel of the Lord arrived on the day of judgment to open the final seal and release pestilence across the land. Jenny described these events as if she were reading out loud a birthday card from a dear friend, and Father Dunn was reminded of the newscasters who announced the most gruesome of disasters with shining teeth and smiling faces.

Following a reading of the Gospel According to Saint Matthew, it was time for the sermon. Here, able to break away from the rigid bones of the service's prescribed format, Father Dunn grew more lively. He loved the church's traditions and rituals, but sometimes they felt to him like a tether keeping him neatly within a circle whose dimensions had been described by someone else. He knew he was supposed to see them more as a set of exercises, the repetition of which cleansed his soul and brought him closer to God. More and more often, however, the collar signifying his obedience to his faith seemed to be choking him.

In his sermons, though, he was free to fly. The church could offer suggestions—and did—regarding appropriate themes, but ultimately it was up to him to create something that would connect with the hearts of his parishioners. And this morning the topic was remembering the dead. He arranged the notes he'd jotted down the evening before and began.

"When I was very small, I remember sitting in front of the television one Sunday night watching Walt Disney's *Fantasia*. Although I liked the dancing hippos and Mickey Mouse as the beleaguered sorcerer's apprentice, I'm afraid overall I found it a little boring. At least until the sequence set to Mussorgsky's 'Night on Bald Mountain.' Watching the mountain come to life, turning into a demonic figure in whose clawed hand danced imps born of the flames, I was fascinated. And when the frantic last notes of the piece blended into the soothing opening tones of Schubert's 'Ave Maria' and the demon was banished by first the sun and then the candles carried by the mysterious pilgrims walking through the woods, I was mesmerized."

He paused, thinking back to that night, to how he had felt staring at the TV screen from his place on the living room floor.

"I had no idea then that what I was watching was the visualization of the ongoing battle between the sacred and the profane. All I knew was that I was held, spellbound, by the music and the feelings it stirred in me. I think, really, it was Walt Disney who set me on the road to the priesthood."

A ripple of laughter greeted his comment. But he was serious. Even at the age of seven or eight, he knew he had discovered something deeply magical, something he couldn't put into words. He understood that the composers of the music and the animators of the film had also been unable to put what they felt into words, and so had brought their experiences to life in notes and images. When he later discovered God and the Church, the feeling was the same. Faith, he had learned that night in front of the flickering television, was most glorious when it was most untouched by reason.

"Today is the Feast of All Saints," he continued. "Last night was All Hallows' Eve. The sacred and the profane. One is a night of mischief, of goblins and ghosts and witches. The other is a day of remembering the spirits of those who have passed on. And that's what I would like each of you to do today. Remember those who are gone from you, those women and men who touched your lives and helped shape who and what you are."

He let this notion sink in. He knew each person in the church was now thinking of names, seeing faces in their minds, remembering moments of love and anger, joy and sorrow. An image came to him as well, but he pushed it away, saving it for later.

"One day all of us will be gone," he continued quickly. "Who will remember us then? Whose lives are we touching with our actions? When ten, twenty, fifty years from now other bodies are occupying the pews in which you sit and another priest is standing in my place, will they remember us fondly or with pain? As you go about your day today, take time both to remember and to be mindful. Thank those people in your life whom you appreciate, reflect on how your actions affect others, and recall the people—the saints of your life—who are no longer here. We are all of us saints in the making. When it's time for us to be remembered, make it be with gladness and love."

He gathered his notes together, slipping them inside his Book of Common Prayer. The church's old, faithful organ lurched to life as the first notes of "Who Are These Like Stars Appearing" filled the air. It was a lovely hymn, one of the priest's favorites, and he sang along loudly.

"Who are these like stars appearing, these before God's throne who stand? Each a golden crown is wearing; who are all this glorious band?"

Again he was reminded of his childhood, although for much different reasons. The words of the hymn made him think of the Swedish supergroup ABBA. He'd had a poster of the band, pulled from the pages of *Tigerbeat,* in his room when he was thirteen or so. The four members were dressed in white satin jumpsuits, lit softly so that they seemed to glow. With their shiny hair and smiling faces, they'd seemed angelic to him. Now, every time he sang the first line of this hymn, he saw that poster in his mind. It was oddly appropriate, he thought: Agnetha, Bjorn, Frida, and Benny as sweet-voiced, Nordic saints of God.

As the last note faded away, he recited a Prayer of Saint Chrysostom before bestowing the Benediction. "May the God of hope fill us with all joy and peace in believing through the power of the Holy Ghost. Amen."

And it was over.

He descended from the pulpit and made his way down the center aisle of the church to the doors, where he took up his position to await the departing congregation. He always felt a bit like a flight attendant at this point, and once or twice he'd been tempted to greet someone with, "We know you have a choice of religions and we thank you for choosing the Episcopal Church for your worship needs. Come again. Buh-bye."

Instead he shook hands and smiled, listened to earnest praise for his sermons and to requests for prayers. He learned the names and faces of the regulars and attempted, mostly successfully, to commit to memory their various ailments, children, occupations, and assorted other bits and pieces of personal information that, when repeated back, created a sense of belonging.

Today the line of well-wishers was mercifully short. Early-morning services, particularly midweek, were not the popular events that

Sundays were. It took only ten or fifteen minutes for hands to be patted, pleasantries exchanged, and promises to see one another again in four days made. Then he was alone.

He shut the doors against the rain and entered the church. Empty, it seemed even colder, and he shivered beneath his robes. He hurriedly blew out the candles that had been lit to provide the illusion of warmth and left the sanctuary for the cozier environment of his own house.

The rectory was behind the church. Erected sometime after the church itself, it was made not of stone but of brick, a simple two-story house in which the keeper of Saint Peter's could be contained. He had inherited the furnishings of the previous priest, who had retired to Florida and left behind a surprisingly tasteful array of sofas, tables, and other items necessary for housekeeping. Father Dunn liked the house very much, and felt both comfortable and safe within its walls.

Once inside he went to the second-floor room that was his study. There was a fireplace there, a twin to the one in the living room directly below, and he'd lit a fire that morning before going to the church. The air was warm, and a cheerful light flickered over the walls. He sank into the well-worn leather chair in front of the fire and closed his eyes.

Away from his duties, from the requirements of his position and the watchful eyes of the faithful, he finally allowed himself to be a man and not merely a priest. He permitted himself to remember. And what he remembered was a face, a handsome face with bright blue eyes, an infectious smile, and cheeks hollowed by approaching death.

Joseph's face had not always been ravaged. It had once been beautiful, was beautiful even as death closed its wings around him and carried him away. The sickness stole his life but not his soul, and he remained a great, shining presence even as the last breath slipped from him.

There was a photograph of him and Joseph on the mantle, but he didn't need to open his eyes to see it. He'd memorized every part of it in the years since Joseph's death. As the sound of his voice and the touch of his fingers had become harder and harder to recall with absolute certainty, Thomas had relied more and more on the few photographs he had of his friend for his memories.

Friend. The word was so inadequate. But what else had Joseph been to him? Teacher. Mentor. Inspiration. He'd been many things. Lover? No, not that. Never that, even if Thomas had sometimes wanted it more than anything. Almost anything. God had always come between them, an irony of the cruelest sort since it was God who had brought them together in the first place.

Thomas had come to see Joseph as his greatest gift and his greatest trial. His temptation in the desert, perhaps. It was Joseph who had forced him to explore his heart's capacity to love, but ultimately he'd had to make a choice between that love and his love for the church. In the end it was God who had won the battle for his affections.

Joseph had never pressed him on the issue, had never, in fact, even discussed it with him except in the vaguest of terms. They'd both been too shy. And when Thomas's decision had been made, it was done in secret, behind the closed doors of his heart.

Even during the months of Joseph's illness and death, when Thomas visited often, they never spoke of those things. Nor did they speak of the cause of the illness, Joseph because it didn't matter to him and Thomas because he feared that he had in some way caused it, or at least failed to prevent it, by making the choice he had.

Thomas opened his eyes. Joseph looked back at him from the photo, his eyes forgiving everything. It was indeed the face of a saint, and gazing at it, Thomas began to weep for his sins.

CHAPTER 4

"Don't drive so fast. The road is wet."

Stephen Darby glanced over at his mother. She was wrapped in her thickest wool coat, her hands in her lap, fingers clasped tightly together. As they rounded a turn, one hand flew out to grip the handle of the door, as if Gail Darby's sheer force of will was the only thing that kept the vehicle from careening over the yellow divider line and into a tree. When they were safely around the bend, she let go and gave a sigh.

Stephen ignored her. His mother was an adept at sighing—perhaps the foremost practitioner of the art—but he'd long ago grown immune to her powers. Well, mostly. After all, she had used guilt to get him to take her to Saint Peter's before dawn, all so she could see Father Dunn. He suspected she had a crush on the priest, as she did on almost any man who embodied what she found lacking in her husband and her sons.

"I read the other day that when the brakes are wet, it takes five times as long to stop in the event of an accident," his mother said.

"Really?" answered Stephen. "Where did you read that?"

He deliberately stepped on the brakes, making the car jolt. His mother's hands immediately went to the dashboard, and he saw her pump her tiny foot, as if she controlled an invisible brake.

"I don't remember," she said breathlessly. "Somewhere. Maybe in *Reader's Digest*."

"Mmm-hmm." Stephen stifled a smile. He knew his mother was lying. For heaven's sake, she didn't even have a driver's license. Yet she wouldn't let that stop her from dispensing driving advice, no more than not having degrees in law or medicine could persuade her that she wasn't an expert on every possible legal situation or malady. She frequently invented facts and then insisted on their veracity, despite all proof to the contrary.

"You can learn a lot from the *Reader's Digest,*" Gail Darby said sagely.

"What did you think of the service today?" Stephen asked her, anxious to talk about anything other than the redeeming value of the world's most-read magazine.

"I thought it was lovely," his mother answered, nodding her head approvingly. "Very appropriate. Father Dunn is a marvelous priest."

"Better than Father Rogan?" Stephen asked maliciously. He knew his mother had doted on the former priest to an extreme, going so far as to invite him to almost every holiday with their family.

"We'll see," replied Mrs. Darby primly. Her thin lips were pressed tightly together as she peered through her glasses at the road ahead, as if watching for oncoming obstacles.

"Will he be coming to Thanksgiving?" Stephen teased.

His mother shot him a look of reproach. "Don't get smart," she said.

"I wouldn't think of it," Stephen told her.

He turned onto the street where his parents lived. Actually, where the whole family lived, in three houses one beside the next. His brother, Alan, occupied the first of them with his wife and three children. His parents had the middle house, where they'd lived since their wedding day forty years ago and where Alan and Stephen had grown up. On the other side, like a familial bookend, was Stephen's house. He lived there alone.

He pulled into the driveway of his parents' house and followed his mother as she walked into the garage. None of the Darbys used their front doors. They were, for all practical purposes, purely ornamental, something on which to hang Christmas wreaths and other seasonal decorations.

They entered into the kitchen, where they found Martin Darby seated at the round table. A newspaper was spread out in front of him and he was staring at it intently. A half-eaten bowl of oatmeal had been pushed to one side, along with a crumpled napkin and a glass of orange juice.

"What's a seven-letter word for 'solid foundation'?" he asked irritably.

Stephen thought for a moment. "Bedrock," he said.

Mr. Darby looked at his crossword, scowling. "No, it has to have a U in it."

Stephen looked over his father's shoulder at the clue. "It's not 'solid,' it's 'salad,' " he said. "And the answer is lettuce."

Mr. Darby's pencil worked its way across the page. "I hate it when they have these cutesy clues," he said. "Why can't they just say what the hell they mean?"

"Because then it wouldn't be any fun," Stephen told him. "That's the whole point."

His father looked at him. "The point is to finish the damn thing."

"Stop swearing," Mrs. Darby said as she went to the refrigerator and opened it. "Stephen, what do you want for breakfast?"

"Oh, nothing," he told her. "I've got to get to work."

His mother looked at him blankly. "You work at home," she said.

Stephen nodded. "And it's still work," he said. "Just because I don't put on a suit and go to an office doesn't mean it's not a real job."

"I didn't say that," said Mrs. Darby. "Don't put words in my mouth. Now, do you want an omelette or scrambled eggs?"

"Why does he get eggs when I had to eat oatmeal?" complained Martin.

"Because I didn't have a heart attack last year," Stephen reminded him.

"Don't get smart," Mr. Darby said gruffly.

"Scrambled eggs or omelette?" Mrs. Darby asked, her voice rising.

"Time to go," Stephen said, standing up. He went to his mother and gave her a kiss on the cheek, then waved to his father. "See you two later."

"You need to eat something!" his mother called after him as he left.

He got into the car, drove the twenty feet to his own driveway, and parked again. Unlike his parents, he did not enter his house through the garage, which was detached. Rather, he walked to the rear of the house and entered there, into a small laundry room where he kept muddy shoes and the recycling. There he hung up his coat before continuing on into the kitchen.

Gathering eggs, butter, and cheese from the refrigerator, he made himself an omelette. When it was done, he sat at the table, a mirror image of the one in his parents' house, and he ate his breakfast from the same plates he'd eaten from as a child. They'd been given to him when his brother, into whose hands they'd first passed, married and received as a wedding present a new set of dishes. Stephen used them without a trace of sentimentality.

When he was finished eating, he washed and dried the dishes he'd dirtied and put them away. Then he entered the downstairs bedroom that functioned as his office and looked at his work for the day. The files he needed were stacked neatly to one side of his computer. Each one contained a tangle of receipts, bills, and assorted other financial debris, the accumulations resulting from his clients' monetary transactions.

Accounting suited him. Numbers were truthful things, completely incapable of deception, and he loved them. True, they could be made to lie, but their intrinsic nature was one of absolute honesty. Left to their own, they would always reveal the truth, and even if that truth was ugly, it was undeniable.

People, on the other hand, were something of a mystery to him. They were influenced by motivations, and seemingly irrational needs, and other things he found troubling and difficult to comprehend. Often, they wished to see anything other than the truth. He saw this frequently in the reactions his clients gave him to the financial truths he set before them. Unable to accept that they did not, in fact, have enough money to send a child to college or retire, they appeared wounded, as if the numbers had somehow betrayed them despite all of their goodwill and encouragement.

Stephen tried to be understanding, but usually he was simply embarrassed for them. He left them with the numbers and with suggestions for remedying their situations as practically as possible, excusing himself as soon as was polite so as to relieve himself of the contamination of their worry. He filed the encounters away in neatly labeled folders, arranged alphabetically by last name.

His own family was well taken care of. He saw to their finances, and knew that his parents would not have to worry about their golden years and that the concerns his two nephews and one niece would have regarding higher education would be gaining acceptance to the schools of their choosing. Everything else was the responsibility of the numbers, and in those he had unwavering confidence.

He sat at the desk and opened the first folder. Within moments he was lost in the rapture of expenses and receipts, his fingers flying over balance sheets and the keys of his calculator clicking as he added and subtracted, bringing order to chaos. When the phone rang an hour later, he looked at it, annoyed.

"Hello?"

"Good morning. It's Russell. I'm calling to remind you about tonight."

"Dinner," Stephen said. "Seven, right?"

"Seven," Russell repeated. "And look good. There's someone I want to introduce you to."

"Russell—" Stephen began.

"Don't start," Russell interrupted. "It's for your own good."

"But—"

"Be there at seven," Russell concluded, hanging up.

Stephen set the phone down and stared at it. His routine had been disturbed, now he was worried, and worry upset him because it was unnecessary. Why was Russell insisting on introducing him to someone? He hadn't asked for such a thing. Why would Russell assume it would be welcome?

He thought for a moment of canceling, of coming up with a plausible excuse to neatly remove himself from the situation. But he disliked lying. Besides, apart from this new surprise, he was looking forward to seeing Russell and John again. He had few friends, and his meeting with the couple had been a happy accident. Referred to Stephen by a teaching colleague of John's, they had come to him for help with their taxes earlier in the year. He had been impressed by John's organization and both intrigued and frightened by Russell's utter disregard for what others thought about him. When they'd invited him out socially, he'd surprised himself by accepting.

Since then they'd become friends. The subject of Stephen's romantic leanings had never been raised; Russell had just assumed and Stephen hadn't contradicted him. Almost immediately, Russell had made it his mission to find Stephen a suitable partner. So far Stephen had been able to put him off. Now, however, it seemed he was cornered.

He tried to forget about it, to lose himself in his work. But the numbers refused to cooperate, and finally he pushed the papers away and leaned back in his chair. Who was this person that Russell had selected for him? On what had he based his decision? They'd never discussed what Stephen was looking for.

And was he looking for anything? Even he wasn't sure what the answer to that question was. Being alone suited him. It prevented complications and made his life easier to manage. Adding someone else to the equation would mean making changes. Still, perhaps it was what he needed.

Romantic attachment was not something he'd permitted himself much of. In high school he'd seldom dated apart from the annual ritual of the prom. Even then, he'd attended with girls he'd befriended in his classes. There had been the awkward kiss or two, but little more. Once, during a long night of studying for a college midterm in statistical analysis, a study partner had unexpectedly professed her love for him and offered to prove it by allowing him to make love to her. He had tried, but the experiment had been a failure and he'd excused himself, citing exhaustion and concern for his grade point average.

He'd been more receptive to the handful of men with whom he'd had infrequent encounters, beginning with a friend in middle school who during a sleepover one weekend suggested they see whose penis was bigger, a proposal that had led to overly enthusiastic discussions of which girls at school they found attractive and culminated with their briefly touching one another's erections before retreating to the safety of their sleeping bags. There had been others since then, mostly in college, where experimentation of that sort was less significant and where he was assured some measure of anonymity due to the sheer size of the student population at the state school he attended.

In the decade since he'd returned to Cold Falls with his diploma in hand, he'd had less than half a dozen partners. Never had he brought anyone home, certain as he was that somehow his parents would find out and demand to know what exactly he thought he was doing. Nor could he stay over at someone else's house, as the absence of his car from the driveway would be sure to raise questions he was unprepared to answer.

The computer had become his way out. There, in the chat rooms he frequented sporadically, he was able to connect. There he could do the things he wanted to do with the men he wanted to do them with. It mattered little to him that they weren't real, or at any rate not physically present. In some ways he preferred that. When he and his partner were done, he simply logged off and was back in his own safe world where his longings couldn't disrupt things.

But tonight he would be faced with a real man, a person who would expect him to interact, presumably, using more than porn film dialogue. The idea of it made breathing difficult. His fingers drummed nervously on the desktop and he stared blankly at the screen. What would he say?

Instinctively, he opened his web browser and typed in an address. Moments later he was scrolling through the names of the men who were waiting, like him, in cyberspace for someone to come along. BoyBlue. GIJoe. JockStrp. Bi9Hrd. So many for being so early in the morning. They read like a menu of sexual appetizers. Some of them he recognized. Some he'd followed into private rooms. He breathed deeply. He was on familiar ground. They were just names. There was no one behind them, no one looking at him and judging. It was all make-believe.

A small window popped open on his screen. He looked at the message from JacknDude: Hey there. Looking for some fun?

Fun. Is that what he was looking for? No, but if that's what his correspondent wanted to call it, he didn't care. He put his hands on the keyboard and began to type.

CHAPTER 5

"Are they hitting it off?"

Russell paused, the pepper on the cutting board only half diced, as he waited for John's answer.

"I don't know," his lover said testily as he took two glasses from the cupboard. "Would you please stop trying to play matchmaker?"

Russell resumed chopping. "Greg is a nice guy," he said. "He's exactly what Stephen needs."

"How do you know what Stephen needs?" John asked. "Have you even asked him?"

Russell scraped the bits of pepper into the salad bowl. "There are some things you don't need to ask," he said. "Besides, I don't think he knows what he needs."

John picked up the drinks he'd poured and turned to leave. "Your obsession with arranging other people's lives is rivaled only by your obsession with rearranging our living room furniture," he said.

"Very funny," Russell answered. "But as I recall, you didn't know you needed me when we met."

"True," John said. "It took a great deal of convincing."

He left the kitchen. When he was gone, Russell set down the knife in his hand and took a long sip from the wineglass on the counter. So far, everything was going well. The roast was almost done, the pie had turned out beautifully, and with a little luck his attempt at setting Stephen up with Greg might just come off.

Then why don't I feel better about it all? he asked himself.

He knew why. It was John. Or rather, it was he and John. More and more he felt as if they simply occupied the same space, orbiting around one another without ever really connecting. They did the same things they'd been doing for seven years, but something had gone from the relationship. The happiness and confidence he'd once felt had been drained away, a slow, almost imperceptible leaching away of joy that hadn't become truly apparent until there was almost nothing left.

Now, though, he felt it strongly. He tried not to. He tried to go on as he always had, pretending that everything was going well and pushing his worries aside. Whenever he felt the prodding of insecurity, he banished it with an attempt at creating merriment, with an evening at the movies, a foray into a new and quickly abandoned interest, or a dinner party.

It was normal, he told himself. Relationships weren't designed to be perpetually exciting. He and John weren't newlyweds. They had a routine, a way of doing things that had developed over the years. That's what couples did. It's what his parents had done. It's what everyone did. He couldn't expect fireworks every day.

Probably, he thought, he was just depressed. He had to admit that work hadn't been particularly exciting either. Maybe a new job would help. And he *was* in middle age, he reminded himself. At forty-three, it was about time he had some kind of emotional crisis. It was practically expected. Hadn't his father come home with a new sports car one day around his own fortieth birthday? Russell, then fifteen, remembered the exasperated sigh his mother had let out upon seeing it roll into the driveway. But his father had been in noticeably better spirits for a long time afterward.

"See," he told himself firmly. "All you need is a Lexus and you'll be fine."

He picked up the salad bowl and headed for the dining room. As he passed from the kitchen, he forced the gloomy thoughts away and greeted his guests with a beaming smile.

"I hope you're all hungry," he said cheerfully as he placed the salad on the table and took his seat across from John. "What have I missed out here?"

"I was just asking John how the two of you met," Greg told him as he put some salad onto his plate.

"Oh, heavens," Russell answered. "It was at a Pride parade in Albany. I was living there and John was visiting some friends for the weekend."

"Under protest," John added.

"Parades aren't his thing," Russell explained. "But they'd dragged him along and I was there cheering for my friends on the gay chorus float."

"I asked him to stop shouting in my ear," John told Greg and Stephen.

"And I told him to get over himself," said Russell. "Then I left. But later that night I went to a party with my friends, and it turns out some of them knew some of the guys John was visiting, so we ran into each other again."

"Literally," said John. "He spilled a drink on me."

"Actually, I sort of threw it at him," Russell admitted. "He was complaining about the Dykes on Bikes who had led the parade, and he was ruining the mood."

"They were shirtless," John said sharply. "They were the only thing the newspeople focused on, and it made us all look like a bunch of perverts. And you never told me you *threw* that drink at me."

"It wasn't really throwing," Russell said quickly. "It was more like dropping. Anyway, we got into a big fight and somehow or other we ended up in bed back at my place. That was seven years ago."

"Opposites attracting," Greg said. "Kind of like *The Way We Were*. I think it's sweet."

"We dated long-distance for a year. Then John got the job here and we decided to move in together."

Greg picked up his wineglass. "I'd like to make a toast," he said. "To John and Russell. You guys are the kind of couple I want to be when I find the right guy."

The four men picked up their glasses and clinked them together. As he took a drink, Russell glanced across the table at John. His lover, busy picking at a spot on his shirt, didn't look at him.

"It must be amazing finding someone you can be with forever," Greg said.

Russell nodded. "Everyone should get to experience it," he said.

"Maybe if the morons who run this country wake up and legalize gay marriage, more of us will," Greg remarked.

"The only thing gay marriage would do is make a lot of money for gay divorce lawyers," John joked.

"Stephen, do you have many gay couples as clients?" Russell asked, ignoring his partner.

"Not really," Stephen said, wiping his mouth on his napkin. "Maybe two or three."

"Stephen is an accountant," Russell told Greg. "He does our taxes."

"What do you do?" Stephen asked Greg.

"I'm in men's underwear," Greg told him.

Seeing the blank look on Stephen's face, Greg and Russell laughed.

"It's a retail joke," Russell explained. "Greg is the manager of men's furnishings at Carter-Beane. You know, socks, underwear, pajamas."

"Oh," Stephen said, nodding. "Now I get it."

"I used to be in handbags," said Greg. "But after a while you just can't look at another Chanel clutch."

"I bet," said Stephen.

"Have you lived in Cold Falls a long time?" Greg inquired of Stephen.

"All my life," Stephen told him. "I went to Cold Falls Central School from kindergarten through twelfth grade. I didn't leave until I went off to college."

"And you came back?" said Greg. "That was brave."

"Not really," Stephen said. "My family lives here."

"Mine live in Pruitt, Kentucky," Greg told him. "Population sixteen, and fifteen of them are directly related to me. I got out as soon as I could."

"How'd you end up here?" asked Stephen.

"God hates me," Greg said. "Just kidding. I actually don't mind it here too much. The real answer is that I was transferred here from a store in Ohio. They offered it to me in the middle of February, and frankly, anything is better than Ohio in February."

"Except Pruitt, Kentucky, apparently," John remarked.

"Exactly," Greg said, ignoring the sarcastic tone of John's comment.

"Well, I wouldn't be here except that the children of Cold Falls Central School are in desperate need of scientific education," John said drily. "Stephen, I don't know how you ever graduated from such a place knowing anything."

"Actually, my chemistry teacher ended up shooting himself in the head in the boys' bathroom," Stephen replied. "Mr. Keller. It turned out he had a huge gambling debt."

"Is that what I have to look forward to?" John said aloud. "At least it would end my misery."

"I'll go get the pot roast," Russell announced. "Stephen, could you give me a hand with the salad plates?"

The two men disappeared into the kitchen, where the dirty plates were deposited in the sink. As Russell ran hot water over them, he asked, "So, what do you think of Greg?"

"He seems nice," Stephen said.

Russell dried his hands and turned his attention to the roast. "Nice as in okay, or nice as in you wouldn't mind going out on a date with him?"

"A date?" Stephen repeated. "That hadn't even occurred to me."

"Not a good sign," remarked Russell as he carved the meat. "I'll take that as a not-interested."

"No," said Stephen. "I just mean that . . . I don't know that . . ."

Russell looked at the young man. "Sweetie, you need to get a life," he said kindly. "You can't just sit around with old people all the time."

"I don't!" Stephen protested. "I go out. I do stuff."

Russell sighed. "When's the last time you had a date?"

Stephen shrugged his shoulders. "I don't know," he said.

"Have you ever *had* a date?" asked Russell.

"Of course I've had dates," said Stephen.

"I mean real dates," Russell continued. "At a restaurant, or a movie, or God forbid, the symphony."

"I don't have time," Stephen said vaguely.

"Like hell you don't," said Russell. "You have nothing but time. And you need someone to spend it with." He spooned the roasted potatoes and carrots into a bowl. "Now, I don't mean to get all Auntie Mame on you or anything, but I do know a thing or two about this particular subject, and I know that you are in desperate need of a love life. So take my advice, and if you like that young man sitting across the table from you, you ask him out before you leave here tonight. Now serve."

He pushed the bowl of vegetables into Stephen's hands and pushed him toward the door, following behind with the sliced roast. The two of them entered the dining room and placed the food on the table. Russell dipped back into the kitchen and returned with several more small bowls, which he added to those already there.

"This all looks—and smells—fantastic," Greg told Russell as they passed the food around. "Do you like to cook?" he asked Stephen as he handed him the platter of meat.

"Not really," said Stephen. "Mostly I eat at my parents' house or throw something in the microwave."

"I love cooking," Greg said. "But it's not much fun cooking for yourself. It's nicer to have someone to cook for."

Russell glanced over at Stephen, who was chewing a mouthful of food, oblivious to the obvious invitation Greg had just thrown his way. The boy really was being most uncooperative, and he couldn't understand why.

"So, tell me what the best part of being in a long-term relationship is," Greg asked, surprising him.

"Stability," John said before Russell could answer. "You always know where your life is going. No surprises."

"Russell?" Greg said.

Russell thought. Stability? Is that what he meant to John, a life that was always the same? It made him sound practical and dependable, like a dog or a good winter coat. There was nothing romantic about stability, nothing to tug on the heartstrings or send the senses reeling.

"I guess the best part is not having to wonder who you'll have sex with next," Russell said.

John's head snapped up and he looked at his lover with a startled expression. Russell calmly stabbed a carrot with his fork and put it in his mouth as Stephen and Greg looked from one partner to the other.

"I mean, you know how it is," Russell continued. "When you're single, you always have to worry about the sex thing every time you're with someone new. Will he be good? Will I be good? What if it's too big or too small? Once you partner up, you always know what you're getting. You don't have to wonder if he's freaked out by rimming or hates the taste of cum or whatever."

John was still starring at him, stunned. Russell swallowed the food in his mouth and put his fork down.

"Now, who wants dessert?" he asked brightly.

A moment later he was standing in the kitchen. John was behind him, fuming.

"I can't believe you said that," he hissed. "That was so rude."

"What?" Russell asked. "You mean I surprised you? I'm sorry for not being stable enough for you."

"What are you talking about?" said John irritably.

Russell whirled around and faced him. "You make me feel like a couch," he said.

"What?" John said again, looking even more confused.

"A couch," Russell repeated. "Or old socks, or, or, or something else dependable and boring and predictable." He started to cry.

"I have no idea what's going on here," said John.

"Neither do I!" Russell said, wiping the tears from his face and staring at his partner. He felt as if he was seeing John clearly for the first time, and he was terrified to discover that his lover's face now bore almost no resemblance to that of the man he'd fallen in love with.

He longed for John to take him in his arms, to hold him and comfort him and tell him that everything would be fine. He waited, the seconds stretching out interminably as John looked at him. Then John cleared his throat.

"I'll take the cake out," he said. "You come out when you've calmed down a little."

CHAPTER 6

"How long have you lived here?"

Mike looked at the man sitting in front of him at the bar. The guy was on his third drink—vodka tonics—in an hour, and his face was showing the signs of drunkenness. Not that he'd looked all that great before he'd started drinking. He'd come in right at four, moments after Mike unlocked the front door, not even bothering to brush the snow from his coat. He hadn't moved since, and a small puddle had formed on the floor around him as the snow had melted in the heat of the room.

"Couple of years," Mike told him. He never got too specific with customers, especially ones he didn't know. The man's face was new to him, and he didn't like what he saw. There was a sadness behind the unfocused eyes and reddened nose, a weariness that spoke of long hours spent in other bars, looking for one thing and avoiding another.

"Nice place to live?" the man tried again.

Mike shrugged. "Depends what you like," he said. "It suits me." He thought about asking the man if he wanted another drink, then decided against it. The last thing he needed was a drunk passed out on his floor.

"I used to live in a place like this," the man told him, pushing an ice cube around his half-full glass with his finger. "Couldn't wait to get out. Bunch of small-town hicks with small-town minds."

"Where'd you go?" Mike asked him. He didn't care what the answer was, but since the man seemed intent on taking up his time with the conversation, he thought he might as well play along. He had nothing else to do until the happy hour rush started.

"Oh, here and there," the man told him, waving his hand around vaguely. "Any big city I could find. Anywhere that wasn't like this place. New York. Chicago. Even Amsterdam for a year."

"And what brings you here now?"

"Business," the man told him, taking a swig from his glass. "Had to fly into Albany, drive up to Syracuse, and now I'm going back again. I needed a pit stop, and this hole was listed in my Damron guide."

"I take it we're not what you're used to," Mike commented.

"I don't mean nothing by it," said the man apologetically. "It's just that being here depresses me. Reminds me of what I ran away from."

"I guess you'll be glad to get back home then," said Mike.

The man drained his glass and set it on the bar. "That's the kicker," he said as he zipped his coat and stood up. "What I found out in all those big cities was that everywhere's the same. You trade the trailers for condos, the blue collars for white ones, it doesn't matter. Only difference is that in a big city it's easier to convince yourself that things are better. If you can keep that up long enough, you make yourself believe it."

He gave Mike a final nod and turned to go. Mike watched him walk unsteadily toward the door, waiting for him to push open the portal onto the snowy night before pocketing the bills the man had left behind for his tip.

The snow was something of a surprise. Usually the cold held off until the end of November, making its grand entrance just in time to create a winter wonderland and get everyone in the mood to face Christmas. But the cold had come early this year, the temperatures dropping overnight and the dawn rising on a landscape whose sharp edges were blunted by powdery wrapping. Now it was a world of plows and rock salt, mittens and scarves.

Mike, for one, was pleased that winter had arrived ahead of schedule. He liked the shorter days and the nights that came early and stayed late. Inside the Engine Room, it didn't matter if the sun was shining anyway. His was a world lit by neon beer signs and low-wattage bulbs. It was warm, an escape from the cold where men gathered for company to stave off both their loneliness and the darkness. Seeing the place packed that evening, Mike thought pleasantly of long-ago days when men crowded into similarly shadowed taverns and alehouses as the frigid winds tore at the world.

Those men spoke to one another of things that occupied their lives, of the sea and whales, farms and flocks. The men in the Engine Room talked of much different things: Cher and *Queer as Folk,* their boring jobs and equally boring love lives. But wasn't it in many ways the same? Hadn't they just traded in their mugs of ale for Cosmos in delicately stemmed glasses, their weather-aged faces for eyes bathed in Clinique?

Mike laughed to himself. It was a ridiculous analogy. But he liked it anyway. No, most of the men who were now coming in and filling the bar with their voices were not exactly the hearty adventurers their ancestors might have been. Yet didn't they rub the cold from their hands the way those men might have? Didn't they, too, find brotherhood in one another?

He was stretching again. He sighed. Where was the adventure in the world? He looked around at the men holding their drinks and chatting about nothing. Didn't they want something more? Didn't they want to *do* something?

He was bored, and he knew it, and that irritated him. His customer with the tired face had been right—everything really was the same. But no, he told himself, he didn't really believe that. There *were* different people to meet and places to see. There was something beyond the WELCOME TO COLD FALLS, NY sign that was planted out on the highway running into town. It was they who chose to stay there, safe within the familiar world. They. He. He had chosen to stay there.

"Mike! Give me a cold one!"

A familiar face greeted him, and he brushed his thoughts away. He would, he knew, lose himself in the patterns of a Friday night at the Engine Room, dive headlong into the currents of chatter, and distract himself with filling orders and making change.

Right up until two o'clock in the morning, that's what he did. And when the final customer was sent to his car, the door was locked, and the cleanup guys were washing the place down, Mike headed out the back door to his waiting pickup.

He drove with the windows down, the chill air filling the cab of the truck, sweeping over his body and escaping through the passenger side window. He felt it cleansed him, carried away the smell of smoke and alcohol that permeated his T-shirts every night and seemed to leave behind a layer of grime he could feel clinging to his skin. He hated touching his own face before he had a chance to shower.

It was still snowing. Although not as heavy as it had been earlier, it still fell steadily, forming an ocean of swirling flakes through which the headlights of the truck cut two thin golden paths. The road had been plowed hours before, and now the tracks of the cars that had passed through since then were almost filled up again.

He turned on the radio and suddenly Hank Williams was sitting beside him, so lonesome he could cry. Mike turned the volume up until Hank's voice drowned out the sound of the windshield wipers with their scratchy click-click-click. It was just himself, Hank, and the snow. The only part of the world that existed was the few feet Mike could see ahead of him; everything else fell away into blackness. Contained in this circle of snow and wind and light, he continued down the road.

He crested a hill and began the descent down the other side. As he neared the bottom, he saw, too late, the blinking red and yellow eyes of a car's hazard lights. Then a face emerged from the snow, eyes tightened against the glare of his headlamps, and arm raised to cover the face.

Mike's foot pressed the brake to the floor and the truck slid, first sliding to the right and then, as he turned the wheel, spinning around completely. The world became a blur of black and white, turning in slow motion until the truck came to a stop with a dull thud and Mike was thrown back against his seat.

His first thought was that he'd hit the figure in the snow. But as his head cleared and he was able to look outside, he saw that he had simply ended up in a bank left behind by a plow. His engine had stalled, but the lights still glowed brightly against the snow and there didn't seem to be any damage.

He opened the door and stepped gingerly to the ground, testing his bones. Everything seemed to be working just fine. Reassured, he walked to the rear of the truck and looked back up the road. The car still sat there, twenty feet away, its hazards unnaturally cheerful. A shadow detached itself and ran toward him.

"Are you okay?"

He couldn't see the face, but the voice was distinctly male.

"Yeah, yeah, I'm fine," Mike said. "But what the fuck are you doing parked in the middle of the road?"

The man came closer, stepping into the light so that Mike could finally see him. He peered at Mike through glasses flecked with snow. His dark hair, too, was capped by a white frost.

"I'm so sorry," he said. "My car just stopped, and I couldn't push it anywhere. I don't have my cell phone with me and—"

"It's okay," said Mike. "We're both fine, right? You just gave me a scare."

The man sighed visibly. "It's so cold," he said, glancing up at the sky and putting his hands in his pockets. Then he looked at Mike, wearing just a T-shirt under his open jacket. "Aren't you cold?" he asked.

"Let's take a look at your car," said Mike. "Do you have any idea what's wrong?"

"I'm not exactly mechanical," the man told him as he fell into step beside Mike. "Are you?" he asked hopefully.

"We'll find out," answered Mike.

They reached the car and Mike opened the door. The keys were still in the ignition. He turned them and the car's interior lights burst into life.

"The battery's not dead," Mike said.

He tried to start the engine. The car gave a sad little cough before relapsing into silence. He tried again and got the same result. He was about to get out and look beneath the hood when his gaze fell on the fuel gauge. The needle was deep in the red zone.

"When's the last time you filled this thing up?" he asked the man, who was standing beside the car and looking at him anxiously.

"Filled it up? Oh, I guess a week or so ago maybe."

"Well, you should have done it tonight. You're out of gas."

"Out of gas?" the man repeated. "Really?" He leaned in and stared at the gauge Mike was pointing to. "Oh, I see."

"There's not a gas station in town open this time of night," Mike told him. "Best thing to do is push the car to the side of the road, leave it here, and hope the morning plow doesn't think it's a drift that needs clearing."

He got out, gently pushing the man with the car door.

"I'll push," Mike told him. "You steer."

The man got in and Mike stepped behind the car. Placing his hands on the trunk, he pushed hard. The car didn't budge.

"Is your foot on the brake?" Mike called out.

"Yes," the man shouted back.

"Take it off," Mike ordered, shaking his head.

He pushed again. This time the car rolled forward easily. The man guided it as far to the side of the road as it would go and stopped. Mike dusted off his wet hands and walked to the driver side window.

"Come on," he said. "I'll give you a lift home. You can come back for the car in the morning."

The man got out, locked the car, and followed Mike to his truck. Once inside, Mike turned the key and was relieved to hear his engine rumble to life. He turned up the heater, which rewarded him with breaths of warm air.

"I'm Mike, by the way," he told his passenger.

"Thomas," the man said. "Thanks for stopping to help."

Mike laughed. "I didn't have a lot of choice," he replied.

Thomas smiled. "I guess you didn't," he said. "Thanks anyway."

"So, where are we going?" Mike asked him.

Thomas looked at him blankly.

"Where do you live?" Mike clarified.

"Oh, right," said Thomas. "Saint Peter's Episcopal Church."

"You live in a church?"

"Not in it," Thomas said. "Behind it. I'm the priest there."

Mike looked sideways at him. For the first time he noticed the white collar peering out from the neck of the man's black jacket.

"What were you doing out this time of night?" he asked.

"One of my parishioners is sick," Thomas told him. "She probably won't live to see Thanksgiving."

Mike nodded, not knowing what to say. Just the idea that there was a priest in his truck was a bit unnerving. He wasn't sure why, really. The man seemed nice enough. But he and religion didn't have much to do with one another, and he preferred to keep the whole thing at arm's length.

"Well, we'll have you back at the church in no time," said Mike.

"I really didn't expect anyone to come along so late," the priest told him. "It's something of a miracle that you did."

"I work late hours," Mike explained. "I was on my way home."

Almost immediately he regretted telling the priest that, as he knew the question it would raise. Sure enough, a moment later Thomas asked, "What do you do?"

Mike hesitated. Should he tell the priest the truth? It probably wouldn't go over very well. But why did he care, anyway? He didn't owe the guy anything. He was irritated with himself for even thinking it mattered what the man thought of him.

"I'm a bartender," he said. "At the Engine Room."

He waited for the priest to say something disapproving. Much to his surprise, Thomas said, "So we're in the same line of work."

Mike looked at him, confused. "How so?"

"Well," Thomas said, "we both minister to people. They come to us because they need something. I'm sure you've had to sit through more than one confession or request for advice. Am I right?"

Mike grinned. "Yes," he said. "You're right."

"Not that I have much experience with bars, mind you," the priest continued, "but I think they have quite a bit in common with churches. People gather there to be part of a community. They look for something they don't find elsewhere."

"You're an interesting priest," said Mike.

"Am I?" Thomas said. "I wonder."

The two of them settled into silence as Mike drove through the snow. Ten minutes later he pulled into the driveway of Saint Peter's. When the truck came to a stop, Thomas turned to him.

"Thank you again for your help," he said.

"No problem," said Mike. "Just don't forget to pick up your car tomorrow. Call any garage and they'll be able to get some gas to it."

Thomas nodded. "I will," he said. "And perhaps one of these days you'll come by and see what it is I do."

Mike laughed. "Tell you what," he answered. "If you come see me at work, I'll come see you." The idea of the priest setting foot in the Engine Room was as ridiculous as him setting foot in a church.

"I just might take you up on that offer," Thomas said as he got out and shut the door. "But for now, good night."

Mike waved at the priest and pulled away. Again he thought about Thomas standing in the middle of a bunch of queens at the bar. He laughed. *What I wouldn't give to see the look on his face,* he thought as he headed home.

CHAPTER 7

He wished he'd worn the rubber boots.
The snow was deeper than he'd expected, and with every step, his feet became more and more damp. He should have known better, he told himself. Walter would have scolded him. "I told you so," he would have said, his voice filled with reproach and love.

At least he'd remembered the scarf. It was red, the only flash of color against the white snow and the black of his greatcoat. The scarf was Walter's last gift to him, finished only days before the end. Unable to sleep, he'd stayed up all night knitting furiously, as if the clicking of the needles staved off death's arrival. When finally it was done, he'd given it to Simon, saying, "It's going to be cold. You're going to need this."

And he had needed it. In the days following Walter's death, he had refused to take it off, wearing it wrapped around his throat like a noose. It had absorbed his tears, soaking them up as they coursed down his cheeks. He saw it as a relic, a holy remnant left behind by the most glorious angel he'd ever known.

Eventually he had been able to take it off, to hang it first on the hook beside the kitchen door where his and Walter's coats hung beside the dog's leash, and then, months later, to take it down and put it in a drawer. He'd taken it out at the first sign of fall, but not until that morning had he put it on.

Immediately the memories of the year before had come back, as if his tears had locked them into the fabric of the scarf and putting it around his neck had released them once more. He smelled the scent of Walter's room, the odor of flowers covering up the acrid stench of decay. He saw again his lover's withered body, consumed by cancer until he resembled a doll made of sticks. But always his blue eyes had sparkled, always they had lit up for Simon, until the moment when they closed forever and Simon had been left holding Walter's lifeless hand in his own.

Death had surprised him with its quickness. Despite the length of Walter's decline, the ending had come as a shock. Nine months he had been ill. It had taken as long for the cancerous cells to multiply and devour him as it took other, less treacherous, cells to bond and bring a new life into the world. How strange it was, the power of those infinitesimal building blocks, to both build up and tear down. Where one blossomed, another took back. What, he wondered, determined their temperament? Why was one body blessed and another cursed?

He'd asked himself those questions while Walter was dying, attempting to make sense of it all. Instead, he should have been preparing himself for the cold rain of grief that came upon him at the very moment of Walter's passing. He'd thought about it, of course, but only in the vaguest of terms. Walter would die. Walter would be dead. Walter would be buried.

But the real pain came not from the death, but from the absence. The death he could handle, had handled, with as much grace as he could muster. The absence, however, was unbearable. One moment they had been together; the next Simon had been alone. There was no gradual transition, no soothing possibility of return. There was simply aloneness.

He had adjusted. He'd had no choice. At first his mind refused to accept the truth, and he'd wandered aimlessly around his house as friends helped him deal with the mundane chores of arranging the funeral, informing relations and other concerned parties, and handling the legal affairs. He had pretended that he was simply organizing a party, a party at which Walter would be the guest of honor.

But afterward, when the funeral was over and the friends had gone home, leaving him in an empty house, he had come face to face with the emptiness Walter had left behind when his spirit had flown. Gone was the warmth of his laughter and the strength of his love, and without them Simon was a ghost. He haunted himself, moving from room to room in search of the past. He sat on the bed, the red scarf around his neck, and wept himself dry. And still it did no good. Still every night he went to bed alone and woke up to a coldness no amount of hot water could ease from his bones.

A year had gone by, and with the turning of the seasons, things had become more bearable. Spring, with its renewing of life, had reawakened in Simon a desire to live. Summer's sun had returned the warmth to his blood. And now he had arrived back at fall more or less intact.

He came to the gravestone and stopped. He'd visited Walter many times in the months following his burial, but he had not been there since late summer. He felt slightly guilty about that, as if he'd stood his lover up, left him waiting, alone, wondering what had happened. This, though, was the important day, the anniversary, and he had come. He stood, looking down at the ground.

"Hey there," he said. "How have you been?"

He reached out and brushed some of the snow from the top of Walter's stone, the way he would have brushed it from his shoulder had they been walking together. His fingertips lingered on the stone for a moment before he pulled his hand back and placed it in the pocket of his coat.

"I guess you want to hear about what's been going on," he said. "Not much, I'm afraid. You haven't missed a thing. Clancy's started barking at the mailman. I don't think he hears very well anymore. Sort of like me, right?"

He smiled to himself, imagining Walter's response to that. He'd almost brought Clancy with him, but the old pug hated the snow and preferred to spend his days curled up on the couch in the spot Walter had once occupied.

He had brought something else, however. In the big pocket of his coat was a CD player. He took it out and held it in his hands.

"It's Brahms," he said. "*The German Requiem.* Only it's in English, Shaw's translation. I tried the original and it was just too much."

He placed the tiny earpieces into his ears and hit the play button. The voices of the Mormon Tabernacle Choir filled his head. He himself would have preferred Mozart, but Walter had always had an affinity for Brahms, frequently quoting the composer's well-known remark, "I never laugh on the inside." Despite Walter's love of life, he'd been fascinated with the darkness that could descend upon even the happiest of souls. Brahms had been one of his favorites, a man who composed soothing lullabies through which ran the merest hint of nightmare. He had listened to Brahms endlessly in the last months, until Simon had found himself humming entire movements even when he was far from the house.

He'd discovered the *Requiem* several months after Walter's death. It was in the CD player Walter had used at night, when he needed the solace of music but didn't want to disturb Simon's sleep. While finally cleaning out the things from Walter's bedside table, Simon had opened the player and seen the CD. At first its significance had escaped him, but when he went to locate the case for the disc, the symbolism had become clear—Walter had been listening to the music of death.

He'd waited another few weeks before putting the disc into the stereo and playing it for himself. He'd wept through the entire performance, sitting on the couch stroking Clancy's head as his body shook. The music, even in the original German, seared his heart. When later he'd bought an English translation and actually understood the words, he'd cried anew.

Now he shut his eyes and listened as the Mormon Tabernacle Choir sang for his dead lover. He knew Walter would appreciate the irony of the notoriously homophobic Mormons serenading him. Besides, the music was heavenly, the soprano soloist angelic. The performance transcended any differences of belief, the orchestra and singers merely acting as conduits for the music.

He stood before Walter's grave, the snow falling gently around him, and he listened for some time. He felt neither cold nor weariness. His feet, wet beyond caring, were numb. All that mattered was his being there, sharing the moment with Walter. Brahms's exquisite creation was the bridge between them, a soaring golden arch across which the worlds of the living and the dead were united.

Half an hour passed, or more. When the choir began to sing the first notes of "How Lovely Is Thy Resting Place," Simon opened his eyes. Removing the earphones from his ears, he placed the still-playing CD in the snow atop Walter's grave.

"Good night, sweet prince," he said softly, then turned to go.

The walk back to the car was mercifully short. Only when he tried to insert the key into the lock did he realize how truly cold he was. His fingers hesitated, and he had to blow on them to get them to bend.

Once inside the car, he sat with the heater at full strength until he felt capable of holding the wheel.

When he reached home, the first thing he did was remove his wet shoes and socks. His toes, like his fingers, refused to feel anything but cold for a long time, despite being wrapped in dry wool socks and slippers. A mug of coffee did its bit to revive his frigid interior, however, and soon he was feeling less like an icicle and most definitely like a sixty-five-year-year-old man who had stayed out in the cold for too long a time.

He sat down on the couch, where he was joined by Clancy, who snuggled into his lap and almost immediately went to sleep. Simon sat, rubbing the dog's ears and listening to him snore. He missed Walter. He missed holding him, and touching him. He missed hearing his breathing as he slept and his singing as he moved throughout the house, forever rearranging furniture and cleaning up.

They were supposed to have grown old together. That had always been the plan. Whenever Simon had thought about his life, he'd always imagined it continuing on and on forever, Walter accompanying him hand in hand. He'd thought about death, of course, but never the specifics of it. They would both die, naturally, but he'd secretly hoped it would be together, in a car accident or even in their sleep.

Now he was left to grow old alone. He supposed to many people he already *was* old. At sixty-five, he was far older than most of the men he knew. Certainly he was far beyond being attractive to them. He knew this, and accepted it. Old gay men were not, in the general scheme of things, hot properties. They could be funny. They could dispense advice. If they were very good, they might be allowed to pay someone younger and more handsome for the privilege of touching his body. But they were not supposed to desire any more than that. It was in poor taste. They'd had their chances, and it was expected that they would now relinquish the rights and privileges of love to those coming up behind them.

No one, in the year since Walter's death, had asked him if he ever thought about finding another partner. It was as if a tacit understanding existed that he had been given his years of happiness and was now supposed to live the remainder of his life comforted by memories. He had cooperated, he knew, by assuming the role of the grieving husband. He had waited the appropriate amount of time and then reappeared at the Engine Room, where he'd been greeted warmly and given a seat of honor at the bar.

But it wasn't enough. Perhaps it was selfish, but he wanted more of what he'd had with Walter. He knew that he'd been given more than most people ever had in a lifetime, but still his heart longed to be filled with the sweet ache of love.

He stood, Clancy sliding gently from his lap and stretching out across the sofa cushion. Leaving the dog there, Simon went upstairs and into the bedroom he'd shared with Walter for more than forty years. Bit by bit, Walter's presence had faded from the room, leaving behind only a faint reminder, like the roses on the wallpaper they'd spent one whole weekend hanging almost thirty years ago. His clothes and personal effects were gone, given to charity or put into boxes and stored in the attic.

But something still remained, something that couldn't be seen or touched or smelled. It was a feeling, a lingering memory that often was difficult to grasp on to but which came into sharper focus whenever Simon entered the room. Here, in the place where they'd spent their most intimate times, he felt closer to Walter than he did anywhere else in the world.

Pictures of him and Walter were placed around the room, images capturing them at various stages of life. The oldest was taken at the party where they'd met, a now yellowing photograph depicting two handsome young men, their arms thrown around one another's shoulders. The most recent had been taken a few months before Walter's death. Walter, overly thin but still smiling, sat in bed while Simon stood beside him.

The beginning and the end, Simon thought as he looked around. And everything in between. He was living in a room of memory, a sacred vault where the life he and Walter had created could be safely stored. Here he felt most alive, here where the heart they'd shared continued to beat softly and steadily.

He removed his clothes, letting them fall to the floor. Standing in front of the full-length mirror that covered the back of the closet door, he looked at his body. His belly was slack, the skin of his arms wrinkled. The muscles he'd once possessed had softened, and the hair on his chest had grayed.

Still, Walter had found him sexy. They had found one another sexy.

Making love for the last time, a week before Walter's cancer had made it impossible for him to do anything other than breathe and speak in short sentences, they had been as enamored of one another as they had been on that first night.

Simon held his penis in his hand, gently massaging it. It was funny how the cock never aged. While other parts of their bodies had begun to suffer the vagaries of age, his and Walter's dicks had remained forever eighteen. Even when various medications and health issues made erections difficult, they had managed. When Simon had taken Walter into his mouth and closed his eyes, he had tasted exactly what he'd tasted four decades earlier, and when he entered Walter, perhaps more cautiously than in those days, he was greeted with the same embracing warmth.

How he'd enjoyed making love with Walter. They'd known everything about one another, and even after years together the smell, taste, and feel of his lover's body against his had been a revelation. Each time they'd come together had made him long for more.

He was hard now, thinking about Walter. His hand moved gently up and down the length of his cock as he lost himself in a daydream. They were in bed. It was afternoon. The sun streamed in the windows and the sheets, hopelessly tangled, hung off the bed. The two of them, sweaty and deeply in love, rolled atop the bed, arms and legs a puzzle.

How old were they? Twenty-one? Fifty-seven? It didn't matter. In his dream they were ageless. All that mattered to him was that they were together, their hands caressing one another, their mouths pressed together.

He came unexpectedly, his body convulsing joyfully as he cried out half in pleasure and half in anguish at having his dream end so suddenly. He reached out, hoping to feel warm flesh beneath his fingers. Instead he touched the cold, smooth surface of the mirror.

He opened his eyes. The mirror was spattered with the results of his orgasm. Behind the milky stain his body was reflected back at him, his rapidly softening cock still held in his hand. Suddenly his knees felt weak. He fell to the floor, kneeling in front of the mirror. He was now level with the streaky smears, his face obscured by the net of pale liquid. The joy he'd felt at the moment of climax had disappeared along with his erection.

Putting his face in his hands, he cried.

CHAPTER 8

"Gina's pissed off again because you didn't give her the Lancôme counter."

Russell looked up from his desk to see Greg standing in the doorway.

"Thanks for the warning," he said. "I'll be sure to be busy doing inventory all day."

Greg sat down in the chair across from Russell.

"What's the matter?" he asked. "You don't seem your usual perky self. In fact, you haven't seemed yourself for a while. Is something wrong?"

Russell put down the order sheets he was going over. Things were very wrong, but he was doing his best to pretend that they weren't. So far, it had been working. But now, with Greg sitting in front of him looking at him with such sympathy, he cracked.

"I moved out," he said.

"Out?" Greg repeated.

"Out of the house," Russell said, his voice hitching. "Away from John."

Greg's eyes went wide. "You moved out?"

Russell nodded toward the door of his office. "Close it," he said.

Greg did as he was asked. Once they were alone, he let out a deep breath, trying to hold back the tears that were forming in his eyes. *I won't cry*, he told himself. *I won't cry*. It had become his new mantra.

"So, what happened?" Greg asked him. "You guys seemed fine at dinner."

Russell laughed. He'd been anything but fine at dinner. After his breakdown in the kitchen, he'd pulled it together enough to sit through the meal without letting on that he was falling apart inside. He'd smiled and nodded, and even said one or two funny things that had made everyone laugh.

Then, after dessert was over and Stephen and Greg had taken their leave, he'd come undone again. Standing over the kitchen sink, he'd burst into tears as John had stood, bewildered, in the doorway looking at him. Finally Russell had turned the water off, turned to John, and announced that he was moving out.

"We need a break," Russell told Greg. "I need a break."

"But what's wrong with the relationship?" Greg inquired.

Russell leaned back in his chair and ran his hands over his face. "That's just it," he said. "I don't know. It's more like what's right with it."

"Do you still love him?" Greg said.

Russell nodded.

"And does he still love you?"

"He says he does," Russell answered.

"Then it's about sex," Greg declared emphatically.

"It's *not* about sex," Russell countered.

"Well, it's got to be about something. You don't just move out after, what is it, seven years? Where did you go, anyway?"

"I'm staying with a friend."

"A friend, or a *friend*," Greg asked, emphasizing the last word meaningfully.

"No, it's not like that," Russell told him. "I'm not having an affair. It's a woman. Cheryl."

"Cheryl from furniture?" Greg said.

Russell nodded. "She has an extra room."

"Have you talked to John since you left?"

"A couple of times," Russell said. "Actually, we're supposed to have lunch in forty-five minutes. I don't honestly know what to say to him. He just doesn't get it."

"No offense, but it sounds like you don't either," said Greg.

"I know, I know," Russell said, shaking his head. "I think I just need some time away from him to figure stuff out. I can't think straight when I'm around him."

"Seven years is a long time," Greg suggested.

"Don't say it," Russell told him before Greg could continue.

"Well, it is."

"I know it is. And there's no reason a gay relationship can't go on for a lot longer than that."

Greg nodded. "I'm not saying it can't. I'm just saying that sometimes the, you know, magic, wears off after a while."

"What's the longest you've ever been with someone?" Russell asked him.

"A couple of months," Greg admitted.

"Get back to me when it's been a couple of years," Russell said.

"I know it's different," Greg continued, waving a hand at him. "I know the fireworks turn into something else and blah, blah, blah. Believe me, I hope I find out. But sometimes relationships just run their course."

Russell shook his head. "I just can't think like that," he said sadly. "I can't. If I let myself think that, then it's all been for nothing."

"I don't know what to tell you," Greg said.

"You don't have to tell me anything," Russell reassured him. "I appreciate you just listening to me. You don't know what it's been like not being able to say anything to anyone. I've barely slept in two weeks. I screwed up these reports three times."

"Let me know if there's anything I can do," Greg told him. "In the meantime, I'll keep Gina out of your hair. There's a sweater display out there that's going to need total refolding."

Russell laughed. "Thank you," he said. "Hey, what about you? Have you heard from Stephen?"

Greg shook his head. "Shot down again," he said. "I've left him two messages."

Russell sighed. "I just don't get him," he said. "I could tell he liked you."

"And I liked him," said Greg. "But as we both know, that's not always enough."

Greg stood up. "Time to straighten out the boxer briefs," he said. "And just about time for your lunch."

Russell looked at his watch. Greg was right. He was due to meet John in fifteen minutes.

"You look fine," Greg said.

Russell blushed. "I feel like I'm going on a date," he said. "It's so stupid."

"You're just nervous," Greg told him.

"I'm beyond nervous," said Russell. "This is the first time we've been face to face since I left."

"It's John," Greg reminded him. "Just talk to him."

Russell nodded. Greg opened the office door and left. Russell waited a minute, put on his coat, and left. Minutes later he was in his car, heading for the restaurant he'd suggested for his meeting with John. Much too quickly, he was there. He scanned the parking lot for John's car, saw it, and felt a wave of nausea sweep over him.

He almost left, but he knew that wouldn't change anything. Finally he calmed his nerves and got out of the car. He walked quickly into the restaurant, found John seated at a table near the back, and walked over.

"Hey," he said, sliding into the bench across from John. "Sorry I'm late."

"You're always late," said John emotionlessly. "I'm used to it."

"Sorry," Russell said again.

He picked up the menu and pretended to look at it. It didn't matter what he ordered; he wasn't going to eat much of it anyway. That's why he'd picked Panda Garden; it was easier to make Chinese food look as if you'd eaten it.

"I don't know why they call this place Panda Garden," he said, his voice tight. "Why would pandas have a garden?"

"Russell, I didn't come here to talk about the name of the restaurant," John said.

Russell closed the menu and put it down. He picked up the packet of wooden chopsticks next to his plate and fidgeted with them. "Right," he said.

John was just looking at him, not saying anything. Russell felt like one of his lab experiments. He wondered what results Russell was expecting from this particular test.

"How have you been?" he asked finally.

"How do you think I've been?" John replied.

"Why do you always answer me with another question?" said Russell defensively. "Why can't you ever just say what you're thinking?"

"You just answered me with two questions," John retorted. "But to answer your original one, I've been fine."

"Fine," Russell repeated. Had he really been fine? How fine could someone be whose partner of seven years had snapped and walked out on him? He looked at John. His hands were folded on the table in front of him and his face was expressionless. He looked as cool as he probably did every day when he faced a room full of students who couldn't care less about what he had to say to them.

"I'm really sorry," Russell said. "I know this is weird."

Again John said nothing. Russell tried to think of something else to say, anything to break the awful silence. He was saved by the fortunate arrival of the waitress to take their order.

"Sweet and sour chicken," Russell said dutifully, listening as John requested beef with broccoli. When the waitress had disappeared, he began again. "I'm sorry about leaving."

"Why?"

He looked at his partner. "What?"

"I asked you why," John repeated. "Why are you sorry?"

"Because it was a shitty thing to do," Russell said. "I just left you there with no explanation."

"But you're not sorry you left."

It was a statement, not a question, and Russell wasn't sure what to say to it. Finally he said, "No, I'm not sorry about the leaving, just about how I did it. I needed to leave."

"Fair enough," John said. "Can you tell me why?"

That was the million-dollar question. Russell looked down at his paper placemat. It was printed with the signs of the Chinese Zodiac. Out of habit, he searched for his birthday and saw that he was born in the Year of the Tiger. John, a year older, was an Ox. He looked at the description for the Tiger and saw that in the love section it said "Most incompatible with the Ox." He moved his plate to cover the image and looked at John again.

"I know you're confused," he said carefully. "I'm confused too. I just feel like things aren't right."

"Things," said John. "You mean our relationship. You don't have to be vague."

"And you don't have to be so fucking scientific all the time."

John's head snapped up and he looked at Russell in surprise.

"I'm sorry for saying it like that," Russell said. "But that's part of the problem. I feel like I'm one of your students. When you talk to me, it's like I'm sitting in one of your lectures."

John said nothing. His fingers idly played with the silverware, straightening the fork and knife until they were perfectly parallel. Russell waited for a response from him, but it was clear none was forthcoming.

"It's like we live in a lab," Russell continued. "Our lives are sterile, perfectly planned, boring."

"So you're bored with me," said John, nodding as if he'd figured out the solution to an equation. "It's time to move on."

"No," Russell said. "I didn't say that."

The waitress reappeared, carrying their lunches, and they each looked away as she set them down. When she left, neither moved to begin eating. Finally, John spoke.

"Russell, ever since I've known you, you've flitted from one thing to another," he said evenly. "You have a new interest every week. First it was photography, then it was gardening. Last year it was yoga, for Christ's sake. You're like a little boy sometimes, always looking for a new toy."

Russell felt himself blushing with anger. The tone in John's voice was exactly the one he hated hearing, the one that made him feel small and silly.

"I can't help it if you don't know what you want," John continued. "Maybe if you had a real job . . ."

"I do have a real job," Russell said, trying to control his voice. "Just because you don't think what I do is important doesn't mean it isn't. And I happen to be very good at what I do, but you wouldn't know that because you never ask."

John sighed and opened his mouth.

"And don't talk to me like a child," Russell continued. "I'm not one. I'm an adult. I'm your partner and I'm your equal."

"I don't think this is getting us anywhere," said John. "Maybe we should just do it some other time."

"You're not running away from this," Russell told him. "You're not walking out just because you're too embarrassed to talk about something other than formulas and reactions and the goddamned Periodic Table. You're going to sit there and talk about *us*. That's what's real, John, not your precious science."

The waitress, passing by, paused and gave them a big grin. "Everything all right?" she asked, eyeing their untouched plates.

"Fantastic," Russell told her, smiling. Giving him a bewildered look, she moved on to the next table.

"I do know why I had to leave," Russell said. "Sitting here with you right now, I know why. I had to leave because I was suffocating. I was constantly holding my breath, afraid to say anything in case it would upset you. I was running out of air."

"I never asked you to do that," said John.

Russell nodded. "You're right, you didn't. But you demanded it by the way you acted. You made me afraid to speak."

"You make me sound like a monster," said John.

"Not a monster," Russell said softly. "Just someone who wasn't paying attention."

He reached across the table and took one of John's hands in his. John looked around nervously and made an attempt to pull away. Russell gripped his fingers tightly.

"See," he said. "You're always afraid. Afraid of what people will think. Afraid of what people will know about you. But John, I feel like I don't even know who you really are, or that you know who I am."

He could feel the tension in John's hand. He knew his lover very badly wanted to put his hand in his lap, where it would be safe from the prying eyes of the other patrons. None of them were even giving the men a second look, but Russell knew that John's heart was racing a mile a minute, fueled by the fear of discovery.

"Can I bring you anything else?"

The waitress's voice startled Russell. He looked up just as John, with tremendous effort, pulled his hand away and stuck it under the tablecloth, out of her sight.

"No," Russell said. "I think we're done."

CHAPTER 9

Pete pulled into the parking lot of the Paris Bookstore and Cinema and cut the engine. A dozen other cars were already there. In the dark it was difficult to tell if any of them were recognizable, but it didn't matter anyway. There was no reason he shouldn't be at the Paris. It wasn't a fag place, even if some of the men who came there weren't completely interested in the variety of porn offered for sale inside. Most of Pete's buddies had been there, some regularly, and there was no shame in it.

He got out and walked through the lot to the door. In deference to their clientele's privacy, the Paris had wisely placed the entrance at the rear of the building, invisible to curious passersby on the street. Not that many people drove by it without purpose. The bookstore was located in one of the city's more run-down areas. Anyone going there would be going there for a reason.

Pete opened the door and entered. A hallway lined with video booths offering five minutes of video time for a quarter led to the interior, and he walked by these quickly, noting that they were all unoccupied. Inside, the Paris resembled a remodeled fast-food establishment, which in fact it was. In better times it had been a Red Lobster restaurant, a barn-like building painted bright red, where families gathered to feast on all-they-could-eat popcorn shrimp and crab legs. Now the windows were boarded up, the tables removed and replaced by shelves filled with videos, magazines, and sex toys. Where the kitchen and storage areas had once been, a small theater now resided, reached by passing through a faded velvet curtain.

Pete looked around the main room. A handful of men wandered

around, reading the backs of video boxes and flipping through magazines. Behind a cash register a bored-looking kid with bad skin and a
nose ring watched cartoons on a snowy black-and-white television, ignoring the middle-aged man who perused the display of lubricants
and rubber vaginas housed behind the counter's glass front.

The crowd was the usual, a mix of young blue-collar types in dusty
work clothes, sad-looking men whose wives thought they were at the
store picking up ice cream for dessert, and the occasional older man.
Each type had their own way of behaving. The younger guys looked
without reservation, opening magazines and flipping through them to
see which images of overly enhanced breasts and spread, pink-lipped
vulvas most excited them. Pete knew most of them would find something fairly quickly, buy it, and leave, taking it home to enjoy with a
couple of beers.

The older men, too, were unembarrassed about their activities. Too
old to attract actual partners, they were searching for an alternative.
Most shunned the magazines and videos, going for the more tactile offerings of the fake pussies and rubber lips made for replicating the experience of a blowjob. They openly fondled the toys, not caring who
knew what they desired.

It was the men in between who were secretive, the ones with wedding bands and the thick middles of the married and settled. They
moved awkwardly, dressed in their corduroys and ill-fitting sweaters,
going from one rack to another as if they were merely searching the
shelves of the local video store for something to take home to the
kids. These were the men who longed for something they couldn't
have. Weary of their bland wives with their sagging breasts, sensible
haircuts, and demands for help with the chores, they wanted to lose
themselves in the fantasies promised by the magazines and tapes.
They looked at the girls who looked back with eager eyes and open
mouths and thought about the lives they once dreamed of having, the
lives the young men around them still dreamed of and the older men
knew would never come.

These were the men Pete despised the most. He despised them for
their air of sad desperation and their shame. He despised them for
their irritating way of holding the magazines open just enough to peek
inside, as if they were fooling anyone. And mostly he despised them
for the way they reminded him of his father. In their faces he saw the

defeat he saw in his father's face, the look of resignation to a life that was the same day after day, an acceptance of what they had achieved as being the most they would ever have. They'd given up, and he hated them for it.

Having noted the possibilities, he walked toward the velvet curtain. He wasn't wasting time in the outer room, which as far as he was concerned, was simply there to provide a pretense for those too timid to venture directly into the Paris's darker regions. That was where the real appeal of the establishment lay.

Behind the curtain the room was shadowy, and Pete paused to allow his eyes to adjust. On the far wall a porn film was projected, a grainy image of a woman giving a blowjob. The cock was as tall as Pete was, and the woman's red-lipped mouth moved up and down it energetically as the penis's owner gripped her blond hair tightly.

Like the main room, the theater held less than a dozen men. They sat scattered throughout the theater, slumped in the seats. Below the slurping of the woman on the screen, Pete heard the faint groan of tired springs, the telltale sign that one or more of the audience were busily whacking off along with the action.

In the dark it was difficult to tell what the occupants of the theater looked like, but he didn't care. He never hunted; he let them come to him, and decided when they were near enough to see whether they would be allowed to have what they wanted. Sometimes, if they were lucky, he would take them into one of the private booths that lined the hallway out front.

He chose a seat halfway down a row in the middle of the theater. The rows in front of and behind him were empty, meaning he could avoid the glances of anyone he didn't want to have watching him. Sitting, he leaned back and tested the seat's give. Unlike most of the theater's chairs, it didn't let out an audible groan, which pleased him.

He turned his attention to the action on the screen. The blowjob was still going on, the man's cock shiny with spit as the woman, using her hand now, attempted to bring him to orgasm. Pete looked at the man's nuts, enlarged to the size of beach balls, each hair visible in their magnified state. They bounced vigorously as the woman jerked the man off. Then the man came, a fountain of cum shooting from his dick and hitting the woman in the face.

The scene did nothing for him, and he was glad when it ended and a new one began. In this one, two men were fucking a woman in a living room. One man sat on an impossibly ugly orange couch, legs spread, as the woman knelt on the floor between them and sucked him off. Behind her, knees buried in the white shag carpet that covered the floor, the second man was busily pumping himself in and out of her.

Pete felt his dick begin to stiffen inside his pants. Reaching down, he unbuttoned the fly of his jeans and placed his hand inside, squeezing the swelling head of his cock. He kept his eyes on the screen as he played with himself, watching the two pricks filling the woman's mouth and pussy. The men seemed connected through her, almost as if they were making love to one another, using her simply as a conduit for their union.

He was distracted by some motion taking place to his left. Glancing over, he saw that he had been joined in his row by someone else. Instinctively, he put his cock back in his pants, not wanting to advertise his arousal if his potential partner turned out to be undesirable.

The man looked young, which was a good sign. But in the dark it was difficult to tell. Pete had been fooled before. Still, it was light enough that he could see that he wasn't being approached by one of the old trolls who frequently tried to use the darkness as a cover for their wizened faces.

The man looked at him and nodded briefly before turning his attention back to the screen. Pete waited to see what he would do. On the far wall, the trio had changed positions. The man from the couch now lay on his back on the snowy carpet, his legs pulled up. The woman sat astride him, facing him and riding his cock. Somehow, the other man had managed to insert his dick into her ass, so that she was being entered simultaneously by both men.

Pete took a chance, freeing his cock once more and stroking it openly. He didn't know if the man beside him was watching or not; the scene had excited him beyond caring. His eyes focused on the two dicks, so close they were almost touching as they slid in and out of the woman's eager holes.

He sensed the movement of shadows and realized that the man in his row had gotten up and moved over into the seat beside his. That was all right. He glanced over and was pleased by what he saw reflected in the light from the projector. He was indeed young, and not that it mattered, but he wasn't bad-looking either.

The man looked at Pete, then down at the cock in Pete's hand. Tentatively, he reached out and touched it. Pete let him, feeling fingers close around his shaft. He leaned back and let the other man take over the job of getting him off.

The motion of the man's hand combined with the images on the wall, blending into one continuous sensation. Pete became one of the participants in the film. He felt the warmth of the woman's ass surround him, sensed the tightness of her. More than that, he felt the other man's cock moving in time with his. He felt its thickness against his own as they pressed together somewhere inside her. Their dicks were one united organ, tying them together so tightly that their heartbeats became one.

Too soon, the men in the film came. Pete was not ready, and when the clip suddenly faded out, he was left frustrated and disappointed. He needed more of what he'd felt watching it. He wanted to be back there, entwined with another man. He needed the release.

"Let's get out of here," he whispered to the man, who was still jerking him off.

The man released him and stood up. Pete tucked his still-hard dick into his pants and followed as his partner exited the theater. Stepping into the brightly lit main room, he barely looked at him as he led him down the hallway and into a private booth, first making sure that no one was watching them.

It was a tight fit. The booths were designed to hold one person. The two of them were close together, almost touching. Pete fumbled in his pocket for some quarters and plunked them into the video machine. A film began, but he ignored it. He knew what he wanted, and he needed the video only as background noise.

He unbuttoned his pants and pushed them down. Immediately, the man dropped to his knees and began sucking. But that's not what Pete wanted. He pulled the man up.

"I want to fuck you," he whispered.

The man hesitated. Pete turned him around in the small space and reached for the buttons of his jeans. He found them and pulled them open, tugging the man's pants and underwear down. He pressed his cock against the man's ass.

"You want me to fuck you, don't you?" he asked.

The man said nothing, but didn't pull away. Pete spit into his hand

and slicked his cock. Pressing the head between the man's asscheeks, he pushed forward until he felt himself begin to enter the guy's hole.

"Slower," the man said, the first word he'd spoken.

Pete ignored him, pushing himself inside. The tightness was intoxicating, and he couldn't wait. He felt the man tense and he pushed harder, breaking through the resistance.

The man cried out and Pete put a hand over his face, covering his mouth as he started to fuck him. It was so warm, so tight. He felt the man pressing back against him as he fucked him. He wanted Pete's cock inside him, wanted to be used by him.

The man was groaning through Pete's hand. That was better. That was what he wanted to hear. He removed his hand so he could hear his moans. He felt his balls slapping against the man's ass and fucked him harder. The man had braced himself against the door of the booth, and Pete used this leverage to push deep inside him.

"I'm gonna fill your ass with cum," he told the man.

"No," the man gasped. "Not inside me. Pull out."

Pete ignored him. He could feel himself about to explode, and he couldn't stop. He gripped the man's waist and steeled himself for the release.

"I said pull out," the man said again. "I don't want to get anything."

The man lurched forward, dislodging Pete's cock. Pete came, but instead of emptying himself into a warm ass, he saw his load shoot out and splatter against the wall. His partner was hurriedly trying to pull his own pants up.

"What the fuck?" Pete said, looking down at his still-twitching cock.

"I said not to come inside me," the man said. "I don't want to get AIDS."

"You think I have AIDS?" Pete said angrily. "You think I'm some sort of dirty fag? You're the one who was getting fucked, faggot."

The man was trying to unlock the door so he could leave. Pete grabbed his hand and twisted it, making the man cry out.

"Shut up, faggot," Pete ordered. "Tell me you wanted it."

The man let out another cry as Pete squeezed his hand again.

"Tell me you wanted it, fag," he repeated.

The man tried to pull away. Pete hit him, his fist connecting with the man's nose. His head flew back and smacked against the door with a crack. Pete saw blood begin to flow from the man's nose as he raised his hands to cover his face.

Seeing the fag try to hide made him even angrier. Why wouldn't he fight back? He hit him again, this time in the mouth. He felt the man's lip split, felt warm blood on his fingers. The man groaned.

"Help," the man called out softly. "Somebody help."

Hearing his cry, Pete was shocked back to reality. What was he doing? He pulled up his pants. Shoving the man out of the way, he unlocked the booth and looked outside. No one had heard anything.

The man had crumpled to the floor, holding his face. Before he could cry out again, Pete dashed for the door at the end of the hall. He hit the door and flew out into the night, not looking back. His car seemed impossibly far, miles away, as he ran through the parking lot, praying that no one saw him.

He reached the car. He seemed to have hundreds of keys in his hand, none of which would open the door. But then it was open and he was sliding into the driver's seat. He looked anxiously at the door to the theater, expecting at any moment to see people running out, looking for him. But no one came.

The engine started and he tore out of the lot, not even bothering to turn on his headlights.

CHAPTER 10

"What can I get you?"

"Cranberry juice and tonic."

Mike, who had been busy cleaning up the bar, looked up to see who his customer was. When he saw the smiling face of Father Thomas Dunn looking back at him, he stopped. The last person he'd expected to see at the Engine Room on a Saturday night was the priest.

"I told you I just might stop by," Father Dunn said.

"You sure did," Mike said as he put together the priest's drink.

Father Dunn looked around the bar. Mike wondered what he was thinking. Surely he had to know now that it was a gay bar. Probably he was wishing he'd never stepped foot inside. Mike was wishing the same thing. He really hadn't expected the priest ever to show up, and now that he had, Mike was more than a little embarrassed.

"Looks like I came on a good night," Father Dunn said, noting the packed room.

On the bar's stage, two drag queens were lip-synching to ABBA's "Take a Chance on Me," their bewigged heads bobbing in unison. *Thank God they're not wearing the nun outfits,* Mike thought as he handed Father Dunn his drink.

"You're surprised I'm here," the priest said.

"A little," Mike answered. "Okay, a lot."

"I wanted to thank you for helping me out the other night, and I figured my staying up late on a Saturday night was a lot more likely than your getting up early on a Sunday morning."

Mike laughed. "You're probably right about that," he said. "I'm not much of a morning person."

Father Dunn took a sip of his drink. Watching him, Mike realized he was dressed in ordinary clothes.

"You're in disguise," he said jokingly.

"Pardon?" the priest said.

"Your clothes," Mike explained. "You're not wearing your priest outfit."

Father Dunn nodded. "I didn't want to scare anyone," he said. "Besides, the Episcopal Church pretty much lets us make up our own dress code. I only wear the suit when I'm working."

"I didn't mean to make fun of you or anything," said Mike.

Father Dunn raised a hand. "It's not a problem," he said. "Besides, I sort of like the idea of being in drag."

Mike wasn't sure what to make of the man standing across the bar from him. He wasn't like any priest he'd ever met. Not that he'd met very many, but still, Thomas Dunn seemed like a normal guy. If Mike didn't know about his occupation, he wouldn't have seemed any different from the men standing around him, oblivious to the fact that there was a man of God in their midst.

"So, how do you normally spend your Saturday nights?" Mike asked him.

"Well, usually I go over the notes for my sermon," the priest told him. "Then I flog myself a little, pray for a couple of hours, and wait for a vision."

Mike stared at him.

"Now I'm the one who's kidding," Father Dunn said after a moment. "See, priests can have a sense of humor too."

Mike nodded. "Point taken," he said. "Hang on. I'll be right back."

He went to the other end of the bar to attend to some customers. When he came back, he found Father Dunn engaged in conversation with a young man.

"So I told that bitch to give me back my Cher CDs and get the fuck out," the man was saying to the priest.

Mike closed his eyes and groaned. *I should never have left him alone.*

"And did he?" Father Dunn asked.

"Damn right he did," his companion said. "I don't care whose cock he sucks, but you don't fuck with my Cher CDs."

"Apparently not," replied the priest.

"How are we doing here?" Mike asked.

"I need another voddy," the young man told him. He looked at the priest. "Can I get you another?"

"Thank you, but no," Father Dunn said. "I'm afraid it's a school night for me."

The young man nodded absentmindedly, looking around the bar. Mike gave him his drink, took his money, and prayed he would leave. To his relief, the guy saw someone he knew across the room and took off, leaving Father Dunn alone.

"Sorry about that," said Mike. "I didn't mean to leave you alone so long."

"It's all right," the priest told him. "This is—fun—for me. As you can imagine, I don't get out all that much."

"You're not freaked out by it?" asked Mike.

"Why should I be?" Father Dunn said.

Mike shrugged. "I guess I'm just not used to the idea of priests hanging around gay bars."

"This is a *gay* bar?" the priest said, suddenly looking around with a terrified expression.

Mike started to say something, then stopped when he realized that Father Dunn was laughing.

"I wasn't sure you knew," said Mike.

"I didn't when I came in," admitted the priest. "But I figured it out pretty quickly."

Mike wasn't sure how to continue the conversation, and there were customers trying to get his attention. He wanted to talk to Father Dunn some more, but he had work to do.

"I should let you go," the priest said, seeming to sense his dilemma. "I just wanted to come by and say thank you. Besides, I have church in the morning."

"It's good to see you," Mike told him. "Thanks for coming."

"My pleasure," said Father Dunn. "And now I'll expect to see you in my congregation one of these days."

"If you can come here, I think I can manage getting up early one Sunday out of the year," said Mike.

The priest stood up and buttoned his coat. "I look forward to it," he said. "Good night."

Mike smiled. "Good night, Father," he said.

"Thomas," Father Dunn said. "We don't want anyone to get the wrong idea now."

"Thomas," Mike said.

They nodded goodbye and Thomas left. Mike watched until he was out the door, then turned to the men clamoring for drinks. The visit from the priest had been unexpectedly pleasant. And he hadn't seemed at all bothered by the whole gay thing. *He's an interesting man,* Mike thought as he began filling glasses with ice and alcohol.

Driving home in his car with a full tank of gas, Father Thomas Dunn was thinking the very same thing. He'd surprised himself by going to the Engine Room. He hadn't planned on doing anything of the sort. As he'd told Mike, he'd been sitting in his study, going over his notes, when suddenly he'd been seized by a desire to find the man who had helped him, to see him again. He had no logical reason for doing so, but the need had been overwhelming.

Now, making his way down the same road on which he and Mike had met a week before, he feared he knew why. Seeing Mike, he had felt a tugging at his heart, an unreasonable pulse of joy that had both shocked and embarrassed him. He'd gone to the bar only with the intention of thanking the man for assisting him; instead he had discovered that he'd been unconsciously engaging in a fantasy, imagining that Mike would be as happy to see him.

He hadn't known that the Engine Room was a gay bar. That it was made everything even worse. It would have been easier to go there and find Mike surrounded by giggling women anxious for his attentions. Knowing he wasn't so inclined created an impossible situation.

He couldn't let himself go there. He'd done it once and it had almost killed him, may, in fact, have killed the very one he had wanted more than anything to save. He'd sworn he would never do it again, would never open himself up to the possibility of such pain and anguish.

Besides, it was foolish, the daydream of a child. He could not allow himself to entertain even the passing thought. He had to drive it from his mind, focus on the work to which he'd dedicated his life. To deviate from that would be to fail both himself and God, God who made it possible for him to be strong.

He drove home and hurried into the house, relieved to be back in the safety of his familiar world. As he stood in his living room, however, he sniffed the air and realized that he'd carried home with him the smells of the bar. Breathing them in, he was taken back to the ride in Mike's truck. He closed his eyes, remembering the proximity of Mike's body to his, the comfort of the warm cab and the sound of the music coming from the radio.

He needed to rid himself of the memories. Going upstairs, he stripped his clothes off and dumped them into the basket inside his closet. Naked, he padded to the bathroom and turned on the hot water, waiting until the bathroom began to fill with steam before stepping into the tub. He sank into the uncomfortably warm water, letting it close over him until he was immersed in it, only his head left free of the tiny, lapping waves.

The water cleansed him. He felt it stripping away the coat of shame he'd wrapped himself in on the way home, tearing it from his body with soothing fingers and leaving him new. He lowered himself even more, allowing the water to close over his face, until he was wholly baptized in the cleansing heat. He held his breath, not wanting to leave the protected womb of the bathtub until he was forced to by his need for air. The longer he stayed, the more cleansed he would be.

He felt his chest begin to ache, and against his will, he sat up. Fresh air streamed into his lungs as he inhaled deeply. The warm water rushed away from him, replaced by the colder air, and he longed to sink again into the water. But it was tainted now, dirty, and he had to get out of it.

He stood up, grabbing a towel and wrapping himself in it as he opened the drain and watched the water run out. He felt better now that he had rid himself of the bar's touch, more himself. He would sleep now, and in the morning he would get up and minister to his congregation. All would be well again.

Returning to his bedroom, he dressed in pajamas and pulled back the covers of his bed. Sliding between the sheets, he got in and laid his head on the pillow. He was where he belonged, in the place he never should have left. Outside he heard the wind howling, but in his house he was protected from everything—the cold, the wind, the world.

He fell asleep quickly, weary from the evening's events and from staying up several hours past his usual bedtime. As he drifted off, his

conscious mind shutting itself up tightly and the other, more danger-
ous, part of himself taking wing, the room fell away and he found himself in another room, in another place, in another time.

It was Joseph's room, the one in which he'd spent his last days.
Knowing he had little time left, he'd demanded to be taken from the
hospital and allowed to die in his own room. The doctors, knowing
nothing could be done to stop the inevitable, had acquiesced.

It was night, and the room was lit only by a small lamp on the table
beside Joseph's bed. Joseph himself was sleeping, his hands atop a
book that had fallen open across his chest. Looking at him, Thomas
thought perhaps he was not sleeping at all, that he had arrived at the
very moment following Joseph's last breath. For this was how they had
found him, a copy of Dylan Thomas's collected poems beneath his
hands.

But as he watched, Joseph stirred, his eyelids fluttering softly and
then opening. His eyes, at first unfocused, turned to Thomas and
cleared. Joseph smiled.

"You came," he said. His voice was quiet, like a child's. He tried to
sit up, pushing against the mattress with hands that dangled from impossibly thin wrists.

Thomas went to him and helped him sit, propping pillows behind
his back. He sat on the edge of the bed, not knowing if it was real or
not. It held him. Joseph, too, seemed very much alive. Thomas could
smell the scent of sickness about him.

"I waited up for you, but I must have fallen asleep," Joseph said.
"What time is it?"

Thomas looked around. There were no clocks in Joseph's room,
nothing outside the windows to indicate the hour.

"It's late," he said.

"I was reading Thomas again," Joseph said, closing the book. "I
know you think he's depressing, but I can relate."

"How are you feeling?" Thomas asked him. Joseph's face was
drawn, the lesions on his cheeks dark purple islands against the pale
sea of his skin.

"Like someone who's dying," Joseph answered.

"Don't say that," said Thomas. "It's morbid."

"It's the truth," Joseph said. He sighed. "Every time I start to fall
asleep, I wonder if it's the last time."

"Joseph, please," Thomas pleaded. "I can't."

Joseph took his hand, his twig-like fingers clasping Thomas's. "It's all right," he said. "I'm ready."

"But I'm not," Thomas said.

Joseph laid his head back against the pillows. "It's not your fault," he said. "I know you think it is."

Had Joseph really said that to him that night? He couldn't recall now. No, he was sure he hadn't. But this dream Joseph was right—he did blame himself.

"If only I could have . . ." His voice failed him and he fell into silence.

Joseph squeezed his hand, making Thomas look into his eyes. Despite the sickness, his eyes were alert, untroubled by the disease that raged behind them.

"It isn't your fault," he said. "I chose my own path."

"But I wanted to love you," Thomas whispered, barely able to get the words out.

"I know you did," said Joseph. "But it still wouldn't have saved me."

Thomas fought back tears. Joseph was wrong. He *could* have saved him, if only he'd allowed himself to follow his heart. If he had, Joseph would never have looked elsewhere for what Thomas couldn't give to him.

"Stop," Joseph said. "We don't have much time. Don't waste it on tears. Listen to me."

Thomas wiped his eyes and calmed himself. Again he looked at Joseph. The light in his eyes was failing, growing dim. He seemed less substantial, lighter, as if he were dissolving into ether. Thomas thought he could see the bed through his body.

"Stop hiding," Joseph said. "Let someone in besides God."

Thomas could no longer feel Joseph's fingers in his. He was disappearing. He grasped at the fading image, his hands meeting nothing.

CHAPTER II

"You fell on the ice?"

Stephen nodded. His mother was reaching for the bandages on his face. He pulled away. He didn't want her touching him.

"You should sue that supermarket," his father said. "For negligence. They should have cleared that sidewalk."

"It was just an accident," said Stephen. "I slipped is all. I should have been more careful."

"Why didn't you call us from the hospital?" Mrs. Darby asked her son.

"I didn't want to bother you," said Stephen. "Besides, I'm fine."

"A broken nose and thirty-six stitches is *not* fine," said his mother. "You should have called."

Stephen was sitting on the sofa in his parents' house. He almost wished he'd just stayed at the hospital. At least there the nurses hadn't kept asking him what had happened. They'd taken his story about falling on the sidewalk at the supermarket at face value, not even asking how he'd managed to drive himself to the emergency room with one eye almost totally shut and hands covered in blood. They'd simply stitched him up and sent him on his way.

He was relieved at their lack of interest. He'd had enough trouble getting out of the Paris Cinema without incident. Hearing his calls for help, several people had discovered him lying on the floor in the hallway. They'd been helpful, offering to take him to the hospital, but he had refused. He just wanted to be away from there, away from the memory of what had occurred. As soon as he could, he'd retreated to his car.

"That must have been a huge patch of ice," his brother said. "You look like shit." Alan was standing in the doorway, eating directly from a carton of ice cream he'd snagged from the fridge. Mrs. Darby looked at him.

"Stop swearing," she said. "And get a dish."

"I think I should just go home and sleep for a while," said Stephen. "The hospital gave me some pain pills. I'll take a couple of those."

"You're not going anywhere," his mother told him. "We'll put you in your old room."

Stephen started to protest, but his mother simply took him by the hand and pulled him to his feet. He knew better than to fight with her when she was like this, so he allowed her to lead him down the hallway to the bedroom he had shared with Alan for most of his life.

Little had changed in the room since first Alan and then Stephen had left it for college. Their twin beds still sat on either side of a shared bedside table. Posters of sports and music figures fifteen years out of fashion adorned the walls. Even the books on the bookshelf remained the same.

"It's like a museum in here," Stephen said as his mother gently pushed him onto his old bed.

"Take off your shoes," she said.

He bent to untie the laces, his head throbbing so badly he almost blacked out. He almost asked his mother to do it for him, but he knew she would enjoy it too much. Willing the pain away, he pulled his shoes off and then collapsed onto the bed.

"Give me the pills," his mother ordered. "I'll get you a glass of water."

Stephen took the plastic bottle from his shirt pocket and handed it to her. His mother left the room. Forcing himself to sit up, he pulled back the bedspread and got into bed, not bothering to remove his clothes. He'd at least changed before coming over to tell his parents about his alleged accident, throwing the blood-spattered T-shirt and jeans into the trash in the garage. He couldn't stand even to look at them, and after handling them, he'd washed his hands repeatedly, convinced there was blood staining his skin.

He couldn't decide which was worse, his nose or his mouth. They'd injected something into his lips to make them numb while they sewed them up, and he guessed its effects were lingering, because there was only a dull ache there. One of his teeth seemed loose, too, but the doctor who had examined him thought perhaps it would be fine if he just left it alone. But his nose, his nose definitely hurt. Protected by a metal splint and crisscrossed with white tape, it looked like the nose of a hockey player after a particularly nasty fight.

He tried not to think about what had happened. As far as he was concerned, he really had slipped on some ice outside the A&P and landed on his face. The reality was too dreadful to recall. Every time he relived even a second of it, he felt a terrible churning in his stomach. No, he had not been beaten up. He had fallen. On the ice. Outside the A&P.

His mother returned with his pills and a glass of water. Taking them from her, he gratefully swallowed the two little blue tablets, following them with a long drink.

"It says you should take them with food," his mother said. "I'll get you something."

She left again. Stephen waited for her to return. He could feel the pills in his stomach, swirling around. How long would it take them to kick in? He wanted to sleep, to sleep and to forget everything.

His mother came back with a bowl, which she handed to him.

"It's applesauce," she said.

Applesauce. The sick food of his childhood, the cure-all for everything from fevers to measles, earaches to broken bones. It was the only time his mother ever gave it to the boys. He associated it with pain and nausea, but also with the comfort of being taken care of. And she had sprinkled cinnamon on top.

He spooned some of the applesauce past his battered lips. It tasted odd, metallic, most likely a by-product of the anesthetic and medication he'd been given. But it was sweet enough for him to stomach, and he swallowed eagerly. Just as it had in childhood, it calmed his stomach, made him feel as if everything would be all right in a couple of days.

"Now get some rest," his mother told him. "When you wake up, I'll make you some dinner."

Stephen nodded. His mother left, shutting the bedroom door behind her. Alone in his old room, he almost felt okay. And really, he wasn't that badly hurt. In time, everything would heal, and no one had to know that he had really been beaten by a man whom he wouldn't let come in his ass.

He put the bowl of applesauce down, suddenly feeling as if he might vomit. He hadn't told the nurses or doctors about his ass, about the pain that burned there. He couldn't. Why had he done it? Why had he let someone do that to him in the first place? It was stupid, he knew it, foolish to let someone fuck him without a rubber.

Even more disturbing to him were his reasons for being at the theater in the first place. He had never gone there before, but he had wondered about it, wondered what went on inside the dark place where men congregated. He could imagine, and he wanted to know.

Then there was Greg. He had called, left messages that Stephen had been unable to return. Several times he had picked up the phone, intending to dial the number he had written on the pad beside the phone. But each time he had hung up and instead turned to his computer, finding release in the faceless rooms in which he felt most at home.

But always Greg had been in the back of his mind. Stephen liked him. He was attracted to him. He knew he should pick up the phone and call, suggest dinner or a movie. But he knew, too, that he wouldn't do it. Greg was not a onetime event; he was someone Stephen could see himself being with. And that couldn't happen. Not now. Not when his life was so complicated.

Still, the need to touch someone else had become overwhelming, and he'd found himself pulling into the Paris Cinema parking lot and going inside, where he knew men were waiting for him. Then he'd found one, one who seemed willing to give him what he wanted, to connect with him momentarily without the need for knowing names or even faces. Without complications.

That in itself had been enough for him to let down his guard. And for a time it had been much as it was in his chat room fantasies, at least until he'd realized what the man intended to do to him. Then he'd tried to stop it, and it had all fallen apart.

That's what he got, he told himself, for not being content with what he had. It's what happened to bad little boys who strayed from the path. He'd wandered into the forbidden woods and come face to face with the wolf itself, the vicious beast disguised as a woodsman. He had failed to see the sharp teeth and wicked eyes, too enchanted to notice the claws ripping his flesh.

It didn't matter now. It was all over, and he would never again go in search of what he didn't need. He would change. He would make his life as safe as it could possibly be, protect himself from harm in whatever way he had to. No one would ever hurt him again.

He slept then, drugged into oblivion. He did not dream, and when he felt someone shaking him, he only reluctantly rose up through the dark clouds of sleep and opened his eyes. His mother had returned, and she was not alone.

"Stephen?" she said. "Stephen, wake up. Someone is here to see you."

As his sight cleared, Stephen saw that the figure he'd taken to be his father or brother was instead someone unknown to him, a figure in a blue uniform and hat.

"Mr. Darby?" the officer said. "I'm Officer Chenoweth. Could I speak to you for a minute?"

Stephen looked at his mother, as if she were somehow the reason for the policeman's presence in his room. She looked back blankly, her eyes worried.

"Sure," Stephen said groggily. "Just let me get up."

"You can stay there, sir," Officer Chenoweth said. "Mrs. Darby, would you mind leaving us alone?"

"Stephen?" Mrs. Darby said. "Is everything all right?"

"It's fine, Mom," said Stephen. "I'm sure Officer Chenoweth just has to ask me some questions about the accident."

Mrs. Darby nodded, eyeing the policeman suspiciously as she left the room. When she was gone, the officer looked at Stephen.

"Those are some nasty injuries," he said.

"How did you find me?" Stephen asked him.

"The hospital gave me your address," Officer Chenoweth told him. "I was knocking on your door and your father saw me. He told me you were here."

"I don't understand," Stephen said. "Why would the hospital call the police just because I fell on some ice? I don't plan on suing the store or anything, if that's what they're worried about."

"The hospital didn't call us," said Officer Chenoweth. "We called the hospital."

Stephen looked at him, still not comprehending. "About me?"

"About an attack on someone at the Paris Cinema," the officer answered. "They called and said a man had been beaten by another patron and left, refusing medical attention. In such cases we routinely call the hospitals to see if anyone has come into the emergency rooms with injuries that might fit the description. Yours did."

Stephen shut his eyes, not knowing what to say next. Could he get into trouble for not reporting the incident? He didn't see how. It was his choice to leave, and he hadn't started the fight. But the police didn't know that. If he admitted to being the one who was attacked, there would be a lot of other questions he would be expected to answer.

"I wish I could help," he said. "But I just slipped on some ice."

"You weren't at the Paris Cinema?" Officer Chenoweth asked.

Stephen shook his head. "I don't even know what it is," he said.

The policeman nodded. "It's an adult bookstore," he said. "You're certain you've never been there?"

"I think I'd remember something like that," Stephen said. "Especially if someone clocked me while I was in it."

"Okay then," Officer Chenoweth said. "I'm sorry to bother you. I was hoping you were the guy."

"Why's that?" Stephen asked.

"Because we think we have the guy who beat him up," the officer said. "Someone saw him driving away and got his license plate number. We ran it and got a name and address."

"You caught the guy?" Stephen said, forgetting that just moments ago he had denied all knowledge of the incident.

"We're talking to him now. But the only one who saw him was the victim, and without a positive ID, we can't do anything."

Stephen almost blurted out the truth, stopping himself as the door opened and his mother looked in. Seeing her face, he gritted his teeth.

"I almost wish I was your man," he said to Officer Chenoweth. "This guy sounds like a real jerk."

Officer Chenoweth nodded again. "Thank you anyway," he said. "I hope you're feeling better soon. Watch out for that ice."

"Will do," Stephen said as the policeman left, walking by Mrs. Darby and saying, "I can let myself out, ma'am. Sorry for the intrusion."

"What did he want?" Mrs. Darby inquired of her son.

"He thought I might know something about a crime he's investigating."

"Crime?" his mother parroted. "What would you know about a crime?"

"Nothing, Mom," Stephen said. "He had me confused with somebody else."

"I should say so," Mrs. Darby said, coming to sit beside him on the bed. "You and your brother were never a bit of trouble."

She put the back of her hand on Stephen's head, the way she had when he was little and she wanted to see if he had a fever. Her skin was cool and dry, like paper.

"You need to sleep some more," she said, as if she could somehow sense this by touching him. "That officer shouldn't have disturbed you."

Stephen said nothing. He was thinking about what Officer Chenoweth had told him. Had they really located the man who had attacked him? What if he had agreed to identify him? He wasn't sure he would even be able to recognize him. He'd only seen him in the light for a short time, and even then he'd been trying to remain as inconspicuous as possible. He remembered short brown hair, a muscular build, rough hands. He remembered the way the man's cock had felt entering him, the way his voice had sounded in his ear. And he remembered the crack of bone against bone.

None of these memories would serve him well in a lineup. He could hardly tell the police that he didn't recognize his attacker because he'd met him in the dark, had seen him mostly from the back. He certainly couldn't ask them to have the suspects drop their pants and show their cocks.

He imagined the questions they would ask him. What were you doing there? Why did he attack you? Do you frequently let strangers fuck you in seedy porn theaters, Mr. Darby, and don't you think maybe you were asking for it when you let him stick his dick up your ass? Don't you think that maybe men who let other men fuck them in the ass deserve to get smacked around a little when they change their minds?

No, he couldn't face questions like that. He had been right to lie to the policeman. Besides, if anyone should decide whether or not this man was prosecuted, it should be him. He, after all, was the one with the broken face.

His mother was stroking his hair, rubbing his forehead and humming. He closed his eyes and pushed all the troubling thoughts from his mind. She would take care of him. She would make him feel better. Everything would be all right again. He just needed to sleep.

CHAPTER 12

"Do you believe in God?"

Simon sipped his drink and thought for a moment before answering Mike's question. "I'm too old not to," he said. "At my age you need to keep all your options open."

"I'm serious," Mike said. "Do you?"

Simon sighed. "What's gotten into you?" he asked.

"I've just been thinking about it lately," Mike answered.

"And what have you decided?"

"I don't know," Mike admitted. "My mother used to drag us to church when we were kids, but I stopped going when I was old enough to have better things to do. I haven't thought about it much since then."

"So why now?" asked Simon.

"No special reason," said Mike evasively. "Maybe just the time of year and all. You still haven't answered my question."

"Yes," Simon said.

"Yes what?" said Mike.

"Yes, I believe in God," Simon told him. "I believe that there is an omnipotent being who created us all and who moves us about like figures on a chess board, manufacturing dramas for his amusement and laughing at us when we behave in ridiculous ways."

Mike fixed him with a look.

"What?" Simon said. "You asked me and I've told you."

"You don't really believe that we're toys for some invisible force that lives up in heaven," Mike said.

"Don't I?" Simon replied. "No, well, I suppose I don't really. That was the God I was raised to believe in, however. I'm afraid we parted on bad terms shortly after he discovered that I liked other boys."

"What do you believe about him now?"

Simon paused again, thinking. "I believe that God—if he exists at all—is what we want him to be. The true God is unknowable, and so we dress him in costumes that make him visible to us. Then we come up with a lot of very silly rules that we attribute to him and tell everyone that if they don't follow those rules, they can't be part of the gang."

"That's oversimplifying religion a little, don't you think?" said Mike.

"Religion *is* simple," Simon answered. "It's the religious who make it complicated. Everybody wants to be right."

"Okay, then, how do you see God?" Mike continued.

"I'll need another drink if we're going to continue this conversation," said Simon. "And this one is on you."

Mike laughed, taking Simon's glass and refilling it. Simon took it back and stirred the ice cubes before speaking again. When he did, his voice was serious.

"Walter was raised Catholic," he told Mike. "He loved the church. He went to Mass every week. I never understood how he could, given what the Pope and his boys have to say about us sodomites. But every Sunday he'd be up and ready for the early service. He tried to get me to come with him, but I wanted none of it, so while he toddled off to church, I stayed home and pondered how I'd managed to marry such a fool."

Mike smiled, knowing Simon was being his usual teasing self. He'd seen Simon and Walter together many times, and knew the deep affection and respect they'd had for one another.

"Normally I could forgive him this eccentricity," Simon continued. "But one night we were watching television and the then-Archbishop of New York was on, Cardinal O'Connor. This was in the midst of the plague, mind you, and several of our old friends had succumbed to the virus. And there was that hateful man talking about how AIDS was God's punishment on homosexuals. I turned to Walter and said, 'That's the God you visit every week.' It was a cruel thing to say, but I was angry."

"What did Walter say?" asked Mike.

"Nothing," said Simon. "He got up, went to the stereo, and put a CD in. It was Bach's *Saint Matthew Passion*. He let it play while I sat, not understanding. Then he said to me, '*That* is the God I visit every week.'"

"I don't get it," Mike said.

"He meant the God behind the music. The inspiration. Not what men had turned God into, but the God behind everything. Think about it. The most beautiful art, music, even architecture—most of it was inspired by a devotion to the divine."

"Maybe because they were sick of painting cows and building huts," Mike remarked.

Simon ignored him. "In every civilization, the greatest achievements in the arts were celebrations of the gods," he said. "The Egyptian pyramids. The Aztec temples. The Sistine Chapel. The compositions of Handel. The works of Milton and Donne and many, many others. All created because the artists were attempting to understand God in some form. Imagine the power of the force that could inspire such things."

"It still doesn't prove that God *exists*," Mike insisted. "Just that people want him to."

"And that's why it's called faith," countered Simon. "You have faith, you believe, against all reason. If it could all be proven, what value would your faith have? It's easy to believe in things that can be seen, or touched, or measured. But believing in the face of all the evidence, that takes more heart than most of us have."

"It sounds as if Walter converted you," said Mike.

"No," Simon replied. "He still never got me to go with him. But I did understand him better after that, and I confess that in comparing myself to him, I found myself wanting. I envied him his ability to believe."

"I think it's all about a fear of death," Mike said. "I think people want to believe that there's something better out there."

"Possibly," Simon agreed. "But does it really matter if they think that?"

Mike nodded. "Sure," he said. "Then religion is just a safety net. You sin, you say you're sorry, and God makes everything okay. You see it all the time with these evangelists who steal money, screw around, and break all the rules they set for everyone else. Then they say they're sorry, God forgives them, and six months later they're doing it all over again. It's just bullshit."

Simon shrugged. "Perhaps it is," he said. "One day we'll all find out."

"That's another thing I resent," Mike said angrily. "They tell you that you don't have a choice. You either believe in God and go to heaven or you don't believe in him and you go to hell. What the fuck kind of options are those? What if I don't want to go to heaven? What if I just want to die and be done with it?"

"For someone who's never been interested in God, you seem to be awfully interested in him now," Simon remarked.

Mike waved a hand at him. "It's nothing," he said. "It's just this guy."

"Oh," Simon said. "Now this is getting interesting."

"No," said Mike. "It's not like that. I picked up this priest the other night."

Simon arched his eyebrows, only half feigning the shock.

"Bad choice of words," Mike said, noting the expression. "I literally picked him up. He had car trouble and needed a ride."

"Go on," Simon encouraged him.

"Well, he came in here the other night to say thank you."

"In *here?*" Simon said incredulously.

Mike nodded. "He's a strange guy. Not strange weird, but strange interesting. He invited me to come to his church."

Simon nodded. "Hence the whole God thing. I see now. Well, my boy, you don't have to believe in God to go see your priest friend."

"No, I know I don't," Mike said. "It just got me thinking is all."

"Tell me more about this priest," Simon said. "Is he humpy?"

"No!" Mike exclaimed. "He's a priest."

"Devotion to God does not preclude humpiness," said Simon.

"I guess he's good-looking," Mike said. "In a priest kind of way. I hadn't really thought about it."

Simon said nothing, watching Mike's face. He could tell the young man was thinking about it now, and he was fairly certain he knew what conclusion Mike was coming to.

"Anyway, I'm not going to go," Mike said. "I mean, what's the point?"

"What's the point of anything?" Simon suggested.

"What are you two talking about over here? You look so serious."

Mike and Simon greeted Russell, who took the seat beside Simon, giving him a peck on the cheek.

"Mr. Monaghan and I were discussing the nature of God," Simon told Russell.

"And what did you decide?" Russell asked, taking the drink Mike had poured for him.

"We decided to postpone our verdict until after our deaths," said Simon.

Russell nodded. "Cheery," he said. "What shall we talk about next, the thrill of stomach cancer?"

"How about what's going on with you and John," suggested Mike.

"That will take another couple of these," said Russell, holding up his glass.

"Where is your other half?" Simon asked.

"Long story," Russell said. "The short version is that we're on a break."

"Any progress?" Mike inquired.

"We tried to talk on Wednesday," said Russell. "It didn't go very well."

"Why does no one tell the old auntie what's going on anymore?" said Simon, sounding hurt.

"I assumed you knew," Mike said apologetically. "You usually know everything that goes on around here."

"I haven't really talked about it with many people," Russell told Simon. "It's sort of embarrassing."

"That's why you *have* old aunties," Simon reminded him. "If you can't talk to us, who can you talk to?"

"Not John, apparently," said Russell. "I don't know what I'm going to do."

"What do you want to do?" asked Mike.

"I don't know," Russell told him. "I wish he would at least talk to someone about what he's feeling, but he's basically just disappeared. None of our friends have seen him."

"Have you considered that perhaps that's because he thinks of them as your friends?" said Simon.

Russell looked at him. "But they're not just my friends."

"Not as far as you're concerned," Simon explained. "But maybe in his mind they are. Does he have any friends he sees apart from you?"

"Just the other teachers at school," said Russell. "And they're all straight. He only talks to them about work."

"There you go," Mike said.

"But he could talk to you guys," Russell protested. "Or to Stephen, or . . ." He stopped talking, realizing that there really weren't many people in John's life apart from the friends Russell had made for them.

"He's probably just sitting in the house waiting for something to happen," Mike said.

"Thanks," Russell told him. "Now I feel a lot better."

"I'm just saying," said Mike.

"He wouldn't talk to anyone anyway," Russell said defensively. "That's part of his problem. He doesn't talk."

"He probably doesn't know what to say," Simon said.

"He just has to tell me what he feels," replied Russell. "What's so hard about that? How can he not know what he feels?"

"Shall we go back to the God conversation?" asked Mike. "It might be easier."

"I've got to figure something out," Russell continued, ignoring him. "I either have to go back home or find somewhere else to stay. Cheryl's been great, but I think we're starting to get on each other's nerves."

"Come stay with me," Simon said.

Russell looked at him. "Really?"

"As I said earlier, what are old aunties for?" said Simon. "I have a big old house with just me and Clancy in it. You're more than welcome."

"Thanks," Russell said. "I think I'll take you up on that."

"You can move in tomorrow," Simon said, patting him on the back. "Just in time for Thanksgiving week."

Russell groaned. "I don't even want to think about Thanksgiving," he said. "Work is going to be hell until after the New Year, and this whole thing with John . . ." Again his voice trailed off. Mike and Simon saw his shoulders begin to shake.

"All right," Simon said, putting his arm around Russell and pulling him close. "We can't have that. Mr. Monaghan, what are your holiday plans?"

Mike shook his head. "I don't have any," he said. "Apart from being here in the evening."

"In that case, you are both invited to my house for Thanksgiving dinner," announced Simon. "It will be a family affair."

Russell cleared his throat. "Can I invite John too?"

"You may invite anyone you like," said Simon.

"In that case, I may bring a guest as well," Mike said.

"It will be a full house then," Simon said happily, already planning the menu in his head.

CHAPTER 13

"Mr. Ellison?"

John looked up from the copy of *Scientific American* he was reading to find a policeman standing in the doorway of the teachers' lounge.

"Yes?"

"Could I speak with you for a moment, sir? In private."

John looked around at his colleagues, all of whom were looking from him to the officer. He put the sandwich he'd been eating down on the table and wiped his hands on his napkin. Ignoring the glances of his fellow teachers, he stood and followed the policeman into the hallway.

"What's this about?" he asked when the door was shut.

"Are you the owner of a 2001 Pontiac Grand Am?" the officer inquired. "License plate HEJ-387?"

John nodded. "That's my car," he answered. "At least, it's registered to me. Why?"

"Were you driving the vehicle this past Friday evening?"

John shook his head. "No," he said.

"Does anyone else have access to the vehicle?"

"Just myself and my partner," John answered.

"Your partner?"

"Yes," John said. "It's registered in my name, but he's the one who drives it. I have another car that I use."

The policeman was looking at him strangely. "Your partner is a man?" he asked.

John felt himself reddening. He was annoyed at the cop for asking him such personal questions, especially when he still didn't know why they were being asked.

"Would you please tell me what's going on?" he said, rather than answering the officer's question.

"Do either yourself or your partner frequent the Paris Cinema?"

"What's that?" asked John irritably. "A movie theater? Sure, we go to the movies. I don't know if we've ever been to that one or not though. You'd have to ask Russell."

"Russell?" the man said.

"My partner. Russell Harding."

Again the policeman wrote on his pad. He looked at John. "Was your partner driving the car on Friday evening?"

"I don't know," John answered.

"You don't know if he was driving the car?"

"We aren't exactly living together at the moment," John said reluctantly.

"May I ask why?"

"No, you may not," John said sharply. "Look, I've been very patient here. Now unless you tell me why you've shown up at my place of work to ask me a lot of very personal questions, I'm going to have to ask you to leave."

"Please try to remain calm, sir," the officer said. "Your car may have been involved in an incident at the Paris Cinema on Friday evening. We're just trying to figure out what happened."

"I guess it's possible that Russell could have been at a theater on Friday night," said John. "But you'd have to ask him. I'm sure you can reach him at work."

The officer closed his pad and nodded. "I'll do that," he said. "If I need anything else, I'll let you know."

John nodded and started to go back in the lounge, but the officer stopped him.

"One more thing," he said. "Are either yourself or Mr. Harding acquainted with a gentleman by the name of Stephen Darby?"

"He's our accountant," John said. "What does he have to do with this?"

"Probably nothing at all," the policeman said. "Good afternoon, Mr. Ellison."

John watched the cop leave, then opened the lounge door and

went inside. All eyes were on him as he entered, but he said nothing. He simply sat down, picked up his sandwich, and resumed eating his lunch. He could feel the stares of the people around him, but he wasn't going to give them the satisfaction of knowing what the policeman had asked him.

He was grateful when the bell for the next period rang, giving him an excuse to leave the room. He knew it was all a big mistake. Still, he was bothered. Along with everything else that was going on, he didn't need to be publicly humiliated in front of his coworkers.

He went to his classroom. Twenty overactive juniors greeted him, talking loudly. Their voices grated on his nerves. He wished they would all just shut up. They were always talking, always making noise. He shut the door to the classroom and took his place behind the desk.

"All right," he said loudly. "Let's get started."

"Hey, Mr. Ellison, what was that cop talking to you about in the hallway earlier?"

John looked up to see who had spoken. Eddie Jessup, the school's star quarterback and resident class clown, was grinning at him. All the other students, too, were now staring openly at him, waiting for his answer. Leave it to Eddie, he thought, to be wandering around the halls when he shouldn't have been.

"Considering the grade you currently have in this class, Mr. Jessup, I think you should concentrate on the material for today's lab, and not on things that are of no concern to you."

A loud "ooh" swept through the room as the other students looked at Eddie and laughed. Eddie, incapable of embarrassment, grinned even more broadly.

"You all have the assignment for the lab," John said, trying to regain a little of the control he'd just lost. "Please get together with your lab partner and begin. I'll be observing your work."

The students got up and immediately resumed talking. For once he didn't tell them to stop. As long as they left him alone, he didn't care what they did. As they filed into the rear of the classroom to start their experiments, he sat behind his desk and began grading their last round of homework.

He picked up his red pencil and put it down again. Why was all of this happening? Things had been going along just fine until Russell had become irrational and announced he was leaving. It had been almost three weeks since that morning and he still didn't understand what was going on. And now the unsettling visit from the policeman. Why, he wondered, couldn't things just go back to the way they were?

He found himself thinking about his car. It was possible they had the wrong vehicle, of course. Mistakes happened. Even if they did indeed have the right car, what kind of incident could Russell have been involved in?

No, it was ridiculous. He went back to grading, making it through half of one paper before the questions returned. Why had the policeman mentioned Stephen Darby's name? What could he possibly have to do with the matter of the car? It seemed completely coincidental. But was it? Was it possible that somehow Russell and Stephen were indeed involved in whatever had occurred?

Russell and Stephen. He'd never thought of it before, but now that he had, he wondered if perhaps he'd overlooked the obvious. Russell had insisted during their lunch that there was no one else. Had he been lying? He himself had said that Stephen needed someone in his life.

He put the pencil down. Was Russell having an affair? Is that what the sudden changes were about? It made sense. It was logical. There was cause and effect. These things he could understand. Suddenly in his mind the pieces all came together, the formula unfolding clearly and unmistakably. Russell had left him because he was in love with Stephen.

"Mr. Ellison, was this stuff supposed to crack the test tube?"

John glanced at the shattered tube being held out by Stacey Koopman. Green goo oozed from it and dripped onto the floor. Stacey, looking at him wide-eyed behind her safety goggles, held it away from her as if it were a poisonous snake.

"You just added it too quickly," John told her. "Clean it up. And you're in charge. I have to go do something."

Stacey looked at him, puzzled, as he took his coat from the rack by the door and put it on. He left her standing there, praying she wouldn't let anyone burn down the school, and walked quickly down the hallway and out of the building.

It was irresponsible, he knew, but he had to do it. He had to see if his theory was correct. If so, it would answer all the questions he had, and although it would mean the end of everything, at least he would have something tangible to deal with. At least he wouldn't be left wondering.

He drove as quickly as he could to Stephen's house. He couldn't ask Russell; Russell would be too inclined to spare him the truth. But Stephen, Stephen was a practical man, like himself. Stephen would understand that he needed to know.

He pulled into the driveway. Stephen's car was there. He got out and walked to the door before he could convince himself that what he was doing was irrational. He rang the doorbell, hearing it echo somewhere inside the house. A moment later he heard Stephen's voice ask who was there.

"Stephen, it's John," he said. "John Ellison. I need to talk to you."

The door opened and Stephen peered out. John, seeing his face, stepped back. "My God, what happened?"

"I had a little accident," said Stephen. "Come on in."

He opened the door wider and John entered the house. He couldn't keep from looking at Stephen's face, which was swollen and bruised.

"It looks a lot worse today," Stephen said. "The doctor says it means it's healing."

"How did it happen?" John asked again.

"It was stupid," Stephen said. "I fell on some ice. It was just a dumb accident. So, what can I do for you? Do you have a financial question, or is this a social call?"

John had momentarily forgotten the purpose of his visit to Stephen. Seeing his face, he suddenly felt like an idiot. The poor man was clearly in a bad way, and now John was just going to make things even worse by demanding to know if he was having an affair with Russell.

"This is going to sound really crazy," he said slowly. "I guess you know Russell and I are having some problems."

"No," Stephen said. "I didn't know that. I'm sorry."

"You didn't know?" John asked. "Russell didn't tell you."

Stephen shook his head. "I haven't spoken to him since your party," he said. "Things have been kind of crazy with work and all."

John rubbed his head. Suddenly his perfectly constructed theory was revealing its weaknesses. If Stephen was telling the truth, then he was right back where he started.

"You weren't with Russell on Friday night?" he asked.

"No," Stephen said.

"And you weren't at the Paris Cinema?" John continued.

Stephen hesitated. "No," he said. "I wasn't."

John sighed. "I'm really sorry," he said. "I'm really sorry I bothered you. I should go."

"Why would you think I was with Russell on Friday?" asked Stephen.

"It's a long story," answered John. "I just thought maybe you were with him, that's all."

"At the Paris Cinema?" Stephen said.

John nodded. "I don't even know where that is, do you?"

Stephen shook his head. "Are you okay?" he asked John.

"I'm fine," John told him. "I'm really sorry for bothering you, Stephen. I should get back to the school. I hope you feel better soon."

"And I hope everything works out with you and Russell," Stephen said. "Give him my best."

"I will," John said. "Thanks."

Safely ensconced in his car, he sat and thought. Something, somewhere, wasn't making sense. Maybe Stephen didn't know about him and Russell. Maybe he and Russell weren't having an affair. But Stephen knew *something*. He could tell that Stephen was uncomfortable talking to him. There was something he wasn't saying.

There was only one other thing to do. He started the car and started driving toward the mall.

CHAPTER 14

"The car's out back, right where I parked it."

Buck Iverson led Officer Wayne Chenoweth, John Ellison, and Russell Harding around the side of the garage to his lot. The Grand Am was sitting exactly where he'd left it on Friday afternoon, parked in between Doreen Baker's 1996 Toyota Celica with its dented fender and Trace Grueland's Jeep 4X4 that was awaiting new shocks. All three cars were covered in snow.

"I'm sorry it's taking so long, Mr. Harding. Like I told you, I had to order the heating coil."

"It's okay, Buck," Russell told him.

"You say someone was driving the car on Friday night?" Buck asked the police officer.

"Someone reported seeing it, yes," replied Officer Chenoweth. "Can you show me where you keep the keys to these vehicles?"

Buck took them back inside and indicated a box in the shop where a tangle of car keys nested.

"That's not very secure," remarked the officer. "Anyone could come in here and take those."

"We lock 'em up at night," said Buck defensively. "Someone would have to break the lock off to get at those keys."

"And you're the only one with access to the box."

"Me, Pete, and Ronnie," Buck answered.

"Can I speak to those men?" asked Officer Chenoweth,

"Ronnie's gone up north to visit his wife's folks for the holiday," Buck said. "Been gone since last week. Pete don't come in until later."

"Do you have an address for him?"

Buck nodded. Officer Chenoweth took out his pad and wrote it down as Buck recited it. "Pete's a good kid," he told the officer when he was done. "Can't imagine him taking a customer's car for a joyride."

"Let's hope he didn't," the policeman said. "Thanks for your time."

Russell and John walked with Officer Chenoweth out to his car. They'd followed him from the mall, where he'd gone to question Russell about his whereabouts on Friday evening. John had come in just as Russell was explaining that the car had been at Iverson's Auto Body since Friday morning, suffering from a problem with the heating system. After an awkward couple of minutes, the cop had suggested they all go over to the garage together to substantiate Russell's story.

"What do you think?" Russell asked him now.

Chenoweth looked at him and shrugged. "Your guess is as good as mine. I'll talk to this Thayer kid and see what I can find out. I'll let you know."

The two men thanked the officer and he departed, leaving them standing together.

"Come on," John told Russell. "I'll drive you back to the store."

They got into John's car and drove away from the garage, neither saying anything for several blocks.

"This is weird," Russell said finally.

"Very," agreed John.

"They must just have the wrong car," said Russell.

"Probably," John said.

"Did that cop really come see you at school?"

John nodded.

"And you left your class to come tell me?"

John hesitated. He hadn't told Russell the full reason for his appearance at the store, mainly because he didn't want Officer Chenoweth to hear, but also because he was feeling more and more stupid about the whole thing.

"That was nice of you. Thanks."

John shrugged. "You would have done the same thing," he said.

"Still," Russell said. "Thanks."

"Did he ask you about Stephen?" John inquired.

"Stephen?" Russell said. "Why would he ask me about Stephen?"

"He asked me if either of us knew Stephen Darby," John told him.

"That doesn't make any sense," remarked Russell.

"I didn't think so either," John said.

"I haven't spoken to Stephen in weeks," Russell continued. "I keep meaning to call him."

"I saw him today," John said.

"Really?" Russell asked. "Where?"

"I, um, went to his house," John told him.

Russell turned and regarded him oddly. "You're just full of surprises today," he said. "Why on earth would you go to Stephen's house?"

"I just thought it was odd that Officer Chenoweth brought up his name," John said, more or less truthfully. "So I went over there."

"How is he?" asked Russell.

"He banged up his face," John said. "He fell on the ice."

"Did he have any idea why the police would be asking about him?"

"No," John said, not mentioning that he'd never actually told Stephen that the police were asking about him.

"It's all too bizarre," Russell said. "And now I'll have to stay late to make up the time. This sale is going to be the death of me."

"You love it," said John.

"Excuse me?" Russell countered.

"You love it," John said. "You're never as happy as when there's some big crisis."

"What's that supposed to mean?" Russell demanded.

"It's true," John said. "Whenever you have a big sale to deal with, you get all giddy."

"Giddy?" Russell said, offended. "I do not get giddy."

"Okay," John said. "Whatever you say. But you do."

"All right," Russell said after a minute. "Maybe I do get a little excited. But it's the only time I really feel important."

They'd arrived at the mall. John pulled into a spot outside the Carter-Beane Department Store. "This is your stop," he said.

"Thanks again," Russell said as he prepared to leave.

"When are you coming home?"

Russell looked at him, surprised at the outburst. John was watching his face, waiting for an answer. Russell swallowed hard.

"Not yet," he said. "I need some more time."

John turned away and nodded.

"Simon is having everyone over for dinner on Thursday," Russell said. "You're coming, right?"

John said nothing. Russell leaned over and kissed him on the cheek. "I want you there," he said.

Again John was silent. Russell waited for a minute, hoping he would say something—anything—to break the awful silence. Finally he put his hand on John's arm.

"Be there at noon," he said. "You don't have to bring anything."

He got out of the car and walked quickly toward the store entrance. He didn't want to watch John leave. For a brief moment, sitting there talking, everything had seemed normal. And that was the problem. He had too easily slipped back into the old routine, the old way of thinking. It had all been so familiar, and he had welcomed it like an old friend. Also, John's question had thrown him off guard. It had been a peace flag, he knew, John's way of saying he was sorry. But Russell doubted his lover even knew what he was apologizing for, and until he did, it meant nothing.

Across town, Officer Wayne Chenoweth was pulling up to the home of Pete Thayer. He was on a wild-goose chase, he knew. For Christ's sake, he didn't even have a victim, at least not one who would come forward. But things were slow, and following up the leads on the Paris Cinema incident beat the hell out of writing traffic tickets. Not that he cared all that much about someone getting roughed up at a porno theater. Guys who went there were asking for trouble anyway, as far as he was concerned.

He walked up to the door and knocked three times. When there was no answer, he knocked again. Finally he was rewarded. The door opened and he was looking at a young man dressed in faded jeans and nothing else.

"Sorry, man, I was in the john," the kid said. "What can I do for you?"

"Are you Pete Thayer?"

The man nodded. "Hey, if this is about those tickets . . ." he began.

"Mr. Thayer, may I come in?"

"Oh, sure," Pete said. "Don't mind the mess."

Officer Chenoweth stepped into a living room cluttered with clothes, pizza boxes, and empty beer cans. It wasn't the worst he'd seen by far, but the disarray didn't improve his opinion of Pete Thayer. In his experience, people's houses reflected a lot more than their taste in furniture.

"I'll make this quick, Mr. Thayer. What were you doing Friday night?"

"Friday?" Pete said. He rubbed his hair, as if trying to recall. "I guess I was here watching television. Some movie on the Sci-Fi channel about aliens invading Los Angeles."

"So you weren't out riding around in a Grand Am you borrowed from the garage where you work?"

Normally Wayne Chenoweth preferred the subtle approach, but he'd discovered that sometimes hitting fast produced the best results.

"Fuck, no," Pete Thayer said. "I'd never borrow a car from the lot. Ask Buck."

"I did," replied the officer. "He told me you're the only other person in town besides himself with access to the key box."

Pete nodded. "Yeah," he said. "But I wouldn't do something like that."

"I guess you wouldn't be inclined to beat the hell out of someone at the Paris Cinema either then," Chenoweth said.

Pete Thayer looked at him, dumbstruck. "No," he said. "No, I didn't do that. Why? Who said I did?"

Officer Chenoweth shook his head. "Nobody," he said casually. "Just asking. Thanks for your time, Mr. Thayer."

"That's all you came here to ask me?" Pete asked as the officer went to the door.

"That's all," Chenoweth answered. "Unless there's something else you'd like to tell me."

Pete shook his head. The officer nodded at him and walked down the steps, not saying anything. It was always better to leave them wondering if they'd really seen the last of him. Besides, he'd gotten his answer. Thayer was lying. Not that it mattered. Without a victim he still didn't have anything to bring the kid in on.

Inside the house, peering out from behind a curtain, Pete Thayer watched him go. His heart was only now starting to slow down. He couldn't believe he'd made it through the conversation without puking. His stomach was twisted into tight knots of anxiety.

How had they found him? Someone must have seen him leaving the parking lot, and they'd traced the car. Jesus Christ. All because he'd punched some faggot in the face. Had the queer gone to the police? He found that hard to believe. What would he tell them, that he was getting his ass fucked in a porno theater and things had gotten a little too rough for him? The cops would laugh him out of the station.

No, if the guy had gone to the police, they would have him sitting in a jail cell answering questions. They wouldn't just send someone to his house to nose around. He might not be the smartest tool in the shed, but he knew something about how the cops worked, especially small-town cops like whatever his name was. Chen-something.

Still, he'd need to be careful. Hopefully if he just laid low, it would all blow over. He just had to hope that little fag didn't decide to shoot his mouth off. He'd also have to stay away from the Paris, not that it would be any big hardship or anything. There were always queers who wanted to suck his cock. He could find them lots of places.

The more he thought about it, the madder he got. Who did that faggot think he was? He was the one who came after Pete. He was the one who grabbed his cock and started playing with it. He was the one who followed Pete into the booth. Hadn't he let Pete fuck him? Hadn't he wanted his ass fucked hard? It wasn't Pete's fault he hadn't asked about a rubber. And then all that shit about not wanting to get fucking AIDS? If anyone should have been worried about it, it should have been *him*. Who knew what the pansy had crawling around in his ass.

Yes, he'd deserved the beating. Maybe it would teach him a lesson, teach him not to be a goddamned cocktease. He was like those girls who went down on you and then bitched when you came in their mouths. They were all a bunch of cockteases, every last one of them. They should be fucking thankful to get a taste of his cum.

He looked at the clock. Buck would be expecting him at the shop soon. He needed to calm down, come up with some story about how dumb the whole situation was, how funny it was that someone had reported a car driving around when they—Buck and Pete—knew damn well it had been sitting in the lot all weekend. Yes, they'd laugh about how fucking stupid people could be sometimes.

He went into the bathroom and started the shower. Everything was going to be fine. He just had to play it cool. They didn't have anything on him, couldn't prove he'd used the car or been to the Paris. He was home free.

He got into the shower and began soaping himself. He wondered how badly he'd beaten the fag up, anyway. He'd hit him pretty hard, and there had been some blood. But he couldn't have done too much damage. After all, he'd only hit him because of what he'd said.

That part had gone all wrong. But the stuff before it, that had been good. The fag's ass had been tighter than any pussy he'd ever had his cock in. Warm and tight. If he hadn't fucked everything up talking his AIDS shit and trying to pull away, it would have been perfect. If he'd just let Pete finish.

He closed his eyes and thought about how it had felt. His fist closed around his stiffening dick, the soapy water gliding under his fingers. Yeah, it had felt like that: hot and tight and sweet.

He pumped harder, remembering, and waited for his reward.

CHAPTER 15

"Would you mind saying the blessing, Father?"

Thomas, seated across the table from Simon, nodded. It was an occupational hazard, always being the one asked to say grace. He'd long ago learned not to refuse; no one else would volunteer to do it, fearing they would make a mess of it in front of the professional. He accepted the responsibility with good humor, assuming the role of Man of God like some sort of holy superhero identity.

"Heavenly Creator," he began. "Thank you for this opportunity to come together and celebrate those things with which you have blessed us: friends, family, health. We share our joy with one another and with you. Amen."

"That was short and sweet," Mike remarked when Thomas finished. "My father used to go on for a good five minutes. Of course, he only said grace once a year, so I suppose he had to save it all up for the occasion."

"A good prayer gets to the point," Thomas said, laughing. "God has no more time to waste than we do."

He still couldn't quite believe he was sitting at a table with five gay men on Thanksgiving. He'd been surprised and delighted to get a phone call from Mike earlier in the week, asking him if he had any plans for the holiday. He did have plans, an invitation from one of his parishioners to join her and her family, but he'd told Mike he was free. After accepting the invitation to dinner with Mike and his friends, he'd called his original hostess and complained of a fever and chills. He'd thrown in a hacking cough for good measure, knowing that above all else Posey Severing feared sickness. She'd readily accepted his regrets and promised to send over a plate with her husband.

And now here he was, surrounded by men he didn't know, invited by a man he knew only slightly. How ironic, he thought as he looked around. It was the church that preached welcoming the stranger. But now he was the stranger, accepted by men some in the church would have turned away.

"I don't want to hear any griping about lumps in the gravy," Simon said as he began passing bowls around. "Russell wanted me to buy *canned* gravy, but I wouldn't hear of it. So if you get lumps, too bad. At least this is the real stuff."

"He had me whisking that stuff all morning," Russell countered, holding up his wrist and letting it dangle. "I think it's broken."

"Please," Mike teased. "Your wrist has always been like that."

"Do you see what I have to put up with?" Russell said plaintively to Thomas. "He's like that kid in *The Sound of Music*. Kurt. What did he tell Maria he was?"

"Incorrigible," Simon answered. "Thomas, you'll have to excuse these children. They're not always this much trouble. I think they're acting out because we have a guest."

"I feel honored," Thomas said. "When I was a kid, my mother always made my sister and me be on our best behavior for company. It was terribly dishonest, since we never behaved at any other time."

"I don't think I've ever met a priest," said Greg. Invited by Russell, he sat beside Mike on one side of the table while John and Russell sat across from them. Thomas and Simon occupied the positions of honor on either end.

"It's not like I'm the Archbishop of Canterbury," Thomas said. "I'm just a priest."

"This bunch doesn't get out much," John told him, spooning cranberry sauce onto his plate and passing the bowl to Thomas.

"What's it like being celibate?" Greg asked.

The others looked at Greg in shock, then began laughing.

"What?" Greg asked. "It's a perfectly reasonable question."

"No, my dear boy, it is not," Simon said.

"But since you've asked it—" Russell said mischievously.

"Episcopal priests aren't required to be celibate," Thomas said, try-ing not to smile. "Only the Catholic ones."

"But only if you're married, right?" Greg prodded.

Thomas nodded. "That's correct."

"Are you married?"

"No," said Thomas, buttering a roll. "I'm not."

"Well, then—" Greg said triumphantly.

"If you continue with this line of questioning, you will get no pie," Simon said firmly.

Greg started to say something else but Simon held up a warning finger. "No pie," he said sharply.

Greg settled into reluctant silence while the others laughed. Thomas began eating. He was having a remarkably good time, even if Greg's questions had hit uncomfortably close to home. He glanced at Mike, wondering if he, too, was curious about Thomas's romantic ex-perience.

"What time do you have to be at the bar tonight?" Russell asked Mike.

"Four," Mike replied. "I got Luke to open up for me so I could get another two hours off."

"I don't see why they can't just stay closed," John commented.

"Money," Mike said. "The place is packed on holidays. Guys either don't go home or they do go home and want to forget about how awful it was."

"You make it sound like every gay man has a horrible relationship with his family," said John.

"You don't see any of us flying off to visit ours," Mike argued.

"That's not because we don't like them, though," John said. "It's be-cause they're too far away."

"Mine aren't that far," Greg said. "I just can't stand being around them on holidays. All my siblings are married, and all they do is ask me when I'm going to be next."

"They don't know?" Russell said, sounding surprised.

"Please," Greg said. "My father is an ex-Marine. They don't have gay sons, especially in Kentucky."

"Don't they ask about your life?" Simon inquired.

"We talk about the weather and about my parents' dog," Greg

replied. "Then I tell them I have to go because someone is beeping in. It works for us."

"My family doesn't mind at all," said John.

"That's because you never actually talk about it," Russell said to him. "They know, but they don't ask." He looked around the table. "Not once in seven years have they sent a Christmas card addressed to both of us. It's always just to him."

"That's just efficient," John said testily.

"Then how come when your mother calls and I answer, she immediately asks to speak to you?" asked Russell.

"She has nothing to talk to you about," John said.

Russell made a noncommittal noise in response, stabbing a piece of turkey and putting it in his mouth. He and John ate in silence, not looking at one another.

"What about you, Mike?" Thomas asked, trying to redirect the focus in the room. "Where's your family?"

"Dead," Mike told him simply.

"I'm sorry," Thomas said. "I didn't mean to—"

"It's okay," said Mike before the priest could apologize. "It was a long time ago. A car crash."

"You don't have any relatives?" Greg asked.

Mike shrugged. "Some cousins somewhere, I guess. We never really associated much with them. No brothers and sisters."

"You have us," Simon said brightly from his end of the table. "And that's family enough for anyone."

Thomas returned to his food, every so often sneaking a look at Mike. He couldn't imagine not having any family. Although he didn't often see his sister or parents, he was comforted to know that they were out there, reachable if he needed him. To not have that, to be all alone, he couldn't imagine it.

Can't you? A voice echoed in his head. Joseph's voice. *Can't you imagine what it's like to be alone?* He willed the sound away. It wasn't the same, he told himself. It wasn't the same at all.

Besides, he had all he needed. He had his church, his congregation, his God. They were his family. They cared about him, loved him. That was enough for anyone, more than enough for him.

The remainder of dinner went by smoothly. The talk turned to movies and pop culture, things Thomas knew little about. He was content to sit and listen, to lose himself in the playful banter that flew back and forth across the table. It surprised him that the men seemed so unselfconscious in his presence. He wondered what he represented to them, whether they saw him as something alien to their world or just another dinner guest. If so, they showed no signs of it. They talked freely, and even when the subject turned to subjects normally not discussed in front of clergy—such as the relative appeal of the asses of George Clooney and Russell Crowe—they didn't refrain from lively debate.

After the promised pie had been served up and eaten, Simon stood up. "I should start on the dishes," he said.

"Oh, no, you don't," Mike told him, standing up himself. "You already did too much work. I'll do the dishes. You just sit."

"I'll help you," Thomas said quickly.

Mike looked at him. "You're sure? You don't have to."

"I know I don't have to," Thomas told him as he stacked several pie plates on top of one another. "I want to. It's the least I can do."

He and Mike carried the dishes into the kitchen while the other men scattered to the living room to sit and let their dinners settle. Simon had already taken care of most of the cooking dishes and utensils, so the pile of plates, silverware, and glasses needing their attention wasn't so daunting.

"Wash or dry?" Mike asked, turning on the sink.

"How about dry?" Thomas suggested.

Mike nodded. He added soap to the water streaming from the faucet, and soon the sink was filled with bubbles. Mike dunked a plate into the water and scrubbed it with a cloth.

"I hope we weren't too much for you," he said as he cleaned the plate with circular motions.

"Not at all," Thomas told him as he took the proffered dish and wiped it dry. "It was actually refreshing. Usually people hide who they really are around me."

"Not this group," said Mike. "Sometimes I wish they would."

"They all seem very nice," Thomas remarked.

Mike nodded. "They are," he said.

"I sensed a little tension between John and Russell," Thomas said.

"They're going through a hard time right now," Mike told him. "Russell's trying to—find himself, I guess."

"He's not alone there," said Thomas. "I see people like that every day."

"I guess priests are sort of like unofficial therapists," Mike said as he dropped a handful of forks into the sink.

"In my case I'm an actual therapist," Thomas informed him. "A psychologist, to be exact."

"Really?" Mike said, looking at him with new respect. "And here I thought you were just . . ." His words trailed off as he returned to the dishes.

"Just a priest?" Thomas said, completing Mike's sentence.

"I didn't mean it that way," Mike apologized.

"I know what you meant. It's okay. Besides, it's not like I have a practice or anything. When I decided to enter the priesthood, I pretty much closed the book on that chapter of my life, at least in an official capacity. But you'd be surprised what people tell their priests."

"Who am I to talk?" Mike said. "I pour drinks for a living."

"But you like doing it, don't you?"

Mike shrugged. "It's a job," he said. "I guess I like it. I've been doing it for long enough. Do you like being a priest?"

The question took Thomas aback. "Yes, I like it very much."

"Who would have thought that you'd be having Thanksgiving dinner with me and my friends?" Mike continued, apparently satisfied that Thomas was telling him the truth.

"The Lord works in mysterious ways," Thomas said, assuming a mock-serious tone.

"So do Volkswagen Jettas," Mike said. "At least when you forget to put gas in them."

"I won't make that mistake again," said Thomas, laughing. "Thanks to you." He paused for a moment. "I guess I have you to thank for several wonderful events in my life lately, don't I?"

"Hey, like you said, the Lord works in mysterious ways. Maybe I'm really one of those angels he was always sending to bring people good news."

"Maybe you are," Thomas said, drying the last of the spoons.

"How long have you been in Cold Falls?" asked Mike.

"Just under a year," Thomas said.

"And before that?"

"I was the Assistant Rector at The Church of the Epiphany in Burlington, Vermont, for three years. Would you like the rest of my résumé?"

"I think that's good," said Mike. "You're hired."

"So when will I see you in church?" Thomas asked. "I came to see you, and now here I am again. I think it's your turn."

"I don't know," Mike said, wringing out the dishrag before tackling a bowl that had held stuffing. "God and I, we don't really have a lot to say to each other."

"You don't have to come to see God," Thomas told him. "You could come to see me."

"Wouldn't the big guy get jealous?" Mike teased.

"I can handle him," said Thomas. "He's not as tough as people say he is."

Mike laughed, almost dropping the bowl he was rinsing. Thomas caught it. For a moment their hands touched, Mike's underneath Thomas's, supporting it. Then Thomas pulled the bowl away, drying it hurriedly.

"I haven't been to church since my parents' funerals," Mike said, picking up another dish.

"How long ago was that?"

"Fifteen years the end of next month," said Mike instantly, as if the number were burned into his memory. "New Year's Eve. They were killed by a drunk driver." He handed the dish to Thomas. "Ironic, huh?"

"That you're a bartender?" Thomas said, getting his meaning. "Not really. A shrink might say you're trying to understand the enemy. Or trying to save the world because you couldn't save your parents."

"Maybe," Mike said.

"I noticed you didn't have any wine at dinner," Thomas said carefully.

Mike shook his head. "I don't drink," he said. "I used to, a lot after the accident. Then one day I woke up, dumped everything down the drain, and haven't touched it since."

Thomas finished drying. He looked at the pile of clean dishes, the result of their teamwork. Then he looked at Mike. "You get more and more interesting," he said.

Mike dried his hands on a towel. "Not really," he said. "I'm just an ordinary guy with an ordinary life. There are a lot more interesting people out there."

Not in my world, Thomas thought as Mike led the way out of the kitchen, shutting the lights off behind them.

CHAPTER 16

Stephen stepped inside his house and locked the door behind him with a sigh of relief. He'd escaped. Almost a week at his parents' house with his mother looking after him had quickly become monotonous. Several times he'd insisted that he felt well enough to return to his own bed, but each time his mother had taken his temperature and declared that he still had a fever. What a fever had to do with a broken nose, he didn't know, but to his protestations his mother had simply said, "I read it in the *Reader's Digest.*" Confronted with the power of the most widely read magazine in the world, he'd given up and stayed in bed.

But now he'd broken free. Busy with cleaning up after the Thanksgiving dinner, his mother had barely noticed when he'd said good-bye and left, taking his pills with him. He knew she'd call as soon as she was done tucking the leftovers into their Tupperware beds and putting them to sleep in the refrigerator, but he just wouldn't answer. His father would keep her from actually coming over. He hoped.

It was good to be in his own house. He missed his bed, and his privacy. He was feeling immensely better than he had been a week earlier. His lip was healing nicely, and his nose hurt only on the few occasions when he'd had to sneeze. Other than that, the pills had kept him in a state of mild euphoria while his body had healed itself.

He walked into the office. Luckily, not much happened around Thanksgiving, and he wasn't facing a mountain of work he would have to catch up on. Still, he hadn't checked his e-mail in a long time. There might be something there requiring his attention. He sat down at his desk, turned the computer on, and waited for it to run through its warm-up of beeps and whirs. When it was done, he signed on.

His mailbox, like his desk, was almost empty once he deleted the seventy-three messages promising him a bigger dick and the best teen lesbian sex on the Net. There was an e-mail from Russell, asking how he was, and a couple from his bank, but otherwise he was free of any pressing correspondence. He was about to sign off when an instant message box popped up. He looked at it. HrdAtWrk: Hey, buddy. It's been a while.

HrdAtWrk. It certainly had been a while. What was it, two or three months? Stephen couldn't remember exactly. He did recall that it had been toward the end of summer, an unpleasantly humid night when he hadn't been able to sleep. He'd encountered HrdAtWrk in a chat room. The guy had said he was in his office and needed a break. They'd had a good session.

He typed a message back: Still hard at work? It was completely un-original, but it would do.

The response came back instantly: Always. U?

Stephen looked at the screen. Suddenly he was very much aware of the fact that he hadn't jacked off in a week. He'd thought about it once or twice, but the idea of doing it in his old bed, while his parents were asleep down the hall, sent his erections screaming. Even when he was thirteen and horny as hell, he'd been able to do it only if they were out of the house.

Now, looking at the box on his screen, a week's worth of need came crashing down on him. He felt his cock jump and thought, *Why the hell not?* He typed a message back to his online buddy: Ready when you are.

While he waited for HrdAtWrk to start, he quickly removed his clothes. Naked, he leaned back in his desk chair. The leather felt good against his bare skin, and it was warm enough in the room that he didn't feel at all cold. His balls rested between his spread legs, and he idly played with his cock, waiting.

HrdAtWrk: Feel like something different 2nite?

Different? What did he mean by different? Stephen had no idea. Sure, he wrote. What do you have in mind?

HrdAtWrk: I'm going to tell you a story.

Stephen gave a short laugh? A story? It was different all right. But if this guy wanted to tell him a story, that was okay by him. I like bedtime stories, he typed back.

HrdAtWrk: You're driving home. You're speeding. You see a cop car in your rearview mirror. The lights are flashing.

Stephen pictured it. He was in his car. It was early evening. Summer. He had the window down. Maybe he was going a little fast, but not too much. Not enough to worry about. Suddenly something in the rearview mirror caught his eye. Lights. Red and blue. But surely they couldn't be for him? He was only going five miles over the limit. But the car pulled right up behind him.

HrdAtWrk: A cop gets out and walks toward you. He asks to see your license and registration.

Stephen opened the glove compartment of his car, searching for the red AAA folder that held his proof of insurance and his registration card. A map of New York fell out.

"I know it's right here," he told the cop, who was watching him through the window. He was a young man, handsome, with stern eyes and a square jaw. The name tag on his uniform read CAFFREY.

Stephen found the folder and opened it, retrieving the card. He handed it to the waiting officer.

"License, too, sir," Caffrey said.

Stephen pulled his wallet from his back pocket and took his license out. The cop took it in one gloved hand and looked at it.

"Mr. Darby, do you realize that you were speeding?"

"No," Stephen said. He felt himself blushing. "Well, I mean I knew I was going a *little* fast, but—"

"You're either speeding or you're not, Mr. Darby. There's no in between. Do you understand?"

"Yes, sir," Stephen said.

HrdAtWrk: Officer Caffrey takes your license back to his car. He gets in and sits there. You wait, wondering what he's doing. Then he gets out and comes back.

Officer Caffrey put his hand on the door. "Would you step out of the car, Mr. Darby?"

Stephen looked at him, not comprehending.

"Step out of the car, Mr. Darby."

"But—"

"Now," the officer said.

Stephen did as he was told. Opening the door, he stepped out and stood up. Officer Caffrey turned him around and spread Stephen's legs by placing a knee between them and shoving. Taking one wrist, he held it behind Stephen's back. Stephen felt the cold kiss of metal on his skin.

"What—" Stephen began.

Officer Caffrey pulled his other wrist back and cuffed it. "I need you to get in my car, sir," he said.

"Am I under arrest?" Stephen asked as he stumbled forward, Caffrey's hand hard on his back.

The cop said nothing as they walked to the cruiser. He opened the back door. "Get in."

Stephen ducked and slid into the rear of the patrol car. A wire screen separated it from the front. The black leather seats smelled faintly of polish.

HrdAtWrk: The cop gets in after you and shuts the door.

As the door shut, Stephen noticed that the car's windows were tinted. No one could see in. He looked nervously over at the policeman as he locked the doors.

"Now, let's talk about your difficulty with obeying the rules."

Officer Caffrey leaned back, spreading his legs. Stephen could only stare at him, not understanding what was going on. The cop put one leather-gloved hand in his crotch and squeezed.

"I think you need to be taught a lesson about respect for the law," he said.

Slowly, the cop pulled the zipper on his uniform pants down. Stephen watched as he reached inside the open fly and pulled out his cock. Long and thick, it rose up from a tangle of dark hair. Caffrey's gloved hand slid up and down it slowly.

HrdAtWrk: The cop leans forward and pulls your head down.

The fat head of Caffrey's dick hit Stephen in the mouth. With his hands cuffed, he had a difficult time balancing, but he forced himself up and opened his mouth. His lips closed over the swollen head and he tasted the salty flavor of Caffrey's skin. The cop, his powerful hand on Stephen's head, pushed him down.

Stephen choked as several inches of thick cop meat slid into his throat. He felt his air cut off, and inhaled through his nose. Caffrey ignored his distress, rising up to shove more of his cock into Stephen's mouth. Stephen felt his nose press against the rough hair of the officer's crotch.

"That's right," Caffrey said. "Take it all."

Stephen moved back up the cop's dick, leaving just the head in his mouth. His throat ached from being penetrated, but the taste left behind by Caffrey's cock lingered, and he wanted more of it. He ran his tongue around the head of his cock, teasing him.

"You like that, don't you?" Caffrey said.

Stephen answered him by going down on him again. This time it was easier. The cop's tool slipped into his throat easily, wet with his spit. Stephen slid up and down it, feeling every inch as it passed over his tongue and lips.

HrdAtWrk: The cop holds you by the hair, feeding you his prick.

Caffrey's fingers pulled at Stephen's hair, holding him in place. He raised his hips a little at a time, each movement pushing more of himself into Stephen's mouth.

"Tell me how bad you want it," he ordered.

Stephen, unable to speak, looked up into the cop's face. His dark eyes were cold, hard. He looked at Stephen with a mixture of lust and hatred.

"Tell me," Caffrey repeated. "Do you want my cop cum in your mouth?"

Stephen nodded. Caffrey rewarded him by shoving himself roughly into Stephen's throat. Stephen expected to feel him shoot his load, but instead the officer pulled out again.

"My cum is too good for your fucking mouth," he said. "Now get up."

He fumbled with his belt, pulling it open and lowering his pants. Freed from the confinement of the uniform, his cock stood up from his belly. His big balls hung over the edge of the seat. He reached for the belt at Stephen's waist, pulling it open as well.

"Sit up," he demanded.

HrdAtWrk: He pulls your pants down.

When Caffrey saw Stephen's hard cock jutting up from between his legs, he reached over and squeezed it painfully. Stephen let out a moan.

"You like it rough, do you?" the cop asked. "Sit on me."

He leaned back, putting his hands behind his head. He'd unbuttoned his shirt so that it hung open. His chest was covered in light brown hair that swirled around his pecs and down his belly.

Stephen straddled him as best he could, kneeling on the seat and trying to keep his balance. He was facing Caffrey, the head of his erect cock touching the cop's chest. The feel of his hair on Stephen's sensitive dickhead made Stephen shudder.

Caffrey spit into one gloved hand and used it to wet his cock. He spit again, this time rubbing one finger between the cheeks of Stephen's ass. His finger probed roughly at Stephen's asshole, then pushed inside. Stephen gasped.

"My cock is next," Caffrey informed him as he removed his finger. "Fuck yourself with it."

Trembling, Stephen lowered himself until he felt the tip of Caffrey's dick against his hole. Steeling himself, he sat, feeling himself spread open. He closed his eyes.

"Look at me!" Caffrey barked.

Stephen's eyes flew open. He looked into the cop's face as he inched more of him inside his burning asshole. It hurt like hell, but he wasn't going to let Caffrey know that. He kept going until he felt himself resting on Caffrey's thighs.

HrdAtWrk: You start to move up and down his thick tool.

His cock was being dragged through the fur on Caffrey's chest. The sensation was almost unbearable, riding the edge between pleasure and pain. Also, he had started to leak precum, and the cop's chest was wet with it, little swirls of hair sticking up in moist tangles.

"Fuck yourself, faggot," Caffrey said.

Stephen's face burned red at the slur, but somehow it made him even more excited. He lifted himself up on Caffrey's dick and then pressed back, filling himself. Caffrey put his hands on Stephen's ass, gripping them painfully. He slapped one cheek hard with his gloved hand.

"I said fuck yourself, cocksucker," he growled.

Stephen moved faster. Caffrey's prick filled him again and again. He was getting close himself, but he knew that if he came, it would be a mistake. Caffrey would punish him for it somehow.

"Do you want my load in your faggot ass?" asked Caffrey.

Stephen nodded.

"Say it, then," Caffrey told him. "Tell me to fill your faggot ass with my cum."

"Fill my faggot ass," Stephen said softly.

"Louder!" Caffrey said, slapping his ass again.

"Fill my faggot ass with your cum, sir," Stephen said.

Caffrey leaned back and arched upward. Stephen felt the cock inside him swell, then twitch. Caffrey groaned and thrust into Stephen several more times as he unloaded in his ass.

HrdAtWrk: He pulls out and orders you to lick him clean.

Stephen couldn't control himself. His cock exploded in a blast of warmth as his body shook with the joy of release. He saw Caffrey's chest covered in the proof of his inability to control himself, and he immediately felt shame come over him. Yet still his body quivered, the electricity taking control of his motions.

He felt Caffrey's hand connect with the side of his face. His head flew sideways, the sting of the slap soaking into his skin. But still the joy washed over him.

"Goddamn faggot," Caffrey said. "Now you're really in trouble."

Stephen opened his eyes. A trail of rapidly cooling cum trickled down his stomach, dotting the hair around his cock with sticky pearls. He'd come a lot. His hand was covered with it, and the leather of his chair was spotted in places.

He looked at the computer screen. HrdAtWrk had signed off. The instant message box still remained, however, his last message flashing red: Thanks. See U around.

He reached over and pulled some tissues from the box on his desk. Wiping himself off with one hand, he clicked the instant message box shut with the other. *Yeah,* he thought. *See you around.*

He turned the computer off and stood up. It was time for another pill. He was starting to feel the pain too much.

CHAPTER 17

"I think this is the best time," Simon said, stretching his feet and letting out a contented sigh. "The afterglow, so to speak."

Russell stretched. "I agree," he said. "And it was great. Thanks."

"What is a house for," Simon replied "if not to fill it with friends."

They were in the living room, Simon lying on the couch and Russell sitting in one of the armchairs, Clancy on his lap. The log in the fireplace was burning low, filling the room with its glow. The guests had all left an hour earlier, and now the two men were enjoying the comfort of a house that still retained the feeling of warmth generated by the company they'd shared.

"Do you ever wish you weren't gay?" Russell asked.

Simon, who was on the verge of nodding off, opened his eyes and regarded the younger man. Russell was staring into the fire intently.

"No," Simon said. "I don't. Why would I?"

Russell sighed. "I don't know," he said. "Sometimes it just seems like it would be easier."

"Easier," Simon said, "or just more convenient?"

"Isn't it the same thing?"

"No," replied Simon. "What you mean is that you think being straight would make your life more convenient because you'd be more like the rest of the world."

"Wouldn't it?" asked Russell. "Don't you ever get tired of being in the minority?"

"Sometimes, of course," Simon answered. "But this is who I am."

"How did you and Walter do it?" said Russell. "Figure out your relationship, I mean."

"Figure it out?" Simon said. "What was there to figure out? I loved him and he loved me."

"But it's not that easy," Russell protested. "You can love someone more than anything in the world and still not be able to make things work."

Simon groaned. "You make it so hard," he commented.

"Who does?" Russell said defensively. "Me?"

Simon shook his head. "All of you," he said. "All of you who think there's some secret formula to life. I blame it on gay liberation."

"What are you talking about?" asked Russell. "Gay liberation? Who says that anymore?"

"I do," said Simon. "And it's true. Ever since everyone started running around waving signs and demanding attention, things have been complicated."

"So you're saying we should all have just shut up and stayed in the closet?" demanded Russell.

Simon put another pillow beneath his head so that he was half sitting up. "What I'm saying is that it used to be so uncomplicated. Do you know how many friends I had when I was your age who had been together for years and years? Couples found one another and stayed together because we needed one another. Nowadays you just flit from person to person as your mood changes."

"That's not true about everyone," Russell said.

"No, it's not," said Simon. "But most people don't value marriage anymore."

"Marriage?" said Russell. "We can't even get married."

"I don't mean that legal nonsense," Simon argued. "I mean the notion itself. Do you know we used to hold weddings when I was young? Long before any of you thought about asking the courts for permission."

"Where?" Russell asked him.

Simon waved his hands. "In our homes," he said. "Wherever we wanted to. Walter and I attended many weddings. We got married ourselves."

"What?" Russell exclaimed. "You never mentioned that."

Simon got up and walked over to one of the many bookshelves that lined his walls. He scanned the rows for a moment and then pulled out a photograph album. He carried it back to the sofa, where he sat and put it on his lap. Russell joined him.

Simon opened the album. The first page was filled with faded black-and-white photographs. Simon flipped past them. Several pages later he stopped and pointed to a shot showing a couple dressed for their wedding. The bride wore a short white dress, the groom a smart tuxedo. They smiled at the camera, holding hands.

"Those are our friends Emma and Patience," he said.

"Those are two women?" Russell said. He peered more closely at the photo and saw that, indeed, the groom's face was feminine in features.

"We didn't call her Patience," Simon informed him. "She was Hank."

Russell laughed. "She makes a good-looking guy."

"Yes, she did," said Simon.

"When was this taken?"

Simon thought for a moment, doing the math in his head. "Nineteen fifty-nine," he said. "Hank died a few years ago."

"And Emma?" Russell inquired.

"She lives in Florida," said Simon. "With another widowed friend of ours."

"Do you have any pictures of you and Walter?" asked Russell.

Simon turned a few more pages, watching the faces of friends passing before him like leaves in the wind. So many of them were gone now. He missed them. A few he still spoke to by telephone from their homes scattered around the country, but more and more the days passed without hearing a voice from the old days. Every so often he would receive word that another one had passed, that their numbers were dwindling.

He came to the page he was looking for and stopped. He hadn't looked at these photos in some time. For years he'd been meaning to take them out, have them enlarged, perhaps, so that he could display them. Walter had wanted that. But Simon had never gotten around to it, and after Walter's death he hadn't been able to bring himself to do it.

"That's you and Walter?" said Russell.

Simon nodded. The first photograph showed the two of them,

both dressed in dark suits, standing on the porch of a house. Subsequent ones showed them surrounded by friends, big smiles on their faces as they congratulated the couple.

"Who did the ceremony?" Russell wanted to know.

"We took turns," Simon said. "It didn't really matter. We were doing this for ourselves, not for God or the state."

"I had no idea this sort of thing happened," said Russell.

"Every generation thinks they invented being gay," Simon replied. "The past is not something most young people care to learn about."

"But this is important stuff," said Russell. "This is our lives."

"No, it was *our* lives," Simon corrected him. "You have your own."

"But don't you see?" Russell said. "If we had these kinds of role models, it would give more of us hope that we could do it too."

Simon closed the album and set it on the coffee table. He understood what Russell was saying, but he knew it wasn't entirely true. Explaining why was going to be difficult.

"We did this," he said, "because we wanted to prove we could do it. It was a noble idea. But it was also flawed."

"What do you mean?" Russell asked.

Simon weighed his words carefully. "As much as we would have denied it, we were in some ways attempting to copy the world around us," he explained. "I said that we did it for ourselves, and that was true. But also we were doing it because it made us feel better about who we were. It gave us a sense of normalcy."

"And that's bad?" said Russell.

"Not necessarily," Simon continued. "But some of us were fooled by the notion that we were indeed becoming more like everyone else. When we discovered that this wasn't true, it was very difficult to handle."

"You're contradicting yourself," Russell countered. "First you tell me your relationships were so much better. Now you're telling me they were harder."

"I'm saying that sometimes our expectations were unrealistic. When we told ourselves that the world might be kinder to us because we looked more like those around us, we discovered too often that this was not true."

"So now we're back to staying in the closet," Russell declared impatiently.

Simon closed his eyes. How could he make the young man understand? It had been wonderful then, but also terrible sometimes. He wanted Russell to know what it had been like, to know why, despite everything, he wouldn't trade those years for anything in the world.

"Hope has to come from inside," he said finally. "It has to be something you find in your heart, not something you take from others. Walter and I created our own hope. We knew we belonged together. We knew we needed one another. Even when it was terribly, terribly hard, we knew that. No one can guarantee that something is going to work. No piece of paper, or ceremony, or promise. When you come to a place where you have to decide to leave or stay, the only thing that will keep you there is knowing that it's where you belong."

He looked at Russell. He was staring at the photo album and nodding silently. He turned and looked into Simon's face.

"You're right," he said. "I've been looking for something to tell me what to do, something to help me make a decision. But I just have to make it."

"Walter left me once," Simon told him, surprising himself. He'd never told anyone the story of their one separation.

"Why?" asked Russell.

"He thought I was having an affair," Simon said.

"Were you?"

Simon shook his head. "No," he said. "But I wasn't showing him enough interest. He panicked and assumed the worst."

"Is that what I'm doing?"

"Do you think John is having an affair?"

Russell shook his head. "John? No. I almost wish he was. Then I'd have something to point a finger at."

"But you're not happy?"

"No," Russell admitted. "I'm not at all happy. I love him. I love him more than anything. But something just isn't there. I just can't figure it out."

"Is it something missing in him, or is it something missing in you?" asked Simon quietly.

"Me?" Russell said. "I told you, I love him more than anything."

"Maybe that's the problem," said Simon. "Maybe you need to love yourself more than you love him."

"Great," Russell said. "He thinks I don't love him enough and you think I love him too much. I feel like fucking Goldilocks. This one's too hard; this one's too soft. How do I find the one that's just right?"

"Two halves can only make a whole when those halves are already complete in themselves," Simon said.

Russell looked at him blankly. "What the hell does that mean?"

"It means don't expect either John or your relationship to make you feel good about who you are," Simon explained. "You need to be happy all by yourself."

"Where do you get this stuff?" Russell asked him.

"Dr. Phil," Simon answered. "There's not a lot to do around here in the mornings but watch *Oprah.*"

He waited a moment to see if Russell would catch on that he was joking. Russell just nodded, however, apparently thinking about what Simon had said.

"What is it you want from your life?" Simon asked him after a minute had passed.

"That's just it," said Russell. "I thought I had it. I like my job. I like my partner. But it's just not coming together somewhere."

"Find the missing piece and you'll find your answer," said Simon. He knew it wasn't what Russell wanted to hear, but he also knew it was the truth.

"Are you happy with your life?" Russell asked him.

"No," Simon said. "I'm not." Again, he knew it wasn't what Russell wanted to hear, but again, it was the truth. He wasn't going to lie just to make his friend feel better. "I do not like being alone."

"You have all of us," Russell said kindly.

Simon put a hand on Russell's knee and squeezed. "And I love you all dearly," he said. "But it's not the same as having someone to share your life with."

"I guess we both need something more," Russell said. He looked thoughtful. "I'll make a deal with you."

"What kind of deal," Simon asked suspiciously.

"By New Year's both of us have to do something about getting what we want," said Russell. "If we haven't, we'll spend the rest of our lives together."

Simon laughed. "I think I'd be getting the better half of that deal," he said.

"Come on," Russell said. "I'm serious. Not about living together forever, but the other part. I'll figure out what it is I want and you'll look for someone you can date."

"Date," Simon repeated. "It sounds so modern. It's a lovely idea, Russell, but I think maybe I'm too old for that kind of challenge."

"So you're giving up?"

"No," Simon answered. "I'm waiting patiently."

"Now you're the one avoiding the issue."

"Really," Simon said with exasperation. "Where do you think I'm going to meet someone around here?"

"You're not going to if you don't look," Russell said. "That's why we're making this deal. By New Year's Eve I will have figured out what to do about John and you will have gotten a date for the big party we're going to have."

"Party?" Simon asked. "What party?"

"The one we're throwing to celebrate our success," said Russell.

Simon groaned. "You're too much," he said. "I don't think—"

"Say yes," Russell interrupted.

"But—"

"Say yes."

"Fine," Simon capitulated. "Yes. Yes, I will agree to make a complete fool of myself for your amusement."

"Excellent," Russell said cheerfully. "It's settled then."

He leaned over and kissed Simon on the cheek. "And now I'm going to bed. You've worn me out."

"It's been a long time since anyone's said that to me," Simon joked.

"With a little luck, it won't be the last," Russell told him as he stood up. "I'll see you in the morning."

Simon waved good night. "I'm going to sit here for a while longer."

Alone in his living room, he looked into the flames, thinking about Russell's suggestion. New Year's Eve was what, about five weeks away? Would he be able to find someone to ask out by then? It was a silly notion. He was sixty-five, hardly what the men he saw at the Engine Room were interested in. Even the ones who were closer to his age were looking for partners many years their juniors. He was last year's model, worn out and dented. Who was going to want him?

What would Walter think of the deal he'd made? He smiled to him-self, imagining the look his lover always gave him whenever he men-tioned some plan Walter thought was overly ambitious.

"You're right," Simon said out loud. "I'm an old fool. So perhaps it's time I acted like one."

CHAPTER 18

"I can't believe you've never done this," Mike said.

Thomas, panting and sweating, stopped to catch his breath. "How am I doing for my first time?"

"Not bad," said Mike. "You need to get your legs moving more, though. Really push."

Thomas looked down at his skis. He thought he *was* pushing. His thighs and calves ached, and they'd been out for only twenty minutes. If he pushed any more, he'd have a heart attack.

"The good news is that we're going downhill now," said Mike. "You can just coast. But remember to bend your knees."

"Bend the knees," Thomas echoed. "Got it."

Mike poled ahead and began his descent down the gentle slope. Thomas sent up a silent prayer and followed after him, trying to keep his skis in the tracks made by Mike's. He dutifully bent his knees as his rate of speed increased, but still he felt wobbly. He was glad they were only cross-country skiing. He supposed trying to attempt downhill maneuvers would result in his death.

He made it to the bottom of the hill, where the ground flattened out and his speed decreased. Ahead of him, Mike turned to watch his progress.

"That was perfect," he told Thomas as the priest skied up behind him. "Ready for another one?"

"Does it mean going *up* first?"

"Afraid so," said Mike, plunging a pole into the snow and setting off. "Come on. Trust me, it will be worth it."

Thomas had his doubts. The notion of skiing, as it turned out, was much easier than the actual doing of it. When Mike had suggested a day of outdoor activity, it had seemed like a novel way to spend an afternoon. Now, though, he was wondering if he'd be able to walk when it was all over. His muscles hadn't had such a workout in years.

He doggedly plodded after Mike, managing to keep up as they tackled another hill, this one, thankfully, smaller than the first. And despite how tired he felt, he was having a good time. For one thing, it was absolutely gorgeous. They'd had another storm, and everything was sparkling in the afternoon sun. The snow was dry and powdery, swirling in billowy wisps across the ground. They were skiing through a valley, and on either side a forest surrounded them, walls of green reaching up to the sky. The peaceful quiet was interrupted only by their occasional conversation and the chirping of the birds that foraged in the tree branches, cocking their heads and staring with small, dark eyes at the intruders in their world.

"How often do you do this?" Thomas asked as they crested the hill and paused again to rest.

"Whenever I can," answered Mike. "It's one of the advantages of having an early and long winter."

He must have legs like iron, Thomas thought to himself, immediately blocking out the mental image that had formed in his mind of Mike's legs. He'd been troubled enough by his thoughts of late; he didn't need to add to the problem by picturing Mike naked.

Still, he wondered in spite of himself, what *would* Mike look like beneath his clothes? The only men he'd ever seen naked, besides the boys in his high school gym class, were other priests, and then only in the seminary locker room. His frame of reference for what constituted male physical beauty was limited mostly to religious paintings of Christ preparing for his crucifixion. Those came in either the emaciated version or the well-muscled version, or Scrawny Jesus and Musclebound Jesus, as Joseph had referred to them once as he looked over a book of Christian-themed art.

Given Christ's occupation as a carpenter, Thomas believed he probably would have tended to the latter body type, although perhaps not to the ideal portrayed by many of the painters and sculptors. Their visions of him verged on the sexual. Then again, so did much of religious art, what with all its saints in ecstasy and whatnot. Devotion to religion had long been the favored outlet of expression for the sexually frustrated, and the intermingling of the two came as no shock, particularly to someone who had intimate knowledge of the religious life. Undoubtedly, there was something about Jesus that brought out the erotic in artists. Probably, Thomas thought, it was not a coincidence that so many of them were rumored to be queer.

Mike didn't resemble Jesus in any way, of course. But Thomas had some idea of what he might look like out of his winter coat and ski pants. He could picture Mike, his captivating smile flashing as he pulled a sweater over his head. He could imagine him stepping out of a shower, his hair tousled. He could see—

He drove Jesus, and Mike, from his mind before he went too far. He needed to concentrate on his balance, as he was having difficulty keeping his skis in the ruts left behind by Mike. Twice he had slipped out of them and almost fallen. Only by catching himself with his poles had he avoided doing a face plant in the snow.

They skied for another half hour without saying more than a few words. Then, just as Thomas thought there was no way he could handle another hill, Mike came to a stop. A large boulder sat in the middle of the field, completely out of place, as if an alien ship had come along and dropped it there for some secret purpose.

"Isn't this thing strange?" said Mike, bending down to undo the bindings of his skis. "I discovered it a few years ago."

"Who put it here?" Thomas asked, copying Mike and releasing the clips that held his boots in place.

"Your buddy," Mike answered.

Thomas looked at him, not understanding.

"God," said Mike as he shucked the backpack he'd been carrying from his shoulders and pointed to the rock. "Actually, a glacier left it behind when it made this valley, but it's sort of the same thing, right? Climb on up."

Thomas put his foot on a small outcropping and pulled himself up to the top of the rock. Its surface, warmed by the sun, was free of snow. It was also flat. He sat down and watched as Mike climbed up beside him.

"What's in the pack?" asked Thomas.

"Lunch," said Mike. "But we don't have to eat it if you're not hungry."

"Oh, I'm hungry," Thomas said quickly. "But I didn't know lunch came with the outing."

"This is a full-service operation," Mike said, unzipping the pack and pulling out two brown bags. "I just hope you like peanut butter and jelly."

"It's my favorite," Thomas said, accepting the bag Mike held out. "Thanks."

"There are also a couple of Power Bars in here," said Mike, opening his bag and taking out the sandwich. "And water."

Thomas bit into the sandwich, tasting peanut butter and strawberry jam. It was the most delicious thing he'd ever tasted. His stomach growled its appreciation as he chewed.

"It's beautiful up here," he told Mike.

"I come here in the summer, too," said Mike. "Actually, I come out here all year round. It's a great place to think. On a clear night the stars spread out and it's like being on your very own planet."

"The universe in the palm of God's hand," Thomas said thoughtfully."

"Did you make that up?" Mike inquired.

"Me? No. Sylvia Tressier did."

Mike raised an eyebrow. "Who?"

Thomas smiled. "An eighteenth-century mystic. She wrote about experiencing nature in its purest form. My favorite is her description of standing in a thunderstorm naked. At those moments she said she knew that the entire universe was held in the palm of God's hand."

"She sounds like my kind of girl," Mike remarked.

"She wasn't the church's," Thomas told him. "They called her a pagan."

"I've noticed you guys do that a lot," said Mike.

"Hey, I wasn't there," Thomas said jokingly. "Don't blame me. Besides, that was the Catholics."

"Ah," Mike said, nodding. "Nothing like a lifelong rivalry to bring out the bitterness."

Thomas laughed. "Some of my best friends are Catholics."

"And some of my best friends are straight," replied Mike. "I guess we're both sort of fraternizing with the enemy here, aren't we?"

"Enemy?" said Thomas. "I don't understand."

"You and me," said Mike. "The church and the sinner, the saved and the unsaved."

"Oh," Thomas said uncomfortably. "I guess I hadn't thought about it like that."

"Really?" Mike asked. "It never crosses your mind that you've been spending time with a gay guy?"

"That's not important to me," Thomas said quickly. "You're just you. I'm just me. I could just as easily ask you if it ever crosses your mind that you've been spending time with a priest."

"Every day," said Mike. "Don't tell me you don't think about it."

"I don't," Thomas lied. He felt a heavy weight descend on his shoulders as he spoke. Suddenly, he didn't feel so much like eating.

"You're a better man than I am," Mike said, patting him on the back.

Thomas didn't reply. He took a long drink of water, trying to clear the block that had formed in his throat. Mike, seemingly oblivious, continued to eat his sandwich.

"Can I ask you something?" Thomas asked when he was able to speak again.

"Shoot."

"Have you ever had a, you know, partner?"

Mike didn't answer right away. Thomas was afraid he'd somehow offended his friend by asking. He was on the verge of apologizing when Mike answered him.

"Once," he said. "Before I moved to Cold Falls. It wasn't a long thing, only about three years."

He stopped talking. Thomas wondered if it would be impolite to ask more. He didn't want Mike to think he was prying. But another part of him desperately wanted to know.

"What was his name?" he asked tentatively.

"Jim," Mike said. He said the name without either fondness or anger, giving Thomas no clue as to how he felt about the man.

"He was a bartender too," Mike continued. "We worked at the same place. I had a rule about never dating customers, so I figured my only option was to date another bartender."

"You're joking," said Thomas.

Mike shook his head. "Dating customers is a big mistake," he said. "A lot of your tips depend on customers thinking you're available. Having a jealous boyfriend hanging around puts a real cut in your take.

Besides, when you break up, either the bar loses a customer or you lose a job. But another bartender gets how it is, so it's okay."

"I had no idea it was so complicated," Thomas joked.

"Jim and I got along really well," said Mike. "Until the end."

"Can I ask what happened?" Thomas assumed the story would have something to do with an affair, a lapse of judgment involving a customer, perhaps.

"He was an addict," answered Mike. He'd finished his sandwich. Now he balled up the baggie it had been wrapped in and stuffed it into the paper sack. "Not street drugs. Prescription."

"I'm sorry," said Thomas, starting to wish he'd never asked.

"He was using them the whole time we were together," Mike said. His voice had taken on a new tone, one that made Thomas sad to hear. "It turned out he was trading some doctor free drinks at the bar for prescriptions. Vicodin. Demerol. Anything that would get him high."

"How did you find out?"

"One night he crashed his car into a lamp post," said Mike. "He was conscious enough to have the hospital call me. When I got there, the doctor told me blood tests had shown abnormally high levels of narcotics in Jim's blood. I told them they were crazy. But the more I thought about it, the more it added up. I guess I'd been ignoring the signs. That night I went to his place and did a little looking around. I found garbage bags filled with empty pill bottles in one of his closets."

"So you broke things off?" said Thomas as Mike looked off into the distance.

"I confronted him," Mike said. "At first he told me that he was just selling the drugs to other people. Believe it or not, for a minute that actually made me feel better. But deep down I knew it wasn't the truth. So then I decided to save him. I convinced him to go from the hospital to rehab. I went with him to a couple of NA meetings. He seemed to be doing everything right. But he wasn't. He'd started using again as soon as he was out of the hospital."

Thomas was listening intently. Although their stories were dissimilar in many ways, he could relate to a lot of what Mike was saying. He badly wanted to tell him about Joseph, but he couldn't bring himself to do it. So he sat and listened as Mike finished his tale.

"We stayed together for a year after that," said Mike. He gave a little half laugh. "Looking back, I can't believe I was so stupid. A year." He shook his head sadly. "What an idiot. Anyway, finally I had enough of the broken promises, the worrying, the waiting up for the next phone call from the hospital or the police. One Saturday morning after he hadn't come home all night, I packed up my truck and left."

"Did you ever see him again?"

"No," said Mike. "No one knew where I went, so he had no way of reaching me. That's when I came here. He could be dead for all I know. He might be better off if he was."

Thomas looked up at the bright blue sky. Tattered bits of cloud chased one another across the azure field, the sun peering through them and turning them into ghosts. How strange it seemed to him that anything horrible could go on beneath such a sky. The story Mike had just told him saddened him deeply. He felt for both Mike and Jim, for different reasons.

"That's strange," Mike said, drawing Thomas's attention back to him. "Usually people tell *me* their sob stories."

"Well, this time it was your turn."

"What about you?" asked Mike. "Any tragic tales of love you need to get off your chest?"

Thomas looked up at the sky again, letting the sun dazzle his eyes. There was so much he wanted to tell Mike. But he knew he wouldn't. He turned to his friend. He knew Mike would accept the terrible lie he was about to tell.

"I've never been in love," he said.

CHAPTER 19

"Look at the tits on that one."

Pete turned to see what Ronnie Boudreaux was staring at. Behind them, leaning against the pool table, a blonde with big breasts and bigger hair was talking to some girlfriends. The girls, noticing Pete and his friends staring at them, giggled and turned away.

"Man, she wants you," Ronnie told Pete. "She's been staring at you all night."

Pete's buddies hooted. Having downed at least three beers apiece, they were feeling no pain. The jokes had been flying back and forth, and all of them were in the mood for a little fun.

"Bet she could suck the chrome off a fender," Gary Pitt said, putting his mouth over his beer bottle and feigning a blowjob. "Bet she'd suck the suds down too."

Pete took a sip of his own beer before replying. "Give her a couple more drinks and I bet she'd do all of us."

The comment earned him another round of laughs from his friends and a high-five from T.J. Donnley. Ronnie, shaking his head, said, "Man, if my wife heard us talking this shit, she'd never let me out of the house."

"Just 'cause she won't go down on you's no reason to be a ball buster," T.J. taunted him.

Ronnie flipped his middle finger at T.J. The guys crowed, knowing they'd hit upon one of Ronnie's sore spots. His wife, Julie, was a great woman, but she hated giving head. He'd made the mistake of telling them all about it one drunken night, and they'd never let him forget.

"Dude," T.J. said, leaning forward as if he were about to share a secret. "I was with this girl last week, biggest fucking tits you've ever seen. I mean porn star big. And she wanted me to titty-fuck her. Man, it was like fucking an ass, these things were so huge."

"You're full of it," Gary said.

"Like shit I am," T.J. said angrily. "I met her at the High Spot over in Herkimer. She took me back to her place. It was fucking amazing."

"Bet that one would like a titty fuck from Pete," said Ronnie, cocking his head toward the girl at the pool table.

"Cool it," Pete said.

"What's the matter?" Ronnie asked. "You giving up on chasing pussy or something?"

"Maybe he's turned queer on us," Gary said.

"Fuck you," Pete spat back. "I'm just not into her."

"I'd be into her," said T.J. He made a circle with his finger and thumb and poked another finger through the hole.

Pete laughed, but inside he was fuming. Fucking Gary, he thought. What kind of shit was that, asking if he'd turned queer? He knew it was just a joke; they all called each other queers whenever they were acting stupid. Still, it pissed him off. Maybe he *should* bang the blond chick, just so they'd all shut the fuck up.

"Another round, boys?"

Pete looked up at Sherrie, the Briar Patch's lone waitress. She was collecting their empty bottles and placing them on the tray in her hand. She swept up the wet napkins and added them to the pile.

"Sure," Pete said. "Bring it on."

Sherrie nodded and walked away. Pete, sensing an opportunity to reclaim his reputation among his buddies, followed her with his eyes. "Now there's an ass I'd like to get into," he said.

"No shit," T.J. seconded. "I've been after her forever. That girl won't give it up for nothing."

"Probably a dyke," Gary remarked.

"Hey," T.J. said. "That's fine with me, as long as she lets me watch."

Sherrie came back a moment later with four Buds. As she put them on the table, Pete, looking at Gary across the table, made a V with his fingers and held it to his mouth. His tongue flicked back and forth lewdly in the opening. Gary tried not to crack up as Sherrie asked if she could get them anything else.

"No thanks, honey," Ronnie said, also trying to hide the big smile that was crossing his face. "That'll do it."

When the waitress left, the boys let out a roar, wailing with laughter. Pete's spirits had lifted considerably. He felt like one of the gang again, one of the guys. He could mix it up with the best of them, he told himself. There was nothing the matter with him.

They sat through two more rounds, bullshitting about nothing. This was what Pete liked, a night out with the boys. His friends were pretty damn cool, he told himself. Regular guys. He could easily sit there all night with them, just talking shit and drinking. Except that right now he had to take a major piss.

"Be right back," he said, standing up. He was a little unsteady on his feet, but putting his hand on the back of his chair steadied him.

"Going to the can?" T.J. asked. "I'll come with you."

The two of them made their way through the bar, attempting not to look as intoxicated as they really were. As they passed the table where the blonde and her friends were now sitting, T.J. gave them a nod. "Evening, ladies."

When he and Pete burst into the men's room, they were laughing. Pete was high on the feeling of camaraderie. "Man, you crack me up," he told T.J. as they lined up at the two urinals.

T.J. unzipped his pants. A moment later Pete heard the heavy sound of his piss hitting the water in the urinal. As he held his own dick, releasing what seemed to be a gallon of pee, he quickly glanced to his left.

T.J.'s cock was big. Even soft it hung low. He held it casually between his thumb and forefinger, aiming the head into the bowl. His other hand was on the wall, supporting him. His eyes were closed. Pete kept staring. The piss poured from T.J.'s prick in a thick stream. T.J. had unbuttoned his Levi's, and in the V formed by the blue denim Pete could see the blond hair of his stomach, the heavier patch around his cock.

T.J. finished and groaned. "That felt good," he said. He shook his cock, a few final drops flying into the urinal. Then he tucked his prick away and buttoned up.

Pete, staring at the wall, finished up as well. He hurriedly zipped up and flushed, not looking at T.J. Going to the sink, he washed his hands thoroughly, trying not to think about what he'd seen. But the image of T.J.'s cock, his hand gently caressing it, was burned into his mind.

Back at the table, he tried to blot the image out with the help of another beer. His head was swimming. He'd had too much. But still he hadn't been able to rid his head of his thoughts. They were still there, teasing. He kept stealing glances at T.J., thinking about what he'd seen. He needed to do something else to banish them, something that would bury them deep and keep them there. He stood up.

"Are you leaving, man?" Gary asked.

Pete shook his head. "I'm going to get myself some pussy," he said, grinning wickedly.

Turning away from his friends, he walked over to where the blonde and her friends were sitting. He stopped beside her and put his hand on her shoulder. She looked up.

"Hey," Pete said. "How are you?"

"Fine," the girl said. Her friends tittered.

"I couldn't help but notice how good you look tonight," Pete told her, giving her a smile.

The girl looked at her friends, who laughed some more. Pete ignored them, focusing all of his attention on the blonde. He knew his buddies were all watching him, waiting for him to score.

He considered his options. The girl had been drinking. She was probably just looking for an excuse to get busy with him. He decided to go for it.

"How'd you like to go somewhere with me and party?" he asked.

The girl seemed to consider his offer for a moment. "No thanks," she said.

Pete looked at her, the smile still on his face. He'd heard her wrong.

"I said no thanks," the girl repeated, this time in a less-friendly tone. "Now would you mind leaving us alone?"

Pete blinked. The girl and all her friends were looking at him. He sensed three other pairs of eyes behind him, taking in the situation. He removed his hand from the girl's shoulder and turned away without saying a word. As he walked back to his table, he saw his friends preparing to give him a hard time.

"Sherrie's not the only dyke around here," he said before they could start in on him. "That cunt's as frigid as a Buffalo winter."

Gary, T.J., and Ronnie smirked but said nothing. Pete's anger radiated from him, and his friends felt it. Pete snatched his jacket from the back of his chair and put it on.

"I'll see you guys later," he said.

He stormed out of the bar, ignoring the table of girls, who teasingly called good night to him as he passed them. Outside, he stopped to take a cigarette from his jacket pocket and light it. He blew a cloud of smoke up at the moon. *Fucking bitches,* he thought. *Who the fuck did they think they were fucking with?*

He got in his car. It took him several tries to get the key into the ignition, but on the third attempt he did it. He pulled out of the parking lot with a squealing of tires and headed for the highway.

Halfway home he saw the lights of the lone truck stop on that stretch of the road. Consisting of nothing more than public rest rooms and a couple of picnic tables—now covered with snow—it was rarely used except by teenagers needing a place to party late at night. And, Pete knew, men looking for some action. Although he'd never been there himself, he'd heard stories about the place ever since he was in high school. Tucker Flatley, when they were sixteen, claimed to have been offered a blowjob by an older man while stopping there to smoke a joint. Pete hadn't believed him then, thinking queers lived only in New York and San Francisco, but he'd never forgotten the story.

The parking lot of the rest stop was deserted save for one lone car, parked directly in front of the rest room, its lights dark. Probably it was just a couple of horny teenagers going at it, Pete thought. Still, he found himself pulling off the road and coming to a stop next to the car. Looking at its windows, he saw that they were empty and unclouded. The car was empty.

He got out, still not quite able to stand without swaying, and looked toward the men's room door. It was closed, but from underneath he saw a line of light extended out to the frozen sidewalk. He walked toward the door and pushed, hearing it bang against the inside wall from the force of his entry. If anyone was inside, they definitely would know he was coming.

The room smelled like piss and dirt. Probably, he thought, it was cleaned only occasionally. And it was cold. His breath formed clouds in the unheated air as he walked toward the sinks that lined one wall, the mirrors over them cracked and covered with filmy streaks, residue splashed there by patrons using the little tubs of pink soap to wash their hands after relieving themselves.

To the right of the sinks there was a row of urinals, five of them side by side with no dividers. A single stall was situated at the far end, its door closed. Beneath the door he could see a pair of shoes.

He walked to the farthest urinal, the one closest to the stall. The walls of the stall were made of some kind of hard plastic, and someone had made a small hole in the wall at waist height. He'd seen such a thing before. Fag Holes, he and his friends called them. Queers looked through them, hoping to get a glimpse of the cocks of the men who used the urinal outside. He couldn't imagine anyone taking the time necessary to drill such a hole through solid plastic. It was the act of someone desperate. But that's what fags were, wasn't it? Desperate and pathetic.

The shoes inside the stall shifted, scraping on the dirty floor. Pete wondered if the guy inside was making himself comfortable, peeping through the hole to get a look at who had come in. *I'll give him a show,* he thought as he undid his pants and pulled his dick out.

Standing at the urinal, he first pissed. Then, his bladder once more empty, he slowly stroked his cock to hardness. He made sure to keep the action in line with the hole in the stall wall. The occupant had made no further noise, and Pete was pretty sure he wasn't there to take a shit. There had been none of the usual movement, no unrolling of toilet paper, no sounds or smells of elimination. No, whoever was in the stall was there for other purposes.

Pete saw one shod foot slip halfway out of the stall. Slowly, the toe was raised and lowered, tapping the floor. Pete ignored it, forcing the faggot to give him more proof of what he wanted. It came a moment later, when the foot emerged farther and tapped again, three times. Then Pete heard the sound of the stall's metal lock being pulled back. Behind him, the door swung inward.

He pushed it open, looking inside. Sitting on the toilet was a middle-aged man. His brown hair was graying at the temples, and he wore the generic gold-rimmed glasses typical of men his age. His brown corduroy pants had been pulled down, and his winter jacket was open, revealing a faded blue button-down shirt and an undershirt beneath it. Only his thighs and upper legs were bare, spread to allow him access to his erect penis, which was short and perfectly undistinguished. The hand wrapped around it featured a gold wedding band on its ring finger.

The man looked at Pete, saying nothing. He just held on to his dick as he stared at the cock in Pete's hand. Pete pumped it a few times, seeing the man's face twitch in anticipation. Then Pete stepped closer, until his crotch was right in the man's face, and slapped his mouth with his cock.

"Suck it, fag," he said.

The man's mouth opened, eagerly accepting Pete's tool. He sucked anxiously, inexpertly, his tongue flicking the head. Pete put a hand behind the man's head and pulled him toward him. He gagged, unable to take the thickness of Pete's cock, but Pete held him there until he calmed down. Then he began fucking the man's mouth.

He didn't look at the man. Instead, he thought about T.J., about his big cock and blond hair. It was T.J. servicing him, running his tongue along the length of Pete's cock. It was T.J. sitting there, jerking off while he waited for Pete to come in his mouth.

He shot, filling the warm mouth with his load. He felt the man swallow, choking. When he was done, he pulled away. The man looked up at him. Cum dribbled from the corner of his mouth.

"What?" Pete said. "What are you looking at?"

The man continued to stare at him. He was pulling on his own dick, his hand moving frantically up and down. He had started to breathe more heavily, filling the stall with puffs of air. Then he groaned. A spray of white shot from between his legs, covering the floor beneath him.

Pete looked down and saw that some of the man's load had landed on his boot. With a shudder of repulsion he glared at the man. "Clean it off," he ordered.

The man reached for the toilet paper dispenser.

"Lick it off," Pete said.

The man looked at him. Pete grabbed him by the collar and pulled him off the toilet. He fell awkwardly to his knees, his bare ass scraping the edge of the toilet. He was kneeling in his own cum, as well as the accumulated dirt of the stall's previous patrons.

"Lick it up, faggot," Pete said again.

The man, clearly shaken, leaned forward, his hands on the filthy floor. Bending his head, he licked at Pete's boot, removing the offend-ing stain. When he was done, he looked up at Pete again, as if waiting for a critique of his work.

Pete spit on him, the liquid spattering the man's glasses and mouth. "Goddamned fag," he said.

He exited the stall, leaving the queer sitting on the floor. His buzz was starting to wear off, and he was going to be sick. Outside the men's room door it hit him, a wave of nausea rising up from his stom-ach. He leaned over and puked, the contents of his stomach landing on the hood of the fag's car. Three more times he heaved, emptying himself completely until he was only retching. The mess on the car's hood steamed. He recoiled from the smell.

Let the queer wash it off, he thought as he got into his own car. *It serves him right.*

CHAPTER 20

"Look at the tits on that one."

Mike looked up. His friends were gawking at a well-muscled man who had just entered. Immediately he'd shed his jacket, revealing a white tank top underneath. Now he was cruising the room, obviously enjoying the attention he was getting.

"He must be freezing," Greg said. "It's twenty degrees out there."

"If his nipples are any indication, he is indeed quite chilly," remarked Simon.

"I couldn't look like that if I went to the gym for six hours a day," Russell lamented.

"You could if you injected as many steroids as he probably does," said Mike, comforting him.

"I'd do it if I thought I'd get a body like that," Russell told him. "In a heartbeat."

"Yes, and your dick would shrink to the size of a peanut," said Greg.

"Who says it isn't already the size of a peanut?" Russell replied. He looked at Simon. "Maybe you should ask him out for New Year's."

Mike and Greg looked at the two of them. "What's going on on New Year's?" asked Mike.

"Simon and I just have a little bet going," Russell informed them. "He has to find a date, and I have to decide if I'm getting divorced."

Mike eyed Simon. "You agreed to this?"

"Under protest," Simon answered, sighing. "It was the only way to get him to leave me alone. He was impossibly tenacious."

"I think it's a great idea," said Greg. "I wish I had a date for New Year's."

"Would you like to be mine?" Simon inquired.

"No," Russell said firmly. "It can't be a friend. It has to be a real date."

"What makes you think Greg isn't interested in me as more than a friend?" Simon asked. "Perhaps he finds me wildly attractive."

"That's true," Mike said. "I've seen the way he looks at you."

"Simon, perhaps we should tell them," Greg said seriously. He looked at the other two men. "Simon and I have been seeing each other for some time. We didn't want you to know."

"Nice try," Russell said. "I happen to know you have the hots for that new stock boy. Gina told me all about it."

"Cunt," Greg hissed, then grinned. "But I can't help it. Have you seen him?"

"Body of death," Russell informed Mike and Simon. "And the most beautiful face. Unfortunately, he also has the most hateful gum-popping girlfriend you've ever seen."

"Why do all the hunky straight boys have girlfriends from hell?" Greg whined.

"To keep them away from queens like you," Mike told him. "Stick with your own kind."

"I've been trying," Greg said. "It's not exactly like this place is crawling with eligible fags."

"And you want *me* to find one?" said Simon, addressing Russell.

"Tits is going into the men's room," Greg said, getting their attention. "Russell, come on."

Taking a protesting Russell by the hand, he dragged him toward the men's room. Mike and Simon watched them go.

"Greg is good for him," Mike said to Simon. "I haven't seen Russell have fun in a long time."

The two of them locked eyes. "Are you thinking what I'm thinking?" Simon asked.

"Could be," answered Mike. "It would make sense."

"Hmm," Simon said cryptically as he sipped his drink.

"Did you really promise him you'd find a date for New Year's?"

Simon groaned. "It seemed like a good idea at the time."

"I think it's an excellent idea," said Mike. "Russell's not the only one who hasn't had fun in a while."

"I'm old," Simon replied. "I'm not supposed to have fun. I'm supposed to wither quietly and make way for the young ones."

"Bullshit," Mike said. "You know better than that."

"Yes, I do," Simon said. "Unfortunately, the rest of the world doesn't seem to agree with me."

"Do you have anyone in mind for this little endeavor?" Mike asked.

"Not a one," said Simon. "I was rather hoping a likely candidate would simply drop out of the sky onto my porch. So far, the gods have not indulged that request. But I am hopeful."

Mike laughed. "You'll find someone," he said. "And what exactly are these big New Year's plans?"

"That has yet to be determined," said Simon. "I'm assuming there will be festivities here?"

"The usual," said Mike. "Drag queens, tiaras, and noisemakers all around. You guys are more than welcome."

Before Simon could express his opinion on the matter, Russell and Greg returned. They were giggling like children, laughing so hard they could barely speak.

"What happened in there?" Mike asked them.

Russell held his fingers up, barely an inch of space between the thumb and forefinger. "Peanut dick," he said, causing Greg to launch into a new round of convulsive hysterics.

"You should have seen Russell," he said. "He couldn't stop staring at it."

"It's just so *small,*" Russell said. "I couldn't help it."

"He saw us laughing at it," Greg said.

"Well, that's what he gets for letting people get a look at that thing," said Russell. "He should keep it in his pants if he doesn't want anyone to know."

"That's why the tits are so big," Mike said. "He thinks no one will notice his tiny tool."

"Tiny is right," Greg said. "That thing belongs on a two-year-old."

"Now that that pressing matter is settled," Simon said, "we were discussing the options available to us for New Year's Eve."

"I told Simon you guys can always come here," said Mike. "I have to work anyway, and I'd appreciate the company."

"Sounds good to me," said Russell. "I'll see what John has in mind."

"Are you two getting along better?" Mike inquired.

Russell nodded. "We are," he said. "We're sort of dating again, taking it slow."

"Has he put out yet?" Greg asked him.

"If you must know, we're not doing the sex thing," Russell told them. "I told him I thought we needed to start over. I have to give him credit, he's really trying."

"Don't look now," Mike announced, "but Tinky Winky is heading this way."

The man with the big chest approached the bar, standing right next to Greg. "Jack Daniels," he said. "Neat."

As Mike poured the man's drink, he watched his friends out of the corner of his eye. Russell and Greg were trying very hard not to laugh, while Simon was pretending he didn't know them. Mike turned back to the man, handing him his drink.

"That's a little short, isn't it?" the man said.

Mike shot Russell and Greg a look as they hid their faces behind their hands. "I'll top it off for you," he told his customer.

The man gave him exact change and left with his drink. Russell and Greg, their eyes streaming with tears, pounded their fists on the bar as Mike capped the bottle of Jack and returned it to its place on the shelf.

"A little short?" Greg howled. "A little short? Honey, I've seen bigger worms in the bottom of a tequila bottle."

"Getting back to the topic of holidays," Simon said. "Since our Thanksgiving was such a success, shall we plan something for Christmas?"

"I'll be in Kentucky," Greg said, sounding dismally unhappy. "My mother called and laid a guilt trip on me a mile long. The only way to get her to hang up was to agree to come. So I'll be spending two glorious days in redneck heaven."

"I'll be here, and John doesn't go anywhere, either," Russell said.

"I'm in," chimed in Mike.

"How about your boyfriend?" Russell asked Mike.

"Boyfriend?"

Russell put his hands together and looked heavenward, attempting to assume a pious expression. Getting the hint, Mike took a swipe at him with his bar towel.

"Knock it off," he said. "Besides, he's probably doing something. That is the big day for the church, you know."

"Ask him anyway," said Simon. "I found him to be delightful."

"Okay," Mike said. "I'll ask him."

"Did you know Jesus was actually born in March?" Greg said, taking a handful of peanuts from the bowls Mike was setting out and popping them into his mouth.

They all looked at him.

"Why do you know that?" Russell asked.

Greg shrugged. "It's just one of those useless bits of trivia I have floating around in my head, like how many Oscars Bette Davis won or something."

"Actually, he's correct," said Simon before anyone could contradict Greg. "Historical evidence does suggest that Christ was born in March."

"Then why do we celebrate Christmas?" asked Russell.

"In order to make Christianity more acceptable to the pagan communities they wanted to control, the church simply inserted religious holidays over the existing pagan ones," Simon explained. "December was the time for celebrating Yule, or the return of the light. By substituting the Christ child for the sun, they provided a neat compromise. The pagans could continue to celebrate their holidays and the church could gradually wipe out the heathen traditions. It was really very clever on their part, so successful that even most Christians don't realize that the trees they put up each year are, in fact, symbols of pagan rebirth."

"Leave it to religion to fuck up something good," Russell said, shaking his head. "Is there anything they haven't gotten their fingers into? They should just wipe out all the churches and start again."

"We'd just fuck it up all over again," Mike said.

Russell nodded. "Maybe," he said. "But at least this time *we* would be in charge. We could make heterosexuality a sin and see how they like it."

"This conversation has gotten kind of heavy," Greg said. "Can we talk about Teeny Peeny again?"

"You started it," Russell accused him. "You and that stuff about Jesus being a Pisces instead of a Capricorn."

"Whatever," said Greg. "Let's get back to the tits. Do you think he's a top or a bottom?"

"Bottom," Mike and Russell said in unison.

"With a dick like that?" Russell added. "I certainly hope so."

"I don't know," said Greg. "I think he *thinks* he's a top, but really he wants someone to bend him over and give him a good, hard ride."

"It sounds to me like *you* want to give him a good, hard pounding," Mike told Greg.

Greg grinned. "He does have a great ass," he said.

"Oh, for the love of God," said Russell. "If you tell me you're going to try to pick that man up, I'm going to have to reconsider being your friend."

"I didn't say I wanted to marry him," Greg objected. "I just said he had a great ass."

"Go," Russell said, shooing Greg away as if he were a pesky dog. "You've already decided you're going to, so just go. But when you get him home and he says he wants to put that little thing of his in your butt, don't say we didn't warn you."

Greg stood up. "I'll see you boys in a little while," he said, marching off in search of his quarry.

"Can you believe that?" Russell asked Mike and Simon. "What on earth would possess him to go after that?"

"He's a man," Simon said knowingly. "And he's had several drinks. If successful, he will indeed regret it in the morning. We have all of us bedded someone we later regretted."

"Even you?" Mike asked, interested.

"Even me," answered Simon. "My friend Patrick used to call them Monets."

"Monets?" Russell repeated. "I don't get it."

"False impressionism," Simon clarified. "Good from far, but far from good. Every gay man has a few Monets in his romantic gallery."

"I have more than a few," Russell admitted. "But even I wouldn't go after Mr. Tits."

"It sounds to me like you're a little bit jealous," Mike teased.

"Of Greg?" Russell exclaimed. "Please."

Mike and Simon looked at one another. Simon nodded. Russell, noticing the exchange, looked horrified. "You guys think I have it bad for Greg?"

"We've just noticed that the two of you seem to get along awfully well," Mike said. "That's all."

"I am *not* interested in Greg," Russell declared. "Not at all."

"But he does have a great ass," said Mike.

"Doesn't he—" Russell began, stopping when he saw the huge grin on Mike's face. "You asshole," he said, trying hard to sound angry.

Giving Simon a wink, Mike took Russell's empty glass and refilled it. "This one's on the house," he said as he handed it back. "Bottoms up."

CHAPTER 21

Thomas looked at the faces staring back at him. They were waiting for him to tell them something. Some of them fidgeted in their seats, scratching their heads or noses; others looked around the room, completely ignoring him. This, he knew from experience, was the toughest kind of audience for a minister. He was going to have to be good.

"Can anyone tell me why Mary and Joseph were going to Bethlehem?" he asked.

Several hands shot up. He picked one at random. "Yes, Alexa?"

"It was their vacation," the little girl said confidently. "We go to visit my grandma at Christmas. Probably they were going to visit Jesus's grandma."

"That's not why they were going," a boy beside her said. "They went because of the centipede. Isn't that right, Father Dunn?"

The boy, Hamish McTooney, looked at Thomas triumphantly. Thomas wasn't sure what to tell him. The centipede? Where on earth had the child gotten such an idea? Thomas didn't want to make him feel foolish, but he was at a loss for words.

"What's a centipede?" someone else asked, sparing Thomas for the moment.

"It's when people count you, stupid," Hamish said knowingly.

Suddenly Thomas understood. "I think what Hamish means is a *census*," he said, ignoring for a moment the fact that Hamish had insulted the asker.

"Right," said Hamish. "That."

"Hamish is correct that a census is a counting of people," Thomas continued. "Mary and Joseph were going to Bethlehem because there was a census going on. They went there to be counted."

"Why did they have to go to Bethlehem to get counted?" asked Lily Parsick. "Couldn't they do it by telephone?"

"They didn't have telephones back then," Thomas explained.

The children all nodded, as if this made perfect sense to them. Thomas thanked God that there were some things five-year-olds took at face value.

"Mary and Joseph went to Bethlehem to take part in the census," he said. "And when they got there, they tried to find a room at an inn. But there weren't any to be found."

He waited for one of the kids to ask why they hadn't made a reservation. Apparently, this small detail escaped them completely, however, because they remained quiet.

"Finally they found someone who would let them stay in his stable," Thomas said.

"We have a stable," Jeb Ritner said brightly. "We keep horses in it."

"There were horses in this stable, too," Thomas said quickly, sensing that some of the other children were about to discuss in detail the contents of *their* stables. "And cows, sheep, and donkeys. There were lots of animals. Mary and Joseph made a bed in the straw, and that's where Mary gave birth to Jesus."

The children stared at him. One yawned. He'd just come to the climax of his story, and they couldn't have cared less.

"Did the donkeys lick him?" Alexa asked. "My grandma has a donkey and it licked me once."

"Probably a donkey did lick Jesus," Thomas assured her. "And later, the shepherds and the three wise men came to see him. Do you know how they knew he was there?"

The children shook their heads as one.

"An angel told them he was there. And the wise men followed a star."

"And the wise men brought him presents," Hamish said suddenly, as if he'd just remembered it. "Gold and something."

At the mention of presents, the class perked up considerably. Thomas knew they were envisioning their own ideas of what constituted acceptable Christmas gifts, and he wasn't about to divest them of their notions. It was easier this way.

"So that's what our pageant is going to be about," he said cheerfully. "And all of you are going to be in it. What do you think about that?"

"Can I be Mary?" Alexa asked immediately.

Thomas looked over at Mrs. Evelyn Siggs, their Sunday school teacher. She rolled her eyes and came to his rescue.

"You all are going to be shepherds, angels, and animals," she said enthusiastically. "The older classes will be the other roles."

"But I want to be Mary," Alexa insisted.

"Maybe next year," Mrs. Siggs said kindly.

Alexa mulled over this news. "Then can I be a pig?" she asked.

"Yes," Mrs. Siggs said, beaming. "You can be a pig. And you all get to sing 'Silent Night' as part of the angel choir."

Gladdened by this news, Alexa immediately began snorting. The other children followed her cue, making various animal noises. The room filled with bleating, mooing, oinking, and assorted other sounds, all of which sounded decidedly odd coming from a bunch of rosy-cheeked first graders.

"It's like this every year," Mrs. Siggs told Thomas. "Thanks for coming to talk to them. It makes them feel important."

"I hope the next bunch is easier," Thomas told her. "It's the teen class."

"They'll just be surly," Mrs. Siggs assured him. "And secretly all the girls will want to be Mary. They always do."

Thomas left her with her charges and exited the room. The smaller children had their Sunday school sessions in the church's basement, while the older ones were upstairs. He went up and walked into the room where they were meeting with Saint Peter's music director and de facto pageant organizer, Gavin Bettelheim. In his sixties, Gavin was a portly, bearded man who favored music many in the congregation found slightly depressing. But his skill as an organist and his ability to draw moving performances from the choir were unchallenged, and he had been a fixture at the church for coming on three decades.

"Ah, Father Dunn," Gavin said as the priest entered the room. "I was just telling these young people about my plans for this year's pageant."

The young people in question were a dozen teens ranging in age from eleven to seventeen. None of them looked particularly enthusiastic about the idea of being in a nativity pageant, and a few seemed to be on the verge of mutiny.

"He wants us to sing in *German*," one of the girls wailed.

"It's Brahms!" Bettelheim said, exasperation strangling his voice. "It's supposed to be sung in German."

"No one will even know what it means," the girl argued.

"No one *cares* what it means," said the director. "They'll all be too busy looking at the shepherds wearing their fathers' bathrobes."

The group retreated into sullen silence, the girls folding their arms over their chests and the boys looking off into the distance. Looking at them, Thomas was thankful to be free of the years when acne and a fragile sense of self rendered every interaction with an adult a potential for disaster. He took the fuming music director aside.

"Gavin, how about if I talk to them alone for a while," he suggested. "I'll see if I can warm them up to the idea of the whole thing."

"Thank you," Bettelheim said. "Maybe they'll listen to you. Do you know one of them dared to suggest that we perform 'Winter Wonderland'?"

Thomas rewarded him with a look of shared disappointment in the musical tastes of the church's youth. Gavin, casting a final, disapproving glance in the direction of his mutinous actors, walked off, muttering to himself.

"So," Thomas said once the man was gone. "What seems to be the problem here?"

They all began talking at once, the air clotting with their competing complaints. Thomas held up his hands to silence them. "Why don't we all sit down."

They sat. He took a chair and placed it in front of them, so that he was the focal point for their attention. Once they were settled, he tried again.

"I know this pageant stuff isn't exactly cool," he said. "When I was your age, I had to do them, and every year I got stuck being a wise man because I was the tallest."

This revelation earned him a reluctant laugh from the kids. He knew they were having a hard time imagining a priest who didn't want to be in a Christmas pageant, but he was telling the truth.

"Mr. Bettelheim is right about parents coming to see their kids,"

Thomas continued. "This is more about them than it is about you guys. And there are a bunch of little kids downstairs mooing and clucking their heads off. They can't wait for Christmas Eve to get here. Do they care that this is supposed to be about the birth of Christ? No. They just want to be in a play. They look up to you guys, just like you probably looked up to whoever was in your shoes when you were five. So what do you say? Will you stop giving Mr. Bettelheim a hard time?"

"It's just so dumb is all," said a boy seated in the front. Tall and thin, with shaggy hair and a pimple-scarred chin, he reminded Thomas of himself at the same age.

"What do you mean, Rick?" he asked.

"The whole thing," Rick said, pushing his hair away from his eyes. "Mary being a virgin. The wise men coming. Come on. It would have taken them months to get there. The whole thing is just a big story."

The other kids looked at him with a mixture of respect and horror. Then, as if their minds were connected on a subconscious level, they turned to see what Father Dunn's reaction was going to be. Thomas could tell they expected him to be angry at the young man's attack on the nativity story.

"I can't vouch for Mary's virginity," Thomas said. "And you're right that the elements of the Christmas story have been sort of pushed together for the sake of convenience. But the basic message holds true. Christmas celebrates the birth of the one who saved the world, the birth of hope. The rest of it is just, well, wrapping paper."

The teenagers looked at him as if he'd just declared the Bible to have been written by Stephen King. Probably, he thought, they'd never heard anyone question the absolute truth portrayed in the gospel. He himself had always been taught that the birth of Christ happened exactly as it was depicted in nativity plays across the world. It wasn't until he was in seminary that he had started to question things.

He remembered, suddenly, a Christmas Eve spent with Joseph. It was before Joseph's diagnosis, before they knew that he was carrying death inside him. They were in seminary, halfway through their second year, and neither had the money to go home for the holidays. Instead, they decided to spend them together.

They'd taken the train from Boston to New York on the afternoon of December twenty-fourth, planning on attending the midnight service at the Cathedral of Saint John the Divine. Both adored the towering church, with its cavernous central nave and its smaller side chapels, each dedicated to the memory of a different group of people: poets, freedom fighters, those claimed by AIDS.

It was snowing when they exited the subway that had taken them uptown. Running up the steps to the cathedral's huge wooden front doors, they'd paused inside, entranced by the glow of hundreds of candles that had been lit by visitors to the church. Their light rose up, somehow filling the emptiness of the ceiling high above them. All around them, people shuffled in respectful silence.

Waiting for the service to begin, they had wandered through the various chapels, looking at the tokens left behind by earlier pilgrims. The AIDS chapel, in particular, was decorated with gifts in memory of those who had died: notes written with trembling hands, photographs of the dead, inexplicable talismans (impossibly large high-heel shoes, the sheet music for "In the Still of the Night," a Barbie), and other mementos whose individual meanings were lost on Thomas and Joseph but whose accumulated effect was numbing.

Thomas, in particular, had been anxious to leave that particular chapel. Joseph, sensing his unease, had shepherded Thomas into the cathedral's gift shop. There, among the gargoyle replicas, CDs of sacred music from around the world, and displays of soaps and (most perplexing) snow globes containing miniature plastic cathedrals, Thomas had discovered a Christmas tree decorated with a multitude of ornaments. He had been particularly drawn to the figure of an angel. Unlike its blond cousins, it had black hair streaming out over a dress of deepest purple dotted here and there with gold. Its wings were like those of a bird, and in its hands was a candle, as if it were lighting the way for its brethren.

Hearing the sounds of music heralding the start of the service, they had rushed back to the nave and taken their seats. Thomas, caught up in the service, barely noticed when Joseph excused himself to use the bathroom.

Only later, as they were sitting, exhausted and blissful, on the train back to Boston early on Christmas morning, did Joseph reach into the pocket of his coat and produce a small bundle, which he handed to Thomas with a "Merry Christmas." Inside was the angel.

"I saw you looking at it," Joseph said. "You had the most beautiful look on your face."

He'd then leaned over and kissed Thomas, lightly, on the cheek. Thomas, holding the angel in his hands, had felt a moment of absolute hope and joy. At the time he'd thought it was a response to the holiness of the day and the lingering effects of his time spent in the cathedral. Only later, when it was too late, had he realized the true cause of his happiness.

"Father Dunn?"

Thomas looked up and saw the wondering faces looking at him. How long had he sat there, silent, in front of them? It felt as if he'd been lost in thought for hours, but surely it could only have been a minute.

"Right," he said, trying to remember what they'd been talking about. "So, as you can see, it . . . it . . ." He had no idea what he was saying. The kids were looking at him with expressions of increasing puzzlement. Then he remembered. Christmas. The pageant. Jesus.

"It may be just a story," he said quickly. "Who knows. But people like stories, and they're expecting a pageant, so just do it, all right?"

The teens looked at one another. For a moment Thomas thought they might demand to know just what it was he thought he was doing being a priest. Instead, they nodded.

"Sure," Rick said as the others murmured their assent. "It's cool."

After a moment a girl in the back raised her hand. "Can I be Mary?" she asked shyly.

CHAPTER 22

The phone rang. Stephen ignored it. Probably it was one of his clients, calling to ask where their monthly statements were. They'd been leaving messages for the past two weeks, at first mildly puzzled, then concerned, and now just plain upset. He didn't even play the recordings anymore, letting them pile up until the machine, its electronic stomach bloated, vomited them away. The blinking eye of the message light was nothing more to him than an angry red beacon warning him to stay away. He was happy to oblige.

He opened the bottle of pills that now sat continuously on his desk and took two, washing them down with Diet Coke. The combination was vile, but he'd long ago stopped tasting anything. It was all cardboard to him. He ate resentfully, because his body demanded it, chewing absentmindedly and filling his mouth until whatever can he'd opened was empty.

He made regular appearances at his parents' house, out of necessity, and had managed to convince them that everything was fine. He answered his mother's questions, accompanied her on the occasional errand, and was in every way the dutiful son. As soon as possible, he returned to his house and to the computer.

The computer. It had become his refuge. There, logged into a chat room, he could forget about himself. He was no longer Stephen Darby. He was PoundCk. It was a silly name, but it amused him with its combination of sweetness that after a moment's thought took on another, darker meaning. As PoundCk he prowled the various rooms, sometimes just looking, sometimes joining in, always searching.

Ever since his encounter with HrdAtWrk, he had waited for another meeting with him. But although he remained logged on at all hours and checked his buddy list constantly, he had yet to run into him again. He contented himself with other men, attempting to create with them the thrill he had experienced at the hands of his faceless partner. Sometimes he came close, but afterward he felt the disappointment of having settled for second best.

He couldn't explain, had he been asked, what it was about HrdAtWrk that called out to him. It was something he feared, a seed of darkness that, once planted within him, had blossomed into a need that gnawed at his heart. He thought almost constantly about the leather-gloved hands, the excitement he'd felt in being forced to serve the cop. He knew it was a fantasy, but it didn't matter. It existed in his head. It was real enough. And it was safe.

He never looked at his face. The bruises, midway through their healing process, had turned an ugly purplish-yellow. His lip, too, was a deep purple, and it was becoming evident that he would carry a scar there. He occasionally caught an accidental glimpse of himself in some shiny surface—the side of the toaster, a pane of glass, even the back of the spoons he dipped into the cans of chili and cold pasta he consumed. For a moment he would stare at the distorted, monstrous visage, not recognizing it as his own. Then, realizing that he was seeing his own reflection, he would look away in disgust and shame.

He knew he was a monster. Only a monster would do what he'd done. Only a monster deserved what he'd received. Only a monster could live a life of furtive searching for something so cancerous. After many hours of thinking through his experience, he'd come to understand this. Since then, an uneasy peace had settled around him. He knew what he was, even if he couldn't face that thing directly in a mirror. He knew that, soon, he would have to try to slay the monster.

Until then, he searched. The pills helped him. They silenced the voices that told him to get into the shower, to get dressed, to return to his old life. They told him the truth, that he was destined to remain in the darkness, a pawn to be used for the pleasure of others. Each time he felt the pain returning, he held some of them in his hand, looking down at them as if beholding the secrets of the universe. He marveled that so much solace could be contained in the tiny spheres.

He no longer knew or cared what time it was. The clocks, like the answering machine, were meaningless. The hands swept around in an endless bid for his attention, but he ignored them. He measured his days by the appearance of familiar names on his computer screen. He'd memorized their habits and patterns: who favored the morning, who was on only during his lunch hour, who came out in the small hours of the morning.

These were his landmarks, the signposts by which he traveled. Although his destination remained out of sight, he moved ever on-ward. Thankfully, the pills did little to dull his sexual appetite. He was almost constantly hard, his hand never far from his waiting cock. Touching it reassured him. Coming was more refreshing than sleep. He jerked off half a dozen times in a single session at his desk, some-times accompanied by someone in another room, sometimes alone, thinking about the back of the police car. The trash can, and now the floor, was littered with crumpled wads of tissue, the paper hardened into perverse origami by his dried seed.

But still there was no sign of his dark knight. That's how he had come to imagine HrdAtWrk, a figure cloaked in shadow, sent to draw him deeper into the world he longed to live in. Only he could take Stephen by the hand and take him down the dim-lit alleys and danger-ous byways of his own mind. Only he could show him the way.

And then, one night as he was battling the call of sleep and forcing his eyes open by staring at the blinking cursor on his computer screen, a miracle occurred. Hearing the familiar ding that signaled the arrival of a message, he turned his gaze to the box and saw there the name he had been waiting for.

HrdAtWrk: U R up late.

Stephen stared at the words until they blurred. He was afraid to blink, lest he open his eyes and discover that he had only imagined the message.

HrdAtWrk: U there?

He reached for the keyboard and typed back a response: Hello. It was the only word he could bring himself to write.

HrdAtWrk: Up 4 some fun?

Stephen's hands trembled as he tried to compose himself. His fin-gers twitched anxiously as he replied: Anything you want.

He held his breath, awaiting his master's response. He was captive, a bird held in the hands of a hunter. All thought stopped, and he heard only the beating of the blood in his head and in his cock.

HrdAtWrk: U R walking home late at nite. You pass a house, and in the window you see a naked man. He's hard.

Stephen closed his eyes and began to dream. He was on a street. It was past midnight. He was walking quickly, wanting to get out of the darkness and into the safety of his house. The houses around him were dark, asleep, the occupants safe in their beds.

In one house, though, a light glowed. Noticing it, he stopped and looked up. There, on the second floor, someone stood in the window. A man. He was naked, his powerful body illuminated by the moonlight. His hand moved up and down a long, thick cock.

Ashamed, Stephen tried to turn away. But something about the man held his gaze. It was then that he realized that the man was looking back at him. His eyes met Stephen's, and Stephen felt his heart stop.

HrdAtWrk: He motions for you to come up to him.

Stephen walked to the front door of the house. About to knock, he instead tried the handle. At his touch the door swung open into darkness. He saw a stairway, the top lit with pale light that tumbled down the steps, growing fainter until at the bottom it was only a flicker.

He knew the man was waiting for him up the stairs. He knew that he still had a chance to turn and leave. Instead he shut the door behind him and took the first step.

At the top, he looked into a bedroom. The man had turned to face him. He was even more beautiful and terrible than Stephen had realized. His thick legs were spread wide, his balls hanging down between them. The muscles of his chest rose and fell as his hand continued to squeeze his cock. He looked at Stephen and sneered.

"What do you want, faggot?"

Stephen licked his lips, unable to speak.

"Well? Tell me or get out."

Stephen choked on his words. "I want to suck your cock."

The man laughed. "Then get over here and do it," he said.

Stephen walked toward him and dropped to his knees. The man's dick taunted him, waving in front of his face as the man moved it back and forth. It was impossibly large. He knew there was no way he would be able to take it in.

The man's hand flew out and hit him in the cheek. He gasped, surprised at the shock of it.

"Suck it," the man ordered.

Stephen opened his mouth and obeyed. The man showed him no mercy, stuffing himself into Stephen's throat. Stephen accepted it, knowing that his only purpose was to do as he was told. He sucked greedily, lapping at the flesh that filled his mouth.

After a few minutes the man pulled out of his mouth.

"Stand up," he said.

Stephen scrambled to his feet, anxious to please his master. He found himself being spun around.

"Drop your pants."

He did, exposing his ass to the man behind him. Then he felt a push and he found himself sprawling facedown on the bed.

"On your hands and knees."

He assumed the demanded position, legs spread. He sensed the man behind him, and waited to feel his cock pressing against his ass. Instead, he felt a finger slide inside him.

"You want your faggot ass fucked?"

"Yes, sir," he said.

The man slapped his ass hard, making Stephen cry out in pain.

"You don't deserve to have me fuck your ass, faggot. Do you?" He slapped Stephen's ass again.

"No!" Stephen bleated, biting his lip.

"That's right. You don't. But maybe I'll fuck it anyway if you take what I'm going to give you."

Stephen didn't understand. Then he felt a second finger add itself to the first. His asshole stretched open as the man spread it. A third finger went inside him.

Suddenly, he understood. The realization filled him with horror. But it was too late. It had begun, and he had no choice. He felt the man's hand squeeze together momentarily, and then a burst of pain shot through his insides as he was penetrated by the thick, hard fingers.

"What a good faggot," the man said. "Your ass was made for this, wasn't it, fag? Made for using by real men."

"Yes, sir," Stephen gasped.

The man pulled on Stephen's balls, making the erection between Stephen's legs slap against his stomach.

"I'm making you hard, aren't I, faggot? Your fag dick is all stiff over me."

"Yes, sir."

The man pulled his fingers out, leaving Stephen empty.

"Tell me you want the whole thing, faggot."

"I want it, sir."

The hand returned. This time the man pushed into him quickly. Tears came to Stephen's eyes as he was invaded. He'd never known such pain. Yet he welcomed it, accepted it as his punishment for opening the door. He felt the man's fingers curl into a fist inside him and push forward. He had become a puppet, controlled from the inside by the man's hand and will. He was his to do with as he pleased.

"You're mine, faggot. Do you understand that?"

Stephen nodded.

"I can do what I want with you. I could kill you if I wanted to. Do you understand?"

Again Stephen nodded. The man pulled on Stephen's balls again until he cried out for mercy.

"Answer me when I ask you a question, faggot. Do you want me to fuck you now?"

"Yes, sir," said Stephen, eyes blinded by tears of pain. "Please fuck me, sir."

He felt the man's hand retreat. He moaned, not for the relief but because he wanted more. He was dirty, a whore, and he knew it.

"Here's what you want, faggot," the man said as he shoved his cock into Stephen's ass. "Milk my cock."

Stephen let out a moan of joy. He was once again complete. With the man's cock inside him, he was fulfilling his purpose in the world. He pushed himself back, impaling himself on the thick tool. He felt the man's balls smack against his own.

Suddenly he felt something cold against his neck. The man had leaned forward, was holding a knife against the soft surface of Stephen's skin. The edge bit into him.

"Keep fucking yourself, faggot," the man told him. "Don't stop or I'll open you up."

The man held the knife there as Stephen continued to move back and forth, the two of them rocking together. With each push, Stephen felt the blade threaten to peel back his skin. He felt the hot breath of his master on his neck, felt himself enveloped by the muscles of the man's body as it covered his.

"You fags deserve to die," the man said. "Don't you?"

"Yes," Stephen whispered, afraid anything else would result in his being cut.

"You like having a real man's cock in your ass," the man said. "You like being a filthy faggot for me, don't you?"

"Yes, sir."

"You want me to come in your useless ass, don't you?"

Stephen tried to nod. The man tightened his grip on Stephen's throat. "Beg me to come in your ass."

"Please, sir," Stephen said as loudly as he could. "Please come in my ass."

The blade pressed against Stephen's neck as the man thrust several times, quickly and mercilessly. He let out a groan of triumph.

"Ooh," he said as the first wave shook him. "Take it, faggot."

Stephen felt himself blacking out as the man's arm tightened like a vise around his throat.

"Take my fucking load."

Stephen's vision faded. He tried to breathe.

"Fucking faggot," the man yelled as he gave one final pump. Then he pulled out. He released Stephen, who collapsed onto the bed, gasping for breath.

The man got off the bed. Picking up Stephen's pants, he threw them at him.

"You're lucky I didn't kill you," he said, holding up the knife he'd used and snapping it shut. "Now get the fuck out before I change my mind."

Stephen jumped to his feet and fled. As he ran down the stairs, he put his hand to his throat. Where the knife had touched his skin, it burned as if he'd been branded.

The blinking of the computer brought him out of his reverie.

HrdAtWrk: See U soon.

He put his hand to his neck. Closing his eyes, he could feel the knife there, waiting to open him up and reveal his true self.

"See you soon," he whispered.

CHAPTER 23

The Cold Falls Public Library had once been a grand building. Now it was a faded, tired, old lady, the victim of a shrinking budget and a decline in interest on the part of the very people she had been built to serve. Still, Simon loved her. Every Monday for the past fifteen years he had arrived there shortly after ten o'clock, carrying the three (or sometimes four) books he'd taken away the previous Monday. These he returned at the library's enormous wooden front desk before venturing into the stacks in search of new reading material.

Until her death in October, the head librarian had been a woman named Millie St. John. She'd held that post during all the years Simon had been coming to the library. Ancient even to Simon's aging eyes, Millie had been a small, shriveled woman with the face of an apple-head doll and a mind that contained the whole of the universe. Not surprisingly, she'd read voraciously, and on each of Simon's visits she'd had one or two suggestions as to books he might enjoy. Only rarely had she been mistaken.

Millie had passed away in her sleep. She'd been discovered, according to local legend, with a copy of William Faulkner's *As I Lay Dying* open on her chest. Whether this was or was not true, what was true was that Millie had somehow during her lifetime amassed a small fortune, all of which she'd bequeathed to the library with the stipulation that it be used to renovate the building and pay the salary of her replacement.

Although the renovations had yet to begin, the replacement had been found. Alistair Wainwright had arrived in November from Potterton, Missouri. Not as small as Millie St. John, he was nonetheless not a large man. Compact, Simon had called him when describing him to Russell. Buttoned-down. He wore sweater vests over starched white shirts and oiled his hair. Despite his age (he was perhaps in his early fifties, Simon guessed), he seemed to have stepped out of a 1940s black-and-white film into the real world.

Alistair's taste in reading material was not as extensive as Millie's had been. More refined, he favored the classics, where Millie had been far more egalitarian, as likely to recommend the latest John Grisham novel as she was to suggest *To Kill a Mockingbird* or *Cannery Row.* Alistair accommodated the tastes of his clientele by purchasing the latest best sellers, but his interest in their reading habits stopped short of encouraging their interests in Anne Rice and Danielle Steel.

Simon had introduced himself to Alistair on his first Monday visit following the new librarian's arrival. Alistair, looking at the books Simon deposited in the return box (Anthony Trollope's *Barchester Towers,* a volume of Virginia Woolf's diaries, and a battered copy of Mark Twain's *The Innocents Abroad*), had sensed a kindred spirit and marked Simon as someone to watch. Simon, in turn, had been relieved that Millie had not, as he'd feared, been replaced by someone right out of library school who would try to revive interest in reading by holding Oprah-esque book discussions.

On this particular Monday, Simon had brought with him for return Mark Helprin's *Winter's Tale* and Truman Capote's *The Thanksgiving Visitor,* both of which he'd enjoyed before but been inspired by the season and the recent snowstorms to revisit. After stamping his feet to remove as much of the attached snow as he could, he duly placed the books in the return box.

"As good as you remembered?" Alistair asked him.

"As good and better," replied Simon. "Helprin should be taken to court for not producing another book in so long. And Capote, well, what can I say? Every one of these so-called wunderkind writers should write a quarter as well as he did."

Alistair chuckled. "I wonder what he'd think of chick lit," he mused.

"Chick lit?" asked Simon.

Alistair held up a copy of a book he'd just finished installing library coding labels on. *"Boyfriend in the Shop, "* he said drily. "Apparently it's about a woman who has it up to here with her imperfect boyfriend. She opens an agency where women can bring their equally unsatisfying men and have them turned into the ideal mates. It is, I am assured by *Library Journal,* destined to be an enormous hit with women from seventeen to seventy. I bought three."

Simon looked at the cover, a vibrant cut-paper collage. The author's name occupied the entire top half. He had never heard of her.

"I have a waiting list for it," Alistair said, giving the book a sour glance. "If you want it, you'll have to wait until February."

"However will I cope?" asked Simon.

"Maybe this will be some comfort," said Alistair, reaching under the counter and producing another book, which he slid across the desk to Simon.

"The new Wallis Simpson biography!" Simon exclaimed. "I didn't even know it was out."

"It's not," Alistair told him. "I received an advance copy from a librarian friend who had an extra. The perks afforded those of us who tend to books for a living may be few, but they're mighty."

"I'm indeed indebted," Simon said happily, opening the book and running his hand over the virgin page. "If there's anything that makes the season bright, it's the reopening of an old scandal."

"I understand Wallis comes across as quite the shrew in this one," Alistair commented. "According to the author, the poor king never stood a chance once she got her claws into him."

Simon gave a murmur of pleased agreement. "The bitch of all bitches," he said. "Quite a woman."

Alistair laughed. "Keep it as long as you like," he said. "I can't imagine anyone else will be asking for it."

Simon closed the book. "Thank you," he said. "And now I will go into the forest and see what other tasty nuts I can gather."

He left Alistair affixing labels to the other new books and entered the library's stacks. Although the city budget of Cold Falls had always been stingy in the funds it bestowed upon the library, Millie had used them wisely. Like a homemaker forced to feed a family of six on a husband's meager salary, she'd cut corners here and stretched resources there, managing during her tenure to acquire a collection that would have impressed any serious reader of literature, had more than a handful existed in the town.

Simon, being one of the few who appreciated Millie's abilities, wandered leisurely among the tall wooden shelves. He seldom came to the library with any particular goal in mind. He preferred to rely on serendipity, the accidental stumbling upon of the perfect book for the perfect time. In this way he was never disappointed. Whatever he took home with him accompanied him because it spoke to him at the time.

Today, though, his mind was occupied with other thoughts. Christmas was only two weeks away, and New Year's Eve a week beyond that. He hadn't yet had even a vague thought as to who might be his date on that night. That wasn't entirely true. He *had* thought in passing about several of the men from the Engine Room. But that had been more in the way of fantasizing than it had been anything he could seriously consider. The men he'd considered were, he knew, much too young. Even if they were to say yes, he wouldn't know what to do with them. Although their physical charms might be considerable, he was old enough and wise enough to know that at some point the intellectual inequities would wear on his patience and result in ugliness.

He had never been one to celebrate youth. Always he had looked forward to being older. Now that he'd arrived, he saw no need to wish he could turn the clock back. The only benefit he could see to being, say, fifty again was that Walter would still be alive. Apart from that, he liked who he had become.

The problem, of course, was finding someone else who appreciated what he'd become. He realized that he was something of a rarity among gay men, an older man who preferred the company of older men. He was familiar with the other variety, the men who longed for the smooth skin of men half their age. He didn't look unkindly upon such men. He understood them. They didn't want to die. They wanted to embrace youth and, by doing so, perhaps slow their own inevitable decline.

It was the same, he believed, as straight men who left their wives for women younger than their daughters, a kind of male survival instinct that revealed itself in pitiful displays of romantic desperation. Still, as long as there were young women and men willing to play along, it would continue to happen. And who cared, really, if people wanted to make fools of themselves. Maybe some of them were even happy together. You never knew what slaked the heart's thirst.

What he wanted, though, was something different. He wanted someone who would help him not forget his age but revel in it. He wanted someone with whom to share the moments of his life that most pleased him, the small everyday occurrences that brought him joy precisely because he was old enough not to take them for granted. He wanted someone who would understand those things.

He looked at the spines of the books he was surrounded by, thinking about their authors. So many of them, he knew, had been both sustained and destroyed by their relationships. He thought of Sylvia Plath and Ted Hughes, perhaps the most brilliant and pathetic of all literary unions. How they'd tortured one another, but also how they'd inspired each other to greatness. He thought, too, of Shirley Jackson and her husband, academic Stanley Hyman. Hyman had encouraged Jackson to write when her own family told her it was folly, had fueled some of her greatest work. But he'd also destroyed her sense of self-worth with his affairs and bitterness, despite Jackson's determination to portray him in her work as the kindest of men.

There were more positive examples, of course. Percy and Mary Shelley. Robert and Elizabeth Barrett Browning. Gertrude Stein and Alice B. Toklas. He and Walter, too, had worked so well together because they complemented one another. Could he find that again? Part of him felt he was too old. He wasn't prepared to make the concessions he'd made in his younger years. He was set in his ways. Could he find someone willing to fit himself into that world?

He sighed. It was a depressing train of thought. Even more depressing, though, was the notion that his only option was solitude. Was that all that was offered to a man his age, particularly a gay man? He thought of his aunts, his mother's sisters, and how as their husbands had died off one by one, the newest widow had moved into a house with the others, until after the death of the last husband (Simon's father), the four of them had comprised a perfectly contented quartet that lived out the remainder of their years with only one another for company.

Had they really been willing to give up on romance, he wondered? He didn't entertain the question of sex. Romance was what he truly missed, those moments of togetherness when both partners knew that the other wanted nothing more than to be there. Hadn't his aunts and his mother longed for such times? They hadn't, after all, been much older than he was now. Some had been even younger. As a boy, he'd never wondered about their lives, seeing them only as sources of birthday gifts and pinched cheeks, not as women—or even people—

who might have personal needs. Now, though, he found himself experiencing an unexpected kinship with those women, most of whom had continued living on after their husbands for nearly twenty years. Surely at some point during that time they had yearned for what they'd lost.

He looked at the book in his hands. Even the ill-starred romance of American divorcee Wallis Simpson and the disgraced Edward VIII had been possessed of a kind of magic, an all-encompassing enchantment that drove them to stay together despite the fact that it had cost Edward a kingdom. What, Simon had often wondered when reading about the affair, had Edward seen when he looked into Wallis's eyes? A handsome and powerful man with many mistresses, he had given them all up for her, even when she tired of him and moved on to other lovers, one of whom, an heir to the Woolworth fortune, was homosexual.

That kind of unhealthy devotion Simon feared. As much as he'd loved Walter, he knew he would have left at the first sign of decay in the relationship. Thankfully, theirs had been a thriving union, even when it was sometimes difficult. That's what he longed for again.

He was tired of looking for something to read. The Simpson biography would have to be his lone treasure for the week. Standing there among the books, he was feeling more and more alone. Finding one that would bring him joy reminded him of the difficulty he was having in finding someone to spend his time with. Like the Simpson book, he decided, the right one would simply have to come into his life by chance.

He walked back toward the desk, preparing to check out. Alistair was still there, carefully taping the identifying labels to the spines of the books, methodically stamping the name of the library onto the inside covers. He seemed perfectly content, at home among the odds and ends of his craft.

Alistair, Simon thought suddenly. *It could be Alistair.*

He stopped in the middle of the room, looking at the man behind the desk. It had never occurred to him before to consider Alistair as a potential partner. Now, looking at him, he wondered why? He was old enough. He was handsome. And certainly they shared mutual interests. Simon looked at him closely. Yes, he could see it.

Nervously, he approached the desk. Alistair, looking up, smiled and put down his stamp. "What did you find this week?"

"Just this," said Simon, setting the book down.

Alistair picked it up. "That's not like you," he said. "Have we run out of books that interest you?"

"No," Simon said as he took his wallet from his pocket and removed his library card. "What with all the holiday fuss and bother, I don't think I'll have much time for reading this week."

He hesitated, not sure how to say what he wanted to. It had been many, many years since he'd asked someone out. Walter had been the last, and Simon couldn't even remember how he'd done it.

"Do you have any New Year's Eve plans?" he blurted out, surprising himself.

"I usually just stay in," Alistair said as he stamped Simon's book and placed the checkout card in the file on his desk. "How about you?"

"Oh, I think I'm going to get together with some friends," Simon answered. "If you're free, you're welcome to join us."

"That might be fun," Alistair said. "We don't know many people in town. It would be nice to meet some."

"We?" repeated Simon, a sinking feeling growing inside of him.

"My wife and I," Alistair said. "Meg."

"Meg," Simon said. "Excellent. Well, let me confirm that everything is still on, and I'll let you know next week."

"I'll see you Monday," Alistair told him.

Simon hustled out into the cold, hoping the frigid air would explain away the redness he knew was coloring his face. *How could I have been so stupid?* Married. Why had he assumed that Alistair was gay? "Probably because he's named Alistair," he said out loud. "And he works in a library."

He was ashamed of himself, both for making such stereotypical assumptions, but more for his apparent inability to distinguish a straight man from a queen. What chance did he stand if he couldn't even do that?

"Maybe you've been out of the game too long," he told himself as he hurried for home.

CHAPTER 24

"Holy shit, they look like rabid monkeys."

Russell and Greg peered over the stack of Estée Lauder gift boxes, looking toward the front doors of the store. Outside, a group of women waited impatiently in the early-morning snow. Every so often one of them tried one of the doors, rattling it loudly to see if perhaps the woman who'd tried before her simply hadn't done it correctly.

"Are you ready for this?" Russell asked.

"I'd feel better if I had a taser," replied Greg. "They look totally out of control."

"This place will be declared a disaster area by seven forty-five," said Russell. "The Red Cross will have to be called in."

It was seven twenty-five. In five minutes, Russell would walk to the front doors and open them, launching the store's before-Christmas sale. With only two shopping weekends before the holiday, they had decided to lower their prices in an attempt to save the season, which so far had been dismal. Now, circulars and credit cards in hand, fifty agitated women waited for their chance to snatch up as many bargains as they could possibly carry.

"Remember," Russell told the assembled staff, "keep your heads down and watch out for flying objects. Everyone ready?"

The staff, eyes wide with terror, nodded. Although several of them were veterans of the Christmas madness, most of them were green. This would be their first, and in some cases last, holiday retail experience. Russell had assigned each of the old-timers a group of virgins to command. Greg he'd put in charge of menswear, where he was overseeing three very nervous young recruits who stood beside their Polo,

Nautica, and Calvin Klein posts, fidgeting with their name tags and sending up silent prayers to their gods.

Russell took a deep breath and walked to the door. The women, sensing the imminent opening of the store, began clamoring with excitement. Their eyes were glassy with the thrill of the hunt, already scanning the store visible through the glass for 30% off signs.

Russell paused before inserting the key in the lock. He turned and nodded at the leaders he was counting on to keep things more or less under control. They nodded back. He pushed the key in and turned, feeling the bolt slide free. An instant later he felt a rush of cold air as the doors flew inward and coated bodies swarmed past him.

The group of women dispersed as they each ran for the section that interested them the most. Many headed for the perfume counter, where they began spritzing the air with abandon, trying out the different scents. Others made for shoes and women's apparel. But by far the majority of them made a beeline for menswear, determined to find gifts for the husbands, brothers, boyfriends, uncles, and sons in their lives.

Russell stepped out of the throng, protecting himself behind a mannequin. Almost immediately the entranceway was turned into a slushy, slippery mess as hundreds of booted feet dragged melting snow inside. He prayed no one would slip and become injured, as had happened recently at a Kmart when overzealous shoppers had practically stampeded through the store to get their hands on Hokey-Pokey Elmo dolls advertised for sale at only $17.99. All he needed was one mother with a broken ankle to make his Christmas bonus fly away.

As the flow of women slowed to a trickle, he risked coming out from behind his hiding place and taking a walk through the store. One of the many advantages he enjoyed as manager was that he didn't actually have to ring any customers up. Although he was frequently subjected to questions from angry shoppers as to the lack of sizes and colors of various articles that they wanted, he didn't have to contend with the temperamental registers and all that accompanied such transactions. He was free to roam and take in the carnage that was ensuing around him.

Ladies shoes was abuzz with excitement. The two staffers who had been assigned this particularly treacherous duty were scurrying in and out of the stock room, their arms piled high with boxes, as women in stockinged feet flitted from shelf to shelf, finding yet more styles they simply had to try on. It would be a good day in shoes, Russell though happily.

Menswear, as expected, was a war zone. Already the neatly folded Polo displays were in disarray, shirts thrown open and left for dead by rapacious hands. One harried-looking clerk was attempting to perform triage on them, roughly folding them and piling them back in their places, but it was hopeless. As quickly as he got them fixed up, someone swooped down to undo his work.

"It's okay," Russell whispered to him as he walked by. "Just keep them off the floor. We'll straighten them out after the first wave leaves."

There would be no distinct "waves"—no ebb and flow—and he knew it, but he had to give the poor young man some hope of respite or he would quickly be overwhelmed. The truth was that they were in for a continuous flood of shoppers. And it would only get worse as the weeks went on. The closer Christmas came, the more of their minds consumers lost. Bedeviled by Christmas cheer, they would go into a frenzy, attempting to manufacture the perfect holiday with the help of wallets stuffed with plastic cards. They would fill the coffers of Carter-Beane with holiday bounty, only realizing the extent of their folly when the bills came in January. By then it would be too late. Returns were not accepted after twenty-one days.

He witnessed the first fight of the day moments later. Two women had both grabbed the last spruce plaid Pendleton flannel shirt, size XXL. Probably they both wanted it for an overweight husband who would hate it because the wool flannel made him itch. He would wear it once to please her and then relegate it to the rear of the closet, where both of them would quickly forget about it.

For the moment, though, the shirt was the most prized possession in the store, and the women were arguing over it like hyenas worrying a particularly meaty chunk of zebra. Each of them had half of the shirt in her hands. Their voices rose above the general din as they attempted to establish dominance.

"I saw it first," said one, her piggy face worked up into an agonized grimace.

"I got to it first," argued the other, who was attempting to maintain her hold on several other items while struggling valiantly with the Pendleton.

Russell was steeling himself to intervene when he saw Greg walk briskly toward the combatants. He watched as Greg laid a hand on each woman's arm and said soothingly but firmly, "Ladies, why don't I take this in the back and see if maybe we don't have another one."

The women glared at one another as Greg smiled at them. Then, apparently calmed by his attention, each let go. Greg took the shirt, smoothed it out, and folded it over his arm.

"I'll be right back," he said.

The women stood several feet apart, arms across their chests and not looking at one another. A minute later Greg returned, another identical shirt in his hands. He handed each woman one of the shirts. Smiling, they went their separate ways.

"Good work," Russell said as Greg came over, rolling his eyes. "I thought we were going to have bloodshed on our hands."

"I told the boys to keep a couple of each size in the back in the event of emergencies," Greg explained. "That way they think we've worked a miracle." He nodded in the direction of the bathrobes. "Speaking of which, I sense trouble in pajama land. I'll see you later."

Russell gave him a pat on the back as he walked away. As he watched Greg go, he thought back to what Simon and Mike had said the other night at the bar about his being jealous when Greg had shown interest in someone. At the time it had seemed ridiculous. After all, wasn't he the one who had tried to set Greg up with Stephen? Wasn't he the one who told everyone what a great catch Greg would be for the right guy? Why, he had made finding Greg a boyfriend practically his mission.

Then why, he asked himself, had he been so annoyed when Greg had pursued the man at the Engine Room? He still didn't know whether or not Greg had been successful. He'd left before Greg had, and he hadn't asked him since what had or had not occurred. Greg hadn't volunteered any information, either. Normally they talked about everything. Why was this one area of discussion apparently off-limits?

As he watched Greg assisting a woman who was searching for something among the boxer briefs, he forced himself to reassess his feelings about his friend. Did he perhaps have more than a passing interest in him? All the while he'd been doggedly looking for someone for Greg, had part of him been hoping Greg wouldn't find anyone and turn his attentions closer to home?

Something had been holding him back from completely reconciling with John. Although their times together had been pleasant, he still didn't feel ready for a full reunion. He was still living with Simon. No date had been set for his return to the house he shared with John, even though John had asked him several times if he was coming home.

Was Greg the thing standing between him and his relationship? He considered the possibility. They got along famously. They shared interests and sensibilities. And Greg *was* attractive. Although he'd never considered him in a sexual way, now that he entertained the notion, Russell found that it wasn't unappealing. Maybe he owed it to himself to give Greg a chance.

"Mr. Harding? I need your help."

His thoughts were interrupted by the arrival of a young woman with panic-stricken eyes, her alarm made even more visible by the copious amounts of shadow and liner she wore. She resembled a disquieted raccoon. Russell waited for her to tell him what the problem was.

"We advertised a one-ounce bottle of the new Elizabeth Taylor perfume, but all we have under the counter are after-bath splashes. I have a lot of angry people over in fragrances."

Russell put his hand on the girl's shoulder and steered her back to her station. As they approached, he saw the remaining fragrance clerk point in his direction. Immediately, the women at the counter turned upon him, outrage in their countenances.

"Now then, what seems to be the problem?" he said cheerfully.

Half an hour later, after soothing ruffled feathers with rainchecks and coupons good for an additional 40% off any item in the store, Russell retreated to the safety of the staff break room. There he found a handful of his employees, looking worse for wear, slumped in the hard plastic chairs that surrounded the room's lone table. Most looked shell-shocked. One was sniffling, apparently on the verge of tears.

"Just keep thinking happy thoughts," Russell joked. "And remember, it could be worse. It could be December twenty-sixth."

A collective groan went up from the troops. December 26, better known as I Don't Have My Receipt Day, was even worse than the pre-Christmas debacle. By then a third of the staff would have quit, swearing never to work in retail again. The rest would band together to fight the hordes who came in the day after Christmas, worn-out and irritable, to return or exchange much of their Christmas take. It was a tedious time, but it at least signaled the end of the holiday season, and if an employee survived it, Russell was almost guaranteed of having her or him the following year.

Russell retrieved a cup of coffee from the much-used machine in the corner. He was seated at the table, stirring cream and sugar into the coffee, when Greg came in. Getting his own cup, he sat down opposite Russell and let out a sigh.

"Halftime," he said wearily.

"What's the score?" Russell inquired.

"Home team is ahead," answered Greg. "But just barely. We're going to need reinforcements."

"How about this," Russell said. "I'll take you to dinner tonight."

Greg brightened. "Now you're talking," he said. "It's a date."

Russell was quiet for a moment. He was hesitant to bring up personal matters in the company of his employees, but most of them had left the room shortly after his appearance. The only one there besides himself and Greg was the girl with the raccoon eyes, who was gazing dazedly off at nothing and paying no attention to their conversation.

Finally he spoke. "Speaking of dates, I never asked you how things went with the guy from the bar."

Greg sipped his coffee before answering. "What guy?" he asked.

Russell cupped his hands over his chest, symbolizing breasts.

"Tits?" Greg said. "You know, we talked a little."

"Just talked?" asked Russell.

Greg grinned. "Maybe a little more than that."

Russell nodded. "Good for you," he said, feigning approval. "It's about time you had some fun."

"I wouldn't exactly call it fun," said Greg. "More like fast food."

"Fast food?" Russell repeated, not getting his meaning.

"Yeah," Greg said. "You know how every so often you just need a Big Mac? That's sort of how it was. I wouldn't want it every day or anything, but that night it hit the spot."

Russell nodded, finally understanding and wishing he didn't. He couldn't help but picture Greg with the man, and it made his stomach churn unpleasantly. What had they done? He immediately pushed the question out of his mind. It wasn't any of his business what they'd done. Besides, he really didn't want to know.

"You took off pretty fast that night," Greg said. "I didn't even see you leave."

"I was sort of tired," said Russell. "It was a long day."

"I thought maybe you were horrified by my sluttiness," Greg said, laughing.

"Why would that bother me?" Russell said quickly.

"I don't know," admitted Greg. "It's just that sometimes when you see people in a new light, it can be a shock. You've never really seen me do something like that."

"It's okay," said Russell. "Really. You're a big boy. You can do what you want."

"But?" asked Greg.

"But what?" Russell retorted.

"You're holding something back," Greg said. "I can tell."

Russell looked down into his coffee cup. "I just think you could do way better."

"Oh, I know I could," Greg said. "But have you seen anyone better banging down my door? I haven't. If you know of someone, I'd love to meet him."

Russell looked up. "I think I might," he said quietly.

"Really?" Greg said. "Who is he?"

Russell started to speak, but was interrupted by someone rushing into the break room. A panting, anxious-looking young man confronted him.

"Russell? There's a woman out there hyperventilating in the handbags. I think she's going to pass out. We can't get her to let go of the Dooney and Bourke she's got her hands on."

Russell looked at Greg. "We'll talk about this tonight over dinner," he said as he got up.

CHAPTER 25

"Thanks for letting me crash here, man."

Pete turned on the lights as he and T.J. entered the house. "No problem," Pete said.

They stood in the kitchen and shook the snow from their coats. Outside, a new storm was raging. It had come unexpectedly, starting while they were inside the Briar Patch downing some beers after work. By the time they'd left, just after ten o'clock, there was a foot of snow covering their cars and the world was a blurry swirl of white. Although a plow had come through and dutifully pushed the snow to the side of the road, eager flakes had swept in to take the place of their vanquished comrades. Driving was treacherous, and even in their inebriated condition, the men had recognized that trying to go too far would be foolish. Pete had suggested that T.J., who lived the farthest away of all of them, and who had the least reliable car, stay the night with him.

They hung their coats up. T.J. sat down on one of the kitchen chairs and unlaced his work boots, pulling them off and placing them to the side, where the melting snow could collect on the linoleum. Pete, following his lead, did the same before walking to the refrigerator and opening it.

"Want a beer?" he asked, scanning the largely empty interior.

"Sure," answered T.J.

Pete pulled out two beers and handed one to T.J., who twisted the top off and took a deep sip. He wiped his mouth with the back of his hand.

"I'm gonna put on something dry," Pete said. "You want some sweats or something?"

T.J. held up a hand. "I'm good," he said.

"Why don't you turn on the TV," Pete suggested. "I'll be out in a minute."

He went into this bedroom while T.J. got up and headed for the living room. He heard the television go on, the sound of voices filling the room with background noise. Setting his beer down, he stripped out of his jeans, the cuffs of which were uncomfortably damp from walking through the snow. He pulled a pair of sweats from a dresser drawer and pulled them on. Almost immediately he felt more relaxed.

Picking up his beer, he went into the living room. T.J. was sitting on the couch, his feet propped up on the coffee table. He was staring at the TV screen, and when he heard Pete enter the room, he looked at him and grinned.

"Nice tape collection," he said.

Pete glanced at the television. On the screen a porn film was playing. A redhead was bent over a couch, getting fucked hard by a man wearing a UPS uniform. His cock stuck out of the fly of the uniform pants. The redhead, who was wearing a string of pearls that bounced against her breasts as she got plowed, was holding on to the sofa cushions with long, red-lacquered nails.

"I guess that's what they mean by special delivery," T.J. joked.

Pete said nothing. He must have left the tape in the VCR, he thought. It was a stupid thing to do. Normally he kept the porn tapes in his bedroom, but he'd felt like jacking off in the living room the night before, so he'd moved in there. After he came, he totally forgot to take the tape out.

He had no idea how to explain the tape's existence to T.J. He felt he should say something, but any excuse he could come up with for why the tape was in there sounded ridiculous. So he just stood there, watching the redhead get reamed.

T.J. didn't seem to care why the tape was there or what Pete was doing with it. He continued to watch, sipping his beer and every so often giving a little laugh as the redhead made a particularly impassioned face or the man smacked her ass. Pete glanced at him, wondering what he was thinking, afraid to ask. Finally, he took a seat on the couch, as far away from T.J. as he could get.

"Man, I wish women liked that as much in real life as they do in these things," he remarked. His voice was a bit slurred, and when Pete looked over at him, he saw that T.J.'s eyes were slightly closed.

The man in the film pulled out and came, spraying jism on the woman's back. When he was done, he zipped up and tipped his cap to her before leaving the room. T.J. laughed again, seemingly at nothing. Pete took a drink from his beer bottle and waited to see if T.J. would tire of the video or let it play out.

The film continued and T.J. made no move to turn it off. He left the remote where it was on the coffee table, apparently content to watch porn. His feet were crossed at the ankle and his beer bottle was nestled in his crotch. His head rested against the back of the couch.

On the screen a new scene was under way. In this one a woman in an office answered a telephone. As she took the call, the man from the earlier scene entered, carrying two large boxes, which he set on the floor beside her desk. He waited for her to finish her phone call.

"Delivery for Mr. Smith," he said in a monotone as he held out a clipboard. "Can you sign for them?"

The girl, a brunette with her hair in a bun and severe glasses that made her look matronly, smiled coyly. "Sure," she said in a squeaky voice. "Do they need any special handling?"

It was typical bad porn film dialogue, but it didn't matter. The talking was just an excuse for what came next. As Pete watched, the man stepped behind the desk and reached for the woman's glasses. Off they came, revealing a pretty face. The girl did her part, unzipping the delivery man's pants and pulling out his already-hard cock. Her red-lipped mouth closed around it as she began giving him head.

The man's dick was in close-up. Pete stared at it, watching the woman's mouth caress it sensuously. The man's balls, large and smooth, banged against her chin as she took him all the way in. His big head, slick with her spit, seemed to fill her whole mouth as she sucked on it eagerly.

Pete was suddenly aware of an uncomfortable feeling in his crotch. He realized then that he'd become hard. His cock was pressing up against the fabric of his sweatpants, making the material tent out obviously. He pressed down on his prick, trying to hide his erection, and looked nervously at T.J.

His friend was paying no attention. But one hand was in his own crotch. His fingers moved slowly, as if he was gently massaging himself. In the other hand he held his beer, taking periodic sips.

The man had removed his uniform shirt. His bare chest was covered in thick, dark hair. He had also undone the woman's bun, removing the clip that held it in place so that her hair tumbled over her shoulders. Her shirt, too, was open, her breasts exposed.

"Look at those fucking tits," T.J. said appreciatively.

The hard-on in Pete's pants wasn't going away. He did his best to cover it up, but the head of his dick was threatening to push past the waistband. He tried willing it down, but he knew it was no use.

The girl in the film dropped to her knees and continued to suck the man's cock. He gripped her hair as he fucked her face, while she wrapped her hands around his ass. The camera, positioned underneath them, showed the man's big tool in glorious detail as it moved in and out.

Pete risked another glance at T.J. His hand was moving more steadily, and it was obvious that he was hard too. His cock swelled hugely beneath the material of his jeans, pushing down the side of his leg. Pete could see its outline clearly, and he knew T.J. must be incredibly uncomfortable with his dick confined that way.

"Look at her take that thing," T.J. said as the girl deep-throated her partner. "That's fucking amazing. How come I always get the chicks who choke?"

Pete laughed nervously. The tension in the room was thick, and he didn't know what to do. What he wanted to do was lean over and touch T.J., feel his cock, maybe even take it out and do what the girl was doing. He remembered how it had looked that night in the men's room, so long and thick. What did it look like hard? He wanted to know. But he couldn't bring himself to move his hand from his lap and into T.J.'s.

T.J. made the decision for him. Draining his beer bottle, he set it on the coffee table and looked at Pete. "I'm beat," he said drunkenly. "Shall I just crash on the couch?"

Pete thought quickly. "Nah, we can share the bed," he said. "It's big enough. This couch sucks for sleeping."

He expected an argument from T.J., but his buddy just nodded. "I'm gonna take a piss," he said, standing up.

Pete avoided looking at T.J.'s crotch. With his friend in the bathroom, he turned the tape off and went into the bedroom. Before T.J. could come back, he shucked off his sweatpants and got into bed in just his boxers. A minute later T.J. appeared. Without saying anything, he removed his clothes and got into bed on the other side, also wearing just his underpants.

"Man, I am wiped out," he said, yawning loudly as he turned off the light. "See you in the morning, dude."

Pete rolled away from him and shut his eyes. His mind, dulled by the beer, refused to sink into oblivion. He kept picturing T.J., holding his cock and pissing. His own hard-on still refused to back down. His hand snuck down past the elastic waistband of his boxers and wrapped around his cock.

Next to him, T.J. seemed to have fallen asleep immediately. He snored roughly, deep inhalations and exhalations that filled the room with his rumbling. He was on his back, arms at his sides. Pete could sense him less than a foot away.

He turned onto his back, terrified that T.J. would be awakened by his movements. When the snoring continued unabated, Pete slowly moved his foot to the left. When it came in contact with T.J.'s, he held his breath. Again, T.J. didn't move.

Pete's cock was aching as he stroked it. He felt the first stickiness seep from the head, coating his fingers. He used this to slick his skin, making his movements silkier, more intense. Was T.J. still hard, he wondered?

He couldn't hold back. Moving painfully slowly, he let his left hand move beneath the sheet toward his sleeping buddy. When he felt the first touch of T.J.'s skin, he stopped. His heart beat in his chest madly, and at any moment he expected to feel the viselike grip of T.J.'s hand around his wrist as he demanded to know what the hell Pete thought he was doing.

But no resistance came. Pete moved his hand higher, feeling the rough hair of T.J.'s belly beneath his fingers. His skin was warm, his stomach moving up and down as he breathed deeply. Pete allowed himself to put his hand flat against T.J.'s stomach, feeling the muscles of his abdomen.

He moved south, and shortly after his fingertips dipped into the indentation of T.J.'s navel, he felt the tip of T.J.'s cock brush his hand through the thin cotton of the boxers he wore. He was still hard. Pete's balls gave a jerk as he realized he was touching T.J.'s rod, and he had to pause to calm himself down.

His mind racing, he pushed his fingers through the fly of T.J.'s boxers. He opened his hand and cupped the head of T.J.'s cock in his fingers. It was hot, and as his fingers closed around it, he felt it twitch. Now he couldn't stop. He slid his hand down T.J.'s shaft, feeling the thickness of it. He moved all the way down, until his fingers met thick hair. Then he went back up, jerking T.J. off in time with the movements on his own dick.

T.J.'s snoring slowed, and Pete sensed him move. His legs opened slightly, and he pressed himself up into Pete's hand. But still he didn't wake, didn't open his eyes. Could he, Pete wondered, really be asleep? Did he think he was dreaming, his subconscious continuing the film they had been watching?

He didn't care. Touching T.J.'s cock, he wanted more. He couldn't be content to just hold it in his hand. The heat radiating through his palm was so intense he felt he might burn himself. He wanted to taste it.

Rolling toward T.J., he ducked his head beneath the sheet. There, under the covers, the world was hot and stuffy. He smelled the scent of sweat and oil from their skin. He felt the warmth emanating from their bodies. Holding his cock in his hand, he bent toward T.J. His cheek brushed against hair as he moved his mouth to the waiting cock.

He pulled T.J.'s cock out, maneuvering it through the opening in his shorts. Parting his lips, he closed them around the head of T.J.'s dick. He tasted heat and salt. He remained still for a moment, just feeling the way T.J. filled his mouth. His tongue gently circled the crown of T.J.'s cock and dipped into the slit at the center.

He couldn't believe he had another man's dick in his mouth. At the same time, he was overcome by the excitement of it. His fingers around T.J.'s shaft, he pushed more of him into his throat. He felt his airway become blocked as the head filled it, and for a moment he didn't know what to do. Then he realized he could breathe through his nose, and he continued on.

Above him, T.J. moaned in his sleep. Pete, emboldened, pressed closer to him and began moving his head up and down T.J.'s dick, sucking him off. He imitated what he'd seen the women in porn films do, using his hand to jerk T.J. off as his mouth worked on his head.

He felt he must be dreaming. He was blowing his best friend, taking his cock like some hungry bitch who couldn't get enough of the big prick between T.J.'s legs. He sucked the fat head and stroked the shaft, wanting to feel T.J. come. He wanted to taste his load.

When T.J. did come, it was in thick jets that spurted into Pete's throat. The musky taste of T.J.'s cum filled him as the sticky liquid gushed from his balls. Pete swallowed greedily as more and more of it erupted from T.J.'s cock. He waited until the last throb died away, then gently squeezed the remaining drops of cum from T.J.'s shaft, milking it with his hand. Reluctantly, he let the softening dick slide from between his lips. Taking one last sniff of the rich smell that came from between T.J.'s legs, he rolled back to his side of the bed.

T.J. grunted in his sleep and turned away from Pete, throwing one arm over himself like a child snuggling deeper into his blankets. Alone, Pete lay in the darkness, tasting the cum that coated his tongue and throat and remembering what T.J.'s cock had felt like in his mouth. What had he done? He'd sucked off another guy. He'd blown T.J.

The mattress shook gently beneath him as he jerked himself off. It didn't take long. Within minutes his hand filled with heat as he came, hard. He gritted his teeth to keep from crying out, and when his orgasm subsided, he wiped his load off on his sweatpants.

Suddenly the excitement he'd felt was replaced by shame and horror. The taste in his throat no longer aroused him; it sickened him. He'd done something terrible, something he couldn't allow himself to consider. Beside him, T.J. slept on, oblivious. But Pete knew—would always know—what he'd done. Every time he looked at T.J., he would be reminded of how he'd lowered himself, how he'd become like one of the faggots whose mouths and asses he'd used. He had become one of them.

He was drunk, he told himself. It was the alcohol that had made him forget himself. That was all. He'd done a lot of stupid things while drunk, hadn't he? This was simply one of them. He had to put it out of his mind, forget everything. He would sleep, and in the morning it would never have happened.

He closed his eyes and willed himself to sleep. His beer-soaked mind obliged him, drawing the dark curtain of exhaustion over his eyes. But as he drifted down into the obliterating blackness, he began to dream, and in his dream he saw himself kneeling before T.J. Kneeling and waiting.

CHAPTER 26

"I'm starting to think that all it does here is snow."

Mike, looking out the window at the continuing blizzard, laughed. "Sometimes it feels that way." He handed Thomas a mug of cocoa and sat down at the kitchen table opposite him.

"I guess this means skiing is off?" Thomas asked.

"We could do it," Mike said. "But it wouldn't be much fun. I suggest we find something else to do."

"And what do you have in mind?" said Thomas. "Making snow angels? Tobogganing?"

"I was thinking more like putting up a tree."

"I'm intrigued," Thomas said.

"I know it's a little late in the game for a tree," Mike admitted. "But there are still five days left before Christmas, and suddenly I'm feeling sort of festive."

"May I ask what brought this on?" Thomas inquired.

"I saw *It's a Wonderful Life* on NBC last night," said Mike. When Thomas gave him a doubting look, he fessed up. "Okay, I just need a little Christmas spirit."

"That's a good enough reason for me," Thomas told him. "I'm in."

"Good. As soon as you're done with that hot chocolate, we'll head out."

"Head out?" Thomas said skeptically. "That sounds suspiciously like what you said when we went skiing."

"What?" Mike said innocently. "It will be fun. Trust me."

Half an hour later, bundled up in their winter coats against the heavily falling snow, the two men were trudging through the snow, making their way through a field of pine trees. Mike carried a saw in one hand.

"I thought we were just going to go to a lot and pick one up," Thomas said as he lifted one booted foot out of the snow. "I didn't realize we were going to track one down."

"Lot trees are for sissies," Mike informed him. "Real men hunt their own."

They stopped and examined several trees, all of which Mike rejected for various reasons. Finally, on the ninth try, he declared the tree they were standing in front of acceptable.

"Hold the trunk while I saw," he told Thomas.

A couple of minutes later the two of them were walking back to the truck, a beautiful evergreen pulled along behind them. The tree cut a wide swath through the snow, covering up their footprints.

"I feel like we're bringing our catch back to the tribe," Thomas remarked as they reached the road and heaved the tree into the back of the truck.

"It's not quite the same thing as a buffalo," Mike commented as they climbed into the truck. "But it's more fun when you get your own. My father used to take me out to get one every year."

Back at Mike's house, they unloaded the tree and shook the snow from its branches before taking it into the garage, where Mike set it in a bucket of warm water.

"This relaxes the branches," he told Thomas when he seemed puzzled by the bucket. "We'll bring it inside in an hour or so."

Once in the house, they shed their coats and went into the living room. Mike lit a fire, and then he and Thomas rearranged the furniture to make room for the tree in front of the big window that looked out on the house's front yard.

"I'll be right back," Mike told Thomas, disappearing down the stairs leading to the cellar.

Thomas waited, warming himself in front of the fireplace. He'd quickly come to enjoy the days spent with his friend. Particularly now that the holidays were upon them, it felt good to have people he enjoyed around him. Christmas was one of the most hectic times around any church, and Saint Peter's was no exception. Although he'd been able to bring about a truce in the matter of the upcoming nativity pageant, there were still a million things occupying his mind, chief among them the memories of Joseph that had been coming back to him more and more strongly.

"Here we are," Mike said, interrupting Thomas's thoughts.

Thomas turned to see Mike, his arms laden with a stack of cardboard boxes. The boxes seemed very old, and were covered in a thick layer of dust. When Mike set them down, the dust rose into the air, settling onto the floor.

"What's in them?" Thomas asked.

"Decorations," answered Mike. "The ones we had when I was a kid. I've been lugging them around all these years, but I've never opened them."

"Never?" asked Thomas, surprised.

Mike shook his head. "Christmas hasn't meant much to me since my folks died," he said quietly. He looked up at Thomas. "But I think it's time to change that."

He sat on the couch and pulled one of the boxes toward him. Hesitating, he reached out and pulled the flaps open. He reached inside and took out a smaller box. Lifting the lid, he revealed a dozen blown-glass ornaments, each one shaped like a fruit. Pears, apples, blackberries, strawberries, peaches, and lemons—two of each—were nestled in cocoons of fragile tissue paper.

"I haven't seen these in fifteen years," Mike said softly as he picked up one of the peaches and let it dangle in front of his face. The pale pink globe was frosted with white, its leaves a brilliant green. "My mother loved these things. I always thought they were silly."

He gazed upon the ornament with an expression of sadness. Looking at it, he couldn't help but picture his mother as she trimmed the tree. Her face radiated happiness as she found the perfect spot for each one, creating a scene of Christmas magic. As a boy, Mike had enjoyed helping her, feeling privileged whenever she allowed him to handle one of the more delicate ornaments. As he'd grown older, the tree had become less and less important to him, and he'd been content to let his mother decorate it more or less alone. Now, beholding the peach, he regretted ever letting a single year go by when he didn't join his mother in her annual ritual.

He put the peach down and returned to the box. This time he lifted out a plastic star. Plain to the point of ugliness, it was three-dimensional, with a hole in the bottom. Mike held the star in his hands and stared at it, not saying a word.

"What is it?" Thomas asked him finally.

Mike held it up, his finger inserted into the hole so that the star stuck up from his hand. "A tree topper," he explained. "My mother bought it the first Christmas she and Dad were married. They didn't have much money, and she saved up for it. I think originally it had a light inside of it and it glowed, but somewhere over the years that broke or fell out. I never understood why she wanted something so ugly on top of the tree. One year I decided to surprise her with a new one. But when she saw it on top of the tree, she started crying. I didn't get it. Not until a long time after."

"It was her tradition," Thomas said, looking at the battered star and seeing it through the eyes of Mike's mother.

Mike nodded. "It reminded her of that first year together. But when you're thirteen, you're too stupid to understand things like that."

He put the star down and sighed. "Let's get that tree," he said. "Before I change my mind."

Together they carried the tree in and set it into a stand Mike dug out of another box. After positioning it several ways, they finally decided on one and stepped back. The tree reached almost to the ceiling, its graceful branches spreading out and filling the room with its scent.

"Lights first," Mike said, removing several boxes of newly purchased lights from a bag. "That was always my father's job. I guess it's mine now."

With Thomas's help, he'd soon encircled the tree with the strings of lights. When Mike plugged them in, the tree burst into color, twinkling all over in red, green, yellow, and blue. Even dressed in just the lights, the tree took on an air of jollity, enlivening the room with its spirit.

"I don't suppose you have any Christmas music," Thomas asked.

Mike regarded him coolly. "Do I look like I would have Christmas music?" he asked.

"Sorry," Thomas apologized. "I thought maybe Madonna had a holiday album or something."

Mike grinned. "Congratulations," he said.

"For what?"

"That's the first queeny thing I've heard you say," Mike told him.

Thomas blushed. "I was just kidding," he said. "I didn't mean—"

"Relax," Mike interrupted. "I'm giving you a hard time. As it so happens, I did pick up some CDs at the mall the other day."

"You really do have the Christmas spirit," Thomas told him as Mike went to the stereo cabinet and returned with a handful of discs.

"Hey," Mike said, "if you're going to do it, you might as well go all out. We've got Christmas albums by Ella Fitzgerald, Louis Armstrong, Etta James, the Andrews Sisters, and Elvis. Which do you want to hear?"

"Elvis," Thomas answered immediately. "Classic."

"These were all records my parents played," said Mike as he slipped the CDs into the stereo. A minute later Elvis started in on "Blue Christmas."

"I'll have a blue-ew-ew-ew-ew-ew-ew Christmas," Mike sang, imitating the King's background singers. "That was always my part. My father sang the lead."

Thomas looked at the boxes of ornaments that were spread out on the coffee table. "Where do we start?" he asked.

Mike picked up an ornament, a red wooden bird painted with white and blue decoration. "Anywhere you like," he answered Thomas.

As Elvis sang, they trimmed the tree. One by one the ornaments went on and the boxes were emptied. In addition to the birds and the fruit, the tree was hung with glass pinecones, angels, several Santas, and assorted elves, stockings, gingerbread men, and stars. When the last of them was placed on the only bare branch remaining, Mike took up his mother's beloved plastic star and, using a chair to reach the uppermost branch, placed it atop the tree.

"And there we are," he said as he stepped down and surveyed their handiwork. "My first Christmas tree since the accident."

"It's a beautiful one," Thomas said. Instinctively, he put his arm around Mike and gave him a hug.

"Thanks," Mike said. "For helping. For coming over. For everything."

He turned to look at Thomas. Thomas, looking into his friend's eyes, felt suddenly unable to move. He stood there, his hand still on

Mike's waist, while Mike stared into his face. Neither said anything. Thomas could feel his heartbeat speed up, until it was pounding so loudly he was sure Mike could hear it as well.

"Have yourself a merry little Christmas."

The sound of Ella Fitzgerald's unmistakable voice floated through the silence. Still, neither Mike nor Thomas moved. It was as if the snowstorm outside had somehow swept them up in its embrace and frozen them in time.

Then Mike leaned forward. Thomas closed his eyes as their lips met. He felt the softness of Mike's mouth on his. Mike's arms went around him, pulling him in closer. Thomas felt strong hands on his back. He kissed Mike back, his hands tentatively reaching up and finding a place against the small of Mike's back.

Too soon, Mike pulled away. He looked at Thomas with an expression of surprise and embarrassment. He let him go and stepped away.

"I'm so sorry," he said, his voice halting. "I didn't mean to do that. Oh, God. I'm really, really sorry."

Thomas put a hand to his mouth, touching the place where Mike's lips had pressed against his. The warmth lingered. He looked at Mike, not able to put into words what he was feeling.

"That was so stupid," Mike continued. "I don't know what I was thinking. I mean, I know you're not—"

"I am," Thomas said.

Mike's mouth stayed open but he said nothing as he stared at Thomas.

"I am," Thomas said again. "I always have been."

Mike blinked. Thomas stepped toward him and took his hands in his own. "I'm gay," he said, thinking perhaps Mike hadn't understood. "And it's okay." He breathed deeply, trying to calm his emotions. "And it's okay."

This time it was he who kissed Mike. And this time neither of them pulled away. Their mouths found one another, tongues pressing against one another. Their arms held one another close, both afraid to let go. Ella's voice serenaded them as they embraced.

When finally they parted, it was Thomas who spoke first. "I guess this is a year of firsts for a lot of things," he said.

Mike, still holding his hand, sat down on the couch, pulling

Thomas down with him. "What's happening here?" he asked. "Are you saying that all this time . . . ?" He looked at Thomas, his question left unfinished.

Thomas nodded. "It's hard to explain," he said. "I'm not even sure I *can* explain it, at least not right now. But you have to understand, I wasn't trying to fool you or your friends or anyone. Well, perhaps myself, but no one else."

Mike rubbed his thumb along the side of Thomas's hand. "Is it true you've never been with anyone?" he asked.

Thomas nodded. "No one," he answered. "I know what you're thinking," he continued. "Another closeted priest. But that's not really it. I—"

"That wasn't what I was thinking at all," Mike interrupted.

Thomas regarded him wonderingly.

"I was thinking that I've never met anyone like you," Mike said softly. "All of this," he said, nodding at the tree, "I did it all because of you."

"Me?" Thomas asked.

Mike nodded. "I didn't understand why, but you made me want to feel alive again," he said, then he laughed. "I thought I was nuts, wanting to spend time with a straight guy. A straight priest. But it didn't matter. I just liked being around you. It never even occurred to me that maybe I was . . ."

"That you were what?" asked Thomas when Mike looked away.

Mike lifted his head. His eyes were damp. "That maybe I was falling in love," said Mike.

CHAPTER 27

The shortest day of the year dawned bleak and gray, as if winter, sensing the eventual loosening of its grip on the world, was trying to obliterate the sun once and for all. The sky remained perpetually dark, clouds obscuring the heavens. Snow fell steadily. There was no hint that, soon, the periods of light would begin to lengthen by several minutes a day as the wheel of the year turned once more.

Stephen Darby didn't know that it was the first official day of winter. Inside his house, a perpetual chill had taken hold many days earlier. In his kitchen, dishes were piled high in the sink. His bedroom floor was littered with discarded clothes. He had some time ago gotten down to his last pair of clean underwear, which he'd now been wearing for six days straight.

Had he bothered to look in a mirror, he wouldn't have recognized himself. Although his bruises were mostly healed, his face hardly resembled the one he'd had before encountering Pete Thayer at the Paris Cinema. Where once he had been handsome, now he was haunted. His eyes were dull, his skin ashen. His hair, uncut and unwashed, hung limply over his forehead. His beard had grown in, covering his cheeks and chin with a patchy forest of reddish-brown.

When the phone rang, Stephen stared at it. It had been ringing a lot lately, but he generally ignored it. There was no one he wanted to hear from, no one who had anything to say to him that was of any importance. Even his family seemed to exist only in the distant past. He'd made a few calls to them, convinced them that he was busy with work and perhaps battling a slight case of the flu. His mother, thankfully, was preoccupied with her usual holiday plans, the undertaking of which outweighed her customary need to oversee every aspect of her son's life. She had left him alone after extracting a promise from him to appear at her annual holiday party, to be held on December twenty-first.

The date was circled on the calendar that hung above Stephen's desk, but it meant little to him. He wasn't sure what day it was, nor did he care. Whenever he had begun to care, even a little, he had taken a couple of pills and retreated into the dull safety of their embrace. There, nothing mattered. He liked it that way.

Now he heard his mother's voice emanating from the depths of the machine. "Stephen? It's your mother. I wanted to remind you that the party is tonight. I want you here by seven o'clock. Oh, and don't forget to bring a gift for the Secret Santa exchange."

Secret Santa. Hearing the words, Stephen laughed. "Secret Santa," he said out loud, enjoying the way the words felt on his tongue, the nonsensical sound of them when they were uttered. "Secret Santa," he said again. "Secret Santa. Secret Santa. Secret Santa."

He laughed again, loudly. What the fuck was a Secret Santa? What did it have to do with him? Nothing, he told himself. Absolutely nothing. It was just something his mother liked to say, another one of her endless, boring topics of conversation, like her perpetually sore back or Stephen's inability to find a wife. Secret Santa. He wondered if she'd read about *that* in the goddamned *Reader's Digest*.

He erased her message. If she wanted him to show up for her goddamned party, he would. Maybe he'd show up dressed exactly as he was, in stained underpants and an old T-shirt. Maybe he'd just walk in like that, a big fucking bow tied around his neck. "Merry Christmas, Mom," he heard himself say. "Merry Fucking Christmas."

He checked the computer screen again. Still nothing from HrdAtWrk. It had been two weeks, two long weeks since he'd heard from him. What was wrong, he wondered? What had he done to drive his master away? He'd been a good boy, hadn't he? He'd done everything that was asked of him. He'd allowed his master to take out his rage on him, to use him the way he deserved to be used. Wasn't that enough?

He lived in front of the computer. Not having heard from his dark lover, and forsaking all others, he'd resorted to searching the web for the next best thing. He'd discovered in his endless wandering several sites that had interested him, places where he could find images that recalled his times with his faceless tormentor. He sat for hours staring at pictures of men who, like him, deserved to be mistreated. He saw their bodies, bound and beaten, their faces twisted in pain as men stronger than they were used them for their pleasure.

These pictures had become the dreamscape of his life. Looking at them, he replaced the bodies of the men in them with his own, superimposed his features over theirs. Soon he was looking at himself, his own body bruised and broken as the man who now controlled his mind ordered him to degrade himself for his amusement. It was his wrists that were tied behind him as a stream of piss, hot and wicked, slashed across his face. It was his back covered in the welts of his master's whip, his chest puckered with the brand of a white-hot iron that seared a mark of shame into his flesh.

He knew he should be ashamed of himself, ashamed of the thoughts that filled his head and the desires that ate at his soul. And he was ashamed. He had no right to exist in the world, at least not the world around him. He didn't belong there. That world was for normal men, men who could hold their heads high and walk with pride. He was not one of those men. He was something small and frail, bent and twisted by a poison that ran through his veins and intoxicated him with its sweetness. He should, he knew, be strong enough to resist it, but he couldn't. He was weak.

It was this poison that had befogged his mind and raised the voice that had told him to go to that place, that place where he'd allowed himself to be taken. It was this poison that made him half a man, incapable of wholeness. He had let it taint him, and now it was eating him alive.

He fumbled for the bottle on his desk. His fingers found it, knocking it over. The pills scattered across the surface of the desk, a rain of small blue tablets. The sound echoed loudly in his ears, and for a long horrible moment he saw the pills tumbling off of the desk and into nothingness. His heart stopped as he imagined the loss of them, and he pawed at the desk anxiously, trying to prevent the pills from running away from him like bugs from the light. He trapped them beneath his palm, where they lay still. When he was sure they wouldn't scurry out of his reach, he lifted his hand and nervously scooped the pills back into the bottle.

He held the bottle up, measuring the remaining number. He

sighed. There were enough to last him for some time. *Unless* . . . The thought returned to him. It had first come a few days before, interrupting his fantasies with its teasing voice. *Unless* . . . He'd ordered it away, terrified by its suggestion. But it had come back, wheedling and coaxing. Each time he screamed at it to shut up, it obliged, but only for a time. Now the periods of its silence were growing shorter and shorter, and it was growing stronger, more insistent.

Unless you take all of them.

He put his hands to his ears, trying to shut the voice out. But it came from within, and now that it had had its say, it felt its power. *Unless you take all of them,* it said again. *All of them. All at once. Unless you take them all.*

He shook his head. No, he wouldn't listen to the voice. It lied. It had lied to him about the pleasures that awaited him in the theater. It had lied to him about the pleasures waiting for him in the arms of men. All it knew how to do was lie. He couldn't trust it.

"Go away!" he shouted, trying to drown it out.

The voice laughed quietly. *Not this time,* it said. *Not anymore. You believed me once. Believe me again.*

"No!" Stephen yelled. He reached for the bottle, took three pills, and popped them into his mouth. His glass of Diet Coke was empty so he chewed, grinding the pills to powder beneath his teeth. The taste was foul, sharp, and metallic, but he didn't stop. Producing some spit, he swallowed. The paste stuck in his throat and he coughed, bringing most of it back up. He swallowed again, harder, and the pills entered his system. He breathed more easily.

What are you waiting for?

Stephen looked up. He'd heard the voice of the dark man, the one he longed for. He looked around the room. Where was he?

What are you waiting for, faggot?

"Where are you?" he called out.

The room behind him was empty. He ran into the hall, peering into the darkness. It, too, was barren. His feet slipped on the wooden floor as he went from room to room, searching. Finally he ended up in the bedroom. The blinds were drawn against the pale light outside, and the sheets on the bed were a tangled nest. A stale smell emanated from them.

Why aren't you on your knees, cocksucker?

Stephen turned around, searching wildly for the man who spoke to him. He found only shadows. Perhaps the man was hiding within them. Perhaps he would emerge to take Stephen in his hands, to use him as he needed to be used.

On your knees!

The voice was harsh, commanding. Stephen was forced to obey it. He dropped to his knees, landing on the floor with a sharp crack of bone on wood. Pain bit at him but he ignored it. He looked up hopefully, waiting.

What is it you want, faggot?

Stephen shook his head, unwilling to speak. He knew what he wanted, but he couldn't say it.

Tell me what you want.

The voice bristled with anger. Stephen trembled, expecting at any moment to feel the slap of a hand across his face, the kick of a boot in his stomach. Anticipating it, he began to cry.

Laughter rang through the room. It came from all around him, mocking and jeering, echoing in his head. It was cruel, cold, and hard.

What a joke you are, the voice said, spitting the words at him. *You're not a man. You're nothing. Nothing. You're a worthless rag for me to wipe up my cum with.*

The tears fell from Stephen's eyes, dropping to the floor. He wiped at his eyes with his hands, trying to stanch the flow. He was disgracing himself, he knew.

Don't bother trying, the voice said. *You're like all the rest of the faggots. Weak. Diseased. Good for nothing. Aren't you?*

Stephen shook his head. He was all those things. He was useless. He had no reason to deny it. The evidence was against him, and he knew it. Didn't his body carry the proof of his weakness? Didn't his mind contain the seeds of disease? Everything the voice said was true.

What am I going to do about you?

The voice spoke not to Stephen but to itself, as if his master was considering what punishment to dole out next. Stephen considered praying for mercy, begging for another chance to prove himself. But somehow he knew that point had been passed. He had failed miserably, and whatever his fate was to be, it was what he deserved.

Maybe I should have you go next door and tell your mother what you've been doing, the voice said thoughtfully.

"No," Stephen whispered.

No? And why not? Shouldn't she know what kind of son you really are? Shouldn't she know what it is you dream about doing? Wouldn't that make her happy?

"No," Stephen said again. "Please, no."

The voice laughed at him. *Look at the little faggot, begging me not to tell his mommy what he really is. Why don't you want her to know? Would she be disappointed in you? Would she be ashamed?*

"Yes," Stephen said, choking back a sob. "Yes." He thought of his mother, seeing him on the floor of the Paris Cinema. He saw her eyes troubled with confusion, wondering what her baby boy was doing there, his pants around his feet, his shame on display for the whole world to see. No, he couldn't let her know. She could never know.

Would it break their hearts? asked the voice, as if its owner had read Stephen's thoughts. *Would it kill them to know that their boy had become a cocksucker? That he wasn't a real man?*

It would kill them, Stephen thought hopelessly. It would destroy them. He'd always been the good son, the one who never caused any trouble. They had always told him how proud they were of him. But they wouldn't be proud if they knew. They would think they had failed.

And you can't be who you are, the voice reminded him. *You can't go on like this.*

Again Stephen knew that the voice spoke the truth. He couldn't live like this, always searching, always looking for men who would use him. He couldn't stay in the shadows forever. Someday he would have to come out from the safety of the world he'd been living in, and then he would be revealed for what he was. Then it would all come crumbling down.

There is one way, the voice said, sounding for a moment like it truly cared about him. *There is one thing you can do, one way to make sure they never find out.*

Stephen looked down. Somehow the bottle of pills was in his fist. Had he carried it with him? Had he clung to it through everything? He didn't remember doing so, but there it was. He shook the bottle and heard the reassuring rattle of the pills inside.

There are enough, the voice told him. *More than enough.*

Stephen sobbed. He was wracked with pain. His whole being ached. All he wanted was for it to stop.

Go on, faggot, the voice said, sounding more like the man he re-membered. *Do what I tell you. You're good at that.*

Stephen nodded, tears blinding him. He looked around the room and saw a glass sitting on the table beside his bed. He crawled toward it, unable to get to his feet. The weight of his burden was pressing down on him, unbelievably heavy. He felt it like a booted foot between his shoulder blades, crushing him to the floor.

He reached the glass and grabbed it. It was still half full. He took a sip. The soda inside was flat and warm, all life sapped from it. He had no idea how long it had been sitting there. He set the glass on the floor and opened the bottle of pills, dumping them into his hand. His fingers closed around the pile, holding it close.

In the other room the phone rang, startling him. He glanced at the clock on the bedside table. It was seven o'clock. He knew the call was from his mother, wondering where he was.

Finish it, the voice said insistently. *She'll be here soon.*

Yes, he thought, she would be there soon. When he didn't answer, she would be there to see what was keeping him. Perhaps she would send his father or his brother. He was running out of time.

He opened his fist. The pills looked small and insignificant, like candy. He put half of them into his mouth.

Now swallow, faggot. Swallow like a good boy.

Stephen obeyed. He took a swig of the stale soda and let it carry the pills down his throat. He repeated the process again, swallowing the remainder of the pills. When they were down, he took another drink.

He didn't feel any different, not at first. Then a warmth began to creep over him, a comforting blanket that shrouded him in darkness and quieted his heart. His eyes grew heavy. He heard the glass in his hand fall to the floor with a dull thud. He felt warmth against his leg.

Where was the man? Had he gone? Stephen looked around, trying to find him. He wanted to see him one last time, feel his touch. But where was he? Stephen felt alone, and for the first time he was fright-ened.

What's wrong, fag?

The voice returned, nearer now. The man crouched behind him, just out of sight. Stephen tried to turn his head to see him, but found himself unable to move.

What's the matter? Isn't this what you wanted?

The voice was taunting him. He could see the man watching him, his mouth twisted into a cruel grin. He felt strong hands close around his throat, cutting off his air. He didn't bother to fight. This *was* what he wanted. It was what he'd wanted when he'd gone into the darkness with the man at the theater. It was what he wanted now. It was what he deserved.

He closed his eyes and allowed his dark master to do what he would.

CHAPTER 28

"Are you okay?"

Russell nodded. "It's just sort of, you know, weird."

"I know," Greg agreed. He played with his fork for a moment, then set it down on the table. "Let's just pretend this is a first date," he said.

"It is a first date," said Russell.

"I mean a real one," Greg said. "Let's pretend we don't know much about one another. Someone—a mutual friend—has set us up."

Russell sat back in his chair. "Okay," he said. "That could work."

"Great," Greg said. "I'll start. So, Russell, what do you do?"

"I'm the store manager for the Carter-Beane over at the Stonesgate Mall," Russell answered.

"Really?" replied Greg. "What a surprise. I'm a manager in menswear at Carter-Beane. I'm surprised I've never run into you."

Russell laughed. "Maybe this won't work after all," he said.

"Just go with it," Greg encouraged him.

"Do you like your job?" Russell asked, trying to think of questions he might ask a date. It had been so long since he'd been on one, he wasn't sure how to do it.

"I do," Greg answered confidently. "But our store manager is kind of uptight."

"Sounds like a drag," suggested Russell.

"I think he just needs to have a little more fun," Greg said. "He's been sort of unhappy lately. What about you? Do you enjoy your work?"

"Most of the time," said Russell. "Some of my employees can be difficult sometimes."

"Maybe you need to discipline them," Greg said suggestively.

Russell laughed. "Let's talk about something else," he said. "What do you like to do?"

"I'm really into oral," Greg said cheerfully, as if answering an interview question. "If we're talking anal, I can go both ways but I usually prefer being on the bottom. As for rimming—"

"I meant hobbies," Russell said, interrupting him.

"Those aren't hobbies?" said Greg.

Russell picked up his knife and pointed it at his companion. "This was your idea," he said. "Play nice."

"All right," said Greg. "Seriously. I like to read, go to movies, concerts, that sort of stuff. I'm not really into sports, although I watch a little baseball in the summer. I'm not much into politics, either, but I voted in the last election."

"Who for?" Russell inquired.

"The guy who lost," said Greg. "Now tell me about you."

"I like to cook," Russell told him. "I'm also into reading and movies. I think I like concerts. It's been a couple of years since I went to one. Don't like sports at all."

"What about your last relationship?" Greg asked. "What happened?"

"That's not fair," Russell said.

"Sure it is," countered Greg. "I ask all my dates that question."

Russell sighed deeply. "I don't know," he said reluctantly. "I guess we just weren't a good match."

"How long were you together?"

"Seven years," Russell said.

"That's a long time to not be a good match," suggested Greg.

Russell took a sip of wine from the glass next to his plate. "Yes," he said simply, "it is a long time."

"Well, I think anyone would be lucky to have you as a partner," Greg said.

Russell put his glass down. "Thank you," he said gratefully. "How about you? Any past loves I should know about?"

"I had a huge crush on Kevin Costner when I was seventeen," Greg answered. "Nothing to speak of since then. A guy here and there, but never for long."

"Trouble committing?" asked Russell.

"Just never found anyone worth committing to," said Greg.

The conversation ebbed as their food arrived. Once the waiter had gone, they began eating. Feeling more comfortable now that he had something to do with his hands, Russell continued the game.

"Are you looking to settle down?" he inquired. "Or are you just interested in something casual?"

"Well, you really get right to it, don't you?" replied Greg. "No wonder all your dates run screaming."

"When you're my age, you don't have time to waste," Russell joked. "I like to know where things stand."

Greg slowly chewed a mouthful of pasta before answering. "Why don't we see how things go?" he said.

Russell looked at him. Greg's expression was serious, and Russell knew they were no longer just playing. Greg meant what he said.

"Okay," Russell said. "We'll see how it goes. How's it going so far?"

Greg nodded his head, grinning. "It's going great," he replied.

The remainder of dinner was easy and relaxed. The two men talked about nothing and everything, from their childhoods to their favorite flavors of ice cream. When the check came, Russell was feeling better than he had in a long time. Although the whole date scenario was sort of artificial, he really did feel as if he were getting to know a potential partner better. There was a sense of anticipation about his interactions with Greg, a fluttering in the stomach that he realized he hadn't experienced since his first dates with John.

"So," Greg said when the check had been paid. "Want to come back to my place?"

Russell hesitated. He hadn't thought about how far their date might go. It had been difficult enough suggesting to Greg that maybe they could consider taking their relationship in a different direction. That had been an awkward conversation, one that had taken most of an evening and a bottle of wine to get out. But once he had, Greg had been surprisingly receptive to the notion. Now, almost a week later, they were at another crossroads. Russell looked at Greg, who was waiting for an answer to his question.

"Sure," he answered. "Let's do that."

They got into their cars and Russell followed Greg out of the restaurant parking lot. As he drove behind him, his thoughts raced from one thing to another. What was he doing? Was he really going to maybe sleep with Greg? He hadn't been with anyone but John since they'd started dating seriously. If he did sleep with Greg, did it mean that he and John were officially over? He hadn't, of course, mentioned his date with Greg to John. He hadn't mentioned it to anyone, not even Simon or Mike. But if they started having sex, didn't that obligate him to tell people?

Again he hesitated. He could simply turn the car around and head back to Simon's house. He could call Greg and apologize, tell him that things were moving too quickly. Greg would understand. They could go back to being just friends.

But he didn't turn around. He followed Greg all the way to his house, pulling into the driveway behind him and parking. He hesitated only slightly before opening the door and getting out of the car. Greg waited for him, and together they walked to the front door.

"Here we are," Greg said as he unlocked the door and opened it. He held out his hand, motioning for Russell to enter ahead of him.

The door shut. Russell turned to look at Greg. For a moment they stood there awkwardly, just staring at one another. Then they were kissing. Russell wasn't even sure who had moved first. One moment they were standing with a foot or more of space between them, the next they were entwined in one another's arms.

As they kissed, they fumbled with the buttons of each other's coats, trying to open them with eager fingers. Russell thought, incongruously, of two overeager children in snowsuits bumping against one another. He felt clumsy, silly, like a little boy. He pulled away from Greg and took a breath.

"What's the matter?" Greg asked.

"I just need to slow down a little," Russell told him.

Greg nodded. "Why don't we start with getting these coats off?" he suggested.

Free of their coats and scarves, they faced one another again. Greg stepped forward and kissed Russell. This time, Russell let himself melt into the kiss. Greg's kisses were different than John's. His mouth was softer, his movements more intense. He used his hands to draw Russell to him, held him with a commanding presence that Russell found arousing.

"Let's go upstairs," Greg said when they parted for a moment. He took Russell's hand, and Russell, not objecting, followed him up the stairs.

Greg walked inside the bedroom, still holding Russell's hand. Russell paused in the doorway, looking in. Beyond Greg he could see the bed, the quilt that covered it pulled back a little at the top. He knew that if he stepped over the threshold, he would be making a decision that could change his life forever.

Greg was waiting for him. His eyes were soft, inviting. His fingers held Russell's in a loose grip. He was leaving the decision to stay or go up to Russell. Russell stepped forward.

Greg led him to the bed. Not speaking, he reached for the buttons on Russell's shirt and slowly undid them, pulling Russell's shirt off and dropping it to the floor. He followed it with his own shirt, then reached for the buckle of Russell's belt.

Moments later they stood in just their underwear. Greg embraced Russell, pulling him toward him. Russell felt the smooth skin of Greg's torso pressed against his own, sensed a hardness at his crotch as they kissed. After hesitating a moment, he slid his hands down Greg's back.

Greg pushed him backward, lowering him to the bed. He was between Russell's legs, and now the bulge in his shorts was undeniable. Russell felt the stiffness of Greg's erection pressing against his own growing dick. He closed his eyes as Greg moved his mouth down to his chin and then to his neck.

Greg kept going, his tongue tracing a lazy path down Russell's neck to his chest. There Greg's mouth paused, his teeth biting gently at Russell's nipple. Russell tensed at the slight pain, then relaxed as Greg replaced teeth with the softness of his warm lips.

Russell was uncertain what to do. His lovemaking with John had quickly fallen into a predictable pattern during the first months of their relationship. John preferred things to go in an orderly fashion, seldom straying from his favored activities of mutual masturbation and the occasional blowjob. He found anal sex messy and distasteful, and the few times Russell had convinced him to try it, the experiment had ended badly. Since then Russell had satisfied himself with what John was capable of.

Greg, unlike John, seemed intent on exploring all the possibilities available to two men making love. When he reached Russell's crotch, he tugged his underwear down and off. Russell's cock, feeling harder than it had in many months, jutted up at an angle. Greg ignored it for the time being, preferring to attend to Russell's balls. He nibbled and sucked on them, letting first one and then the other roll around on his tongue.

When his tongue descended into the crack of Russell's ass, Russell inhaled sharply. When he felt his asshole gently spread and Greg's tongue enter him, he cried out despite himself. Hearing him, Greg probed more deeply. Russell gasped, overcome by the sensation. His cock jerked of its own accord as his body was wracked with spasms of excitement.

Greg continued to fuck him with his tongue, alternately moving in and out and then pausing to languidly circle the perimeter of the opening to Russell's ass. Russell, never having had such attention paid to his butt, pushed his head back against the pillows and prayed it would never end.

When it did, he looked down, disappointed, to see Greg moving back up between his legs. This time he stopped at Russell's cock, gently taking the head in his mouth and sliding down it. Russell's dick was encased in warmth, and again his head went back against the pillows. He lost himself in the movements of Greg's mouth. Then Greg moved onto the bed, turning so that he was straddling Russell's body. Russell opened his eyes to see Greg's prick hanging above his face.

He reached for it, feeling its thickness in his hand. As Greg continued to suck him, he returned the favor. For the first time in seven years he tasted a cock other than John's. He took as much as he could into himself, relishing the rich smell and the way Greg slid against his lips and tongue.

As he was sucking, he felt Greg release his cock and move back to his asshole. This time Greg slipped a finger inside. Russell groaned, Greg's cock deep in his throat, and pressed against the finger that played with him. Greg, taking the cue, fucked him more forcefully. When Russell couldn't stand the teasing any longer, he let Greg's cock fall from between his lips.

"Do you have a rubber?" he asked.

Greg rolled off him and reached for the drawer of his bedside table. Opening it, he pulled out a condom and a small bottle, which he set on the table. As Russell watched, he ripped open the foil packet and removed a rubber, which he quickly rolled down the length of his dick. Then he squirted the contents of the bottle into his palm.

Kneeling between Russell's legs, he slid his finger back inside him.

Russell felt the lube on Greg's finger slick his hole. Greg massaged him for a minute, loosening him up. Then Russell felt the head of Greg's dick pressing against him. He tried to relax.

When Greg entered him, his mouth opened in a silent cry. Seeing it, Greg slowed down, giving Russell time to adjust to him. Then he resumed his progress until Russell felt Greg's balls slapping gently against his ass.

Greg began to move in and out, slowly fucking him. He pushed Russell's legs back. Russell, looking up at him, wavered between laughing and crying. Greg's cock felt wonderful. But Russell also felt guilty. Instead of Greg's face, he saw John's. He was looking down at Russell, confused. Russell wanted to reach up and stroke his cheek, tell him that everything was okay.

But it wasn't okay. He was making love with another man. As good as it felt, as much as he wanted it, something was missing. He'd hoped that doing this with Greg would make him feel whole; instead, it was tearing him apart all over again.

"I can't," he whimpered.

Greg, not hearing him, continued to fuck him.

"Stop," Russell said more loudly.

Greg slowed down. "Does it hurt?" he asked.

Russell sat up. Greg pulled out of him and knelt between his knees, concern on his face. "Are you okay?"

Russell shook his head. "No," he said, an overwhelming sadness building up inside him as he looked at Greg and felt his heart breaking all over again. "I'm not."

CHAPTER 29

"Well, here we are again."

Simon looked down at Walter's grave. Someone had, not surprisingly, taken the CD player since his last visit. A new layer of snow had covered the stone, and the lower half was almost completely obscured by a small drift that had been pushed up against the marker by the wind.

"I don't know how you stand it out here," Simon said, addressing the stone as he pulled his coat more tightly around him. "It's not precisely balmy."

He had brought a bouquet of flowers, red roses that he'd paid dearly for at a shop downtown. He bent down and stuck their stems in the snow. The roses, defying the cold, bobbed their blood-red heads against the wind. It was a futile battle, but Simon admired their defiance.

"I'm sorry," he said, again addressing Walter's resting place.

He waited a moment, as if perhaps Walter's voice would creep up from the grave and answer him. He half expected it to, and when he heard nothing, he was vaguely disappointed.

"I'm sorry for thinking that I could replace you," he tried again. "It was a silly notion. I suppose it's what I get for listening to those young men. They don't understand, really, what we had together. And I can't blame them. They haven't yet had it themselves."

He was talking quickly, letting his thoughts pour out. He'd been thinking about what he was going to say ever since he'd walked away from the library after making such a fool of himself. He owed Walter an apology, an explanation for his behavior. Now that he was standing there, giving it, he felt better.

"I'm an old man," he continued. "An old man who had the great fortune of sharing a life with someone he loved. That's enough for me. I've been selfish. But I miss you, Walter. Oh, how I miss you."

A tear slipped from his eye and fell to the snow. Simon sniffed, trying to prevent any further crying. It was too cold for crying. The moisture froze in the corners of his eyes, painful stabs of iciness that hurt when he blinked.

"You should have seen me," he told Walter, hoping that talking would prevent any additional weeping. "You would have laughed. I know you would have laughed. Didn't you always say that I could never tell one of our kind? Well, it seems you were right."

He looked around him. The cemetery, draped in white, was asleep, its dead nestled safe in their earthen beds. Someday, Simon knew, and perhaps not too many years off, he would join them. He looked at the plot beside Walter's. It was empty, bought at the same time and reserved for him. He remembered the day Walter had brought him the brochure and suggested it. How old had they been then? He counted back. They had been in their thirties. Death had seemed an impossibility, although both of them had already buried their parents and a number of friends.

Simon had laughed at Walter's morbidity, agreeing to purchase the plots in order to maintain peace in the house. He had drawn the line at choosing headstones, however, believing that it could only tempt fate. Walter, unusual for him, had acquiesced. It wasn't until Walter's death years later that Simon discovered that Walter had selected his stone in secret. At the time, Simon had been thankful rather than angry, relieved to have one less decision to make on his own.

He had not yet chosen his stone. Although he appreciated Walter's thoroughness in planning for his inevitable passing, he himself couldn't entertain thoughts of his own funeral. Looking at the blank plot of land beside Walter's grave, however, he couldn't help but feel a small sense of peace knowing that there was a place for him beside his lover. It was sentimental, he knew, but the knowledge that they would be together forever made the idea of dying slightly more bearable.

He knew too many couples who had been separated in death, first by the passing of one or the other, and then later by the family who cared little about the partner with whom the deceased had shared his life. He and Walter, at least, would be reunited in death. He had no belief that they would meet again, walking the world as ghostly lovers or existing as some kind of ectoplasmic energy. Dead was dead, and he was content to become fodder for whatever plant or insect life wished to use his decaying body for its purposes. But he would do it while lying next to the man who had captured his heart, with whom he'd spent the majority of his life.

As he stood, thinking these thoughts, a cardinal detached itself from a nearby branch and landed atop Walter's gravestone. Cocking its head, it looked with interest at Simon. Its black eyes sparkled and it ruffled its crimson feathers, fluffing itself up against the cold. Simon regarded the bird with interest. Cardinals had been Walter's favorites. He had often sat at the window watching them forage in the seed he scattered under the trees behind the house for them.

"What?" Simon said to the bird. "Are you supposed to be some kind of a sign? Because I don't believe in signs."

The bird tipped its head at him, but made no move to fly away. It rubbed its beak against the stone and shuffled from foot to foot. Simon crossed his arms over his chest.

"Walter, did you send this bird to me?" he asked. "If so, I think you've been badly influenced by your friends on the other side. Parlor tricks are beneath you."

The bird chirped loudly. Simon waved a hand at it, shooing it away. The bird ignored him.

"Walter, I'm cold," Simon said, half addressing the bird without meaning to. "I'm going to go home now, where I will sit in front of our fireplace with Clancy on my lap and grow old without any further attempts to be twenty-one again."

The cardinal leaped into the air, flapping its wings. It flew at Simon, who put his arm up to block the attack. But the bird flew by him, landing on a stone some way off. It continued to look at him.

"You are a bird," Simon said loudly. "A bird and nothing more. Go away."

The bird chirped.

"Please go away," Simon repeated. "Leave me in peace."

He stared at the cardinal, expecting it to leave. He was irritated, both by the bird's stubbornness and by his own inability to just turn and leave it there. He looked again at Walter's gravestone, a feeling of annoyance growing inside him.

"Fine," he said. "I'll play your game, but I don't believe for a minute that this bird has anything to do with you. I am simply humoring you, you old bastard."

He walked toward the cardinal. When he was a few feet from its resting spot, it took off again, flying to another stone. Resigned to his role as the pawn in whatever was occurring, Simon followed it. Each time he grew near, the bird continued on. It was leading him down the main road that ran through the cemetery, away from the parking lot where his car waited and deeper into the world of the dead.

He followed the bird as it flew around a bend in the road. The wind had picked up, and the snow was blowing against him. Even with his hands pushed deep into the pockets of his coat, he was chilled. He was too old to be out in weather such as this. He should, he knew, just turn around and walk as quickly as he could back to the car. There he could warm himself and forget about the foolish notions that had taken hold of him.

Growing angry, he decided to do exactly that, the bird be damned. He turned, determined to go, but found himself buffeted on all sides by the wind. It had picked up the snow and was twirling it around him, blinding him. He had no idea which direction he was facing; all was whiteness and cold. He put his hands up to his face, suddenly very afraid. He opened his mouth and cried out in fear.

The snow stopped. He felt the wind die away immediately, and he no longer felt the sting of the snow on his skin. The cold remained, but it was tolerable. He lowered his hands and looked around him, searching for the bird. It had gone.

"Hello, Simon."

He blinked. Standing not more than a dozen feet from him was a young man, a young man with familiar features. He was dressed in brown pants and a blue shirt. His features were strong, his eyes bright. He wore no coat.

"Walter?"

His lover was there. But it wasn't the Walter of those last days; it was the Walter of forty years ago, Walter the way he was when he and Simon had first met. Simon stared at his handsome, youthful face, not believing.

"Where's your coat?" he asked incongruously.

Walter laughed. "Look around you," he said.

Simon did. The snow had gone, and in its place summer reigned. The sun shone down from a clear sky, and all around him the grass was fresh and green. Daisies nodded their bright faces in the pleasant breeze that blew. The tombstones, too, were gone. He and Walter were standing instead in a spreading field that seemed to have no end.

"What happened to the snow?" Simon asked.

Again Walter laughed. "You know I was never one for the winter," he said as he walked toward Simon. "Summer was my time."

Simon regarded his lover with wonder and suspicion. Walter, stopping just in front of him, reached out and touched him. Simon flinched. Walter touched him again, this time leaving his hand on Simon's chest. Simon felt the pressure there, as real as the sun on his face and the scent of the grass.

"Walk with me," Walter said.

He took Simon's hand, his fingers curling around Simon's. They were warm, beating with blood. Simon held on to them tightly, afraid that if he let go, Walter would float away from him.

"The roses are beautiful," Walter said. "Thank you."

Simon said nothing. He didn't know how his lover had come to be with him, how the world had changed in the blink of an eye, but he wanted to do nothing that would end it.

"It's all right, Simon," Walter told him. "This is my world. Look at yourself."

Simon did as Walter told him. When he beheld his own figure, he was again shocked into stillness. Like Walter, he had grown young. His body was once more strong. He no longer felt the weight of age, the tiredness of his years. The skin of his hands was smooth, the hair on his arms dark. He felt his face and discovered there the softness of youth.

"This is how I remember us," said Walter. "Forever young. Do you remember how it was that summer, Simon? Do you remember what it was like to be two men in love?"

"I remember," Simon answered. "I remember looking at you and knowing that everything was all right with the world. I remember sleeping beside you and being afraid of nothing."

Walter smiled at him. "It was wonderful," he said. He looked into his lover's eyes. "I want you to have that again, Simon."

Simon's face fell as sadness filled his heart. He was looking into Walter's eyes, and in them he saw nothing but love. Yet what he was saying hurt Simon deeply.

"I can't," he said softly. "No."

Walter nodded. "You can," he said. "And you must. I want you to."

"I'm too old," Simon protested. "Too tired to start again."

"You're not," Walter insisted. "You have all the time in the world, even if it's only a day, a month, a year. Don't spend what you have left living with only my memory."

"I miss you," Simon said. "I miss you every day of my life."

"And I miss you," echoed Walter. "That will never change. But it's not a reason to stop living."

"I am living," Simon objected. "I have friends. I—"

"You need more than friends," said Walter.

Simon looked away from him. He knew Walter's words were supposed to comfort him, but they were tearing his heart to pieces.

"Why can't I stay with you?" he asked sadly.

Walter didn't answer. He merely looked at Simon with his great dark eyes. Simon, lost in them, realized suddenly that Walter was fading. His touch was becoming lighter, insubstantial. Simon grabbed at his hands.

"No!" he said plaintively.

Walter continued to diminish, his body growing less and less visible. Simon could see grass through his shirt, sky in the hole where his face had been. He was breaking up, the pieces swept away in the breeze.

Simon grabbed at the air around him, trying to resurrect Walter, to pull him back. His hands found nothing, though, and he was left twirling around, searching blindly for some remaining scrap of his lover. When his fingers found nothing, he buried his face in his hands.

"Are you okay, mister?"

Simon felt a pull on his sleeve. Looking through his fingers, he saw a little boy staring up at him.

"Are you lost?"

Simon lowered his hands. He was standing in the graveyard. Snow was falling. He patted himself. He was once again dressed in his coat. And he felt the heaviness of age once more in his bones.

The boy continued to look at him. Simon smiled at him. "I guess I am a little lost," he said.

"Walter?" A woman's voice echoed through the air. Simon looked up to see a young woman walking toward them. "Walter?" she called out again. "What are you doing?"

Simon turned, half expecting to see his lover standing behind them. But there was no one. He and the boy were alone.

"Walter," the woman said as she reached them. "Where did you run off to?"

"Nowhere," the boy said indignantly. "I was right here."

The woman looked up at Simon and gave him a small smile. "I'm sorry if he was bothering you," she said. "I was putting a wreath on my husband's grave. He must have wandered off."

"I didn't wander," Walter insisted. "I said I was right here."

Simon smiled at the young woman. "It's all right," he said. "Walter was helping me find my way, weren't you, Walter?"

"That's right," Walter said brightly. "I was helping him."

"I was visiting a loved one of my own," Simon explained to the woman. "I'm afraid I got a little bit turned around. I'm sorry about your husband."

The woman nodded. "It's been nearly two years," she said. "But the holidays are always hard."

"Yes," Simon agreed. "They are hard."

The woman looked up. "You have to go on, though, don't you," she said, not speaking directly to Simon. "You have to live your life."

"Can we go?"

Walter was tugging on his mother's hand impatiently.

Simon looked at the boy and his mother. "Thank you for your help, Walter," he said.

The boy nodded, his interest in Simon waning. His mother took his hand and the boy smiled broadly, having achieved his aim.

"Merry Christmas," the woman said to Simon.

"Merry Christmas to you too," replied Simon. It seemed an odd thing to say to someone he'd met in a graveyard, and he almost laughed at the absurdity of it. But the young woman didn't seem to notice the peculiarity of the moment.

Simon watched as Walter and his mother walked in the opposite direction from him. When they were out of sight, he turned and made his way back toward his car. He still wasn't certain what had happened to him there in the cemetery. He wasn't one to believe in ghosts or visions. Still, he'd experienced something. Whether it was a momentary delusion or something else, he wasn't sure.

But did it really matter? As he passed Walter's grave, he gave it a final look. If millions of people could believe that angels appeared to announce the birth of God's son to a virgin, what was one dead queen coming back for a few minutes to deliver a message to his lover? Thinking about it, he felt himself grow lighter. A warmth spread through him, banishing the cold. He began to sing.

"God rest ye merry gentlemen," he sang out to the surrounding graves.

Laughing at his little joke, he returned to the world of the living.

CHAPTER 30

The interior of Saint Peter's Church glowed with the light of numerous candles. The electric lights had been shut off for the evening, and the church was filled with a festive air as the children rushed to and fro, getting ready for the pageant. A handful of adults were there to keep them in line, but by and large their attempts at keeping the confusion to a minimum were unsuccessful.

Father Dunn stood at the rear of the church, silently praying that none of the scampering sheep and angels would tip over a candle and catch something on fire. The church was made primarily of stone, but there were draperies and pews and all manner of other things that could easily combust should an errant flame touch them. Still, despite his low-level worry, he was as enchanted by the beauty of the evening as everyone else.

Christmas Eve services always had their own special magic to them. This particular night the weather was lending a hand, contributing a light snowfall, just enough to be pretty but not enough to raise concerns about driving. The church was filled with people, many of whom Thomas had never seen before. The Once-a-Yearers, he and Joseph had called them, those who made an annual appearance, always at Christmas or Easter, never to be seen again. Thomas didn't care why they were there, though. He had much to be thankful for on this Christmas, the full pews being just one of them.

He looked out into the crowded parking lot, searching for a sign of Mike. He had promised he would come, and Thomas was looking forward to seeing him. But so far he hadn't come, and it was nearing time for the pageant to begin.

"Father, five minutes."

He turned to see the anxious face of Gavin Bettelheim looking at him, his brows knitted up in worry. He knew the music director's nerves were on edge, so when he spoke, he kept his voice low and soothing.

"I'll be ready, Gavin," he said. "And I saw your dress rehearsal this afternoon. It's going to be wonderful. Everything's going to be fine."

Gavin, reassured, brightened considerably. Clutching a roll of sheet music, he turned and hurried off in pursuit of some rogue choristers who had gone by, giggling into the sleeves of their robes.

"Are we on time?"

A figure stepped inside and Mike's face was lit up. Thomas, seeing him, resisted an urge to kiss him. Instead, he took Mike's hand and held it for a long moment. "You're right on time," he said.

"I brought some friends," Mike told him. "I hope that's okay."

Thomas was delighted to see that Simon, Russell, and John were coming up the steps behind Mike. Thomas greeted each of them warmly and ushered them inside.

"We're about to start," he said. "I'm afraid the back row is the only one with any room in it."

"That will be perfect," Simon whispered to Russell as they went in. "This way we can escape if it becomes too much to bear."

Thomas, too excited about having Mike there, failed to notice the lack of enthusiasm. After making sure his friends were situated, he strode up to the front of the church and ascended to the pulpit.

"Good evening," he said. The church grew silent as the murmurings stopped and everyone looked toward the front. "Welcome to Saint Peter's and our Christmas Eve service. Instead of our usual service, tonight we're presenting the children of Saint Peter's in a pageant celebrating the season."

Thomas nodded at Gavin, who was sitting in the first row. As Thomas stepped down and walked to the back of the church to take his seat beside Mike and the others, the music director stood up and walked over to stand in front of the assembled choir of young people. Dressed as angels, they wore white robes and had rings of golden tinsel on their heads. The youngest ones played with the hems of their costumes, looking out at the audience in search of their parents' faces.

Gavin held up his hands. When he brought them down again, the singers launched into "It Came Upon a Midnight Clear." At the same time, a group of fifth graders, dressed as shepherds, emerged from the darkness, herding in front of them several small children wearing sweatshirts glued all over with cotton balls. Seeing them, the audience laughed. One of the sheep bolted, making for her mother in the front row, but was stopped by a keen-eyed shepherd, who collared her and dragged her back into place.

The singers' voices faded out as one of the boys stepped from the back row and took center stage. "And an angel of the Lord appeared unto the shepherds keeping watch over their flocks by night," he said, his voice carrying throughout the church. "Unto you is born this night a savior, which is Christ the Lord."

The shepherds stared at the angel for a moment before filing off-stage. The angel chorus resumed singing as the shepherds were replaced by the three wise men, each dressed in an elaborate robe and long fake beard. One of them carried a telescope, through which he looked into the distance.

"And a star appeared unto them," a voice from the darkness informed the audience. "A sign that in the city of David a child had been born. And then did they set out upon a journey."

The wise men followed the shepherds into the darkness. In the last row, Simon leaned over. "I believe I smell a Tony," he said drolly.

Thomas, sitting beside Mike, reached over and took his hand. As Mike accepted it, Thomas felt a surge of joy fill him. Ever since telling Mike about himself, he'd been happier than he ever had been. The burden he'd been carrying around for so long had been lifted from him. He didn't know what road his life would take now, but he felt confident that everything would be all right. As he sat in the darkness of the church, listening to the greatest story of hope ever told, he understood how the shepherds and the wise men might have felt hearing the words of the angel of the Lord. He, too, had received wonderful news, and his heart resonated with the impact of the message.

At the front of the church a new scene was unfolding. Mary and Joseph, looking tired from their journey, arrived in Bethlehem, seeking shelter. The choir serenaded them with "Oh, Little Town of Bethlehem" as the invisible narrator told of their fruitless search for a room. When finally they found an innkeeper willing to give them space in his barn, the blue-robed Mary seemed genuinely relieved to sit down on the hay bales put there to represent the stable.

"And there, in a stable surrounded by horses, cows, and sheep, she gave birth to the Christ child and laid him in a manger."

"I can't wait to see this part," Mike whispered to Thomas, who stifled a laugh.

The birth was discretely handled, as Mary reached into her robes and removed a baby doll, which she placed in its makeshift bed as the congregation, unable to contain itself, applauded gently. Mary, blushing, bent down to attend to the newborn's needs.

A rustling behind them caused the five men to turn around. There, standing in the vestibule, were the shepherds and wise men. They peered into the sanctuary, awaiting their cue to enter. When it came, in the form of the angel choir's rendition of "Away in a Manger," the shepherds darted forward, filling the aisle between the pews with bleating sheep as they made the long pilgrimage through the church. They were followed in short order by the three wise men, who marched solemnly to their signature tune as they carried their gifts of gold, frankincense, and myrrh, which they laid around the manger as Joseph and Mary nodded appreciatively.

The entire nativity scene having been assembled, the tiniest angels enjoyed their moment in the spotlight, warbling "Silent Night" in various keys and tempos. When they were finished, Gavin turned to the congregation. "Will you now join the angel choir in singing some carols," he instructed them.

Thomas opened the program tucked into the hymnal rack in front of them and held it so that Mike could share it with him. As the first notes of "O Come, O Come, Emmanuel" began, he listened to Mike's voice, a deep, rich sound that melted into his own. On Mike's other side, John, Russell, and Simon formed a trio, their voices fainter but no less important to Thomas. Surrounded by his friends, he looked toward the nativity scene and was almost overcome by the emotions running through him.

He wished Joseph could see him now, see how far he'd come since those days when the very thought of revealing himself to anyone filled him with terror and shame. How had he ever convinced himself that God, in his infinite capacity to love, would turn away from him for reflecting that same ability? How had he not seen, as Joseph had even in his sickness, that to truly serve God he was obligated to welcome life in all its complexity, all of its contradictions?

Now, viewing a children's pageant, he realized the truth. God could not be contained within the teachings of any church, was not waiting to sit in judgment of him. He had been judging himself based on false assumptions, on what he feared others might find wanting in himself, and in the process he had failed in his duty to the one he professed to serve. But no more. Whatever it brought, he was going to live as the man he was. The thought thrilled him, and as he sang, his voice rose up in joy.

Gavin led them in several more carols. Throughout the singing, Thomas held on to Mike's hand, not wanting to let go. But as the final words of "O, Holy Night" faded away, he let go. "I'm on," he told Mike as he stood and walked to the front of the church.

He looked out at the people seated before him. A serenity had settled over the church, a peace and warmth that radiated from the faces looking back at him. In the last row, Mike, Simon, John, and Russell were watching him.

"As our children have shown us tonight, the message of Christ's birth is one of love and wonder," he said. "Hold this message in your hearts as you celebrate the season. Thank you for joining us tonight. As our angel choir sings for us one more time, please join us in the hall for refreshments. May the peace of the Lord and the blessing of the Spirit be with you and yours."

The congregation gathered itself up as the older angels dutifully followed Gavin's direction of the much-debated Brahms piece. Thomas, giving them an appreciative nod, descended into the mass of people making their way to the adjacent hall. He was stopped several times by those wishing to give him holiday greetings, but eventually he made it back to Mike and the others.

"I guess we'll go," Mike said. "We'll see you later at Simon's, though, right?"

"Go?" Thomas asked. "Why?"

Mike looked at the people streaming past them. "You know," he said. "It's not like we belong here."

"Yes, you do," said Thomas firmly. "Now get in there and eat some cookies."

Mike looked back at John, Russell, and Simon for their reaction.

"I, for one, would love some eggnog," said Simon.

"Cookies sound great," Russell seconded.

"I guess we're staying," Mike told Thomas.

"I'll see you in there in a minute," Thomas said happily. "I have some priest stuff to do."

Thomas disappeared into the sea of departing figures, leaving them to find their way into the hall. Mike followed the crowd, and moments later the men found themselves standing beside a table heaped high with cookies, fudge, and candy. They each got a glass of punch and a small plate of goodies and stood to one side, munching and observing the people around them.

"Do you think they know we're from the dark side?" Simon asked.

"What makes you think some of them aren't queer?" Russell said.

"Can you say 'queer' in a church?" joked Mike as he nibbled on a cookie.

"You can, and I'm sure some of them are," John announced firmly. The others looked at him in surprise.

"What?" he said as he popped a piece of fudge into his mouth. "They're *Episcopal*, for Christ's sake. The entire church owes its existence to the fact that Henry the Eighth wanted a divorce so he could marry Anne Boleyn and the Pope wouldn't give it to him. They're practically founded on deviance."

"While not entirely true, that's essentially correct," Simon opined. "Although 'deviance' is perhaps not the word I would use."

"What would you say?" Russell asked him.

"I prefer 'openness,' " Simon answered. "Both in mind and in sexuality. It is true that gays are quite prominent in the church now, although not everyone is happy about it."

"There's a shock," remarked John. "Religious people not liking us."

"Spoken like a true scientist," Simon said, patting him on the back.

Before they could continue the conversation, they were confronted by a beaming woman dressed from head to toe in red. She carried a plate of cookies, and she smiled at them broadly. "I don't believe I've seen you here before," she said.

"It's our first time," Mike told her.

"Well, welcome to Saint Peter's," the woman said. "I'm Beth-Ann Milliman. I'm in charge of the deaconesses."

"It's nice to meet you," said Mike.

"Are you here alone, or are your wives with you?" Beth-Ann inquired.

Mike looked at his friends for help. Simon stepped forward and smiled at Beth-Ann. "I'm afraid we're all single gentlemen," he said.

"Not all of us," John said.

Simon gave a small smile. "That's right," he said. "I forgot. Mr. Harding and Mr. Ellison are companions."

Beth-Ann looked at John and Russell with a perplexed look, not comprehending. "You're friends?" she said.

"That's right," Russell replied. "Special friends."

"Well, we're happy to have you here," Beth-Ann said after a moment. "I hope we'll see you again."

"Oh, I think you just might," Simon said. "We're quite taken with your pastor."

Before Beth-Ann could respond to the remark, Thomas appeared.

"Father Dunn," Beth-Ann said, sounding relieved. "We were just talking about you. These gentlemen—"

"Could you excuse us for a moment, Beth-Ann?" Thomas said, taking Mike's arm and pulling him away.

"What's going on?" Mike asked when they were away from the crowd. "You look like you've seen a ghost."

"I just spoke with one of our members who knows the Darby family," Thomas said.

"Stephen?" Russell said. "I've been calling him all week, but he never answers."

"He's in the hospital," Thomas said.

"Is he all right?" asked Russell.

Thomas shook his head. "He's alive," he said, "but he's not all right. He overdosed on pain pills."

"What?" Russell said. "Why would he do that?"

"I don't know," said Thomas. "It was probably accidental. But it sounds like he's pretty badly off."

"We have to go see him," Russell said. "Right now."

"We can't," Thomas told him. "He can't have visitors. Not until tomorrow."

Russell looked at the plate in his hand. "What a way to spend Christmas," he said sadly. "Poor guy."

"I'm sure he'll be fine," John said, putting his arm around Russell and pulling him close.

"This sort of puts a damper on things, doesn't it?" Mike said softly.

"It's still Christmas Eve," Thomas reminded him. "And we're all still together."

"That's true," said Simon cheerily. "And tomorrow we will all have Christmas dinner together. As a *family*," he added, stressing the last word.

Thomas looked around the room. "I should go mingle," he said. He turned to Mike. "See you later?"

"Come over when you're done here," Mike told him. "We'll wait up for Santa."

"I'll see you boys tomorrow," Thomas said to the others. "Merry Christmas."

When Thomas was gone, Mike put his plate and cup on the table. "Shall we?" he asked.

They left the hall and went out into the night. The snow was still falling, and over the church the moon shone pale and round against the sky.

"All is calm, all is bright, indeed," Simon said as they walked to their cars and prepared to head for home.

CHAPTER 31

"And may all your Christmases be bright."

Pete stared dully at the television. On the screen some teenage pop singer he didn't recognize was singing. Dressed in a white fur coat, she stood surrounded by dancers dressed as carolers. Fake snow tumbled from somewhere above her, littering the stage. The girl beamed, flashing impossibly white teeth.

"Fuck you, bitch," Pete said. He changed the channel. An animated Rudolph pranced across the screen, his nose glowing red. Pete banished him with another press of the remote button, replacing the reindeer with a talking snowman. He ran quickly through some of the other channels. Even goddamned MTV was showing Christmas videos.

He threw the remote down in disgust and reached for the bottle on the table. Pouring a healthy shot of Jack Daniels into the glass in his hand, he drank deeply. The whiskey burned his throat, but after a quarter of a bottle he was used to it. Besides, whiskey was the quickest way to get into a festive fucking mood, wasn't it?

He'd just had Christmas Eve dinner at his mother's house, putting up with her annoying cheerfulness. She'd made too much food, as usual, and the neighbors who stopped by had barely put a dent in it. Pete had stayed as long as necessary, promising to come back in the morning to open presents, then headed home to escape the merriment.

His buddies were all with their own families, doing whatever it was they did to celebrate the holiday. Pete wished it was all over, so life could return to normal. The last couple of weeks had been totally fucked up, what with having to shop for presents for his mother and endure the craziness that came with the holiday season. He couldn't wait for New Year's. Then they'd have a real party. It was going to be at his place this year, and he had plans.

But New Year's was a week away, and right now he had nothing to do but drink and wait for it all to end. There weren't any good movies on. Christ, he thought, he might as well turn the TV off and go to bed. But he wasn't tired. He was just bored. There had to be something to do, some way to amuse himself.

He thought about putting in a porn tape. But ever since the night T.J. had stayed over, he'd been unable to get off from looking at porn. Whenever he tried, he remembered what had happened and felt sick to his stomach. Nothing had happened, he corrected himself, as he had been all week. Nothing. He'd dreamed it all. If anything *had* happened, it would mean he was something he most definitely was not. Only someone like that could do the things he'd dreamed he'd done to T.J. that night.

Then why was T.J. acting all weird, he asked himself. Why hadn't T.J. called or stopped by? Why had he hurried out the next morning when they'd woken up, saying he had to get home to do something? Why hadn't he looked Pete in the eye when he'd said goodbye?

It was nothing, Pete told himself. T.J. had just been in a hurry. And he'd been busy. He'd come around again soon enough. He'd be there for the New Year's party, along with Gary, Ronnie, and everyone else he was inviting. They'd all be there, and they'd have an amazing fucking time. He wouldn't think about that night ever again.

Maybe, he thought, he'd invite the girl he'd been introduced to at the bar the other night, the one who'd looked like she wanted him to do her right there on the table. What was her name? Carolyn. That was it. Carolyn. Pretty face. Nice tits. He'd thought about fucking her, taking her out to his car and screwing her in the backseat. Maybe he'd give it to her good on New Year's, ring in the year with a good hard bang.

He drained his glass and refilled it. He was feeling better. The bullshit he'd been thinking about T.J. wasn't anything to worry about. It was just something he'd imagined, that was all. A really bad fucking dream. He hadn't actually put his mouth on another guy's tool. Only queers did that shit.

He wouldn't mind having a mouth on *his* dick, though, he thought.

He hadn't had his cock sucked in a long time. Not since the faggot at the rest stop. He could use a good blowjob. It would relax him. He'd be able to sleep.

But where would he find someone to blow him on Christmas Eve? Nobody was going to be hanging out in a men's room or a truck stop looking for cock tonight. They'd all be home, even the faggots. They had to take a break sometime, he guessed. They couldn't spend every night on their knees.

He laughed at the image in his mind, a queer on his knees sucking off Santa Claus. It was funny. He pictured Santa's big hairy belly hanging out while some fag pulled on his dick. "You want Santa to come down your chimney?" he imagined old Nick saying.

He stood up, his head swimming a little. Maybe he could find some action after all. Maybe there were some desperate homos sitting around with nothing better to do than give his prong a wash. Taking the bottle of Jack with him, he went into his bedroom and to the computer that sat on his makeshift desk. He'd bought it to play video games and burn CDs on, but he'd discovered it had other uses as well. He sat in front of it and signed on to his online service.

He'd discovered the chat rooms accidentally while poking around his Internet service. He'd been surprised to see rooms with names like BiM4M and M4MJONow. The first time he'd entered such a room, nothing had been going on. It wasn't until a little window appeared on his screen and someone asked him if he wanted to get off that he'd understood. Even then, it had taken some time for him to really get into the game. He'd spent a long time just sitting in rooms, looking at the profiles of other users, waiting for people to approach him.

Finally he'd made up his own profile. It was largely the truth, with a few important details changed. And it seemed to work. Guys liked him. They sent him pictures of themselves, faceless images of them with their hard cocks in their hands. He never sent one back, but it didn't seem to matter. They never turned him down. They always did what he asked them to.

He usually limited himself to rooms with generic titles: M4MJocks, MilitaryM4M, StrtM4JO. But lately he'd been looking at other rooms, ones where men met to meet in real life. He'd never ventured into one, afraid of identifying himself geographically. More and more often, though, he'd found himself wondering what he might find in

M4MUpstateNY. Would there be anyone from Cold Falls, anyone near enough to actually come over and drain his balls or, better, let him come to him? He found the idea exciting, but also terrifying. What if he should encounter someone he knew? Someone like T.J.?

That would never happen, of course. T.J. was no more queer than he was. Still, he'd been cautious. Fucking around with people he couldn't see was one thing; meeting them in the flesh was different. But he couldn't deny the attraction of it. He'd had some hot times with his electronic buddies, with one in particular. He wondered idly what had happened to the guy. What had his name been? Pound-something? Cake? It had struck Pete as a stupid name. But the guy had been into anything. They'd fooled around a couple of times.

Maybe he'd run into pound cake tonight, but he doubted it. Even if he did, he wasn't interested in online play. Having accepted the idea, he now had his heart set on real live action. That is, if he could find any. He still had his doubts that there would be anyone within a two-hour drive of Cold Falls.

He found the list of rooms and searched for M4MUpstateNY. There it was. According to the listing, there were twenty-three people in it. Jesus Christ, didn't faggots take a break even on Christmas? He logged himself in and looked at the list of members. The names were all new to him. Apparently none of them ever ventured into the rooms he frequented.

He clicked on a couple of profiles that sounded promising, but rejected them for one reason or another. Finally, toward the bottom of the list, he came across one that caught his eye: CldFllsGy. Selecting it, he read the details. The man indeed claimed to be from Cold Falls. The rest was immaterial. Pete opened an instant message box and typed a query: Looking for some fun?

He waited impatiently for a response. In his experience, if people didn't reply quickly, they were busy with someone else. He had no interest in reeling someone in; he wanted a hungry one. When a window popped open, he raised a fist in triumph.

CldFllsGy: What's up?

Pete continued the direct approach with his reply: My cock. Want 2 suck it?

He poured himself some more Jack and downed it. His foot tapped against the floor impatiently. What the fuck was taking so long? Either the fag was interested or he wasn't. A ding broke the silence as the answer came back: Pic?

"Fuck a pic!" Pete muttered. He wrote back: No. Got 8 thick and cut. Big balls.

It took very little time for CldFllsGy to get back to him. Where R U? he asked.

Pete knew he had him. They always went for the big cock. And in his case, he wasn't lying. He felt his dick stiffen as he wrote back to his quarry: Cold Falls 2.

It was a risk, he knew. Cold Falls wasn't that big a place, and although it was unlikely, it was possible he was talking to someone who would recognize him. But now he was anxious to have his dick sucked. Besides, he wasn't the one looking to be the cocksucker. He wasn't the fag here. He had nothing to be ashamed of.

CldFllsGy: Come to my place?

A few more exchanges later and Pete had the address. He told CldFllsGy he'd be there in fifteen minutes and grabbed his jacket. He knew he probably shouldn't be driving, but it wasn't far, and he'd be careful.

Right on time, he pulled into the driveway of the house whose address he'd scrawled on the scrap of paper. Decorated with Christmas lights, it looked like all the other houses on the street. But unless someone was fucking with him, waiting inside was a queer who was going to do exactly what Pete told him to do.

He got out and walked to the door. He rang the bell and waited. A few moments later the door opened and he found himself looking at a guy not much older than he was. He was dressed in jeans and a T-shirt.

"I'm Greg," he said. "Come on in."

Pete stepped inside and the queer shut the door. The house was nice, nicer than Pete's. It looked like the fag made some money. The furniture was new and it all looked kind of expensive. From somewhere the sound of a woman singing a Christmas song floated into the foyer. Pete noticed that Greg wasn't wearing shoes, probably so he wouldn't track anything onto the clean floors. Fuck him. Pete wasn't about to take his boots off for any faggot.

"Quite a way to spend Christmas Eve, huh?" Greg said. He was just standing there, looking Pete up and down. It made Pete sick to see the queer sizing him up. He was lucky Pete was going to let him suck him off.

"Just another night," Pete said surlily.

"Yeah," Greg answered. "I guess it is. So, you want a drink?"

"No," Pete said. "Let's get to it."

Greg nodded. "Whatever you want," he said. His words seemed a little dulled, and Pete noticed for the first time a mostly empty bottle of vodka on the coffee table. Apparently he wasn't the only one who'd been drinking.

Greg walked into the living room and Pete followed him. Greg motioned to a leather armchair. "Make yourself comfortable," he said. "Do you mind if I leave Barbra on? She kind of sets a mood, you know?"

"Whatever," Pete said. He assumed the fag was talking about the crappy music that was playing. He didn't care if it stayed on or not. He undid his belt buckle and pushed his jeans down. His cock sprang free and stood out from his crotch. He saw Greg eye it greedily. *That's right,* Pete thought. *And you're going to take it all.*

He sat down in the chair, spreading his legs. He grabbed his dick and stroked it a few times, giving Greg a good view. The queer came over and stood in front of him, looking down. What the fuck was he waiting for?

"Suck it," Pete said.

Greg lowered himself to his knees. Looking into his face, Pete realized that he was drunker than he'd seemed at first. He knelt there, swaying slightly as he stared at the cock in front of his face.

Pete grabbed him by the hair and pulled him down. His dick hit Greg in the face and he opened his mouth, clumsily putting the head of Pete's dick between his lips. When he slid forward, his teeth scraped the sides of Pete's cock.

"Jesus Christ!" Pete said. "Watch it!"

Greg looked up at him, the head of Pete's cock still between his lips. He seemed unable to move. Then he started to cry. He let Pete's dick slip from his mouth and sat back on his heels, bawling like a little kid.

"What the fuck is wrong with you?" Pete asked, growing angry.

Greg shook his head. "Just go," he blubbered. "Go."

"Not until you blow me," Pete said.

"Get out," Greg said, his voice rising. "I don't want you here."

Pete grabbed the queer by the neck and pulled him back toward him. He tried to shove his cock in the man's mouth. "Suck it!" he yelled. "Suck my fucking cock!"

Greg pushed against him, forcing himself away. He sprawled on the floor. "I was supposed to be home," he said quietly. "For Christmas. Then my father called and said he didn't want me there. He didn't want his faggot son to come home." He looked up at Pete with drunken eyes. "I just wanted to be with someone tonight," he said. "That's all. I didn't want to be alone."

"Fuck you," Pete said. He didn't care what the fag wanted, or why he was home alone on Christmas Eve. This wasn't about him. It was about what Pete wanted. He stood up and advanced toward Greg. If the faggot wouldn't suck him off voluntarily, he was going to get what he wanted by force.

He grabbed Greg by the shirt, holding him in place. With his other hand, he whipped the queer's face with his cock, smacking him in the mouth.

"Suck it, faggot," he ordered. "Suck it now."

Greg pushed him away. Pete, enraged, brought his fist down against Greg's face. He heard the queer cry out as his nose crunched. He was just like the cocksucker at the theater, too weak to fight back. Pete hit him again.

He continued to hit, bringing his fist down again and again. At first Greg made an attempt to protect his face, but after a minute he went limp. Blood dripped from his face onto the floor. Seeing it, Pete let the man go and he slumped to the floor. Pete kicked him in the stomach.

"Get up!" he screamed. "Get your faggot ass up!"

Greg didn't move. Pete kicked him again. He felt something snap. Why wasn't the faggot trying to protect himself? Why was he letting Pete beat the shit out of him?

Because it's what he wants, a voice said. *It's what he wants you to do to him.*

Pete knew it was true. All the queers who'd ever sucked him off, that's what they'd wanted, wasn't it? The fag at the theater, the one at the truck stop. They all wanted him to use them. Well, he'd give this one what he wanted.

He continued to kick Greg, watching the blood spatter and enjoying the soft thuds his boot made against the queer's chest. Finally, his
anger drained enough that he saw how much blood there was, he
stopped. Through the foggy haze that enveloped him, he saw that he
had to leave. He'd done what he'd needed to, and the fag had gotten
what he wanted. Their meeting was over.

He left Greg on the floor and walked to his car. Turning the radio
up, he put the car into gear and pulled away, leaving the front door
open. From inside the house, Barbra Streisand wished the world
peace on earth.

CHAPTER 32

At eleven o'clock on Christmas Day, Mike Monaghan unlocked the back door of the Engine Room and stepped inside. Flipping a switch, he brought to life the garlands of twinkling lights that had been strung throughout the bar's main room. Another flip of another switch turned on the bar's sound system, and holiday music filled the air. Mike, standing in the middle of the bar and looking around, had never felt more depressed.

He had been woken up shortly after five by a kiss on the cheek from Thomas, who had spent the night. Rubbing the dreams from his eyes, he'd managed a mumbled "Merry Christmas" as Thomas had dressed and prepared to go to church, where he was presiding over a morning service. Mike, watching him dress, had wished the two of them could spend the morning together. But each had the needs of their followers to attend to, and so they had parted.

Mike had slept awhile longer, enjoying the warmth of the bed and the memory of Thomas's body lying next to his. They'd yet to make love, or even to be naked with one another. But twice they'd shared a bed, sleeping with arms around one another, one's back pressed against the other's stomach. Mike was certain that at some point during their nightly cycles of dreaming, during the shifting of positions that occurred in the deepest stages of sleep, erect cocks had undoubtedly butted against unsuspecting bodies, fingers had unconsciously fallen upon and stroked exposed skin, but for all practical purposes their relationship was as yet unconsummated.

Without ever having discussed it, they were waiting. For what or when, exactly, Mike wasn't sure. He knew only that the time had not yet come. Until it did, he and Thomas were exploring one another, talking and questioning and finding in one another something that delighted them equally. They were like children who, distanced from the world around them by illness, or difference, or the watchful eye of a nervous parent, had spent long hours staring from a bedroom window, watching others at play and longing for a special playmate. Now, having discovered one another, they were caught up in the innocent joy of discovery.

With the realization that he was falling in love with Thomas had come, however, a reawakening of a fear Mike had tried to bury. Along with the excitement of finding someone with whom he felt comfortable had come a flicker of doubt, a tiny nagging worry that it would never last. He had tried to ignore the feeling, but it had been persistent, returning again and again despite his best efforts to push it away. Nothing lasted forever. The freshest emotions would eventually sour. Even the most solid of foundations hid fault lines that, once disturbed, would result in crumbling. It had happened to him before, first with his family and then with Jim. He was not someone who was destined for happiness.

When he was with Thomas, he was able to pretend that the enchantment would last, that the golden light that seemed to surround them at all times would never succumb to the shadows of doubt. But when he was alone, his strength waned, and the demons of worry pounced upon him, pinching at him mercilessly and whispering to him of failure. There was no reason to believe, they said, that things would be different this time. Why should they be?

Because Thomas was different, he argued. Because he was kind, and because he wasn't demanding anything. True, the demons countered in their ugly, hypnotic voices, but there were also many things standing in the way, not the least of which was Almighty God. How, they asked, did Mike think he would be able to stand up to such competition? And even if he should win that battle, how would he fill the hole left in Thomas's heart afterward?

They were right, of course. He knew that. Even if he and Thomas did fall in love, where would it lead them? Would Thomas forsake his church for a man he loved? Would he turn his entire world upside down to pursue a life he'd never even let himself imagine, to become someone he freely admitted he'd always been terrified of?

"You had to go and fall for a priest," Mike said out loud to the empty room. "You couldn't settle for a drunk or a tweaker; you had to find one who's addicted to God. There's no twelve-step program for that."

He walked behind the bar and looked around. The Christmas lights were reflected in the glass of the bottles, tiny, bright stars of color shining against a clear vodka sky. The whiskey glowed warmly, promising forgetfulness. The glasses, lined up like soldiers awaiting deployment, gaped at him with open mouths.

In less than an hour the bar would begin to fill with men seeking solace from the events of the morning. Either having no family or having too much family, they would come in from the cold, leaving outside the memories of strained holiday rituals. With bottles of beer and glasses clinking with the sounds of swirling ice cubes, they would rid themselves of the ghosts of Christmases past and present, until everything around them blurred and the interiors of their heads filled with dizzying warmth. And Mike, like some kind of modern-day Marley, would aid them on their journeys with the tip of a bottle, the squeeze of a lime. Standing behind the bar, he would watch the spectacle play out as it did after every holiday, the participants gamely waltzing through the familiar moves. Sugarplum fairies, indeed.

He couldn't do it. Not again. He was tired of the same old show, weary of the unhappiness and the forced camaraderie he helped perpetuate. Yes, some of the men who came to the Engine Room were his friends. Some of them he cared about, and some cared about him. But by and large the men who gathered there were strangers to one another. They knew, sometimes, one another's names, perhaps a few small details about each other's lives. Just enough to convince them that they were friends.

But that was all. Seldom did their curiosity about one another extend any further than finding out more, unless perhaps it was to seek out the answers to questions answered in the bedroom: How big was he? Did he give it or take it? What secret desires did he have? These things they might display some interest in knowing, might even spend some time and effort into researching, but once they had their answers, the spotlight of their curiosity quickly panned to another face, another crotch, another distraction.

None of them were looking for anything real. They might tell themselves they were, but they lied. Mike had seen enough during his years in various bars to know that ultimately they were simply prisons, cells in which condemned men waiting to die spent their time. Oh, they always hoped for a pardon, for someone to come along and release them from whatever held them there. And sometimes, briefly, they were granted a reprieve. But almost always they came back after a time, looking even wearier than they had before they left. Over time they grew accustomed to their fate, until finally, accepting it, their faces acquired a resignedness that masqueraded as contentment.

Mike looked in the mirror behind the bar. Unblinking, he examined his face closely. Had it changed? Had the years yet taken their toll? It was the eyes that told the story. In the beginning they shined brightly, darting here and there like rabbits crossing a field as they tried to take in everything at once. Gradually they slowed and grew dull as the field of vision narrowed, as the spirit that lit them up from within was drained, until finally they looked out at the world as dull, dirtied windows clouded over with the grime of disappointment.

Did he have eyes like that? He leaned forward and looked closely. No, he hadn't yet come to that point. He was simply tired. Despite the rest he found with Thomas in his bed, his face bore the marks of sleeplessness. He was growing older. The Engine Room, its patrons, were slowly draining him of his soul. How long until it was gone completely? A week? A month? A year?

It wasn't their fault. He understood that. They needed the bar, and the bar needed them. And it wasn't all bad. There was happiness contained in the walls, a sense of place and belonging that kept everything from falling in on itself. But the balance was delicate, and more and more he felt himself tipping the wrong way. He'd been there too long, spent too many hours among the lost and the directionless.

"How about a shot of Christmas cheer?"

Mike turned and saw his first customer of the day. Ernie Cheddum. Ernie walked to the bar and sat down, undoing his coat. Underneath he wore an unflattering burgundy sweater patterned all over with white snowflakes.

"From my mother," he said, noticing Mike looking at the sweater. "I wear it home from her house and then never put it on again."

Mike continued to stare at Ernie's sweater. The snowflakes had begun to move, swirling around and around in front of his eyes, becoming a blinding storm. Through the falling flakes he saw Ernie looking at him with sad eyes.

"It's not *that* ugly," he said. "Now how about that shot?"

Mike reached for a bottle of scotch and set it on the counter in front of Ernie. "It's on the house," he said as he walked from behind the bar and toward the front door.

"Thanks," said Ernie as he poured himself a glass. "Where are you going?"

"Dale will be in in fifteen minutes," Mike said. "Tell him I took the day off."

Ernie watched, confused, as Mike rushed out the door. Climbing into his truck, he started it and pulled out of the parking lot, fishtailing as the truck's rear tires skidded on the ice. Driving as quickly as he could on the slick road, he raced toward Saint Peter's. When he arrived, he pulled up in front of the rectory, got out, and walked to the door. Not bothering to knock, he went inside.

"Thomas?" he called out as he went from room to room.

"Up here."

He heard Thomas's voice, puzzled, calling to him from the house's second story. Bounding up the stairs, he discovered the priest in his bedroom.

"What's wrong?" Thomas asked. "I was just getting ready to go over to Simon's."

Mike stood in the doorway, staring at Thomas. He had apparently just stepped out of the shower. A white towel was wrapped around his waist, and his torso was bare. His hair, still damp, was playfully unkempt. Suddenly Mike recalled one of his early fantasies about Thomas: Thomas getting out of the shower, his hair wet, just as it was now.

"Tell me it will be okay," he said.

Thomas looked at him. "What will be okay?" he asked.

"Me," Mike said. "You. This. Us. Everything. Tell me it won't all fall apart."

Thomas bit his lip, thinking. He regarded Mike for what seemed like far too long. "It will be okay," he said.

Mike shook his head. "Not good enough," he said. "You don't sound convinced."

Thomas crossed his arms over his chest and leaned against the door frame. "I can't promise," he said. "Nobody can. All I can tell you is that I want it to be okay."

"But how do you know?" asked Mike. "How do you know we won't wake up one morning and it will all be over?" He looked at Thomas, feeling his heart struggling not to break. "I'm tired of running," he said.

Thomas stepped forward and held out his arms. "Then come home," he said.

Mike went to him. Thomas's arms closed around him, pulling him close. Mike smelled soap and honey.

"I don't know what's going to happen," Thomas whispered softly. "I've been running too, and I don't know what happens when you finally stand still. Maybe everything you've been running from comes crashing into you. Maybe you fall down and have to get back up again. I don't know. But whatever it is, we'll find out together."

Mike leaned back and looked into his eyes. They were bright, unclouded. Thomas smiled at him. "What?"

"You're so beautiful," Mike said.

He leaned in and kissed Thomas. This time, he didn't pull away when he was done. Instead, he kissed Thomas again, more deeply. His hands went to the towel and pulled it free. It fell to the floor, and for the first time his hands touched the smooth globes of Thomas's bare ass. His fingers ran over warm skin as he pressed himself against Thomas and felt naked muscle meet him.

They moved toward the bed, neither breaking contact. Thomas tugged Mike's shirt from his jeans and helped him pull it over his head. Shoes, socks, and pants followed, until both were undressed. Then they were on the bed, Thomas on his back and Mike atop him, their bodies sliding against each other.

Mike, a veteran of numerous encounters with different men, now felt as if he'd never touched another man before. Thomas, who hadn't, felt each finger, each kiss, each pressing of flesh against flesh, with breathtaking intensity. When his hands, wandering over Mike's body, followed the line of hair down his belly and felt for the first time the thickness of his cock, the heaviness of his balls against his palm, his mouth opened in a cry of delight.

His reaction was repeated moments later when Mike, lowering

himself between Thomas's thighs, took Thomas's dick into his mouth. He was surrounded by warmth as Mike slid up and down the length of him, tugging at the head of his cock, toying with his balls. When Mike wet a finger and slid it up inside him, Thomas clutched the sheets beneath him.

Mike continued to work Thomas's cock with his mouth as he gently eased him open. Thomas, his head spinning with each new sensation, anticipated what was coming and welcomed Mike's fingers. When they retreated and Mike positioned himself, pushing Thomas's knees back slightly, Thomas held his breath, waiting.

Mike went slowly, proceeding only when Thomas was ready. With only the moisture of his own mouth to ease his entry, he knew he had to take it easy. But his desire for Thomas made it difficult, and when finally his stomach pressed against the cheeks of Thomas's ass and he knew he could go no farther, he began to move in and out with more speed. Beneath him, Thomas breathed heavily, not in pain but with excitement. Mike, looking into his face, saw there an expression of rapture.

Thomas's legs went around Mike's waist, pulling him deeper. Feeling himself enveloped by Thomas's thighs, Mike leaned down, kissing him while continuing to pump his hips. Thomas's tongue met his, probing, and Mike felt the hardness of Thomas's cock as it was sandwiched between them.

When he felt himself getting close, he leaned back and pulled out. Holding his dick against Thomas's, he jerked them both the rest of the way. With his balls slapping against Thomas's he came, crying out as a thick jet of cum shot from his swollen head and rained down on Thomas's chest. Thomas was right behind him, his cock pulsing repeatedly as he emptied himself along the length of Mike's dick. Sticky wet heat slathered Mike's fingers and he continued his strokes, their combined loads slicking their still-hard shafts.

Mike continued to hold Thomas against him as they softened, not wanting to let go. Bending down, he stretched himself along the length of Thomas's body, the cum on their bodies cementing them together. Bound like this, they kissed for a long time as the glow of orgasm wrapped them in its cocoon. When they finally parted, Mike rolling over to lie beside Thomas, it was with contented sighs. They remained like that for a long time, holding hands and lost in their thoughts. After a few minutes Thomas rolled onto his side and peered down at Mike.

"Well?" Mike said. "Was it worth waiting for?"

Thomas grinned. "Oh, yeah," he said. "I just have one question?"

Mike raised his eyebrows, waiting.

"Is it as much fun being on top?"

"Why?" Mike asked suspiciously.

Thomas took Mike's hand and guided it down between his legs, where his cock was beginning to swell to life again. "Because I'd really like to find out," Thomas said as he lowered his head toward Mike's crotch.

CHAPTER 33

"What have you two been up to?"

Mike and Thomas exchanged a glance then looked at Simon. He was standing in the doorway of his house, while they waited on the front step, holding a green bean casserole and several bottles of wine. Neither of them answered the question.

"Well?" Simon said, crossing his arms over his chest.

"It's freezing out here," said Mike. "Let us in."

Simon shook his head. "Not until you tell me what's been going on."

"What makes you think we've been up to anything?" Mike asked.

"Please," replied Simon. "You're redder than Rudolph's nose, and this one has a grin on his face a mile wide. You've been very bad little boys, haven't you?"

"Will there be coal in our stockings?" Thomas asked.

"I think your stockings have been filled with much more interesting things," Simon answered primly. "Now get inside before I catch my death of pneumonia."

Thomas and Mike hurried in, where they were greeted by Russell, who hugged them both and said, "You're late. What happened, couldn't get out of bed?"

"Why does everyone think we were doing something?" Thomas asked, trying to sound irritated and doing a very poor job of it.

"You *were* in bed!" Russell exclaimed as John emerged from the kitchen.

"Where's Greg?" Mike asked as he handed Simon the wine and took his coat off. "I hear he decided to stay here after all. How come?"

"He's not here yet," Russell told him, "and don't try to change the subject."

"There is no subject to change," said Mike.

"Like hell there isn't," protested Russell. "So, are you two officially an item now? Won't you get burned at the stake or something?" he added, addressing Thomas. "I mean, isn't it illegal for priests to be queer?"

"There are people in the church who aren't wild about the idea of gay priests, true," Thomas said, taking a seat on the couch.

"That's the understatement of the year," remarked Simon as he returned with wineglasses and one of the bottles Mike and Thomas had brought over. "Look what happened in New Hampshire when Robinson was made a bishop. You'd have thought a serial killer had been installed at Canterbury."

"What is the official position on the subject?" asked John, taking a seat across from Thomas.

Thomas sighed. "The Episcopal Church recognizes that God's children come in many different forms," he said as he took a sip of wine.

"Seriously," Mike said, "what do they have to say about it?"

Thomas held his glass in his hand, staring down at it. "That depends on who you ask," he said. "Different parishes have different views."

"But there must be *some* official opinion," Russell pressed.

Thomas gave a small laugh. "Officially, we welcome everyone," he said. "Unofficially, we would prefer that our priests not talk about what they may or may not do in the privacy of their bedrooms."

"Don't ask, don't tell," John summarized.

"Something like that," said Thomas. "Bishop Robinson's consecration caused a stir primarily because he lives openly as a gay man with his partner."

"And if he stayed in the closet?" asked Mike.

Thomas shrugged. "Who knows? Maybe nothing. The point is, he *isn't* in the closet, and that's what upsets people. Many people in the church are perfectly willing to accept gay people in theory. It's when they actually dare to *be* gay people that there's a problem."

"Love the sinner, hate the sin," Simon said tersely. "Isn't that what so many of our religious leaders are fond of saying when it comes to this particular discussion?"

"It's an easy way around what a bishop of mine used to refer to as the 'Gay Problem.' You can be a homosexual, you just can't engage in homosexuality. At least not if you don't want to make God throw up."

"How magnanimous," quipped Simon as he cut a piece of cheese and placed it on a cracker.

"When you think about it, it's sort of like what the Catholic Church asks of its clergy," Thomas said. "You can have a sexual identity, you just aren't allowed to ever act upon it. The idea is that by fighting temptation, you become stronger spiritually."

"Meanwhile, three quarters of them are sticking their dicks in altar boys' behinds," said Russell.

"It seems to put being gay on a par with, say, alcoholism or drug addiction," Simon mused.

"Really, I think the majority of people in the church really don't care what anyone does in bed," said Thomas. "But the ones who do make such a noise about it that we're forced to make it an issue."

"Which brings us back to where we started," Mike said. "What does this mean for you?"

"Honestly? I don't know," answered Thomas. "I'm trying not to think too far ahead."

"A sensible plan," Simon told him, raising his glass. "In the meantime, welcome to our little family."

"I always thought your were a fag," said Russell, earning him a slap on the arm from John. "What? I did. I'm sorry if the rest of you have defective gaydar. Besides, do you think it's an accident that his car broke down and Mike helped him? No. It was fate."

"The meeting with Mr. Monaghan does seem to be rather providential," agreed Simon.

Thomas looked at Mike. "God works in mysterious ways," he said.

"Speaking of Mr. Monaghan," John said, "shouldn't you still be at work?"

"I sort of took a leave of absence," Mike said. "A mental health break."

"The two of you are filled with surprises this afternoon," said Simon. "What's next?"

"Dinner, if Greg ever gets here," John said, looking at his watch. "Do we know what's keeping him?"

"He's always late," Russell said. "I'm sure he'll be here in a few minutes." He stood and picked up the cheese plate. "I'll go get some more crackers," he said.

"I need a refill," said Mike, looking down at his empty glass. "I'll come with you."

"Check on the ham while you're in there," Simon told them.

Mike followed Russell into the kitchen. As Russell fussed with the cheese and crackers, Mike opened the oven. Satisfied that the ham was taking care of itself, he went to the refrigerator and refilled his glass with iced tea. He drank some and leaned against the counter, watching Russell.

"Want to tell me what's wrong?"

"Nothing's wrong," Russell said, a little too quickly. He sliced some Gouda and placed it on the plate. "Why?"

"You seem edgy," explained Mike. "Are things not working out with John?"

"It's not John," answered Russell, unwrapping some brie. "It's Greg."

"Greg?" Mike repeated.

Russell nodded as he fanned crackers around the edge of the plate. "Remember how you and Simon were teasing me about him a few weeks ago?"

"Yeah," Mike said. "When you got so bent out of shape about him chasing after that trick."

"Well, you were right," said Russell. "Sort of, anyway. I was upset about it. So I thought maybe he and I should, you know . . ."

"Really?" Mike said, surprised, as Russell let the sentence hang, unfinished, between them. "You and Greg?"

"Quiet," Russell ordered, looking toward the kitchen door. "Anyway, it didn't happen. I couldn't do it."

"Why?"

"It just didn't seem right," said Russell, cleaning up the cheese wrappers and dropping the knife he'd been using into the sink. "It's hard to explain. Anyway, he said it was okay, but I think maybe he was angry at me. When he said he was staying here for Christmas, I invited him to come with us last night, but he said he had other plans."

"Maybe he did," Mike suggested.

"It was the way he said it," Russell said. "I think he'd been drinking. And now he's not here."

"I'm sure he'll show up," said Mike reassuringly. "You have too much drama in your life."

"Said the man sleeping with the priest," Russell countered.

"Good point," admitted Mike. "And now probably the man with no job."

"You think they'll fire you for skipping out?"

"Even if they don't, I don't think I can go back," said Mike. "I think it's time to move on."

"To what?" asked Russell.

"Who knows?" replied Mike. "Whatever's next. I haven't thought a lot about it."

Russell looked at him curiously. "Don't run away from him," he said.

"Away from who?" Mike asked.

"Thomas," Russell said. "You're thinking about it. I see it in your face."

Mike laughed. "I'm not running anywhere," he said.

Russell said nothing, but he fixed Mike with a hard look. "You'd better not be," he said as he picked up the cheese plate and turned toward the door.

They returned to the living room, where in their absence Simon and John had gotten into a heated discussion. Thomas, looking bewildered, was sitting quietly on the couch, listening to them.

"What are you girls yakking about in here?" asked Russell as he put the plate on the coffee table. "More church talk?"

"Your lover had the audacity to say that Gwyneth Paltrow is the new Audrey Hepburn," Simon said indignantly. "That stick of a girl wishes she were half as talented as Audrey was."

"Remember that pink dress she wore when she won the Oscar?" said Russell. "She looked so glamorous."

"She looked like an emaciated peppermint stick," Simon said caustically.

"Why is it all you old queens get so angry whenever anyone suggests that a new star is as good as one of your beloved divas?" asked John. "It's so annoying. I'm sorry Bette and Joan and whoever are dead and gone, but get over it."

"I will not get over it," Simon insisted, only half joking. "These new girls have no idea what being a star means. They think they can put on a British accent or play someone with a handicap and that makes them special."

"Unlike Bette Davis, who made a career out of accents and handicaps," John retorted.

"Welcome to gay Christmas," Mike said to Thomas as he sat down. "This little spat will be followed by an hour-long debate on the best way to moisturize."

"Here's an idea," Russell said suddenly. "How about presents?"

The Gwyneth versus Audrey argument came to an end as Simon and John grudgingly agreed to postpone the discussion to a later time. Russell, his excitement restored by the prospect of gifts, acted as delivery man, handing out presents from a pile sitting beneath the tree he and Simon had put up earlier in the week. He read the names on the tags and handed them round.

"And here's one for you," he said as he presented Thomas with a parcel wrapped in red paper and tied with a green bow.

"I'm afraid I didn't get you anything," Thomas said, sounding embarrassed.

"Don't worry," Russell reassured him. "You have until New Year's to make up for it."

"But now you have to make it *really* good," Mike whispered to him. "Otherwise you'll hear about it all year long."

Thomas pulled at the bow on the package. It came off easily, and was soon followed by the paper. Inside was a Carter-Beane box. And inside the box was a scarf. It was cashmere, deep red, and very soft. As he fingered the material, Thomas looked around and saw the others looking down at or holding up the same scarf, in different colors.

"I know, it's a cop-out," Russell said. "But it's been a rough month."

"Can we exchange them?" Mike asked, laughing as Russell threw a bow at him. He wrapped his dark blue scarf around his neck. "This is great," he said. "Thanks."

"Am I the only one who actually got gifts?" Russell asked, looking around at his friends.

"You are not," Simon said. "Mine, however, are upstairs, hidden from the prying eyes of nosy young people. I'll return momentarily."

He stood up and left the room, leaving the others to discuss the possible contents of the boxes he would be returning with.

"I hope it's not homemade jam, like last year," Mike said quietly.

"Or fruitcake," added John. "Remember those?"

They laughed. Then, turning serious for a moment, Mike turned to Russell. "Are you going to see Stephen later?"

Russell nodded. He looked at John. "Will you come with me? I'm sure he'd like to see you."

John hesitated. "I don't know," he said. "He's more your friend."

"He's *our* friend," Russell said.

Before John could answer him, there was a knock on the door. Russell stood up. "It's probably Greg," he said.

He threw open the door, exclaiming, "It's about time, you bitch!"

Officer Wayne Chenoweth regarded him with an expression of shock mixed with irritation. He had been called away from his own family's Christmas to deal with the matter at hand, and his wife had been none too happy to be left alone with two hyperactive children and a pile of new toys, most of which either made noise or required assembly. But he quickly masked his annoyance and addressed Russell Harding for the second time in as many months.

"What are you doing here?" Russell asked, confused.

"You're a friend of Greg Mihalski, is that correct?" the officer asked him.

Russell nodded. "Yes," he said.

"Mr. Mihalski was attacked last night," Officer Chenoweth continued.

"Oh, my God," Russell said. "Is he okay?"

"He was beaten quite severely," answered the cop. "Apparently he has no family in the area, but he gave me this address and told me I would find some of his friends here."

"That's right," Russell said, nodding.

"Could I come in?" the policeman asked.

"I'm sorry," Russell said. "Of course."

He stepped aside and allowed the officer to come in. As Wayne Chenoweth entered the foyer, Simon was coming down the stairs. He was carrying an armload of presents and had put a Santa hat on his head. When he saw the uniformed man standing in the hallway of his house, he stopped.

"I assume," he said, looking from Officer Chenoweth to the distraught expression on Russell's face, "that you have not come bearing tidings of comfort and joy."

CHAPTER 34

The fourth floor of Mercy Hospital—recently rechristened the Binny Sellwidge Houghton Memorial Wing, after the wife of a local auto dealership owner who, moved by the staff's treatment of his spouse of fifty-three years during her three-month battle with and subsequent death from cirrhosis of the liver, had donated slightly more than one million dollars in her memory before discovering at her funeral that for more than half of their marriage his beloved helpmate had been carrying on an adulterous affair with his best friend—smelled, as all hospitals do, of disinfectant and decaying flowers. The fluorescent lights spraying the linoleum-tiled floor with their harsh glare did little to boost its appeal; nor did the grim-faced nurses and orderlies who paced the halls in thick-soled shoes, clipboards in their hands and eyes on the clock, counting the minutes until they could go home.

Nobody liked working the Christmas shift. It was when the suicides came calling, the alcoholics and manic-depressives who, driven to the brink of distraction by the holidays, decided to finally do something about it. They seldom succeeded, and consequently became the problem of the women and men who had been such a boon to Binny Sellwidge Houghton in her final days. They tended to their charges with barely disguised irritation, administering (and sometimes withholding) pain pills, inserting thermometers, and doling out tiny paper cups of gelatin colored red and green in celebration of the season.

It was into this world that Mike, Simon, Thomas, John, and Russell entered, rising up from the lobby past Floors 2 (Obstetrics and its twin, Pediatrics) and 3 (Cardiac Care and Oncology) to 4, and stepping out of the stuffy confines of the elevator and into the twilight realm of General Services. There were housed all those who failed to fit neatly into any specific category, those whose bodies, while not entirely well, were not being attacked by anything precisely nameable, like lymphoma, or suffering from something definite, like a torn ACL or broken vertebrae. In the rooms of General Services lay those afflicted with more general ailments: labored breathing, mysterious rashes, gashes and punctures and scrapes that necessitated looking after but failed to merit the vigilant guarding demanded by more serious injuries and more virulent diseases. Floor 4 was a zoo of the mildly distressed, which accounted somewhat for the lack of interest shown by the employees who staffed it. Had their charges been touched by more exotic maladies, they perhaps would have displayed more enthusiasm for their care, thus truly earning the favorable, if inaccurate, opinion of their attentions shown by Mr. Jerry "The Cadillac King" Houghton, who had apparently visited the ward on one of their infrequent good days.

"I hate hospitals," Russell said as the five men walked down the hallway, searching for Room 448.

"Nobody likes hospitals," countered John. "That would be like enjoying pain."

"Tell that to the leather guys," said Mike as they came to an intersection. Rooms 401–425 stretched off to their left, while a right-hand turn would take them to 426–450. A small waiting area existed in the middle, an oasis of vinyl-upholstered chairs and out-of-date magazines in the midst of sickness.

"We probably shouldn't all go in at once," Russell said.

"We'll wait here," Simon suggested, looking doubtfully at the garish orange chairs. "In Shangri-la."

Russell nodded. "I'll be back in a little bit," he said.

Leaving the others to thumb through old issues of *Redbook, People,* and *U.S. News and World Report,* he walked quickly down the hall to the end, where he found the door to Room 448 and peered in. Greg was the lone occupant, barely recognizable beneath a mask of bandages and bruises. The television mounted on the wall across from the bed blared tinny Christmas carols courtesy of the smiling performers on the screen. An untouched tray of food sat on the table beside the bed.

Unsure whether Greg was awake or not (his swollen eyes seemed to be stuck halfway between open and closed), Russell stepped inside. "Hey," he said.

Greg turned to look at him. He attempted to smile, his face distorting and reflecting the pain he felt from the effort. Instead, he lifted one hand in greeting. Russell walked closer, trying not to register shock at Greg's appearance. In addition to the darkening bruises, there was dried blood on his face, a splint on his nose, stitches in both upper and lower lips, and a cast on his right arm. Beneath the sheet, unseen by Russell but felt acutely by Greg, were four broken ribs and a mosaic of additional contusions. There were deeper wounds as well, invisible but even more painful.

Russell stopped at the side of the bed, unsure of how to proceed. He didn't want to touch Greg, fearing hurting him, and he didn't know what to say. Finally, Greg solved the dilemma by speaking himself. "Sorry I missed dinner."

Russell smiled. If his friend was joking, perhaps things weren't as bad as they looked. He reached out and touched Greg's hair. Greg flinched only slightly. Russell pushed the hair out of his eyes.

"Want to talk about it?"

Greg turned his head to the side, presenting Russell with a cheek the color of a rotting plum. "Santa showed up with some nasty elves," he said. "I guess I was on the naughty list."

He turned back to look at Russell. Tears were slipping from the slits of his eyes. "I did something really stupid," he said softly.

Russell knew the basics. Chenoweth had told them. From the rough story Greg had given the officer, Russell had pieced together the rest. "Was it someone from the bar?" he asked.

Greg shook his head. "Online," he said.

Russell sat down in the chair positioned beside the bed. He took Greg's hand and held it gently, careful not to disturb the IV taped to the back. Locating the remote on the bedside table, he turned the television off, silencing the overly joyful carolers.

"This wasn't your fault," he said.

Greg closed his eyes completely, the bruised lids shielding him from Russell. He didn't say anything, but Russell could see his chest shaking.

"Greg, this guy is crazy. He was looking for someone to hurt. I wouldn't be surprised if he's done it before."

He paused, hearing his own words. Done it before. He looked at Greg's face, the eyes still closed. It was eerily familiar. Suddenly an image of Stephen, his nose bandaged, his skin mottled with broken blood vessels, flashed across his mind. Stephen, who at that very moment was lying in a room two floors above them, whom Russell had planned on visiting when he was done in Greg's room.

He said nothing to Greg about his thoughts. Instead, he stroked his hand, waiting for the shaking to stop. When it did, Greg opened his eyes. "I didn't want to be alone," he said. "That's all."

"You're not alone," Russell told him. "You've got us."

Greg looked at him, the tears in his eyes obscuring the pupils, distorting them as if Greg were looking up from underneath the water. "But I don't have you," he said. "That's why I couldn't spend Christmas Eve with you."

And suddenly Russell understood. Despite his carefree attitude about their aborted date, Greg *had* wanted something to happen. He had wanted Russell, and when Russell had pulled away, it had wounded him deeply. Russell saw that now. He looked at Greg's damaged face and saw that, on some level, he was responsible for it.

"I'm so sorry," he whispered, his throat refusing to let the words out fully.

They sat, looking at one another. Russell could think of nothing else to say, and he prayed Greg would be likewise silenced. He didn't want to talk about the things he was thinking and feeling. He didn't want to believe that he in any way had had a hand in Greg's attack. He had been sitting in a church, watching children dressed in their fathers' bathrobes play at being angels and shepherds. He had been far away. But perhaps he had been closer than he knew.

A nurse interrupted the moment, entering the room with a heavy tread and glancing suspiciously at the two men holding hands. She looked briefly at Greg's chart, saw what was written there, and came to her own conclusions.

"It's time for Mr. Mihalski's medication," she said, her voice flat and authoritative. "He needs to rest now."

Russell glared at her but, seeing her expression, said nothing. Although he resented her intrusion, he also welcomed the opportunity for escape. He looked at Greg and once again touched his hair.

"We'll be back later," he said. "Try to sleep."

"Oh, he'll sleep," said the nurse, producing a hypodermic needle, which she inserted into one of the ports in the IV standing beside the bed. "I don't think he'll be having any more visitors tonight."

She finished the injection, the pale fluid in the needle's barrel mixing with the clear liquid in the IV tube. Russell watched the oily-looking stream float down the tube toward Greg's hand, promising unconsciousness. He gave Greg's fingers a final squeeze and left the room.

Back in the waiting area, his friends had quickly tired of reading yesterday's news and were sitting uncomfortably. Seeing Russell appear, they brightened considerably.

"How is he?" Mike asked.

"Not good," said Russell. "He's pretty wrecked."

"Did he say anything about who did it?" inquired John.

Russell hesitated. Answering the question would possibly bring additional ones, ones he wasn't sure he could answer honestly, especially with John present. But these were Greg's friends, too, and they deserved some explanation. He opted for an edited version.

"Let's just say a date didn't go very well," he said.

Simon let out a groan, while Mike, Thomas, and John shook their heads.

"What was he thinking?" John said angrily.

"It wasn't his fault!" Russell snapped. "He didn't ask for this to happen."

"Did he even know the guy?" asked John. "Or was it just some trick he picked up somewhere?"

Russell faced him. "What difference does it make?" he said. "What are you saying?"

"I'm saying that when you go home with guys you don't know, that . . ." John stopped, looking down at the floor.

"What?" Russell demanded loudly. "That you deserve what you get?" He glared at his lover, anger growing inside him until it exploded. "This is exactly your problem," he said. "You're the most goddamned judgmental person I've ever met. And you know what? You can go fuck yourself. You think you're so perfect? Then why are you so fucking unhappy, John?"

He turned and walked away from them. Mike, running after him, reached out for his elbow. Russell pulled away, but he stopped. He leaned against the wall, not looking back to where John and the others stood.

"You know he didn't mean it," said Mike.

"No," Russell said, "he meant it. He always means it, and I'm tired of making excuses for him." He took a breath before continuing. "Greg is in there because of me."

"What?"

Russell nodded. "He did it because of what happened between us," he explained.

"No," Mike said, taking Russell by the shoulders and making him look at him. "No. That's not why he did it. It may have played a small part, but it's not the whole reason."

"Does it really matter how much it had to do with it?" asked Russell.

"You can't take responsibility for this," Mike said.

"There's something else," said Russell. "I think Stephen might have been attacked too."

"I thought he fell on the ice," Mike said.

"That's what he told everyone," Russell said. "But when I looked at Greg in there, it was like looking at Stephen. I think maybe he was lying."

"Shit," said Mike, running his hands through his hair. "Should we tell the cop?"

Russell shook his head. "Not until I talk to Stephen," he said. "I'm going to go up there now. Can you ask Thomas to come with me? Stephen knows him from church, and it might help."

Mike nodded. "What about John?"

"One casualty at a time," answered Russell. "I'll be back as soon as I can."

He walked to the elevators as Mike returned to the other men. As Russell waited for Thomas, he thought about John. The truth was, he had no idea what he was going to do about him. He pushed that problem to the back burner of his mind, though, as Thomas arrived.

"Mike said you want my help. What can I do?"

As they walked toward the elevators, Russell briefed Thomas on his theory. By the time the doors opened and they stepped once more into the tiny metal box, on their way to the sixth floor and the Psych Ward, the priest was up to speed.

Finding Stephen was easy; they had only to look for the worried faces of his parents and brother. The Darbys were clustered outside of Room 613, having been shooed away by a nurse who could have been the twin of the one in Greg's room. Russell and Thomas approached them.

"Father Dunn," Mrs. Darby said when she saw Thomas. "Thank you for coming."

"How's Stephen doing?"

"The doctor tells us he'll be all right," Mrs. Darby said. "Thank God. He took too many of his pills. It was an accident."

"I'm sure it was," Thomas said kindly. "May we see him?"

Mrs. Darby glanced briefly at Russell, then nodded. "You can go in," she said.

Thomas and Russell entered the room as the nurse emerged, brushing by them without a look as she moved on to her next duty. Thomas deftly shut the door, giving them some privacy from Stephen's family.

Stephen himself was, like Greg, in bed and hooked up to an IV. Unlike Greg, he seemed awake and alert. Seeing Thomas, he gave him a small smile. Then, seeing Russell behind him, he looked confused.

"We met in the gift shop," Russell joked.

"You two know each other?" asked Stephen.

Thomas nodded. "It's a funny story," he said. "We'll tell you all about it."

"But first we need to talk," said Russell.

CHAPTER 35

On the morning of December 26, Wayne Chenoweth pulled up to the house on Meridan Street and got out. He was in no mood for any shit, and when he knocked on the door of the house, he did it without gentleness. When the door was opened by a sleepy-eyed Pete Thayer, Chenoweth wasted no time pushing his way by the kid and into the house, where he produced the handcuffs from his belt and, turning his suspect around, affixed them to his wrists.

"Peter Thayer, you're under arrest for the assault and battery of Stephen Darby and Gregory Mihalski. You have the right to remain silent."

As he read Pete the rest of his rights, the kid, as they all did, protested.

"What the fuck? I didn't do anything! I don't even know those guys you just said."

"Mr. Thayer, if you want to keep talking, you are free to do so," said Officer Chenoweth. "I advise you, however, to shut the hell up until you can consult with your attorney. Now walk."

He left the house, pushing Pete ahead of him. He knew that in just a T-shirt and jeans, the kid was probably freezing, but he didn't give a damn. It wasn't his job to make sure he was comfortable; it was simply his job to bring him in. Let the asshole complain to his lawyer if he was cold.

Pete continued his professions of innocence as Wayne drove back to the station. The officer only half listened as the demands to be let go slowly faded away, replaced, again predictably, by attempts at gaining sympathy.

"I didn't try to kill anyone, man," he said.

Chenoweth stared straight ahead, not replying, but his eyes watched Pete's reflection in the rearview mirror closely. The young man was leaning against the window, his forehead pressed to the glass. The cop had seen hundreds of men, and a few women, do exactly what Pete Thayer was doing. Everything looked different from inside a squad car. Thayer, he knew, was looking at the world with new eyes.

"I didn't do anything!" Pete shouted, a final act of bravado before hanging his head. Sometimes they kicked the back of the seat for emphasis, but Pete left this particular flourish out.

Chenoweth had a choice. He could let Thayer talk himself out and hope he got the truth from him at the station in a formal interrogation, or he could push him a little and see if maybe he'd pop right there in the car. The former would be more by the book, but there were advantages to getting it over with.

"You hate fags, right?" he asked.

Pete looked up. Chenoweth, still watching him in the mirror, saw his eyes dart back and forth as he thought about how to answer the question.

"Fags," Chenoweth said again. "You don't like them, right?"

Pete shook his head. "Who said anything about fags?"

Chenoweth laughed, a light chuckle designed to create an air of friendliness. "Come on," he said. "Those two guys you clocked. You didn't know they were queers?"

He saw Pete hesitate. Answering the question would mean he had to admit to the crimes. Not answering was the smart thing to do. Chenoweth would bet his entire week's paycheck he knew which choice Thayer would make.

"No," Pete said. "I don't like fags."

Bingo. Chenoweth nodded his head, as if agreeing with Thayer. More buddy bonding. They were going to be good pals, he and Pete Thayer. He turned his head and glanced at Pete. "Me neither. Fucking pansies are always calling up the station complaining about getting picked on. State says we have to deal with them. Hate crimes, they call them."

Pete grunted, as if indicating that the fairies were indeed wasting Wayne Chenoweth's very valuable, taxpayer-financed time. Yes, it was a real goddamned shame that the Cold Falls Police Department had to involve themselves in the affairs of a bunch of fruits, just because they weren't capable of defending themselves.

"So you roughed up a couple of queers," Chenoweth continued. "What'd they do, try to get in your pants? Wouldn't surprise me."

He saw Pete studying the back of his head, calculating the risk he was about to take. Again, Chenoweth figured the odds were in his favor.

"So what if I did?" Pete said. "I'm allowed to protect myself, right?"

"Absolutely," Chenoweth said heartily. "Someone tries to feel you up or something, no one's going to blame you for popping them a couple of times."

"Right," Pete said, sounding hopeful. "If I was just trying to keep them away from me, no one can say I was doing anything wrong. They can't just put their hands on you, right? Not if you don't want them to."

"Hey, it works for the ladies when they cry rape," Chenoweth said. "What's good for the goose, you know."

Pete was nodding, a smile forming on his face. His eyes had brightened, and Chenoweth could practically hear the ungreased wheels of his mind clunking along as he saw what he thought was a way out. He decided to give Thayer one last push.

"So that's what happened, right? Couple of fags tried getting sweet with you and you had to push them away?"

Pete started to speak, then stopped. Chenoweth held his breath, waiting for him to crumble. *Come on,* he thought. *Just tell me you did it.*

"No, man, I didn't do nothing," Thayer said.

Chenoweth cursed him silently. Now they were going to have to do it the hard way.

"I don't like fags, man, but I didn't hit nobody," Thayer said. "Wouldn't blame whoever did, though. Like you said."

Yeah, Chenoweth thought, *like I said.*

He pulled into the station parking lot and into the space reserved for his car. Getting out, he opened the rear door and helped Pete Thayer out. Together they walked into the station. Half an hour later, after letting the kid make his phone call, he showed Thayer to a cell and left him there to stew.

Pete, sitting on the cell's cot, stared at the wall opposite him and waited. He congratulated himself on catching on to the cop's trick in the car before he got into any more trouble. He'd been so freaked out that he'd almost let it happen, but he'd stopped himself at the last minute. He had his dad to thank for that. Good old dad, who'd always managed to get him to reveal his sins by making Pete think he was on his side. "So you broke a window. No big deal. What happened, you playing ball in the house? Shit, I did that a million times when I was your age."

Pete had fallen for it time and again, and every time he'd paid dearly for believing that, for once, his father really did understand where he was coming from. After each confession, though, had come punishment: a mouth full of soap, a stick on the backside, a week with no TV. Eventually he'd wised up and stuck to flat-out denials. In his experience, that always worked best. Unless they had proof, all they had to go on was your word against the other guy's.

The cop—the stupid fucking doughnut-eater—had claimed they did have proof. Witnesses. Maybe they did; maybe they didn't. He didn't know, and he didn't really care, either. If they were going to nail him, he was going to make damn sure they worked hard to do it. He wasn't going to give them any fucking help.

He tapped his foot nervously, making the springs of the cot squeak like surprised mice. Where was Ronnie? He'd used his one call to phone his buddy, asking him to come down to the station and bail him out. He'd done it once for Ronnie when he'd been picked up for driving after a few too many beers, so Ronnie owed him one. Pete wished he'd hurry up. Being in the cell made him feel like an animal. Plus, he was fucking cold. The goddamned cop hadn't even let him put on a jacket. He wondered idly if maybe he could sue them for something because of that.

Eventually his anxiety turned to weariness and he dozed, his dreams sketchy and troubled, a disjointed narrative in which he was pursued by something he couldn't see. The projectionist in his head, asleep on the job, failed to keep the image in focus, so that Pete ran through shadowy hallways that shook beneath his feet. His hands went out to steady himself, but the walls retreated from his touch and he fell, feeling the hot breath of his pursuer on his neck as teeth like razors closed around his throat.

He woke up when he heard someone calling his name. In the first moments of wakefulness, he thought he was fourteen, in his own bed, being told by his father to get downstairs for breakfast before he missed the goddamned school bus. Shaking his head, he looked for his clothes before realizing he was dressed, a grown man, and looking out at the face of Wayne Chenoweth, who glared at him from behind the bars.

"Get up," he said as he unlocked the door.

Pete followed the cop down the hallway and back to the front desk of the station. Ronnie stood there, his hands in the pockets of his coat. Pete went to him and gave him a rough hug.

"Thanks, man," he said.

"No problem," Ronnie said. "Let's get out of here."

"Mr. Thayer," Wayne Chenoweth said as he slid Pete's personal possessions to him across the counter, "we'll be seeing you again."

Pete resisted an urge to flip him off, taking his wallet and leaving with Ronnie. It wasn't until he was safely locked inside Ronnie's car that he allowed himself the joy of giving Officer Wayne Chenoweth and the entire Cold Falls Police Force the finger. He did so gleefully, waving his extended third digit around wildly and yelling, "Suck my cock, you fat-assed pieces of shit."

"You owe me twelve hundred bucks," Ronnie said, pulling onto the road. "What the fuck did you do?"

"Nothing," Pete said. "It's total bullshit. I'll pay you back, don't worry."

"At twelve hundred bucks, it must be pretty major bullshit," said Ronnie.

"They think I beat up a couple of homos," Pete told him.

"Did you?"

"Nah," answered Pete. "They've got me mixed up with someone else. What the hell would I be doing around fags?"

"How the fuck do I know?" Ronnie said, turning on the radio. "I'm just asking."

"Like I said, they've got the wrong guy."

"Just make sure you get me that money," said Ronnie. "Julie'll have a shit fit if she finds out I took it out of the bank."

"You'll have it tomorrow, buddy," Pete assured him.

That was the extent of the conversation about the matter. Ten minutes later Ronnie dropped Pete off at his house, and after a quick handshake, he was off. Pete went inside, locked the door behind him, and breathed freely for the first time since opening the door and seeing Wayne Chenoweth standing on his stoop.

The first thing he did was take a shower to wash the jail smell off his skin. Then, dressed in clean clothes, he retrieved a beer from the fridge and sat down in the living room to think. He lit a joint (thank God the cop hadn't searched the house) and drew the comforting smoke into his lungs. He wasn't in the clear yet. Despite almost convincing even himself that he hadn't done anything, he *had* given the two queers a pretty good thrashing. And even if they did deserve it, he knew they'd try to make him out to be the bad guy, the one with the problem, all because he'd taught some cocksuckers a lesson.

He was surprised they'd even told the cops what had happened. That just proved how pathetic they were, running to the police when they couldn't take care of themselves. If they were really men, they'd handle things themselves. Then again, he reminded himself, if they were real men, they wouldn't be faggots.

It had to be the second one, he thought, the one he'd visited on Christmas Eve. He must have gone crying to the cops and that asshole with the badge probably played detective, putting two and two together and thinking he'd see if he could get Pete to crack. That was the only possibility. He'd never given the fruit his real name. The cop—Chenoweth—must have remembered him from the incident at the porn theater, must have had a hunch the two things were connected.

Well, they were, but that didn't mean shit if they couldn't prove it. To do that, they'd have to get both the faggots to ID him as the one who'd knocked their lights out. That would mean admitting they'd wanted to suck his cock, and then who would look bad? Not him. Not Pete Thayer. He was just a regular guy minding his own business. It was those stupid fairies who had gone gay on him, trying to get at his dick. Nobody with half a brain would blame him for trying to keep them away.

Yes, in order to nail him, the cops would have to get the fags to testify against him. And that, he was pretty sure, would never happen. He took another drag on the joint, the mellowing effects of the grass spreading through him. He was already feeling better. Things weren't all that bad. He just had to keep playing it cool, keep reminding himself that he hadn't done anything wrong. It was those two queers who should be ashamed of themselves, who should be worrying about what was going to happen to them.

He wondered if he still had the second guy's address, if he'd kept the scrap of paper he'd written it down on. Not that it mattered; he was pretty sure he remembered where he lived. Maybe, he thought, he'd pay the queer another visit, put another scare into him. That might keep him from talking any more.

He chugged his beer, letting the alcohol mix with the pot, knowing it would make everything smooth as silk. He thought about going back to the fag's house, knocking on his door. "Hi," he'd say. "Remember me? Your friendly neighborhood ass-kicker? How about we follow up on that conversation we had a few nights ago? How about I just step inside and show you a few more samples?"

He laughed, imagining the expression on the queer's face. Would he scream? Would he call for help? Or would he drop to his knees and beg, beg Pete not to hurt his pretty face? Maybe even beg to suck his cock again. And this time Pete would make sure he finished what he'd started.

Pete slid his hand into his pants. His cock was getting hard. He closed his eyes and imagined the faggot, on his knees, begging Pete not to hurt him. He pictured grabbing the queer by the hair, forcing his cock into his mouth. He felt himself slide into his throat.

He unzipped his pants and pulled his dick out. Holding the joint in his mouth, he imagined what he would do if he got another chance to teach that faggot what a real man was made of.

CHAPTER 36

The classical music section at the Sam Goody's in Stonesgate Mall was not what could be called extensive, but Simon had managed to find a handful of purchases, mostly things he already had on vinyl (vinyl—it sounded so old-fashioned, like galoshes, or the croup) and wanted to replace. He was particularly excited about finding Jonas Starker's recordings of the Bach cello suites, which he loved but which he hadn't listened to since scratching one of the albums. This had set him on a Bach tear, and he'd picked up several other CDs of the composer's work. He planned on spending the evening listening to them and trying to forget about the unpleasant events of the past two days.

He was standing, looking at a cardboard cutout and wondering why someone called Marilyn Manson would want to have such unpleasant photographs of herself displayed in public, when he noticed someone else intently perusing the classical selections. Something about the man's face was familiar, and after a moment he realized that he was looking at the director of the nativity pageant he'd attended at Saint Peter's. The man was flipping through the discs, his brow furrowed. Then, unexpectedly, he looked up and straight into Simon's face. Faced with either turning away or acknowledging his own stare, Simon chose the latter. He nodded. The man nodded back.

"I was at your concert on Christmas Eve," Simon said. "Lovely."

The man laughed roughly. "I'm not sure if that's quite the word for it. Passable is more like it. But thank you."

"I was particularly taken by the Brahms piece," Simon continued. He thought suddenly of Walter, and looked down.

"Really?" the man said. He walked closer to Simon.

"Brahms was a favorite of my late partner," Simon explained.

"He's one of my favorites as well." He held out his hand. "I'm Gavin Bettelheim."

"Simon Bird."

"I don't think I've ever seen you at Saint Peter's."

"I'm not a regular attendee," explained Simon. "I was there with some friends."

Gavin looked at the CDs in Simon's hand and his face lit up. "You got the Starker!" he said. "That's what I came in for. I saw it the other day while I was on my way out. I was sure nobody else would ever even notice it, so I didn't rush back."

"And here I stumbled upon it completely by accident," Simon said. "Here. It's rightfully yours."

"I couldn't," Gavin said as Simon held the box out to him.

"Your face says that you could," said Simon. "I insist."

"In that case, I accept," Gavin said happily, taking the CD. "Thank you so much. I've been looking forward to listening to these. I'm afraid my old albums don't sound quite as good as they did in the glorious days of hi-fi."

"Just what I was thinking earlier," Simon told him. "I'm afraid my old turntable is soon to go the way of the dinosaurs."

Gavin laughed. "Say, what are you doing for lunch?"

"Nothing whatsoever," said Simon.

"Then let me take you," Gavin said. "It's the least I can do in exchange for making you relinquish the Starker."

Simon nodded. "All right, then. I think that's a very fair trade."

After checking out, the two men walked into the mall. Filled with teenagers celebrating the week off from school, the cavernous space rang with voices as the kids moved through the shopping center in tight little knots, like sticking with like. Boys in baggy clothes stared at girls in too-tight jeans, trying to look as cool and uncaring as they could. The girls, in turn, ignored them completely, all the while praying that their hair and makeup were doing their part to ensure admiring glances.

"Amazing, isn't it?" Gavin remarked, nodding toward a gaggle of young women trying as hard as they could not to acknowledge three boys who had just turned to watch them walk by. "In ten years they'll have babies of their own and will be complaining to one another about how their husbands never pay them any attention."

"What do you think they'd do if they knew that now?" Simon mused.

"Become lesbians?" Gavin suggested.

Simon shook his head. "Then they'd have cats and complain that their *lovers* aren't paying them any attention."

Gavin laughed loudly, earning a contemptuous glare from the very girls they were joking about. He put his hand over his mouth.

"They can't imagine what two such unforgivably old people could possibly find to laugh at," said Simon as they arrived at one of the several chain restaurants scattered throughout the mall.

"Is this all right?" Gavin asked, nodding at the garish neon sign welcoming them to T.G.I. Friday's. "Given our other options, I think it's the best of the lot."

"I'm game if you are," said Simon, walking into the restaurant and facing the chipper host, a young woman wearing a red and white striped apron and what seemed to be about ten thousand pins of various kinds.

"Welcome to Friday's," she said. "I'm Patty. How many of you are there?"

"I believe the most accurate estimate is about one in ten," Simon said.

The girl wrinkled her brow.

"Two," Simon said.

Picking up two menus, Patty led them to a booth at the rear of the restaurant. Simon was relieved to see that there were no tables of teenagers in sight. Apparently, the section he and Gavin were being placed in was reserved for everyone who didn't fit neatly into the restaurant's preferred demographics.

"Your server will be right with you," said Patty, giving them one last smile before running off, her ponytail bouncing jauntily.

"I think I'll have whatever she had," Gavin said drily.

Simon, looking over the menu, nodded. He was enjoying Gavin's sense of humor, and even if the choice of luncheon location wasn't one he would normally make, it had an air of fun about it. After the previous two days, fun was something he very much needed to experience. As he perused the lists of salads and burgers, chicken-fried steaks and spaghetti bowls, he couldn't help but think about Stephen and Greg. He felt terrible about what had happened to the two young men, but was unsure how he could help them. Since Monday he had remained largely in the background as Russell, more distracted than usual, had raced around the house, making calls and assisting the police in speaking with Greg and Stephen. The resulting arrest of the man responsible for hurting them had only intensified Russell's agitation, particularly when the suspect was freed on bail, and finally Simon had simply removed himself from the house for a day out.

"What can I get for you fellows today?"

Simon looked up and saw Patty's twin beaming at him. So similar was she to the peppy hostess that he had to look twice at her apron (no buttons, he noticed) to make sure she hadn't reappeared. But in addition to the absence of decoration on her apron, this girl's name tag read ALICIA.

"I'll have the chicken caesar and a bowl of the French onion soup," Gavin told the girl, who scribbled furiously on a pad in her hand, as if any second the order would flee from her memory.

"And you?" she asked Simon.

"I think the roast beef sandwich, please."

"Fries?"

"Why not?" Simon answered, earning a bob of the head from Alicia as she noted it on her pad. "And an iced tea, if you would."

"Make that two iced teas," Gavin said.

Alicia frowned as she crossed out Simon's single tea and wrote a two next to it. Then she collected their menus. "Thanks, guys," she said as she trotted off, apparently to join Patty.

"How many of them do you think there are?" Gavin asked. "And do they manufacture them just to work in T.G.I. Friday's across the country?"

"I think it's just us," Simon answered. "Everyone under twenty looks the same to me."

"I know," said Gavin. "My daughter is thirty-five, and I can't believe it. I still remember changing her diapers."

"You have a daughter?" Simon said, surprised. He had assumed that

Gavin was gay. *That's what you get for making assumptions about men who like classical music and direct church choirs,* he chided himself. And what did he expect? After the disaster with the fellow in the library, he should, he thought, know better than to trust his first impressions.

"There's a granddaughter as well," Gavin continued. "She's almost twelve."

"You and your wife must be very proud," Simon said.

"We are," agreed Gavin. "I'm not sure they're so proud of *me,* but that's another story."

"I love stories," Simon told him.

Gavin stroked his beard, as if thinking about how to begin. "I'm gay," he said. Then he laughed. "I'm sorry. That sounds so dramatic. It's just that I heard what you said to the girl—what's her name?"

"Patty."

"Patty. When we came in. About the whole one in ten thing. I assumed you meant that you're gay."

"I did," Simon assured him.

"Thank God," Gavin said. "I was afraid maybe I was going to make a fool of myself."

"By telling me you're gay?"

"It's just that I haven't told all that many people. Outside of my family, that is."

"This does sound like a good story," said Simon as Alicia arrived with their drinks and Gavin's soup.

Gavin waited until she was gone before continuing. "I was married for a long time," he said. "Twenty-five years."

"Good Lord," Simon remarked. "Didn't you know?"

Gavin poked his spoon through the melted cheese covering his soup. "I had some suspicions," he said. "But I was happy. At least I thought I was. Then I fell in love for the first time. I mean really fell in love. I loved my wife, but I realized I was never *in* love with her. Unfortunately, the person I fell in love with was one of my students at the college where I taught music. There was an affair, I felt guilty and broke it off, he went first to my wife and then to the dean."

"How awful for you," said Simon.

"It was," Gavin said. "I can't blame him, though. He was young. I should have been more responsible." He paused. "In the end I lost them both, plus my job. That's when I moved here, to start over."

"And now?" Simon asked. "Do you speak to your ex-wife and daughter?"

"I do. It took a long time, but now we can talk. I think Deborah is still hoping a miracle will occur and Marjorie and I will get back together."

Simon hesitated before asking his next question. "And is there anyone in your life now?"

"No," Gavin said. "After what happened with Ben, I largely turned off my romantic needs. I threw myself into composing. That's how I spend most of my time now, when I'm not orchestrating Christmas spectaculars for the good folks at Saint Peter's."

Again Alicia interrupted, this time with the salad and sandwich. "Can I get you anything else?" she asked, smiling so wildly that Simon almost ordered something just to please her. But he refrained, and soon the girl was gone again.

"What about you?" asked Gavin. "Are you with anyone?"

Simon chewed a fry before answering. He knew from experience that talking about a dead lover could quickly turn maudlin, and he didn't want that to happen. He decided to give Gavin the short version of his story. The longer one could wait for another time.

"I had a lover for many years," he said. "He passed away last year."

"I'm sorry," Gavin said. "You must miss him."

"I do," said Simon. "But I have the memories, and I have the life we made together."

"I wonder sometimes what my life would have been like if I'd understood myself better when I was young."

"Your life isn't over," Simon reminded Gavin.

Gavin shrugged. "I'm fifty-five," he said. "It's not exactly beginning."

"You might be surprised," Simon told him. He thought for a moment before continuing. "What are you doing New Year's Eve?"

"Probably going to some very boring party held by some of the church people," Gavin answered. "Charades and eggnog all around."

"No," Simon said firmly. "You're going to come to my house."

"But I won't know anyone."

"You'll know me," Simon said. "And again, you might be surprised," he added, thinking about Gavin's reaction to seeing Thomas among a group of gay men.

Gavin speared some lettuce and looked at it. "All right," he said. "But only because I feel I still owe you for giving up the Starker."

"After Sunday night you may consider the debt fully repaid," said Simon. He was now thinking about his bet with Russell. Did Gavin count as a date? He wasn't certain of the definition, but decided that he was close enough. In fact, he thought as he looked across the table at Gavin, he was better than a date. He was a new friend.

"So, you really liked the pageant?" Gavin asked.

"I especially enjoyed the magi," said Simon. "Their adoration of the Christ child is unparalleled in the history of the theater."

Gavin accepted the remark with good humor. "I know it's not Shakespeare in the Park or anything, but it's good for me," he said. "Saint Peter's became a home for me when I first moved here. There are a lot of wonderful people there."

"I met some of them the other night," Simon said. "One in particular. Beth-Ann, I believe her name was."

Gavin responded with a roll of his eyes. "Don't hold her against the rest of us. She's special."

"I believe she, Patty, and Alicia would get along famously," Simon suggested. "Perhaps we should invite her to lunch next time?"

"I'd rather we kept it to just the two of us," Gavin said.

Simon looked up. Gavin smiled shyly and returned to his salad, leaving Simon to wonder what, exactly, he'd meant by that.

CHAPTER 37

Stephen opened his eyes. Without moving his head from the pillow, he traced the pattern of the ceiling tiles above him with his eyes. Although at first the tiles all appeared to be completely alike, a closer inspection revealed that every other one had been set into the plastic grid of the support beams facing the alternate direction of its neighbors. The differences in the patterns were subtle, but obvious once you knew what to look for. He had been counting them for hours, and was now fairly certain that the sky of his room consisted of four hundred and twenty-six tiles, although it may have been as few as four hundred and eighteen or as many as four hundred and sixty-eight. He'd counted several times and come up with different numbers, a situation he attributed to the fact that he was floating in and out of sleep.

He was, in fact, in withdrawal. He knew this because his doctor, a young man with beautiful black eyes and the equally beautiful name of Ashak Vinpasa, had told him that he was. He had also given Stephen something to help with the worst of the symptoms, but it had not tamed all of them, and as a result, Stephen's body had reacted by going to sleep. This in itself was not so bad; when he was asleep, he had only to contend with the troubling dreams, most of which involved his running from some large, invisible, but completely terrifying monster.

It was being awake he had difficulty with. When he was awake, he remembered what he'd done. Worse, he remembered that his family was there with him, awaiting an explanation. So far all they'd been told by Dr. Vinpasa was that Stephen had consumed far too many pills and needed to rid his body of the lingering toxic effects. They had not yet been told that the pills had initially been consumed over a period of weeks, and that the final handful had been nothing more than a chaser to bring things to an end.

He wished he had died. That first moment of awakening, when he'd heard someone calling his name and, thinking it was the voice of his dark master, swam up through the haze of death to answer, had been enormously disappointing. Instead of the face of an angel, he'd found himself staring into the eyes of a man named David Farris, one of two EMTs assigned to the ambulance that had answered the 911 call Alan Darby, sent to his brother's house to see what was keeping him, made after finding Stephen unconscious. David Farris's partner, Heidi Winterton, had existed only as a disembodied voice calling out random numbers that buzzed like bees in Stephen's head. They had been his vital stats, and they had not been good.

But under David and Heidi's care, he had survived, and his next memory was of having a tube shoved up his nose and down his throat so that the poison he'd fed himself could be sucked out. The purging had worked, and now he was in a hospital bed, still alive and counting ceiling tiles to prevent himself from thinking too much while the final traces of chemicals worked their way through his skin like worms boring into rotten wood.

Losing count of the tiles, he thought instead of his visit from Russell and Father Dunn. He still had difficulty believing that it hadn't been a dream as well. The effects of the pills had been lingering, and at first he'd assumed he was hallucinating. But Russell and Thomas (he had insisted that Stephen call him by his given name) had been very much real, as had their questions. Stephen had initially continued to deny the origin of his injuries, once again mentioning the ice, the slipperiness, the fall. Then Russell had told him about Greg, who lay two floors down, taking the first steps on the path down which Stephen had so blindly stumbled. He'd recalled Greg's smiling face from dinner, his kindness, and the unreturned phone calls. Perhaps if he'd had the courage to dial Greg's number, neither of them would be where they were.

Father Dunn's—Thomas's—role in the visit had been unclear at first, and when it was explained to him how the priest was connected to both Greg and to himself, Stephen found it difficult to believe what he was told. But Thomas had assured him that what he was saying was indeed the truth, and finally Stephen's barriers had come down. He'd agreed to speak to the police. When, an hour later, Wayne Chenoweth had come in and sat at Stephen's bedside, Stephen related the events of his visit to the Paris Cinema as quickly as he could, never looking at the officer's face.

He had no idea what would happen next. He'd been told that he would likely have to identify his attacker, perhaps testify at a trial. The idea filled him with cold dread. He imagined a jury looking at him as he spoke, as he admitted to willingly following his attacker into a dark booth. He saw his mother's face, her hands covering her eyes as he confessed to wanting to suck another man's dick, felt his father's shame as his son declared to the world that he had allowed someone to fuck him in the ass. He heard his brother's muttered curses, and once more he wished he had died.

"Knock, knock."

He looked toward the door, where his mother was walking in carrying a stuffed bear and yet another bouquet of flowers. As she placed both on the dresser with the other flowers, she chatted steadily.

"These are from the Roepers," she informed him, rearranging the daisies. "And the bear is from your Aunt Sally. I don't know why. I guess she thinks you're still seven. But it was a nice thought, so don't forget to thank her when you see her. Your father and your brother are working on the car—it keeps stalling when you put it into second—but they'll come by later. I cleaned your house this morning. I can't believe you let it get to such a state. It's snowing again, so probably . . ."

Stephen tuned her out. He knew she was talking because she was still upset. It's what she did, had always done ever since he was a kid. Hearing her babble on was soothing in a strange way, a kind of maternal white noise that drowned out other, more troubling, thoughts. He closed his eyes and let her words surround him like rain.

"And the dog just would *not* stop barking. I don't know what he thought was out there. A fox, maybe. Your father saw one last week. But probably it was just a jay. They're all over the suet since the temperature dropped. Oh, the racket they make when a squirrel comes around." There was a pause in the flow, and Stephen opened his eyes. His mother was standing very close, looking down at him.

"What?" he said, startled.

"Nothing," his mother said, turning away.

"You were checking to see if I was alive, weren't you?" Stephen said.

"No, I wasn't."

Stephen sighed. He knew she was lying.

His mother went to one of the vases of flowers and began moving the blooms around. "I never asked you, did you have a nice chat with Father Dunn the other night? And who was that with him? He said he knew you, but I haven't seen him before."

Here we go, Stephen thought. He knew he could tell his mother anything and she would believe it. But he also knew that eventually she was going to find out what he'd really talked to Father Dunn about, and what he'd told Officer Chenoweth.

"Mom, come here," he said.

Mrs. Darby turned, a carnation in her hand. "What do you need, dear?"

"Just come sit down for a minute. I want to talk to you."

His mother placed the flower back with the others and walked to the bed. She sat and placed her hands in her lap, one resting on top of the other.

"About what happened," Stephen began.

"It's all right," Mrs. Darby said. "You took too many pills. It happens all the time. Why, Liz Taylor—"

"Mom, it wasn't an accident," Stephen interrupted.

His mother's mouth shut and she shook her head. "No. You just took too many. The directions were very unclear. I told your father we should think about suing the hospital."

"I took them on purpose."

Mrs. Darby ruffled herself like a hen, shaking her head and pulling herself deeper into her sweater. "Nonsense. Why would you do that? It would kill you."

"That's exactly the point, Mom. I wanted to die."

Mrs. Darby's face registered confusion. Her mouth, the lipstick applied too heavily, was a flat line. She regarded Stephen as if he'd suddenly announced that he was going to launch himself into space on a homemade rocket, or perhaps run for president of the United States.

"Don't be ridiculous."

"Mom, listen to me. This isn't easy for me to say. I tried to kill myself."

"Why on earth would you do such a thing?"

Stephen couldn't look at her when he answered. "I didn't want you to be ashamed of me."

"I'm your mother. I would never be ashamed of you."

Stephen felt tears form in his eyes. Everything was so simple for his mother, so black and white. He was her son, and she loved him. But she had no idea who he was, what he was. She had no idea that he was about to blow her neat and tidy world into a billion pieces.

"Mom, I'm gay," he said before the words could lock themselves inside his mouth.

There was no answer. He could hear his mother breathing, not a foot away from him, but she said nothing. He felt his heart begin to race, beating wildly inside his chest as the seconds stretched out into an unbearable quiet. Nor could he open his eyes to see his mother's face.

"What do you mean?" she said finally.

Stephen forced his eyes open and looked at her. She hadn't moved. Her hands were still in her lap, although now one hand was stroking the other nervously. She fingered her wedding band, turning it around as she waited for him to answer her.

"I'm gay," he said again. He knew no other way of putting it. Surely his mother didn't need for him to tell her what made someone gay, what particular interests and activities defined who he was. "I like men," he added.

His mother nodded her head. "Oh," she said.

"I don't want to be this way," Stephen told her. "I don't want you to be ashamed of me."

"Why would I be ashamed of you?" Mrs. Darby said sharply. "Why would you ever think that? You're my child."

Stephen looked away. Seldom in his life had his mother surprised him, but she had now. He'd expected her to cry, or yell, or at the very least run from the room. But she continued to sit quietly, watching him.

"Listen to me," Mrs. Darby said after a moment. "I know you and your brother think I'm a silly old woman, and I suppose I am. But I am also your mother. There is nothing you could ever do to make me stop loving you. When I look at you and Alan, I see the babies I held in my arms when they were born. And I want those babies to grow up healthy and safe and happy. That's all."

When he turned to look at her, Stephen saw that now his mother *was* crying. But they weren't tears of anger or disappointment, they were the tears of a mother who saw her younger child in pain, pain she could do nothing to relieve. She continued to look at him as the drops rolled down the lines of her face.

"I love you, Stephen," she said. "Whoever you are."

Stephen didn't know what to say to her. He had underestimated his mother, failed to understand the capacity of her heart for acceptance and love. She was right; he had seen her as a silly woman, one whose life consisted of immaterial events and unimportant thoughts. He saw now that he had been wrong about her.

"How did you get so smart?" he asked, his voice cracking.

His mother wiped her eyes. *"Reader's Digest,"* she said.

There was more he needed to tell her, but now wasn't the time. Later she would find out about how he'd been beaten up, and why. For now it was enough that she knew the truth about him. But having told his mother, Stephen now realized something else: He couldn't take it back. He had committed himself to this identity of his. Now that he'd come out, staying in was not an option.

This, almost more than telling his mother, was the real burden. His thoughts flashed suddenly to the nights spent in front of the computer screen, searching for someone to wring desire from his heart. Was that all there was for him? Was the dark man right about him; was he nothing more than a rag to be used by others?

He didn't want that. He didn't want to spend his life in darkness, constantly looking for faces in the shadows, waiting to feel a hand on his neck. He didn't want to live on his knees, looking up into the face of someone who wanted only to destroy him.

"What are you thinking about?"

His mother's voice broke through his thoughts. He couldn't tell her what he was thinking. She had done enough for him. His fears were something he was going to have to shoulder himself. And he would shoulder them, if only because he wanted his mother to be proud of him.

"I was just thinking about what Dad and Alan are going to say," he told her. Although not precisely true, it was a question he had been asking himself.

"You leave those two to me," his mother said. "I can handle them."

Stephen laughed. "You're something else," he said.

His mother smiled at him, arching an eyebrow. "And don't you forget it."

CHAPTER 38

Thomas stared at the notes on his desk, rubbed his temples, and sighed. His sermon wasn't going well at all. He picked up the piece of paper and reread the first line. "On this last day of the year, as we look forward to the next, I want to talk about new beginnings."

He let the paper drop to the desk and groaned. It was awful. But so were the dozen or so other opening lines he'd written and rejected. He pawed through the discarded scraps of paper, hoping maybe one of them would contain a gem he could reconsider, or at least something that didn't sound like a greeting card.

It almost seemed providential, the fact that December 31 fell on a Sunday. His last sermon of the year would also be his opportunity to tell his congregation about himself. He would start the next year as a new man. He hadn't thought beyond that. Several things could happen. Although there was nothing in the church laws that necessitated his stepping down from his position, if his parishioners were uncomfortable attending Saint Peter's under his leadership, he would have to consider removing himself from the pulpit. At the moment, simply thinking about living his life openly was difficult enough; he had no interest in forcing change upon a small-town parish.

And then there was Mike. Thinking about him, Thomas couldn't help but smile. Their meeting had completely altered the course of his life. It was hard for him even to remember what things had been like six weeks earlier, before the snowstorm, before his car trouble, before he'd first sat in the cab of Mike's truck. Since then, his world had been turned on its head. But rather than feeling disoriented, he saw more clearly than ever before in his life.

Sitting back in his chair, he looked at the photo of him and Joseph. How would his life have been different, he wondered, if he'd allowed himself to love Joseph? Where would he be now? What would he be doing? Would he have been able to fill the need Joseph sought to fill in his encounters with other men, the couplings that had resulted in his sickness and, eventually, his death? Would Thomas's love have been enough to save the bright, kind, and funny man who had first stirred his heart?

Joseph's face looked back at him, revealing nothing. Thomas studied it, pondering the questions. He knew he would never have the answers. Wondering what might have been was a game without end. He could go around and around, and still he would be no closer to knowing.

"How's it going, preacher man?"

Mike, entering the study, put his hands on Thomas's shoulders and squeezed. Feeling the strong pressure of his fingers, Thomas relaxed. Mike leaned down and kissed him on the top of the head.

"Not so well," Thomas told him. "This sermon just isn't coming together."

"Anything I can do to help?"

"Write it for me?" Thomas suggested.

"Sorry," Mike answered. "I was never very good at writing. But if you want me to get up there and demonstrate how to make the perfect cocktail, I'll have them eating out of my hand."

"That might work," said Thomas. "They're Episcopalians. They love cocktails."

Mike took a seat in the room's other chair. "Seriously, are you really going to come out to them?"

Thomas nodded. "I have to," he said. "Not just for them, but for me. How can I claim to be their spiritual leader and not be honest with them?"

"It seems to work for the guys on TV," said Mike. "They just ask everyone to forgive them when they get caught."

"Exactly my point. I don't want anyone saying I'm hiding who I am."

"Suppose they don't like who you are. Then what?"

"Then we open a B and B and I learn how to make waffles," Thomas said. "I don't know. This is all I've ever been."

"Then you'd better make sure that sermon is damn good," Mike suggested. "Because I've tasted your waffles, and they suck."

"While we're on the subject of the future, have you given any more thought to yours?" Thomas inquired. Mike hadn't returned to the Engine Room since walking out earlier in the week.

"I was thinking it might be fun to be a porn star."

"Too old," said Thomas.

"Ouch."

"You qualify in every other way, if it's any consolation."

"I'd take that as a compliment, but I know you don't have anything to compare me to," Mike said. "No, I've actually been thinking that maybe it's time I finished my degree."

"You never told me you started one."

"It's one of the many dark secrets of my past," Mike teased. "Actually, I did one year of a teaching program when I was working in Syracuse. I was going to teach high school English."

"Why didn't you finish?"

Mike sighed. "Oh, you know," he said. "There was this guy."

"Jim."

Mike nodded. "It was kind of hard to work, go to class, *and* clean up after him. Then I left and just never got around to getting back to it."

Thomas looked at Mike for a moment, tilting his head to the side.

"What?" said Mike.

"I'm just trying to picture you holding a copy of *The Great Gatsby* and discussing the symbolism of the color yellow."

"I'll have you know my lesson plan for *The Scarlet Letter* had them on their feet," said Mike. "Smart ass."

"Could you really see yourself in front of a class every day?"

Mike nodded. "I think I could. I mean, it can't be any harder than standing behind a bar for eight hours a night listening to a bunch of drunks."

"High school students don't tip you because they think you're cute, though," Thomas remarked.

"I hear some of them do," said Mike, grinning.

Thomas wadded up a piece of paper and threw it at him. He looked out the window at the snow, which had begun to fall again, then back at Mike. "What do you think you'd be doing right now if you hadn't stopped that night?"

Mike looked at his watch. "It's eight forty-five. I'd be pouring drinks and listening to Miss Minnie Skirts and Miss Fellatio Hornblower work their way through 'Any Man of Mine.' "

"And you'd rather be here with me?"

"Hard to believe, isn't it?"

"You've really changed my life," said Thomas.

"No more than you've changed mine."

"I guess the person we really have to thank is Margaret Sorenson."

"Who?"

"Margaret Sorenson," Thomas repeated. "The old woman I was visiting the night I ran out of gas."

Mike nodded. He'd forgotten about the errand that had called Thomas out in the middle of a winter night. "We'll send her flowers," he suggested.

"It wouldn't do much good," Thomas said. "She died a couple of days later. Stomach cancer."

"Thank God she held on long enough to get you out of the house."

"Speaking of getting out of the house, I'm sending you home," Thomas said. "I've got to get this sermon written, and I'll never do it if you keep distracting me."

"Who's distracting you?" Mike said innocently as he got up and went over to Thomas's chair. Kneeling, he looked up with wide eyes. "Forgive me, Father, for I have sinned."

"Out," Thomas said, stifling a laugh. "Get thee behind me, Satan."

"Behind you?" said Mike. "That's exactly what I had in mind."

"Out!" Thomas said again.

Mike stood up. "Okay," he said. "I'm going. But call me later. You can read me your sermon."

"Deal," Thomas said, accepting the kiss Mike gave him. "Now get out."

Mike left Thomas with his notes, heading downstairs to grab his coat before going out to his truck. The falling snow was light and dry. There wouldn't be much accumulation, and what did hang around wouldn't interfere with driving. It was the perfect winter night, pretty without being inconvenient, and it made him happy.

He got into the truck and turned on the radio. The Dixie Chicks started singing "Landslide" to him as he drove out to the road. " 'I took my love, I took it down,' " he sang along softly along with Natalie Maines. "'I climbed a mountain and I turned around.' "

The truck hummed along as he made his way down the road. He wasn't quite ready to go home, and decided to take a drive around town. When he came to the place where he had almost crashed into Thomas and ended their relationship before it had even begun, he slowed down to take a look. It was just a stretch of road, a dip at the bottom of a hill with nothing at all remarkable about it. Yet passing through it in the still of one cold, snowy night had completely altered the course of his life.

He was past the spot and halfway up the hill even before he completed the thought in his head. Just a few seconds was all it took. Just a few seconds, and the whole universe could shift to one side or another, throwing you off your feet and send you tumbling in a new direction. It was amazing.

The truck crested the hill and kept going. The Dixie Chicks were replaced by Tim McGraw. Mike tapped his fingers on the wheel, thinking about what was in the refrigerator at home and wondering if he should stop at the store before calling it a night. He was mentally running through the contents of his freezer when he passed the Engine Room.

Out of habit, he glanced at the parking lot. It was half full. Not bad for a Thursday night. The bar would be busy, especially since Dale was on his own. Mike felt a twinge of guilt when he thought about how he'd just walked out. But it happened all the time in bars. People quit. Usually you never heard from them again. Dale would find someone else.

On an impulse, he swung the wheel and turned into the lot, taking the first spot he came to. Leaving the engine running, he sat and looked at the bar. The sign over the door blinked in red and white, the "M" in Room dimmer than the rest of the letters, so that the name resembled some offbeat children's show about trains. The building itself was nondescript, cinder blocks painted black. Why were so many gay bars painted black? Maybe because it made them blend in with the night, helped them disappear, like so many of the men who walked through their doors.

It was only four walls and a roof with a sign over the door. Before it had become the Engine Room, it had been a VFW. Before that, an Agway farm supply store (and before that, nothing but a rough set of plans drawn by Roy Dimpler on the back of a piece of paper taken from his desk at Dimpler & Sons Construction). The building itself had no identity; it was what went on within it that gave it a purpose.

For six years the building had given Mike a purpose as well. It had been his home, his refuge. The men who came in and out of its front door had been his family; a dysfunctional one, perhaps, but a family nonetheless. He had met Russell, John, and Simon there. He had rebuilt his life, one night at a time, until finally the memories of Jim had become pale ghosts that haunted him only when he awoke in the middle of the night, forgetting that he was alone.

If he felt guilty for abandoning Dale, he felt guiltier about abandoning the bar itself. Now, looking at it, he felt almost as if he were looking at the face of an ex-lover. The Engine Room, more than any other place in Cold Falls, had welcomed him in, allowed him to escape inside its doors and heal, safe from the world outside. Within it was a world in which he, and men like him, were able to live as they wanted to.

But like an ex-lover, he and the bar had outgrown one another. He no longer needed it. Staying together would only keep him in one place, endlessly treading water. It was time to let go and move on. He wished it well, wished its other lovers—the ones who still came to find comfort in its arms—well.

He wondered how many of the men who came to the bar truly understood their relationship with the place, knew why it was, apart from the obvious reasons of alcohol and the possibility of sex, they returned again and again. Probably not. Probably they wouldn't know unless it was taken from them. He imagined a giant, invisible hand reaching down and picking the building up, lifting the roof and walls up into the sky so that the people within were left standing amid the drifts of snow. He pictured the surprised faces of the patrons as they looked around, drinks in hand, trying to figure out what had happened. He saw the drag queens, wigs catching the snowflakes in their blue and purple curls, fluttering their impossibly long lashes as they stared up at the heavens.

Hopefully they would never have to experience such a thing. Hopefully their little world would continue to exist and they would continue to visit it as often as necessary. But for him the journey was ended. There were other worlds to explore, and while someday he might pay this one a return visit, it would be only as someone passing through.

Saluting the bar, he pulled out of the lot and drove toward home, leaving the other travelers to keep searching after whatever it was they were looking for. He hoped they found it.

CHAPTER 39

"Thanks for coming over, dude."

Pete closed the front door as T.J. came into the house. He was glad to see his buddy. The past few days had been difficult ones. Although Ronnie had been cool about his arrest, not everyone had. Word had somehow gotten around (Pete suspected Julie Boudreaux), and a couple of customers had told Buck they didn't want Pete working on their vehicles. On Wednesday afternoon Buck told him to take some time off until things blew over. He'd spent the past forty-eight hours in the house, watching television, drinking, and convincing himself that he was the one being attacked. Finally, he'd called Ronnie, T.J., and Gary to see if they wanted to go to the Briar Patch. Gary hadn't picked up, and when Julie answered instead of Ronnie, Pete hung up on her. Only T.J. had been home.

"So, what's the plan?" Pete asked. "Want to head over to the bar?"

"Nah," T.J. answered. "I thought we could just hang out here."

"Shit, man, I've been in this house for two fucking days. I want to get out."

T.J. nodded. "I hear you," he said. "But I'm not so sure you should be out on the town, if you know what I mean."

"Why not?"

"Dude, you know people are talking," said T.J.

"Let them talk," Pete snapped. "What the hell do I care? I didn't do nothing."

"Come on, Pete," T.J. said, looking down. "Everybody knows you did it, man. For Christ's sake, you used a car from the shop."

"What the fuck are you talking about?"

T.J. looked at him. "Well, you did, right?"

"No," Pete said. "No."

T.J. continued to look at him. Pete, agitated, walked around the living room. If even his friends didn't believe him, how the hell was he going to convince anyone else of his innocence? Suddenly, the confidence he'd been feeling began to crumble. He sat on the couch and hung his head.

"Hey," T.J. said. "It's no big deal."

Pete stared at him. "No big deal? Right. Tell that to the cops. They think it's a big fucking deal."

"They just want to scare you, man. What's the worst that could happen?"

"I could go to jail," Pete said.

"You're not going to jail for beating up a couple of fags," said T.J. "Most you'll get is probation."

"You think so?" Pete asked.

"Shit, yeah," said T.J.

"What about what people are saying? What about Buck?"

"Screw Buck. So a couple of customers are freaked out. They'll get over it."

Pete nodded. T.J. was right; people would get over it. He was worrying for nothing. The knot that had gripped his stomach loosened, and he relaxed a little. He just had to chill, take it easy. A couple of weeks and no one would even remember that he'd been arrested.

"Got any beer?" T.J. asked.

"In the fridge," said Pete. "Grab me one too."

T.J. disappeared, returning a minute later with two cold Buds. He handed one to Pete and sat down on the couch. Holding up his bottle, he clinked it against Pete's. "You cool?"

Pete took a deep swallow of beer. "Yeah," he answered, picking up the television remote. "I'm cool. Thanks."

He turned on the set and flipped to the cable menu, looking for a movie. "How about *Die Hard?*" he suggested, and when T.J. shrugged, he turned to the channel and sat back.

For two hours they watched Bruce Willis fight his way out of a building overrun with terrorists. Every half an hour or so, one or the other of them would make a trip to the kitchen and come back with two more beers, until the coffee table was littered with them. Pete had sunk into a comfortable haze, his thoughts fleeting and unfocused. Mainly he just stared at the screen, imagining himself in the building with Bruce. Man, he'd blow the shit out of those terrorists if he had the chance.

When the movie ended and the credits began to roll, Pete got up to take a piss. He'd been holding it in for a while, and he badly needed to go. "You pick the next movie," he told T.J., tossing him the remote.

He went into the bathroom, unzipped, and let his stream fly. Christ, how many beers had he had? He peed for what seemed like forever, his bladder spitting out an endless flow of urine. Finally, he felt it end. Squeezing out the last few drops, he tucked himself away and flushed.

"What's on?" he called out to T.J. as he went to the kitchen for more beer and then headed back to the living room.

"Nothing good was on, so I got one of your videos," T.J. called back.

When Pete entered the room, he saw that Pete had gone into his bedroom and picked up one of his porn tapes. A muscular guy with a shaved head and massive cock was sitting on a couch, stroking himself. Seeing him, Pete wanted to throw up. T.J. had found one of the movies he'd ordered online, a bisexual film called *Switch Hitters*. He'd watched it once and put it away, telling himself he'd only gotten it because the girl on the cover had such hot tits.

"You don't want to see this, dude," he told T.J. "It sucks." He reached for the remote in T.J.'s hand, but his friend pulled it away.

"I want to see what happens," said T.J.

Pete handed him a beer. Maybe if he got him drunk enough, he thought, he could convince T.J. to turn it off.

"Look at that fucking thing," said T.J. as the man in the film smacked his hard dick against his stomach. "Jesus H. Christ."

Knowing there was no arguing with T.J., Pete took his place on the couch and watched through half-lidded eyes as another guy entered the room. Apparently the first man's roommate, he wore only boxer shorts, and seemed surprised to find his buddy sitting on their couch, his tool in his hand.

"What are you doing?" the man asked.

"I couldn't sleep," the guy with the shaved head answered, speaking as if reading a cue card held off camera. "This beats counting sheep."

The roommate looked down at his friend's huge prick. "Need some help?"

"Sure."

The second man sank to his knees and took his roommate's cock in his mouth. Pete closed his eyes. Why did it have to be a scene with two guys? What the hell was T.J. going to think? He waited for an exclamation of disgust to come. When it didn't, he opened his eyes and looked over at T.J.

T.J. was looking at the screen, seemingly unmoved by the two men going at it. After a moment he looked over at Pete. "Feel like helping me out?"

Pete laughed, thinking that T.J. was mimicking the dialogue in the film.

"Come on, dude," T.J. said, looking down. Pete followed his gaze down and saw that T.J.'s hand was rubbing his obviously hard cock.

Pete shook his head. "I'm not into that," he said.

T.J. laughed. "Like shit. You were into it the other night."

Pete was silent. It was the first mention T.J. had ever made of what had happened between them. Pete had almost convinced himself that it had never even happened. T.J. took a swig from his beer bottle and squeezed his crotch again.

"Nothing happened," Pete said.

T.J. responded by unbuttoning his jeans, exposing the head of his cock. Pete stared at it.

"You know you want it," T.J. said, milking his prick with his hand so that a glistening drop of precum escaped from his piss slit. "Come on."

"T.J., man, I'm not like that," said Pete. "I don't know what you think—"

"What do you think Ronnie and Gary would think if I told them how you put the moves on me while I was sleeping?" T.J. interrupted. "Think they'd believe nothing happened?"

Pete felt as if he'd been slapped. He looked at T.J., his mouth open, not believing what he'd heard.

"Come on, Pete. I don't give a shit. Just do it."

T.J. shucked his jeans down so that his lower half was bare. His cock stretched toward Pete as T.J. scratched his balls with one hand. Pete swallowed.

"Do it, dude."

Slowly, Pete leaned down toward T.J.'s dick. Halfway there, T.J.'s hand came down on his neck, forcing him the rest of the way. Pete felt the thick, warm head of T.J.'s cock against his mouth and opened to it. T.J. groaned.

"That's it," he said.

Pete took as much as he could into his mouth. T.J.'s hand was insistent, pushing him farther down until he started to choke. Still T.J. pushed. Pete resisted, but his buddy's touch was firm, and finally he had to just relax and let T.J. fill him. He felt the rough hair of T.J.'s belly against his nose, smelled sweat and manliness.

"I bet you've been thinking about my cock ever since you sucked it, haven't you?" T.J. said.

Pete, unable to respond, moved his mouth up and down T.J.'s shaft. T.J.'s hand never left his neck, working like a piston to control Pete's movements. Pete's throat began to burn as it was scraped by the thick head. T.J. continued to talk, his voice droning in Pete's ears.

"Suck that big prick," he said. "Suck it nice and slow."

He continued to imitate the dialogue coming from the television set, where the man on the couch was receiving the same treatment from his roommate that Pete was providing for T.J.

"Oh, yeah," T.J. growled. "Milk my fucking balls, faggot."

Pete recoiled at the word. Had T.J. just called him a fag? Pushing against T.J.'s grip, he raised his head. "What did you say?"

"Suck my cock," T.J. replied, trying to push him back down.

Pete pulled away. "I'm not a fag."

T.J. looked at him and laughed. "Tell it to my dick," he said, reaching out and grabbing Pete's T-shirt, pulling Pete toward him.

Pete pushed against him, freeing himself. "Knock it off."

T.J.'s eyes went dark. "Suck my fucking cock," he said.

"Get out," Pete ordered. "Get the hell out of here."

Before he knew what was happening, T.J. had tackled him. Pete was thrown to the floor as T.J. landed on top of him. He felt his hard cock pressing against his stomach. Then T.J. was straddling his chest, pinning his arms down. The head of T.J.'s cock was placed against Pete's lips.

"Suck it," T.J. said, his voice hard.

Pete turned his face away, but T.J. forced it back. He slapped his dick against Pete's lips. "I said suck it."

"Fuck you," Pete said. "Get the fuck off me."

"Okay," T.J. said. "I guess you want it in another hole."

He got off Pete, who tried to scramble away. But T.J. overpowered him, holding him around the waist as if they were wrestling. Pete felt T.J. fumbling with the zipper of his jeans, then felt them pulled down. T.J. pushed forward, and Pete found himself flat on his face. T.J.'s weight held him there, his face pressed into the carpet.

"Is this what you want?" asked T.J. as Pete felt his cock press against his asshole. "You want my dick in your ass?"

T.J. pushed into him and Pete yelled into the carpet as pain ripped through him. He felt as if he were being split in two as T.J. kept going, filling his butt. Pete tried to buck him off, but his motions simply drove T.J. deeper.

"That's it," T.J. said. "That's what you want, isn't it?"

He lay on top of Pete, his thighs pressing against Pete's, his hips moving up and down as he fucked Pete's ass. His breath was hot against Pete's ear, the smell of beer foul in Pete's nose. His hands gripped Pete's wrists, holding him prisoner.

"Your ass is fucking tight," T.J. said, moaning.

Pete closed his eyes tightly, trying to will the hurt away. He felt sick, his ass on fire and his stomach clenched as he attempted to ease the fresh bursts of pain that came with each thrust of T.J.'s invading tool. Even worse, he was hard as a rock, his own cock pressed tightly against his belly, scratching against the carpet. How could he be hard? He was in pain, ashamed. Yet there it was, evidence to him of how right T.J. was.

T.J. increased his thrusts, pounding Pete's ass. Pete could sense his breathing getting heavier, faster. Then there was a loud moan and T.J. shuddered. Pete felt his cock twitch, and knew that T.J. was coming in his ass.

"Fuck," T.J. said simply as he finished. He pulled out and got up. Pete, rolling over, looked up at him. T.J. was pulling his jeans back up.

"How about you help me out now?" Pete said, gripping his still-hard cock in his fist.

T.J. shook his head. "I'm not a queer," said T.J. "Sorry, man. You're the cocksucker."

Pete could only look at him, a mixture of rage and fear flooding through him. T.J. was getting dressed as if nothing had happened, as if he hadn't just held Pete down and fucked him.

"Don't worry," T.J. said as he picked up his beer and drained the rest of it. "I'm not gonna tell Ronnie and Gary. This will be our little secret. You take care of me when I need it and we'll be fine."

Pete was on his knees, standing up and pulling his jeans up, covering himself. He couldn't believe what T.J. was saying. All he could do was watch as T.J. put his jacket on.

"I'll see you later," said T.J., going to the front door and opening it. "Thanks for the beer."

He left, the door shutting behind him. Pete stared at it. Then he looked at the empty beer bottle T.J. had left behind. Picking it up, he threw it as hard as he could at the door.

"Fuck you!" he shouted. "Fuck you! I'm not a faggot!"

He collapsed, falling to his knees. The pain inside him poured out as he cried, hot tears filling his eyes. "I'm not a faggot," he repeated. "I'm not a faggot."

CHAPTER 40

"If anyone else moves into this house, I'm going to have to get a hotel license."

Simon puttered around the guest room, straightening Greg's pillows and opening the curtains. Greg, propped up in bed, watched him.

"You're making me dizzy," he said.

"That's the medication," Simon replied. "Which reminds me, it's time for your pills. I'll go get you some applesauce."

"Applesauce? Thanks, Mom."

"Just for that, I'll make it cod liver oil."

"Do they even make that anymore?"

"Unfortunately for the cod, yes," Simon said. "And for you, too, since I just opened a new bottle. My mother used to make me take a tablespoon of the stuff every morning. It's hardly appetizing though quite health-promoting."

"I'll stick with the applesauce," said Greg. "Thanks. And thanks for letting me stay here."

"Well, we couldn't have you sitting in that hospital another week, could we?" Simon replied. "I'm happy to have you."

"Sorry for ruining Christmas for everyone," Greg said.

Simon waved away the remark. "You didn't ruin it for anyone, except possibly for yourself."

"How's the patient?" Russell, fresh from work, poked his head in.

"The patient is doing just fine, thank you," said Simon. "I was just on my way down to the kitchen to get him a little something."

"Want me to get it?"

"You stay here and keep him company," Simon ordered. "I'll be the candy striper."

As Simon left, Russell came in and sat on the edge of the bed.

"So, honey, how was the office?" Greg asked.

"Slow. Everybody asked about you. I told them you were in an accident. By the way, you look like shit."

"I feel like shit," Greg said. "But I feel a lot better now that I'm out of that hospital room. Thanks for covering for me."

"Well, you *were* in an accident," Russell said. "You can make up the details later."

"I don't suppose getting beat up by rough trade is covered under workers' comp, is it?"

Russell laughed. He was glad to see that Greg's sense of humor seemed to be coming back, especially as there was something they needed to talk about.

"Listen," he said. "About what you said that day, about not having me—"

"I was drugged out of my mind," said Greg. "Forget about it."

Russell shook his head. "I don't want to forget about it," he said. "I want to talk about it. I want you to know that you really mean a lot to me. I'm sorry I couldn't—you know." He stopped, embarrassed, and looked away.

"Get it up with me?" Greg suggested.

Russell laughed despite himself. "Yeah, that," he said. He looked at Greg's bruised face. "Did you really get together with that guy because of me?"

"Not just because of you," Greg said. "I've been lonely for a long time. Sometimes I look for people to help me through it."

"The guy from the bar," Russell said, more to himself than to Greg.

"Him. Whoever. It doesn't usually matter. Sometimes I just need to touch someone. Are you disappointed?"

Russell took Greg's hand. "You're a wonderful man," he said. "And you deserve somebody special. No, I'm not disappointed."

"That's funny," said Greg. "Because I am. I should have known better. Christ, I never even asked for a picture of the guy before he came over. How pathetic is that?"

"We've all done it in one way or another," Russell reassured him.

"You're not the first gay man to pick up the wrong guy, and you certainly won't be the last. It's what we *do*," he added dramatically.

"That doesn't make me feel better," Greg informed him. "But thanks for trying."

Russell released his hand. "The right one is out there," he said. "You just have to keep looking for him."

"Couldn't you just find him for me?"

"I thought I had," Russell said.

"Stephen?" said Greg. "Did he really run into the same guy I did?"

"It looks like it."

"That's too creepy."

"It's a small town," Russell told him.

"At least we have more in common now," said Greg. "It will give us something to talk about if I ever see him again."

"He'll be here tomorrow night for the party," said Russell.

Greg laughed. "My party face is in the shop," he said. "I think I'll stay up here."

"You at least have to come down for midnight," said Russell. "Otherwise we'll all come up here."

"We'll see," Greg told him.

"Will you leave that poor boy alone?" Simon said, coming in with a tray. "He's supposed to be resting."

"I was just leaving," said Russell. "It's time to get out of these clothes."

He left Simon and Greg and went to his own room, at the other end of the hall. He'd been living with Simon for over a month, and he'd come to think of the house as his home. But with Greg's arrival, he was reminded that his home was somewhere else, in another house, where John was living alone while Russell made up his mind about what he wanted from his life. And he knew he had to do it soon, if only to keep from losing his bet with Simon.

He went into his room and shut the door. Removing his tie, he quickly unbuttoned his shirt and hung it up. His pants followed, folded neatly and placed over the back of the chair beside his dresser. He was pulling on jeans and a T-shirt when there was a knock on the door. He opened it to find Simon standing there.

"Are you decent?" Simon asked.

"Am I ever?" Russell answered, opening the door all the way.

Simon stepped into the room and shut the door.

"Is it that serious?" Russell asked, sitting on the bed and pulling on fresh socks.

"Gravely," said Simon. "I want to talk to you about the party tomorrow."

"You had to shut the door for that?"

"I don't want to disturb our patient," said Simon.

"Right," Russell said, not believing a word of it.

"All right, if you must know, I need some advice," said Simon. "Dating advice, if you will?"

"Dating?" Russell said.

Simon nodded. "It appears that I may have accomplished the goal you set for me."

"You got a date for tomorrow?" exclaimed Russell. "Way to go!"

"Shh," Simon hissed, motioning for Russell to keep it down.

"What's the big secret?" Russell asked. "This is great. Who is it?"

"I'd prefer to keep at least that much to myself until I'm sure this is an actual date," said Simon.

"You're not sure?"

Simon sighed. "It's been a very long time," he said. "Forgive me if I'm a little out of practice."

"Okay," said Simon. "What can I help you with?"

Simon looked discomfited. He cleared his throat. "This safer sex business," he began.

Russell gave a hoot and clapped his hands. Once again Simon, glancing at the door as if Russell's voice would penetrate the oak and sail down the hallway, motioned for him to keep it down. Russell, grinning, composed himself.

"As I said, it's been a very long time," Simon said. "Things have changed. I understand there are—things—one needs to be concerned about."

"Sure," Russell nodded. "That's true. But rubbers pretty much take care of that. Do you swallow?"

"Do I what?" Simon asked.

"Swallow," Russell repeated. "You know, when you give head."

Simon blushed deeply. "Well, I suppose I . . . I don't . . . Good heavens."

"It's okay," said Russell. He patted the bed beside him. "Come sit down. We'll start at the beginning."

Simon went to the bed and obediently sat. "I feel like a fool," he said.

"Don't," Russell told him. "I'm glad you came to me instead of believing what all your friends tell you."

Simon glared at him. "If you're going to mock me, I can just ask Mike."

"I'm sorry," Russell apologized. "This is just so after-school special. Besides, I'm never going to have kids, so let me have some fun."

"Very well. But just stick with the basics. I *have* been with a man before, as you know."

"Right. So, what did you and Walter used to do? I mean, did you, you know, engage in anal intercourse?"

"Oh, for the love of God," Simon said. "I'm not your grandfather. You can say 'fuck.' "

"All right, did you and Walter fuck?"

"Yes," Simon answered.

"And who did the fucking?"

"Well, me mostly," Simon explained. "Walter was never very comfortable doing that. He said it made him feel like an overeager terrier."

"Good," said Russell. "So you're usually a top. What about rimming?"

"Rimming?"

"Sticking your tongue in someone's ass," Russell elaborated.

"Can you do that?" asked Simon.

"Don't tell me you and Walter never did."

"It never occurred to us," Simon told him.

"Well, if you're going to try it, just remember that you can get hepatitis and a bunch of other stuff that way."

"This is all starting to sound a little hazardous," Simon said. "Perhaps I should just forget about it."

"Relax," said Russell. "I just want you to consider the possibilities. Chances are you'll be fine. Has this guy been around a lot?"

"I don't think so."

"Good, then he's probably low-risk. Still, if you're going to fuck him, you should use a rubber. Have you ever used one?"

Simon shook his head. "We didn't worry about such things then," he said.

"It's no big deal," Russell said. "Just make sure you don't use any oil-based lube."

"Lube," Simon repeated, as if memorizing a grocery list.

"Lubricant," said Russell, sensing his confusion. "Don't use anything like baby oil, or Vaseline. You want something water-based."

"Where would one purchase something like that?" Simon ventured.

"At the drugstore," answered Russell. "Right by the condoms. It's a brave new world," he added, seeing Simon's surprise at hearing this news.

"When I was a boy, condoms were kept in a locked case in the pharmacy," he said. "You had to ask the druggist for them. I remember my father purchasing some once. The clerk wrapped them in brown paper. For the longest time I thought they must be some kind of candy that he was taking home to surprise my mother."

"Well, I guess they sort of were," said Russell. "But don't worry, you can walk into any store and get them. If you want, I'll do it for you."

"I think I can manage, thank you."

"Okay, well, that's pretty much all there is to it. You just roll it on your pecker and go to town."

"And they're used for both?"

"Both what?"

"Fucking," Simon said, "and the other." He pointed to his mouth.

"That's your call," said Russell. "Most people think sucking someone off without a rubber is pretty safe. But definitely for the fucking."

Simon nodded. "I feel fully prepared," he said. "Thank you for your help."

"You really going to do it with this guy?"

"If I do, you will be the first to know," Simon said.

"Good for you," Russell said, putting his arms around Simon's shoulders. "Really. Walter would want you to find someone."

"Yes," Simon replied. "He would. But I must say, the prospect of starting all over again with someone new is a trifle frightening."

"Tell me about it," Russell said. "I've been thinking about that a lot lately."

"Have you come to any decision about John?"

Russell sighed. "Yes," he said. "And then an hour later I change my mind."

"Where are you right now?"

"In the middle," said Russell. "Smack dab in the middle."

"May I offer you some unsolicited advice?"

"Hey, you sat through my condom talk," Russell said. "It's the least I can do."

"When people are fearful, they shut the world out. They make themselves safe by lashing out at anything they perceive as a threat."

"You mean John? What does he have to be afraid of?"

"You'll have to ask him that," said Simon. "I don't know."

"Why do I always have to be the one to ask?" Russell protested. "Why can't he be the one to take the first step?"

"Maybe he doesn't know how."

"So I have to help him? Why should I?"

"Because you love him," Simon said.

"You sound more sure of that than I am."

"That's because I'm on the outside looking in," Simon said. "It gives me an advantage. Besides, I loved a man for forty-three years. I recognize it when I see it."

"I don't know," said Russell. "It got really hard. I couldn't stay there."

"But the question is, can you go back?"

Russell leaned his head on Simon's shoulder. "Do I have to answer that right now?"

"No," Simon said. "You have until tomorrow at midnight, remember?"

"Can we talk about condoms some more? That's easier for me."

"I think we've covered that," answered Simon. "But I do have a couple of questions about this rimming thing."

CHAPTER 41

At a few minutes past ten on the morning of New Year's Eve, Simon walked through the doors of a CVS pharmacy and stopped. He scanned the helpful signs hung over each row detailing the contents of that aisle's shelves: FEMININE NEEDS, SHAMPOO, PAPER PRODUCTS. What heading, he wondered, would condoms come under? Finally he located it: FAMILY PLANNING. Such a name, he thought with amusement. How coy. Did heterosexual men really sheath their penises to prevent pregnancy? He'd almost forgotten, having come to regard condoms as the province of gay men. Didn't women simply take a pill, or stuff something inside themselves? Did they really leave such an important task up to the men who sweated and panted on top of them? It seemed barbaric.

He walked down the aisle, hoping he looked inconspicuous. A young woman, an employee, was the only other occupant of the row. She was looking intently at tubes of hemorrhoid cream, arranging them into neat stacks. Simon nodded at her in passing and continued on. The condoms were at the very end of the aisle, isolated from the aspirins and cold remedies, like exotic animals in a zoo. He stopped in front of them.

The condoms were in boxes, a rainbow of colors hung on thin metal arms. Scanning the offerings, Simon realized with some dismay that things were not going to be as simple as Russell had led him to believe. There seemed to be an endless array of options: ribbed, colored, and—was he reading correctly?—flavored. A multitude of descriptions assailed him. Reservoir tip. Super-thin. Ultra-Last. Spermicidal. (How violent, he thought. As if trapping the poor sperm weren't enough,

now they needed to be eradicated completely, like unwanted ro-
dents.) There were condoms with bumps, condoms made from the
skin of lambs, condoms for men with extra length and girth and for
men with reduced length and girth (did anyone buy the latter?).

As the length of time he spent looking at the condoms increased,
he grew more and more nervous. He decided to delay his decision by
first locating the promised lubricant Russell had assured him would be
nearby. This proved to be true. There was a small shelf devoted to the
slippery stuff. Again, he discovered that this necessary accessory to
lovemaking came not in one generic form, but in different permuta-
tions. Fortunately, there were only a handful of them, unlike the condoms, which seemed to mutate constantly, creating newer and more
perplexing varieties of themselves even as he tried to decide which
ones to purchase.

He read the information on the bottles. Recalling Russell's edict to
stick with things water-based, he searched for the words. This narrowed his options to three. The first product guaranteed him a feeling
of "skin on skin." The second claimed to produce a sensation of heat.
The third promised nothing, its label generic, almost clinical. Comforted
by its modesty, he chose it with a sense of relief.

He turned back to the condoms. Again their myriad voices clam-
ored at him, each entreating him to give it a try. He was about to just
take one at random when a voice interrupted his thoughts.

"Are you looking for something in particular?"

Shaken, he turned to see the young woman he'd greeted earlier
standing beside him. Apparently having completed her hemorrhoid
cream duties, she had come down to assist him. Now she stood, her
head cocked, waiting for him to answer. He tried to make the bottle of
lubricant in his hand disappear as he composed himself.

"My grandson," he said, thinking quickly. "I'm purchasing him
some—of these," he concluded, indicating the boxes of rubbers. "He's
sixteen," he added as an afterthought.

"That's so cool of you," said the girl, not much older than that herself.

"Thank you," Simon said. "I'm afraid they're slightly more complicated than they were when I was your age."

The girl laughed. "No problem," she said. She reached for a light
blue box. "My boyfriend likes these."

Simon accepted her suggestion thankfully, not even looking at the box. "I'm sure these will be excellent," he said.

"Can I help you find anything else?"

"No. That will be all."

"Okay, then. Have a great day."

Simon hurried away from her, grateful to have the ordeal over with. He was still reeling from the girl's complete lack of embarrassment. Had she really told him that she and her boyfriend were intimate with one another? It seemed inconceivable. Then again, he thought, he had concocted an imaginary grandson as cover for his own needs. Which of them should be ashamed?

In the checkout line he experienced another brush with ignominy when he found himself sandwiched between an elderly woman purchasing numerous cans of cat food and a weary mother with two young children in tow. He placed the condoms and lube on the counter, where they waited between the tins of Friskies and a bottle of Tide and two Snickers bars for the clerk to ring them up. He felt the eyes of all concerned on him, and resisted the urge to blurt out the story about his grandson.

Mercifully, he was able to pay without incident. The clerk barely looked at him as he handed over some bills and accepted his change. When asked if he needed a bag, Simon answered firmly that he did, and moments later he was outside. Clutching his purchases in his hands, he got into his car and sped away, imagining the clerk and the harried mother discussing the foolish dreams of old men as the children devoured their candy bars.

Walking into his house twenty minutes later, he hid the bag beneath his jacket, as if he were smuggling pornography or contraband into his own home. When he entered the kitchen and found Greg in there, standing in front of the refrigerator and peering inside, he was glad he had.

"What are you doing?" he asked. "You're supposed to be in bed."

"All of my nurses deserted me," Greg said, taking out a Tupperware container and opening it.

"Where's Russell?"

"He went out about an hour ago," Greg answered, opening the container and sniffing the contents. "He said he'd be back this afternoon to help you get ready for the party."

"Well, I want you back in bed," Simon ordered. "Go on. I'll bring you some lunch in a little while."

"This is fine for now," Greg said, grabbing a spoon from the dish drainer.

"Take it upstairs," Simon told him. "I have a lot to do for this evening."

"Yes, ma'am," said Greg, walking as quickly as he could out of the kitchen.

Simon waited until he heard Greg clomping around upstairs before going up himself. He snuck by Greg's open door and disappeared into his own bedroom, shutting and locking the door. He went to the bed and sat. Taking the paper bag out from beneath his jacket, he removed the bottle of lube and the box of condoms and looked at them. The box sported a picture of a laughing man and woman. The words "More Pleasure!" were stamped across the bottom in red.

"More pleasure than what?" Simon asked out loud.

Setting aside the lube, he opened the box and dumped the contents into his hand. Six wrapped rubbers tumbled out, landing on his palm. They were encased in plastic. He picked the top one up and the others came with it, falling out behind like the tail of a kite. He dangled the half-dozen little plastic-wrapped packages before him, watching them swing back and forth. Taking hold of the last one, he tore along the perforated edge, separating it from the chain. Collapsing the remaining five back into one another, he put them into the box and put it next to the lubricant on his bedside table.

Tearing the packet in his hand open, he pulled out the condom inside. He was surprised to see that it was a pale brown in color; he had expected it to be blue, like the box. It was wrinkled and damp, like a baby bird or the discarded skin of a large insect. Simon looked at it with distaste, imagining putting such a thing on his penis.

Standing, he lowered his trousers and underwear before sitting down again. His cock hung between his legs, hardly aroused. Holding the condom in one hand, he played with himself with the other, attempting to coax an erection out of his flaccid member. It stubbornly refused to cooperate, so he shut his eyes and tried to think of something exciting. The first image that came to him was Walter, and he rather guiltily pushed it aside. That was the past; he wanted to concentrate on the future.

He could think of nothing else. It had been so long that he had no frame of reference for his own desires, for what stirred him apart from the memories of his lover. Frustrated, he stroked himself harder, as if he could force the blood to flow into his soft tissues. This only resulted in making him sore, and finally he fell back on the bed, annoyed and tired, and stared at the ceiling.

Downstairs, the doorbell rang. Thankful for the reprieve, Simon got up and pulled his pants up. Tossing the still-unused condom onto the bedside table, he left the room and went to answer the door. Assuming it to be one of the boys coming over to help with party preparations, he was surprised instead to find Gavin standing outside.

"I hope I'm not bothering you," Gavin said. "I was going to the market and thought I'd stop by to see if you needed anything for tonight."

"How very kind," said Simon. "I think we've got everything covered, but why don't you come in."

He showed Gavin into the house. Gavin, looking around, said, "I didn't interrupt anything, did I? I wouldn't want to keep you from whatever you were doing."

"Believe me," Simon said, taking Gavin's coat, "you didn't."

"Your house is fantastic," Gavin remarked.

"Walter and I completely redid it," said Simon. "The previous owners had painted all the woodwork in this room a hideous green. It took months to get it all off. Would you like to see the rest of the house?"

Gavin nodded, and Simon began the tour. After the lower level, he took him up the stairs to the second floor. Peering into Greg's room, he found him asleep, so he pulled the door shut and moved on to the other rooms.

"And this is the master bedroom," he said, showing Gavin into his room.

"The moldings are lovely," Gavin remarked. As he turned around, his gaze fell upon the bedside table and lingered. Following it, Simon saw the discarded condom, the bright blue box, the bottle of lube. The paper bag from which all had been extracted lay crumbled beside the pillows.

"I should explain that," said Simon. "I—"

"It's all right," said Gavin quickly. "Really. I understand. I didn't know you were expecting anyone."

"Oh, no," Simon protested. "I wasn't expecting anyone. I was . . . practicing."

Gavin looked at him. "Practicing?"

"Oh, dear," Simon said. "That wasn't quite what I meant. I mean, it *was,* but it sounds so lurid somehow." He was babbling, he knew, and it only increased his embarrassment. "It's just that I've never worn a— I thought that perhaps if I *tried* one before we—" He stopped as Gavin's eyes widened. "Not that I assumed you would want to," said Simon, trying to save the moment.

Gavin looked again at the condoms, then back at Simon.

"This is very awkward," Simon said sheepishly. "If you want to go, I don't blame you at all."

Gavin shook his head. "No," he said. "I don't want to go."

"You don't?"

Gavin picked the condom up. "Shall I show you what to do with it?"

Simon was at a loss for words. But Gavin made them unnecessary as he came to him and put his arms around Simon's waist. They stood, looking at one another for a moment. Then they were kissing. Simon felt the roughness of Gavin's beard against his face. For a moment he hesitated at the unfamiliar sensation. Walter's skin had always been so smooth. But it wasn't Walter he held in his arms. Walter was gone. But Gavin was right there, his mouth warm against Simon's. Simon kissed him back.

Moments later, their clothes were on the floor. Simon was surprised at the quickness of it, but once it began, he found himself caught up in the excitement. He removed his pants and shirt, hesitating only a moment before adding his underthings to the pile. Gavin, too, had stripped, and they stood, naked, looking at one another.

Gavin's body was soft. His stomach, covered in dark hair, formed a pouch over his waist. His cock hung beneath it, nestled in a thicket of hair. His balls, heavy and fat, swung beneath it. He kept his glasses on, examining Simon through them.

Simon looked down at himself, back at Gavin. They were hardly young, hardly what most would consider specimens of beauty. But in Gavin he saw something lovely. They were two men in their later years, with lived-in bodies that had experienced much. Anticipating Gavin's touch, Simon found himself stiffening.

Gavin reached out, wrapping his fingers around Simon's lengthening cock. "Come here," he said, pulling Simon toward him, and toward the bed.

They fell together, arms and legs entwining as they kissed once more. Simon ran his hands over Gavin's body, felt Gavin's roaming over his. His hardness increased, and he pressed himself against Gavin. Gavin responded by spreading his legs, so that Simon was lying between them. Simon sensed Gavin's dick, equally hard, against his stomach.

He moved down, his mouth kissing Gavin's chest, then his stomach. When he came to Gavin's cock, he paused, looking at it. Short and thick, it was the opposite of what Walter's had been, the narrow smoothness of his lover replaced by something denser, weightier. Simon took it in his hand and felt how it filled his fist. He held it while he leaned down and surrounded the head with his lips. He had always enjoyed sucking Walter's cock. Now he took Gavin's into his mouth.

His fingers worked their way between Gavin's buttocks as he sucked him, searching for the tender center. There was hair, and heat, in the veldt of Gavin's ass. He pulled his feet up toward his waist, spreading himself so that Simon could see what his fingers were stroking. There, beneath the plump sack of his balls, his pucker waited.

Simon rubbed a fingertip around the wrinkled eye, probing gently. Then, thinking about his conversation with Russell, he bent down and flicked his tongue against it. Gavin groaned, pushing against him. Simon applied more force, and felt the tip of his tongue penetrate the opening. His cock twitched as an unfamiliar thrill radiated through him.

"Here."

He looked up and saw that Gavin was handing him the bottle of lubricant. He took it and squeezed some onto his palm. This he rubbed into Gavin's asshole, sliding a finger inside. Gavin was tight, and Simon felt his finger pinched comfortably.

"Let me put it on you," Gavin said, and Simon saw that he was holding the rubber.

Gavin sat up. Taking the bottle from Simon, he poured some lube onto his hand and used it to slick Simon's cock. The sensation was intense, and for a moment Simon thought he might come. But then

Gavin released him, and the threatened climax retreated. Then he felt Gavin's hand again, this time rolling the condom down the length of his prick. When he looked down, Simon saw that he was encased in the rubber.

"That's it?" he asked.

Gavin laughed. "That's it," he said. "Go to town."

He lay back again and spread his legs. Simon, his heart racing, positioned the head of his cock against Gavin's slicked hole and pressed in. He watched Gavin's face as he entered him. At first slightly tense, the muscles of Gavin's mouth softened as Simon patiently proceeded, until finally he was all the way in and Gavin seemed relaxed and ready.

He moved in and out slowly, enjoying the smoothness and the warmth. Gavin, reaching down, stroked himself as Simon fucked him, his arm moving in time with Simon's thrusts.

"You're going to make me come," Gavin said after a few minutes.

"Good," Simon answered. "Because so am I, and I didn't want to be rude."

Humor was replaced moments later by heavy breathing as first Gavin and then Simon climaxed. A spray of cum blasted from Gavin's cock as Simon gripped his thighs, pushing himself deep. Simon shook with the force of his own orgasm, filling the rubber with his load. When he was done, he slipped out of Gavin and pulled the rubber off. He rolled onto his side beside Gavin, his cock flushed and sticky.

"I hope you don't think I'm easy," he said as he put his hand on Gavin's chest.

"I do," Gavin answered. "But it's okay. I like easy."

They rested in silence. Simon closed his eyes. Lying beside only the second man he'd made love to since meeting Walter, he felt as if it were his very first time. He felt young again, filled with the thrill of having accomplished something very grand and important.

"What are you thinking?" Gavin asked him.

Simon propped himself up on his side and looked down into Gavin's face. "That it's going to be a very good year," he answered.

CHAPTER 42

"Fuck you, Dick Clark."

Pete gave the TV the finger. Dick Clark, ignoring him, continued to beam. What the hell was wrong with that guy, anyway? Wasn't he, like, eighty years old? Pete had been watching him since he was a kid. Every New Year's until he was old enough to go out with his friends.

He should be out with his friends now, he thought. Instead he was home, sitting in just his boxer shorts alone, stoned, and drunk, watching goddamned Dick Clark and a bunch of bands nobody gave a shit about count down to the new year. Fucking T.J. It was all his fault. Pete couldn't even think about it. Whenever he did, he got so mad he thought about killing T.J. He'd even gone out to the garage and found the gun, the one his father used to keep on the top shelf of his closet, underneath girlie magazines and the flannel shirts he wore when he went hunting. When Pete wanted to impress his buddies, he used to take them into his parents' bedroom and show them the gun.

The gun had passed to him after his father's death from a heart attack. His mother hadn't wanted it in the house anymore, and so Pete had taken it. Now it sat on the coffee table. Beside it was a box of bullets, dug out of one of the boxes stacked against the garage's far wall.

He picked the gun up and examined it. A classic Colt pistol, its surface gleamed a steely blue-black. It was heavy, substantial, a gun meant for business. His father had spent hours polishing it, telling Pete stories about the lawmen and bandits of the Old West who had carried similar weapons: Wyatt Earp, Billy the Kid, Jesse James. Later, when Pete was older, he'd taken him into the woods and shown him how to hold the piece, how to aim and pull the trigger. Once he had allowed him to actually shoot it. The recoil had nearly knocked Pete off his nine-year-old feet, but he had never forgotten the thrill of feeling the bullet lock in the chamber, the excitement of pulling the trigger, hearing the gun roar, and a split second later, seeing the empty beer can he'd targeted fly into the air, its metal skin ripped open.

He imagined taking aim at T.J., pointing the Colt at his shit-eating grin, and pulling the trigger. He saw T.J.'s head fly into a million pieces, the grin disappearing. He laughed. Wouldn't T.J. shit his fucking pants? They'd see who the fucking faggot was then.

"The new year will be here in half an hour, folks. And you'll see it right here."

Pete lowered the gun. Dick Clark was talking to some chick with pink hair. Behind them, a bunch of assholes jumped up and down, waving at the camera. Dick ignored them. He was asking the girl, who had just finished lip-synching her latest hit, how it felt to have the number one record in the country.

Pete picked up the joint he'd been working on and took a toke on it. He blew the smoke out at Dick Clark's face. That's what Dick needed to do; he needed to get high. Then maybe the stick up his ass wouldn't bother him so much. Then maybe he could actually act like he wasn't so damn old and tired.

Pete laughed, pointing the Colt at Dick's head. He imagined pulling the trigger. Blam. With one shot, Dick's head would disappear. "No more Rockin' New Year's Eve for you, asswipe," Pete said to the television.

He put the joint down and picked up a beer. "How about a cold one?" he shouted at the set as he toasted Dick with his beer. He chugged it, draining the half of the bottle that was left. When it was gone, he opened his mouth and belched, tasting pot and Cold Falls Ale.

Dick disappeared and a commercial came on. Burger King. Suddenly he remembered that he was hungry. He'd been drinking since early afternoon, but he hadn't eaten anything since a bowl of Frosted Flakes at breakfast. He decided to see what there was in the kitchen.

He stood up, and immediately sat back down. The room swayed around him. He laughed. "You are majorly fucked up," he told himself. "Majorly."

He tried again. This time he was prepared for the swaying sensation, and managed to keep standing. Moving slowly, he made his way down the hall to the kitchen. It, too, was swaying. The refrigerator seemed impossibly far away. He wasn't sure he'd be able to get there before falling down.

He did, though, but when he pulled the door open, he discovered that the only things inside were more beer and a jar of pickles. He took both out. The beer he set on the counter; the pickles he opened. He reached in and pulled one out, putting it in his mouth. It was sour. Dill. He took one bite and threw the rest of the pickle in the sink. The smell was making him sick.

He put the jar down and took up the beer, twisting the top off and dropping it on the floor. He took a long sip, killing the pickle taste in his mouth. Afterward, he felt much better, although his head was starting to throb. He needed to get back to the couch.

He made it, largely by feeling his way along the hallway wall. Once he was sitting down, though, he was all right. Sitting was good; it was standing up that was tricky. He could sit all night, sight and drink and smoke and fucking ring in the New Year all on his goddamned own.

He considered picking up the phone and calling Ronnie or Gary, but he knew they'd be out. Then he thought about calling T.J. "Hey, faggot," he heard himself say. "Hey, you fucking cocksucker. Why don't you come over here and suck my goddamned cock?"

Laughter poured from him. That's what he should do. Or maybe he should go over to T.J.'s house, go over and knock on the door. When T.J. answered, he would pull the gun out and give him a scare, make him get on his knees and tell Pete what a faggot he was. Tell him how sorry he was for thinking *Pete* was the queer.

Even better, maybe he'd get T.J. on his knees and make him suck his cock. Hold the gun against his head while he pumped his dick in and out of T.J.'s mouth. He'd like that. He'd like seeing T.J. cry like a baby while he shot a load in his mouth.

He picked the gun up again. Holding it in both hands, he closed his eyes and imagined T.J. on the floor. He would make him strip first, so that he was naked. Then he'd hold the end of the gun at T.J.'s temple, right above his eye. He'd hold it there while T.J. took his cock in his mouth, while he put his hand on the back of T.J.'s head and buried his dick in his throat.

"Oh, yeah," he said. "You like that, don't you?"

He slid his hand into his boxers. His dick, fighting the alcohol and pot swirling through his blood, was getting hard. He played with it while he continued his fantasy. He pressed the barrel of the Colt against his own cheek, the steel cool on his skin. He traced the line of his jaw with it while he thought about T.J.'s mouth on his prick.

"That's the way," he whispered, his fingers gripping T.J.'s hair.

The barrel of the gun met his lips. He opened his mouth, darting his tongue into the opening. He tasted the bitter tang of metal. The gun tapped against his teeth. He closed his lips around it, sucking.

"Are you a faggot?" he asked T.J. "Are you a good little cocksucker?"

He moved the gun in and out of his mouth as he pulled his boxers down and off. Nude, he lay back on the couch, putting his feet up on the coffee table. He stroked himself. The fingers of one hand gripped the handle of the Colt; the fingers of the other gripped his dick.

"And now we're just fifteen minutes away from the dropping of the ball!"

Dick Clark's voice cut through the haze of his fantasy. Pulling the gun from his mouth, Pete pointed it at the TV and pulled the trigger. He saw the screen shatter. Smoke fanned out from the place where Dick's head had been. His arm stung.

He looked at the gun, then at the remains of the television. Apparently there had been a bullet in it. For a moment he was shaken. Then he began to laugh. He'd killed fucking Dick Clark. Put a bullet right through his big plastic head. It was pretty goddamned funny, when he thought about it.

He touched the barrel of the gun. It was warm. He put it to his lips, feeling the heat transfer from the steel to his skin. The acrid smell of powder filled his nose.

"That could have been you," he pictured himself telling T.J. as the two of them stared at what was left of the television. "That could have been your head instead of Dick's."

T.J., looking at the TV, begged him to stop. Pete responded by getting on his knees, so that he and T.J. were face to face. He traced the outline of T.J.'s face with the gun's barrel while T.J. shook, trying not to cry. He ran it down T.J.'s neck, circled one of his nipples, and continued down his belly until he reached his cock. It was hard.

"What's this?" he asked T.J.

T.J. shook his head. Pete put the end of the barrel beneath T.J.'s balls, lifting them up. He pressed the gun into the soft place beneath T.J.'s nuts. His balls fell on either side of the barrel, brushing Pete's fingers.

"Am I making you hard, T.J.?" he asked. "Do you like this?"

He opened his eyes and saw that he had the Colt beneath his own balls. The barrel, having cooled, bit into his skin with its cold teeth. He pushed up, pressing his balls tightly against the base of his cock. Then, slowly, he let the end of the barrel slip down.

Moving behind T.J., he placed the barrel of the gun between the cheeks of his ass. "On your hands," he ordered.

T.J. dropped forward, supporting himself on his hands. His ass was before Pete, exposed and unprotected. Pete spread the cheeks with his hand. T.J.'s asshole stretched open. Pete spit on it, beads of saliva catching in the hair on T.J.'s thighs and balls. He pointed the gun at T.J.'s hole.

"Do you want me to fuck you?" he asked.

T.J. whimpered. Pete jabbed him with the gun. "Do you want me to fuck you?" he repeated.

"Yes," T.J. said almost inaudibly.

"Because you're a faggot?" Pete asked.

T.J. nodded.

"Say it. Tell me what you are."

"I'm a faggot," said T.J.

Pete pushed the barrel of the gun into T.J.'s asshole, watching the pink lips part and swallow the steel shaft. He kept pushing until the gun was buried to the chamber inside T.J.'s butt.

"Shall we find out if there are any more bullets?" he asked. "What do you think about that, faggot?"

T.J. didn't answer. He was crying. His head was down, and his body shook. Watching him, Pete felt himself come. Again his eyes opened. The Colt was between his own legs. He had spread them, and the gun, held upside down, was inside him. It wasn't T.J. he was fucking, but himself. The long shaft of the Colt was inside him, where T.J. had once been, and his hand was covered in his own stickiness.

"T.J. isn't the faggot," he said. "You are."

There. He'd said it. He *was* queer. T.J. was right. He had wanted T.J.'s cock, and when he'd gotten it, he'd taken it all in his ass. He was just like the men he despised, a pathetic cocksucker. And like them, he deserved what he got.

He pulled the gun from his ass and brought it to his face. Again he placed it in his mouth. He ran his tongue over it, tasting himself on the barrel. He felt for the trigger. Was there another bullet left? What if there was? It no longer mattered to him. He'd discovered what he was. His cock, still hard, told him. T.J. had told him. He was a faggot, a queer, a cocksucker.

His finger found the trigger. Trembling, he pulled back on it. He heard the mechanism within the Colt start to click, felt the chamber rotate into place. In his mind he saw T.J. look up at him, grinning, and then his soul was flying across the sky.

CHAPTER 43

"How did your father take the news?"

Stephen dipped a cracker into the bowl on the table. "Pretty well," he told Russell. "I think when my mother said she had something to tell him about me, he assumed she was going to tell him I had some fatal disease."

"What about Alan?"

"Him I'm not so sure about. He's been a little distant."

"He'll come around," Russell said. "It took my brother a while too. I think they're convinced that it must be hereditary and that they've got it too."

Stephen laughed. "Wait until they find out about Father Dunn," he said. "Then they'll really think it's spreading."

"Did you go to Saint Peter's this morning?"

Stephen nodded. "It was amazing," he said. "Thomas stood up there and came out to the entire congregation. You could have heard a pin drop when he was finished. Then my mother stood up and started clapping. It was like the ending to one of those John Hughes films, where the geeky girl gets a standing ovation. Except that no one else stood up."

"Ouch," Russell said. "Did anyone leave?"

"A couple of people. But basically we just went on with the service as if nothing had happened, like the good WASPs we are. I'm sure the fallout, if it happens, will take a while."

"And what about you? How are you feeling about everything?"

"Embarrassed," Stephen said. "Stupid. Like a fool. Pick one."

"Don't," Russell said. "You made a mistake. It's over. Now it's time to get on with your life."

"I know," Stephen said. "My new shrink said the same thing. But it's scary."

"That's why you've got friends. We've all been there."

"So why do we always seem to feel like we're the only ones?"

"It's the gay drama gene," Russell said. "I'm afraid you're stuck with it."

Stephen, laughing, dropped his cracker on the floor.

"What's so funny?"

Russell and Stephen looked up to see Greg standing beside the couch. Stephen, who hadn't yet seen him since his run-in with Pete Thayer, stared at his battered face in shock.

"That bad?" Greg asked.

Russell stood up. "I'm going to help Simon in the kitchen," he said, motioning for Greg to take his place. "You boys sit and chat."

Greg took his place on the couch as Russell left. "I hear we went out with the same guy," he said. "We should have compared notes."

"Are you okay?"

"Do I look okay?" Greg said. He put his hand on Stephen's leg. "I'm sorry. I don't mean to be bitchy. It's how I'm dealing with this."

"That's better than my way, I guess," Stephen remarked.

They looked at each other, then laughed.

"We're pretty pathetic, huh?" said Greg.

"You are," Stephen said. "I'm fine."

"Asshole," Greg joked. He took Stephen's hand and held it, neither of them speaking for a while.

"I should have called you," Stephen said finally.

"Yeah, you should have," Greg agreed, nodding his head.

"Is it too late?"

"I don't know," Greg said. "I've sort of been seeing this hot guy. He's got a little anger management problem, but I think we can work it out."

Stephen hesitated a moment, then shook his head. "Now who's the asshole."

"That's enough name calling, children," Simon said as he appeared with a tray of food. "Don't make me send you to your rooms before midnight."

"Where are the rest of the guys?" Greg asked.

"On their way," answered Simon as he fussed with arranging the food.

"By the way, your date's a cutie," Greg remarked. "And from all the noise I heard coming from your room this afternoon, he's a tiger in the sack. Or was that you doing all the grunting?"

Simon, a flush of red moving from his neck and up his face, concentrated on a dish of olives. "You were supposed to be having a nap," he said.

"I was," said Greg. "All the banging woke me up."

"What banging?" asked Russell, entering with another tray, this one filled with glasses of champagne. Gavin was behind him, a plate of deviled eggs in one hand and a bowl of chips in the other.

"There was no banging," Simon said firmly, giving Greg a sharp look. "Greg thought he heard something. It was probably squirrels in the attic."

"No," Greg said. "It sounded more like something getting nailed. Hard."

Simon, blushing afresh, turned away. "I have to attend to something in the kitchen," he said. "Gavin, would you help me, please?"

"What was that about?" Russell asked, nabbing a chip.

"Simon's got a boyfriend," Greg said in a singsong voice.

Russell looked at him, then at the retreating figures of Simon and Gavin. He looked back at Greg. "No," he said. "Really?"

"Well, I don't know if you can call him a boyfriend yet. I guess technically he's still just a trick. But they're pretty cute together, aren't they?"

Russell, thinking back to his conversation with Simon, suddenly had a mental image of him and Gavin, naked. "You go, old boy," he crowed.

The doorbell rang. Excusing himself, Russell went to answer it. Mike, Thomas, and John all stood outside when he opened the door.

"It's about time," he said. "We were starting to think we wouldn't see you until next year."

"I had a call from the bishop," Thomas explained as they came in.

"And what's your excuse?" Russell asked John. "Did you have a call from the bishop too?"

"Worse," John answered. "My mother. She says hello."

"Hmm," Russell said. "So, what did the bishop have to say?" he asked Thomas.

"Apparently word travels fast," said Thomas as they made their way into the living room. "One of my beloved parishioners phoned him as soon as he or she—he didn't tell me who it was—got home and informed him that Saint Peter's was under attack by sodomites."

"It makes us sound like a football team," Russell said. "The Cold Falls Sodomites. We should have T-shirts made up."

"Yes, well, the bishop wasn't exactly thrilled to be the last one to know," Thomas continued. "He and I are having a meeting on Wednesday."

"What's this I hear about sodomites and football?" asked Simon, returning to the room with Gavin, whose flushed face suggested that Simon had told him that their afternoon tryst was no longer a secret.

"It's our new team," Greg told him. "We're playing the Packers on Sunday. Hopefully our tight ends will score."

"Get to your room!" Simon said as Greg laughed. "Now!"

"What do you think the bishop will say?" Russell asked Thomas, who had settled into one of the armchairs.

Thomas shook his head. "I have no idea," he said. "It could go either way. He was pretty annoyed, and he hasn't been supportive of gay clergy in the past. But he's the one who suggested me for the post, so we'll see."

"In the meantime, we're going to have a good time tonight," said Mike, standing behind Thomas and putting his hands on his shoulders. "Right?"

"Right," Thomas agreed.

"Then I suggest we begin the festivities," said Simon. He picked up a glass of champagne and handed it to Thomas. "And for you some sparkling cider," he said, handing a second glass to Mike.

"I wonder how this would mix with my medication," Greg mused, holding a glass up and looking at it.

"Trust me, not well," said Stephen, taking it from him. "Have some cider instead."

"We haven't even had a date yet, and already you're nagging me," Greg told him. "Is this how it's going to be?"

"Good for you," Simon said to Stephen. "Someone needs to keep that one under control."

"John?" Russell said, holding a glass out to his partner, who was standing apart from the others, looking out a window.

"No, thanks," John said. "I'm sticking to cider too. I'm driving."

"One glass isn't going to turn you into a falling-down drunk," Russell said. "Have a little fun."

John looked at the glass Russell was holding out to him.

"Besides," Russell said, "I'll make sure you get home in one piece."

John looked up at him. "What do you mean?"

"My bags are packed," Russell told him.

"You're coming home?"

"If you want me to."

John nodded. "I want you to," he said.

"But we both need to make some changes," Russell said. "It can't be like it has been. We need to meet somewhere in the middle."

"I'll try," said John.

Russell shook his head. "That's not good enough," he said. "You have to want this too."

"I do want it."

"Tell me why?"

John looked confused. He stood for a moment, looking at Russell without saying a word. Then he cleared his throat. "I need you," he said haltingly. "When I thought you were gone for good, I tried to imagine my life. I couldn't. It was just blank."

He took his glasses off and absentmindedly wiped them with his shirt. Russell recognized it as a sign that he was trying to work out a problem in his head. He waited. John put his glasses back on.

"I love you, Russell. I love you more than anything in this world. I guess I don't always know how to say that, but I do."

"You did pretty well just now," said Russell. "And I love you, too."

He held out the glass of champagne once more. This time, John reached out for it. Their fingers touched.

"Thank you," John said, taking the glass.

"Hey, you two, join the party," Mike called.

They went back to the others. Greg had resumed throwing out veiled references to Simon and Gavin's earlier activities, and the innuendoes were flying. Simon, attempting to turn the conversation away from himself, was vainly trying to interest the men in a game of charades.

"And after that, we can roll hoops down the road," said Greg.

"I despise you," Simon told him, trying not to laugh. "You're a hateful little boy."

"You have to be nice to me, though," said Greg. "I'm recovering."

"Much too quickly," Mike suggested, sending them all into fits of laughter.

For the next two hours they talked, ate, and drank, the conversation flowing from one topic to the next like a leaf traversing the rapids of a stream. The eight of them formed ever-changing configurations as the night progressed, sometimes sitting in groups of three or four, others times breaking into pairs as they followed divergent paths of discussion. Always they came back together at some point, sharing and laughing before heading off in new directions.

Finally, as midnight neared, Mike looked at his watch and realized that they were about to miss the transition from the old to the new year. "Hey, boys," he called out. "Get your glasses ready."

They converged from their respective locations. Empty glasses were filled, and as Mike looked at his watch, he began the countdown. "Ten," he said, raising his glass. "Nine."

His cup was joined by seven others, all held aloft. "Eight. Seven. Six." Their voices mingled as, together, they sent the old year on its way. "Five. Four. Three. Two. One."

A collective "Happy New Year!" went up as glasses were clinked together and the ritual kissing began. When they'd gone fully around the circle, Mike put his arm around Thomas and held his glass up again.

"To friends old and new," he said. "And to seeing everyone again same time next year."

EPILOGUE

The waters of Lake Hinckley glistened black and cool in the late June sun. Mike, standing on the dock that stretched out into the lake, took the stone he'd picked up on the shore and skimmed it across the surface. It jumped four times, finally sinking beneath the water.

"Not bad," Thomas remarked. He was sitting on the dock's edge, his feet dangling in the water. "Bet I could get five, though."

"You're all talk," said Mike. "I'll believe it when I see it."

"Later," said Thomas. "I'm enjoying just sitting."

"Chicken," Mike teased.

"What time is it?"

Mike checked his watch. "Almost three," he said.

"We should go soon," said Thomas. "I have to finish my sermon for tomorrow."

"Why do you always put them off until Saturday night?"

"I guess I work best under pressure," said Thomas, laughing. "Why do you always put off your lesson plans until Sunday night?"

"Because I'm a lazy fuck," said Mike.

"Don't forget, we're having dinner with Simon and Gavin tonight too."

"Please tell me Gavin isn't making one of his weird concoctions," Mike said. "I don't know how he's managed not to poison Simon yet."

"I don't think Simon would notice," said Thomas. "He likes everything Gavin makes."

"Is it just us?"

"Maybe John and Russell," Thomas answered. "Greg and Stephen have other plans."

"I can't believe they're actually still together," Thomas remarked, shaking his head. "They're so different."

"And we aren't?" Mike countered. "Besides, don't they sort of have to stay together after what happened? You couldn't write an ending like that."

Thomas stared out at the water. "I know it sounds awful," he said, "but I still feel bad for that Thayer kid. Can you imagine what must have been going on in his head to do that?"

Mike sat beside him. He put his bare feet in the lake, welcoming the coolness on his skin. "He was looking for something," he said, thinking about Pete Thayer and how he'd blown his brains out rather than face trial for what he'd done. "Who knows what it was."

"We're all looking for something," Thomas said. "All of us."

Mike lay his head on Thomas's shoulder, nuzzling his neck. "And some of us are lucky enough to find it," he said.